REBEL

THE DRAAX SERIES
BOOK THREE

ELIZABETH KELLY

EK PUBLISHING INC.

Edited by
L. Nunn Editing

Cover art by
The Final Wrap

REBEL

The black market thief is about to be royally screwed.

Being a lower in Earth's society isn't a walk in the park.

I survive by stealing and selling the Draax healing juice on the black market.

Until I steal from the wrong Draax ship.

It's just my luck I got caught by a gorgeous copper eyed Draax named Galan. Did I mention he's the freaking head of the King's Guard *and* the King's best friend?

Now, a war between two alien races has me trapped on the Draax planet until they can send me back to Earth to await a far worse fate.

I need an escape plan.

Instead, I can't get Galen out of my head. It's his job to protect the king from people like me, but our attraction could put both our lives at risk.

We're growing closer every day, but the clock is ticking. Our love story can't have a happy ending. Or can it?

CHARACTER NAME PRONUNCIATIONS

Dear Reader,

Are you like me and easily distracted by proper name pronunciation when you're reading? Nothing takes me out of a story faster than constantly wondering if I'm reading a character's name correctly. To that end, here is a list of a few of the characters in "Rebel" and the proper pronunciation of their names.

Happy Reading!

Elizabeth

Galan – Gay-len
   Sigan – See-gan
   Teo – Tay-oh
   Melu – May-loo

Jovie – Joe-vee

Jota – Joe-tah

Naceth – Nay-seth

Laos – Lay-os

Quodia – kwo-dee-ah

For a glossary of Draax words, as well as extra tidbits and information about the Draax world, check out my website at www.elizabethkelly.ca

CHAPTER 1

Ellis

I was very good at not being noticed. When you lived on the street and your life depended on blending in, you got real good at it, real fast. Even when I should have stuck out like a sore thumb on the docking bay, I didn't. No one noticed me. Sure, the docking bay was busy, there must have been over a dozen Draax ships alone, not to mention the numerous havoc cruisers waiting to take off, but still… I was the only one in the loading area not wearing a uniform.

I zipped my hoodie to my chin and made sure not a strand of my long blonde hair was showing. I should have cut it short instead of constantly hiding it under hats or hoods, but I was stupidly vain about it even when it was stringy and dirty like it was right now.

Not my fault. The homeless shelters were full the last few days. I'd spent each night huddled in a damn alley under a literal cardboard box, wondering if this would be the night I froze to death. Winters in Iowa were no joke.

Plenty of us lowers froze to death every winter. Hell, I'd almost been an Ellis popsicle myself last winter. I would have been a goner if I hadn't found that land vehicle to break into.

I leaned against the towering stack of shipping containers, keeping my head down and studying the ships that lined the bay. Which one was most likely to have some gallberry juice on board? I mean, they would all have a little, but I needed a big score.

I'd found out two days ago that Richie Bulchanini had put a price on my head. A steep one. The only way to avoid being killed was to bring him juice. A lot of it. Even then, I put my odds of survival around fifty/fifty. One did not fuck with Richie. Not if they wanted to avoid being buried in a shallow grave.

So, why did you do it? You knew this would happen, but you still gave her the juice instead of bringing it to Richie.

I ignored my inner voice. It knew why I'd done it. I knew why I'd done it. We didn't need to fucking discuss it.

Maybe you should just forget all of this, grab one of those havoc cruisers and get the fuck out of Iowa. Go somewhere warm, like Mexico. Richie would never find you there.

It was tempting. There were plenty of cruisers to choose from. But boosting a cruiser wasn't a one-woman job. It required at least three people. There was no way in hell I could disable the tracking device, override all six passcodes, and pilot the ship before the cruiser's alarms went off and alerted everyone on the docking bay to what I was attempting to do.

I swiped a hand down my grubby jeans. For a moment, I was overwhelmed by my sorrow for Torra and the rest of the gang. It was almost two years since they'd gone to prison, but they'd been the closest thing I had to family and it was still a kick to the gut to think about them.

I heard voices and shrank into the shadow of the shipping containers. I suppressed my urge to cough. I'd developed a nasty cough in the last week, and it was getting to the point where I'd need to steal juice for myself.

Two dock bay workers walked by, arguing good naturedly about whose turn it was to go on break. I held my breath, keeping my slender body completely still as they passed by the shipping containers without glancing my way.

When they were gone, I released my breath, coughed into the crook of my elbow to muffle the sound, and studied the ships again. There was only one Draax ship in the bay, and while some of the government ships lined up in a neat row near the landing pad would have juice, the Draxx ship was my best bet. Not only were the odds higher of more gallberry juice being on it, but the cargo hold was open. I could walk right in, find the juice, and walk out. Easy pickings.

No, not easy pickings. The cargo hold is open because the Draax are returning soon. Which means the risk of getting caught is higher.

True, but I'd been honing my skills as a thief for years. I was small and skinny and quick. I wouldn't get caught.

You might.

Also true. But considering the alternative, I didn't see how I had much choice. I'd gotten myself into this mess and now needed to get myself out of it. It's not like I had anyone else to turn to.

I wanted to feel sorry for myself, but I pushed it aside. Now was not the time for a round of self pity. I had a mess to clean up.

I studied the ship, looking for any movement around the

cargo hold. I didn't know for certain that the Draax hadn't returned to it. For all I knew, they could be in the ship, preparing it for take off.

Pick another ship, Ellis. This one is too dangerous.

Yeah, it really was. It had the symbol for Draax royalty etched into its shiny metal. Stealing gallberry juice was a serious crime. I could only imagine how many more years would be tacked on to a prison sentence if it was stolen from Draax royalty.

The icy wind brushed my face, numbing my cheeks and making my eyes water. I blew on my hands to warm them, studying the open space between the shipping containers and the Draax ship.

It was further than I liked, but it looked like I'd gotten lucky, and a shift change was happening. In another ten minutes or so, the bay would be much busier. I had to go now or –

A searing pain behind my left ear dropped me to my knees. I threw my arm over my mouth, muffling my groan of agony. The pain swelled, black roses bloomed at the edge of my vision, and everything went blurry. I curled up on my side, my hand pressed against the side of my head, bile rising in my throat as I waited to either pass out or die.

Slowly, second by agonizing second, the pain diminished. My vision returned and, my stomach churning, I stared at the shipping containers next to my head. My heart was hammering in my chest, sweat slicked my entire body, and the urge to vomit was still powerful.

I swallowed the bitter bile and slowly sat up, leaning back against the containers as I tried to slow my breathing.

Fuck, that was a bad one.

I rubbed gingerly behind my ear. I could feel the bulge of

the translator just below the skin. I was pretty sure I wasn't supposed to feel it at all. But that's what happened when you had Draax translators implanted by a guy named Emilio who worked out of a one-room apartment infested with cockroaches and mold growing on the walls.

I took a few more deep breaths. I'd had the ear and throat translators for almost two years, and they'd been instrumental in helping me score gallberry juice to sell on the black market. Sure, the Draax weren't supposed to sell us the juice, but plenty of them did. They loved sex, and with no female Draax left to bang, they were all over us human females. Myself, I didn't understand the risk of going to prison for life just for a few rounds of hide the salami, but to be fair, I was more interested in not starving to death than getting my hump on.

But trying to pantomime a bargain with them for their magical healing juice got real old, real fast. So, I'd had the translators installed inside my skull and my throat. Being able to understand and talk to the Draax made it a hell of a lot easier to bargain with them.

Especially since they never wanted to bargain with me at first. With my hair hidden, my narrow hips, and the way I bound my small tits, I could pass for a boy and often did. I deliberately kept my tits hidden and dressed in baggy men's clothing. It was safer on the streets if they thought you were a guy. But even if they didn't mistake me for a boy, the Draax had no interest in bargaining for sex with my skinny ass. They liked the curvy girls who had tits for days. Luckily, I had a partner who the Draax drooled over.

I did the bargaining with my second-rate translators. Bailey did the fucking.

It was a good arrangement, mutually benefiting both of

us. I arranged to get the juice from the Draax, Bailey showed him the time of his life in the bedroom, I sold the juice on the black market, and Bailey and I split the profits.

It was perfect.

Until Bailey decided to make some extra cash on the side and help Big Steve with a job. A job that went wrong. Horribly wrong.

I closed my eyes. This time the nausea in my belly had less to do with the lingering pain in my head and more to do with how Bailey looked once Big Steve finished beating the crap out of her.

She was close to death when I forced the gallberry juice down her throat. I spent a few tense nights huddled with her in a dirty motel room, forcing her to swallow sips of juice every half hour until she stopped coughing up blood and screaming every time she moved. By the time our limited funds ran out and we were kicked out of the motel, Bailey could walk again, and I had a price on my head.

I rubbed at the translator again. Bailey had immediately called home. Not even her love for fucking the Draax – and boy, did she love fucking them – was enough to make her stay. Her near-death experience had convinced her that living with her controlling mother was better than trying to survive on the street. She'd told me to do the same. Told me Richie would never find me living in the suburbs, and it was my only chance. She was right. But I couldn't go back. Even if I wanted to, they'd never take me back. Not after what I did.

There was another pulse of pain, and I steeled myself, clenching my teeth and digging my fingers into my thighs. Thankfully, it didn't worsen, and I hissed out a breath. Something had gone wrong with the translator, and I needed to get it out of my head before it killed me.

Too bad Emilio was dead.

I stood up, my knees shaking and the urge to vomit still lingering despite the pain easing off. I was sweating profusely, and I was pretty sure I had a fever. Still, I had to move. I needed some juice to take back to Richie, and with my too-thin body, I'd never convince a Draax to trade some juice for a little playtime in the sack with me. They were desperate for sex but apparently not that desperate.

Stealing it was my only chance.

I tightened the straps of my backpack, straightened my back, and walked briskly across the open area of the docking bay. The key was to look like you belonged here. To act like it was your right to be walking across the docking bay toward a Draax royalty ship with the intention of stealing every last drop of gallberry juice.

Sweat slid down my back despite the cold air, and the area behind my left ear started to throb dully. Shit. That was new. Usually, there was nothing until I got felled by the occasional stabbing pain. I really needed to find someone to get the fucking thing out of my head.

I was almost to the cargo hold now, and I resisted the urge to look around to see if anyone was watching. It would only make me look guilty. Instead, I marched right up the ramp like I owned the goddamn thing, not releasing my pent-up breath until I was on the ship.

"Holy shit. It worked," I said before coughing.

I couldn't help but be delighted with myself.

Yeah, great, it worked. You still need to find some juice on an alien ship, steal it, and get the fuck out of the docking bay without being caught. Save your self-congratulations for later, idiot.

Good point.

I studied the cargo area. It was bare with no containers that might hold gallberry juice. I jogged over to the door that led to the ship's interior and hit the button. The door slid open, and I stepped into the medium-sized room. A long, narrow table was bolted to the middle of the floor, a row of three seats bolted to the left wall next to a metal cabinet, and what looked like a storage area with a narrow door against the right wall.

Best of all, a grey shipping container was on the floor next to the table.

"C'mon, lady luck, cut me a break, would you?" I knelt beside the container and flipped it open. "Holy shit."

I froze and looked around. I'd been too loud, and even with the doors closed, if anyone else was on the ship, they might have heard me. I strained to hear even the slightest noise. I slipped my backpack off and set it on the floor beside me when there was only silence.

I lifted one of the bottles out of the container and stared at it. The pink liquid shone in the bright overhead lights. I'd never tried gallberry juice, but I knew it supposedly tasted a little like strawberries. I'd always wanted to try it, but it was too valuable to waste on me when nothing was physically wrong.

But this time? This time I was taking a fucking bottle for myself. It would help get rid of my stupid cough and hopefully heal whatever the hell the fucked-up translator was doing to my brain.

"I'm gonna be rich," I whispered, then stuffed the bottle into my backpack before reaching for a second. There were two dozen bottles in the container. I could probably fit about a dozen into my bag. Still, even just a dozen would be more than enough to get me the fuck out of Iowa and start a new life. Somewhere hot with a beautiful beach and a crashing blue ocean. I'd never seen the ocean before.

I grabbed another bottle and stuffed it in beside the first. I was reaching for the third when the hollow thud of footsteps in the cargo hold reached my ears. I froze, my brain screaming at me before I snatched up the lid of the shipping container and notched it back into place.

I scanned the room desperately as I shrugged into my pack. I couldn't go further into the ship. It would just be harder to get out without them seeing me. As the footsteps grew closer, I sprinted toward that narrow door, yanking it open and peering inside. As I suspected, it was a small storage space that, thank fucking God, was empty.

I squeezed myself into the space and eased the door shut just as the door to the room slid open. I breathed shallowly as male laughter filled the space.

"Galan, you worry too much. We will be home well before the storm."

My breath lodged in my throat when a deep voice spoke directly outside my hiding spot.

"You worry too little, Krey. Does he not, Sigan?"

A little shiver went down my spine. I was in deep fucking trouble, was now really the time to be thinking about how sexy that voice was?

The third Draax's response was too low to hear. Or maybe I just couldn't hear it over the pounding of my heartbeat. Fuck, I needed to get off this ship before they left Earth.

Stay cool, Ellis. Stay cool. They'll go further into the ship. The minute that door closes behind them, you sprint for the cargo hold, lower the door and get the fuck off the ship.

Easy peasy.

"Sigan," that low and sexy voice was speaking again, "are you not joining us?"

"No. I will sit back here. It is too crowded with all three of us."

"Suit yourself."

My heart stopped. It just fucking stopped in the middle of a beat and, two seconds later, kicked back in. I was trapped. He wasn't leaving, and I was trapped. What the fuck did I do?

Sit back and enjoy your free trip to Draax?

I groaned inwardly as the door to the cockpit slid open and then closed. I listened carefully. Maybe the one named Sigan had decided to join them after all. The creak of the seat as he sat quickly killed my hope.

Adrenaline rushed through my body as the throbbing behind my ear steadily worsened. I'd never even left Iowa before, and now I was about to fly to freaking outer space?

I was one hundred percent fucked.

Galan

KREY FLIPPED THE SWITCH TO AUTOPILOT AND SAT BACK IN THE seat. "Another couple of hours, and we will be home."

I stared at the black nothingness, my stomach still churning from our trip through the jumpgate. Space travel always made me sick, and I stared at the blinking lights on the ship's dashboard as I shifted in the co-pilot's seat. "Did you put in the correct coordinates for home?"

Krey laughed before grabbing the apple he'd bought from the market on the way back to the ship. I did not care for the taste of most Earth food, but Krey loved it. He bit into the red fruit and wiped away the juice from his chin.

"Yes, Galan. I will return you home safely. Besides, we are in our solar system. There is no fear of getting lost."

I rubbed at my roiling stomach. "The Idalia system is one of the biggest in the galaxy. It would be easy to lose our way." I indicated to the lights on the ship. "For all I know, we could be in a completely different solar system altogether."

Krey took another bite of his apple, chewing noisily before swallowing. "The ship's navigation system has not failed, Galan. We are in Idalia and," he tapped a light on the dashboard, "headed straight for Draax. I promise."

I closed my eyes, waiting for the nausea to settle as Krey said, "If you traveled more by ship, the space sickness would not be so bad."

"I do not like traveling by ship," I said.

Although I couldn't see it, I knew Krey was grinning when he said, "You have never enjoyed space travel, not even as a small boy. I thought the mandatory pilot lessons we took when we joined the king's guard might have cured you of your fear, but I believe it made it worse."

"The simulated crashes that Oren made us endure every single day could be the reason for that."

Krey laughed. "They were occasionally… terrifying."

I cracked open one eye and stared at Krey. He had finished his apple and had his feet up on the ship's dashboard, his fingers interlaced over his flat stomach. "You took to flying right away. Why did you not join the Draax Space Division instead of staying in the King's Guard? You know that Oren would have put in a good word for you. You were always his favourite student."

"I always thought you were his favourite," Krey said.

I grinned. "Truthfully, it was probably Quill."

Krey nodded. "You are probably right."

"Why did you not join?" I asked again.

"I love piloting a ship," Krey said, "it is why I volunteer for as many of the trips to Earth as I can, but I love fighting more."

I laughed as Krey patted the handle of the sword around his waist. "Besides, I am a mediocre pilot at best but an excellent fighter."

"Calling yourself mediocre does not inspire confidence that we will arrive safely home."

"Relax, Galan," Krey said. "You must learn to have faith in me. You do not hear Sigan complaining, do you?"

I glanced at the door that separated us from the rest of the ship. "Only because Sigan rarely speaks unless necessary."

"It is true. Our kadana is a quiet Draax. But excellent at healing our sick."

Krey sat up, dropping his feet from the dashboard. "Why did you come on this trip, Galan?"

"Because our king asked me to," I said.

Krey cocked his head. "You have turned down Quill's requests to go to Earth on many other occasions."

I didn't reply, and Krey said, "At first, I assumed it was because you wished to lie with a female. How long has it been? Six moons?"

"Longer," I admitted grudgingly.

Krey shook his head. "Which is why I was so shocked when you disappeared from the Earth bar last evening."

I rubbed at the back of my neck. "I am sorry for abandoning you and Sigan like that, Krey. I should have said something before I left."

Krey waved his hand at me. "Do not trouble yourself about it. Besides, I handled both the little females after you left." He grabbed his crotch and tugged at it. "They were equally sated this morning when I left their bed."

"Did Sigan find a female to bed?" I asked.

"I never asked," Krey said. "Why did you leave?"

I just shrugged. Truthfully, I didn't know why I'd left. For the first time in my life, none of the soft and beautiful human females appealed to me. There were plenty to choose from last night, and while I, Krey and Sigan refused to offer a bit of gallberry juice as an incentive for them to sleep with us, I still would have had my pick of females. Plenty of human females were breeding incompatible with us but still enjoyed taking us to their bed for an evening or two.

"If it was not to fuck, why did you come on this trip?" Krey asked.

"I am head of the king's guard," I said. "With Quill's mate so close to giving birth, he did not want to leave her. It is my duty to take his place at the meeting with Earth's officials."

"True, but Teo is happy to go more often than not."

When I didn't reply, Krey said, "Do you think this new system with the humans will work?"

"I believe it will," I said. "Look how many females have already agreed to work at -"

"Galan?"

Sigan's voice came over the intercom. I pushed the button on the panel next to my head. "What is it, Sigan?"

"We have a problem. There is some gallberry juice missing."

"What do you mean? Did we not deliver all of it to Earth?"

"I brought a few extra, just in case," Sigan said. "I was reviewing inventory, and the case has two bottles missing."

I glanced at Krey, who shrugged. "I did not take it."

I stood up, stretching my spine and ignoring the nausea in my stomach. Maybe I would grab some gallberry juice from the extra case. "I am on my way."

I frowned when Krey stood as well. "Where are you going?"

"Relax, Galan." Krey clapped me on the back. "Autopilot, remember?"

I grimaced but didn't say anything as Krey followed me to the back of the ship. Sigan was standing beside a grey shipping container. I peered inside, studying the empty spots where the bottles should have been.

"Maybe the case was not filled completely," Krey said.

"I checked them myself before we left Draax," Sigan said.

"Well, they did not simply grow feet and walk away," Krey said. "They must -"

"Quiet." My voice was low, but Krey stopped talking immediately, his hand dropping to his sword.

I had heard something, the slightest scrape of metal against metal, and I stared at the door of a small storage space to my right. I withdrew my sword, and Krey did the same. I stepped in front of the door, holding my sword in my right hand as I nodded to him.

Moving quietly, he approached the door and eased his tail around the handle. He jerked it open at my nod, and a young human male fell out of the narrow space and onto the floor at my feet.

Before he could scramble to his feet, I held my sword at his throat. "Slowly, human."

He stood up slowly. He was wearing rough pants, which humans called jeans, and a sweater that was too big. It zipped up at the front to his chin, and he had the hood up and pulled shut so that only his face was visible.

His clear blue eyes were clouded over with pain, and sweat poured down his face. His features were delicate, almost feminine-like, and he made a low groan of pain, biting down on his full bottom lip as he pressed one hand to the side of his head.

"Who are you?" My voice was cold, and I pressed against his chest with the tip of my sword. "Why are you on our ship?"

The male was wearing a backpack, and as he shifted on his feet, his hand still pressed against his head, I heard the distinct clink of bottles.

"I guess we found our thief," Krey said. He studied the man as Sigan moved closer to get a better look. "Do you know what we do with gallberry juice thieves, boy?"

The human opened his mouth, and I stepped back as he vomited onto the floor.

"Krono!" Krey skittered back and stared at his own feet in disgust. "Ugh, there is vomit on my boots now. What is wrong with you, human?"

"He does not understand you," Sigan said. "Not without a translator."

The male wiped his mouth with a shaking hand, and I grunted in surprise when he made a high-pitched scream and grabbed at his head. His eyes rolled back in his head, and he crumpled to the ground.

"Sigan, stay back," I said when the kadana knelt beside the earth male.

Sigan ignored me, peeling back the human's eyelid and studying his pupil. "There is something very wrong with this human."

"There is vomit on my boots," Krey repeated.

Sigan gave him an impatient look as he stood and crossed

the room to a metal cabinet. "Galan, put the human on the table."

I sheathed my sword and crouched, sitting the human up. I took the backpack off of him, leaving it on the ship's floor, before sliding one hand around his back and another under his thighs. I lifted him, frowning at how light he was, and carried him to the table. The ship was too small to have an infirmary, but the cabinet Sigan was rifling through was stocked with a few basic medical supplies and bags of gallberry serum in intravenous form.

I laid the unconscious human on the table as Sigan joined me. He had a pleirdox in his hand and ran the small silver box over the human's body and past his head. He stared at the screen and frowned. "The human is burning up from fever. He will die if we do not get him cooled down."

He pushed another button on the screen. "He has an infection, but I do not know what. The pleirdox does not recognize it, and nothing is coming up from my database of Earth infections. Krey, bring me a needle and a bag of serum."

"Will the serum help?" I asked.

"It should," Sigan said. "I do not know this type of infection, but the gallberry plant cures everything in humans."

"Why are we wasting gallberry serum on a thief?" Krey asked.

I frowned at him, and he held his hands up. "Just a question."

"Bring Sigan his supplies, Krey."

Krey walked toward the cabinet as Sigan pushed a button on the pleirdox. A screen popped up in mid-air, and Sigan read the information printed on it. "Perhaps it is an infection that only Earth males can get. I mostly have studied the female humans."

He glanced at the human. "Galan, remove his outerwear, please. We must get him cooled down as quickly as possible."

As Sigan scrolled through the screens of the pleirdox, I untied the laces holding the hood tight and pulled down the zipper. The hood loosened, and I might have been surprised by the long blonde hair that was now visible if I hadn't been distracted by the white bandaging around the male's upper chest.

"Sigan, look at this," I said. "It looks like he was previously injured. Perhaps that is the cause of the infection?"

Sigan moved forward and studied the bandaging. "I do not see any blood or smell any signs of infection."

He reached into his pocket and produced a pair of small, sharp scissors as Krey returned with the gallberry serum. Sliding the scissors between the bandaging and the human's flesh, Sigan carefully cut his way upward. He snipped the last bandage, and the material slid down to pool on the table.

The breath whooshed out of my lungs in a harsh rush, and I heard Sigan's grunt of surprise.

Krey leaned over my shoulder and stared at the unconscious human. "Krono, is that…"

"Yes," I said as I stared at a set of small, pert, and utterly perfect breasts. "The human is female."

CHAPTER 2

Galan

K rey had barely set the ship down on the landing pad outside the castle before Sigan opened the door to the cargo hold. "I will return with a stretcher."

I picked up the small female carefully. "I will carry her to the infirmary. It is faster."

I followed Sigan through the maze of corridors to the infirmary, nodding to the Draax we passed and ignoring their curious glances at the female.

"Put the female on the bed," Sigan instructed as we entered the infirmary. The castle we both called home was massive, and the infirmary was large enough to house a dozen beds.

"She is still feverish." I set her down on the closest bed. I could feel the heat radiating from her pale skin. I brushed her hair away from her face, studying her delicate features.

She was much too thin, the skin on her cheeks stretched

tight, and her body barely heavier than a maluken's. I wondered when she'd eaten last.

"Why is the serum not helping?" I said.

"It is," Sigan said. He was crossing the infirmary, turning on lights and various machines. "She is still alive, is she not? Without the serum, she would be dead. There is something very wrong with the human."

My stomach clenched oddly at the thought of the small female dying. My tail flicked agitatedly. Why should I care if she lived or died?

"Can you find out what is wrong?" I said.

"Now that we are home, yes." Sigan went to lift the female off the bed, and I put my arm out to block him.

He frowned at me. "Galan, I must get the human into the scanner immediately."

"I will carry her."

"Fine by me. I have never met a human female who smells so terrible," Sigan said.

Sigan was right – the little female did smell terrible – but I ignored the smell and carried her fragile body to the scanner. I set her down, and Sigan straightened her limbs before locking her wrists and ankles to the bed.

"In case she wakes," he said. "It is doubtful. She is barely clinging to life as it is, but if she did wake and thrash around, my scans would be ruined."

I stepped back and watched Sigan turn on the hrotti connected to the scanner. He typed rapidly, and the scanner hummed to life. A long silver wand attached to the scanner swept the human's body from her head to her toes. Her pale skin glowed in the blue light as the wand made another sweep.

The machine quieted, and a hologram screen popped up

above the hrotti. Sigan studied it before making a grunt of satisfaction.

"What?" I said. "What is it?"

"Move her back to the bed, Galan." Sigan returned to the long counter at the back of the infirmary and rummaged in a cupboard above the counter.

I unlocked the cuffs around her wrists and ankles and returned the female to the bed, easing her onto it with infinite care. Her face was pale, and her breathing incredibly shallow.

"She is barely breathing," I said.

"I know."

Irritation washed over me. Sigan was being slow and callous with the human's fate, and I didn't like it.

"Tell me what is wrong with her," I said.

He glanced at me, surprise showing on his face. My tone was angry, and that wasn't like me, but my worry for the little human made me feel odd.

"Sigan?" The door behind us opened. "I'm here for my... Galan? What's wrong? Why is your tail whipping back and forth like that?"

I turned and bowed. "My queen."

She rolled her eyes. "How many times do I have to tell you to call me Sabrina? This 'my queen' shit is getting old."

"My queen," Sigan said with perfect timing and bowed from his spot by the counter. "Forgive me, but I need a few extra minutes before beginning your scan."

"That's fine," Sabrina said. "Quill is supposed to be joining us, and he's somewhere with... whoa. Is that a human?"

She hurried forward and peered around me. "Who is this? I don't recognize her from the database of women we hired."

"She is a thief," Sigan said.

I grimaced. "We found her aboard our ship shortly before we arrived home, hiding in the storage space."

"She had stolen two of our bottles of juice," Sigan said.

"Seriously?"

Sigan nodded as he joined us.

"What's wrong with her?" Sabrina said. "She looks and smells awful."

"She is dying," Sigan said. He was back at the hrotti, and he pushed a few buttons. "She has a cancerous tumour on her spine. A few more moons and the tumour will constrict her spinal cord and paralyze her."

"Oh my God," Sabrina said. "That's terrible."

"Indeed," Sigan said. "It appears to be quite an aggressive form. The scanner indicates it has already spread to her lungs. It will take a large amount of juice to heal her."

He frowned at the hrotti screen before pushing a few more buttons. "Humans are so fragile. So many of you seem to have this cancer disease."

"Poor thing," Sabrina said. "No wonder she's so thin and pale."

"Oh, that is not from the cancer," Sigan said. "It is doubtful she has yet to feel any symptoms from it other than perhaps some discomfort in her back and a mild cough."

He turned the female's head until her ear faced upward and brushed back her hair before folding her ear forward. "She is dying because of this."

"What is that?" Sabrina leaned in, both of us staring at the small lump behind the female's ear.

"A translator," Sigan said.

Sabrina touched behind her own ear. "Why can you see it like that? Mine isn't visible at all."

"It is an older model, not installed properly, and leaking flux fluid into the human. It is why she is dying."

"Jesus. Can you get that thing out of her?" Sabrina said.

Sigan nodded. "I can, but I must speak with the king first. He may not wish to save the life of someone who stole from him."

My tail thwacked against the floor. "Take it out of the human immediately, Sigan."

"I cannot do so without the king's permission, Galan."

My hands clenched into fists. "She is dying."

"I am aware," he said. "But until the king says I am allowed to do so, I cannot -"

"I'm telling you to do it." Sabrina's hand rested on my back. "Your queen commands you, Sigan."

"As you wish, my queen." Sigan bowed and returned to the counter. He scrubbed his hands at the sink as Sabrina rubbed my back.

"Galan, are you all right?" she said.

"I am fine," I said.

I wasn't, and I had no doubt that our queen knew that, but she didn't question my deception as Sigan returned. He set down a syringe of pink coloured liquid and placed a white cloth over the human's head, arranging the hole in the center to expose her ear.

"What is that pen thing?" Sabrina pointed to the device in Sigan's hand.

"It is a turing carver," Sigan said.

"Carver?" Sabrina made a face. "That doesn't sound... pleasant."

I frowned at him when he bent over the human. "Should you not give her more serum for the pain?"

"There is enough serum in her system to help with the

pain. Besides, just removing the translator may kill her, so I will not waste more gallberry serum on her. She is weak and severely malnourished," Sigan said.

I glared at him, and Sabrina squeezed my arm. Sigan bent over the female. We watched as a small blue beam of light at the tip of the carver sliced open the female's skin behind her ear. Even unconscious, she groaned with pain, and I placed my hand on her slender thigh, rubbing back and forth as Sigan took a pair of forceps and removed the translator. It was coated in a black liquid and I could see the same black liquid oozing out of the human's flesh.

"Gross." Sabrina covered her nose with her hand. "It smells terrible."

"It does," Sigan said. He syringed the pink liquid into the open wound in the human's head, flushing out the black liquid.

"Is that gallberry juice?" Sabrina asked.

"Serum," Sigan said. "It will help heal the infection faster if applied directly to the area. I will leave the wound open for now to allow more of the flux fluid to empty. Do I have your permission to remove her voice translator as well? No doubt it is just as old as the ear translator."

"Yes," Sabrina said. "Get it out before it does the same thing."

Working quickly, Sigan removed the translator from her throat. No black liquid coated this one, and he flipped a switch on the carver. The light went from blue to violet, and Sabrina watched in fascination as Sigan ran the carver along the cut he'd made, and the human's flesh fused.

"Okay, that's cool. Did we get this technology from the Vokine?" Sabrina asked.

The Vokine were one of our trading partners whose technology was far more advanced than ours.

"Yes," Sigan said. "The gallberry serum would eventually close up the wound, but this device is convenient. I enjoy using it."

Sabrina laughed. "I doubt you have to use it very much what with you guys drinking gallberry juice daily."

"True," Sigan said. "But with the addition of the fragile humans who now live in the castle, perhaps I will have more use for it."

His face brightened with hope as Sabrina laughed again. "Maybe. Our skin isn't as thick or tough as yours."

She glanced at my hand that was still resting against the female's thigh, and, feeling oddly embarrassed, I pulled my hand away.

Sigan removed the cloth from her face and covered her thin body with a blanket. He hooked up a fresh bag of the gallberry serum to the female. "We will leave her for now. The serum will help keep her alive until she can be returned to Earth."

"Will there be permanent damage from the translator?" Sabrina said.

Sigan shrugged. "There may be. The flux fluid is toxic, and I do not know how long it leaked into the human."

"But the serum should heal it, right?" Sabrina said.

"Maybe, maybe not. It heals, but it does have limitations. If a human lost a limb, they could drink unlimited juice, but the limb would not grow back," Sigan said. "It may be the same with the damage done to the human's brain. She may never wake from her sleep, or she may wake and be unable to talk or walk."

"Jesus, that's awful," Sabrina said.

"We have done everything we can for her," Sigan said. "Now, are you ready for your scan, my queen?"

"I am." Sabrina rubbed her belly before grinning at me. "I feel like I've been pregnant for about a year and a half."

"That is biologically impossible," Sigan said.

The door swung open, and Sigan and I bowed when our king, Quillan, entered the room. He nodded to us before nuzzling the cheek of the toddler he held in his arms. "You see, my little queen, I told you your mama was here."

The toddler's tail flicked back and forth, and her purple skin darkened with excitement as she stared at Sabrina. The young girl clinging to Quill's hand said, "Quill, can we go swimming again?"

"The next time you visit, Bella," Quill said.

"But Mama says you are too busy now that it's the warm season, and we can't visit as much," the little girl said. Her skin was the same shade of purple as Quill and Sabrina's daughter. "I won't see you again for at least a moon."

"Then you will enjoy the pool that much more, meena," Quill grinned.

Bella pouted a little but brightened when she saw me. "Hello, Galan!"

She ran forward, and when she jumped at me, I caught her and set her in the crook of my arm before kissing her soft cheek. "Hello, Bella. You are looking well today."

"Quill said you weren't here. He said you were on Earth with Krey."

"I was," I said. "We have only just returned."

"I'm glad you're here." Her smile was shy, and I kissed her cheek again. While I had no desire for my own children, I enjoyed spending time with them, and Bella was a sweet girl. She'd developed a small crush on me over the last few moons and, whenever she visited, sought me out.

"Will you go swimming with me, Galan?" Her tail flicked out and wrapped around my forearm, squeezing tightly.

"Not this time, Bella. But when you visit next, I will join you in your swim."

Her tail squeezed again. "All right. Guess what?"

"What?" I said.

"I am skipping a grade in school. Papa says it's because I'm very smart."

I smiled at her. "Good for you."

"Uda is worried that the older children will be cruel to me because I talk like Mama and I'm small, but I'm not worried. I will punch them in their face if they're mean to me."

"Bella, we spoke with you about proper behaviour, my love."

The human female entering the infirmary looked remarkably like our queen. Her long dark hair and curvy body were similar to Sabrina's, and her skin was the same pale shade. The woman standing next to her was curvy as well, but her hair was a striking shade of pink, and her skin a warm brown.

"Sorry, Mama," Bella said, although she didn't sound sorry at all. "I wouldn't actually punch them in the face."

The woman smiled at her before turning to me. "Hello, Galan. I didn't expect to see you on this visit. Sabrina said you and Krey were on Earth."

"We just returned now. It is good to see you, Evelyn. You look well. How are your mates?"

"Busy now that the warm season has begun. The crops are starting to come in, and they spend most of their days in the field," Evelyn said. "Have you met my friend Candala?"

"Not formally," I said. I'd seen her in the training room, she was one of the females employed to clean it, and she was impossible to miss with her pink hair, but I hadn't spoken to her. "Hello, Candala."

"Hi there." The woman shook my hand in the traditional Earth greeting. "You can call me Candy."

"I prefer Candala," I said.

All three women laughed, and I glanced at Quill who just shrugged. Despite being mated to Sabrina for three years, he sometimes understood the human females no better than I did.

"I thought Court was picking you up at three," Sabrina said to Evelyn.

"He's on his way," Evelyn said. The baby in her arms made a short cry, and she swayed back and forth. "He messaged me to say he was running a bit late."

"Well, in that case, hand that baby over for one last snuggle," Sabrina said. She held out her arms, and Evelyn gave her the baby.

I moved closer, shifting Bella to my other arm to see the baby.

"Bella, come stand with me and Candy," Evelyn said. "You're too heavy to be held for so long."

"Nu-uh." Bella flung her arm around my neck in case I decided to listen to her mama. "Galan is really strong. He can hold me. Right, Galan?"

I smiled at her. "Yes, Bella. What is your brother's name again?"

"Naceth," Bella said. "It is a name from Uda's family. I forget from where, though."

She glanced at Evelyn, who said, "It is Uda's grandfather's name, meena."

"Right."

We studied the baby as Sabrina propped him above her round belly and cooed at him. "He looks so much like Court," she said. "Seriously, he's a mini Court."

Evelyn laughed. "I know. And even though he's only a month old, his personality is already fully Court, too. He's such a laid-back baby. I swear he only cries when hungry or needs his diaper changed."

"He smells really bad sometimes," Bella said. "It makes me wanna barf, but Papa says that I smelled just as bad when I was a baby."

"What does barf mean?" I said.

Bella mimicked throwing up, complete with retching noises and hand gestures. Quill laughed so hard that his daughter stared at him with wide eyes.

"Sorry, Jovie," Quill said to her, "I did not mean to startle you."

He kissed his daughter's cheek, and she patted his face before holding her arms out to Sabrina. "Mama, hold."

Sabrina handed Naceth back to Evelyn before cuddling Jovie. "Did you have fun with your daddy, sweet girl?"

Jovie rested her head on Sabrina's breast, her thumb inching toward her mouth. "Yes, Mama."

"My king, your meeting with King Raynor of the northern province will start in less than an hour. Have you read over the briefing I sent you?" The old Draax entered the infirmary, his tail waving agitatedly behind him and his grey hair sticking up like he'd been running his hands through it.

He bowed to Sabrina. "My queen. You are looking well this morning."

"Hello, Teo," Sabrina said.

The king's advisor studied the people in the room before turning to Quill. "Have you read it? I swear if you have not, I will leave you to fend for yourself in the meeting."

Only Teo dared speak to Quill so disrespectfully. Although, as the oldest Draax in the castle and king's advisor to not only Quill but to Quill's brother and father before him, I supposed he had earned the right to be a bit impatient from time to time.

"Relax, old friend." Quill clapped him on the back. "I read it over last night. I am well prepared."

"Good," Teo said.

Another Draax entered the infirmary – the room was starting to feel a bit stuffy and overcrowded despite its large size – and Bella squealed in delight before wiggling in my arms. "Uda!"

I set her down, and she skipped toward the large Draax, who picked her up and kissed her cheek. "Hello, meena."

He leaned down and pressed a kiss against Evelyn's mouth. "Hello, Evie."

"Hi, Court." Evelyn took his hand.

"Uda, guess what I did today?" Bella said. "I went swimming and played with Roden and the other children in the garden. I won three rounds of jorken."

"Speaking of which," Candy said, "I should head to the garden and find Roden. He has homework to finish."

"Bye, sweetie. It was good to see you. I'll hologram you tomorrow with that recipe," Evelyn said.

"We must go as well," Court said. "Bran was planning to have supper ready by six thirty."

Evelyn kissed Sabrina's cheek. "Message me if you go into labour, all right?"

Sabrina laughed. "Bite your tongue, Evie. I'm not due for another month, remember?"

"True, but Jovie was two weeks early, and you look about ready to pop, so…" She kissed Jovie's forehead. "Bye, Jovie. Una loves you."

"Bye, Una," Jovie said.

Court set Bella down and took the baby from Evelyn. Bella waved and blew a kiss to us before taking Evelyn's hand and following her and Court out of the room.

Teo glanced at the vertex in his hand. "Forty-five minutes, my king. Perhaps you should take one final look at the briefing."

"I will join you when my mate's scan is complete."

Teo groaned, and Quill grinned at him. "You worry too much, Teo," he turned to Sigan, "you must be more like Sigan, who is… what is that?"

He peered at the female lying on the bed. "One of the females we hired is sick?"

"No, my king," Sigan said. "This female was discovered on our ship as we were returning home. She was attempting to steal gallberry juice, and we caught her."

"Why did you not leave her on Earth?" Quill covered his nose with his hand. "And why does she smell so awful?"

"We were halfway home when we discovered her hiding," Sigan said. "As for the smell, I believe it's mostly from her clothing, although," he prodded at one leg, "she could use a bath. I will get her cleaned up."

"No," Sabrina said. "She can have a shower when she wakes up. She won't want a strange male bathing her while she's unconscious."

"I have no sexual interest in her," Sigan said. "She is much too small and skinny. Even if she were not malnourished, she would be too thin. No Draax will want to mate with her."

"That's not the point," Sabrina said. "It doesn't matter if you're attracted to her or not. She won't want you bathing her, even for medical purposes. Being dirty and smelly won't kill her. Just leave her until she wakes. Trust me on this."

"Yes, my queen," Sigan said. "Although she may not make it through the night. The gallberry plant is working but slowly."

"What is wrong with her?" Quill asked.

Sigan quickly filled him in. I gritted my teeth but kept quiet when he referred to her repeatedly as the thief. She *was* a thief, and my weird reaction to the little female didn't negate that she had stolen juice.

When Sigan finished, Quill glanced at Teo. Teo was typing into his vertex, and he said, "I will alert Earth's authorities that we have caught a thief and will return her for punishment."

He turned to me. "What section of Earth were you visiting when she boarded the ship?"

I had the oddest urge to refuse to tell him, which didn't make sense. Earth had many prisons, and she could be thrown into any of them. I had taken Earth studies throughout my schooling and knew the fate awaiting the little female. Stealing gallberry juice meant imprisonment of at least forty Earth years. She would be an old woman when she regained her freedom.

"The province of Iowa, in a city called Des Moines," Sigan said when I didn't answer.

"State of Iowa," Sabrina said. "We call them states, not provinces."

Teo made a note in his vertex. "When will she be ready for transport, Sigan?"

Sigan shrugged. "Tomorrow. If she does not die in the night."

"What if she's not," Sabrina paused, "normal? Like, what if her abilities are impaired because of the flux fluid? And what if the gallberry plant doesn't completely cure the cancer by tomorrow?"

"It will not be cured," Sigan said. "She would need more of the plant than I can give her in twenty-four hours, even by serum. She will be dead in six moons." He studied her prone body. "More likely three moons with her tiny and fragile body."

His careless tone grated on my nerves, and I had to work very hard not to thump my tail against the floor and betray my annoyance.

"So, she'll die in prison," Sabrina said.

"That is not our problem, my queen," Teo said. "The little female has broken Earth laws. The Planetary Treaty requires she be returned for her punishment regardless of her state."

Sabrina bit at her bottom lip, her hand stroking Jovie's hair as she studied the sick female. Our king's mate was soft-hearted, and a part of me hoped she would convince Quill to...

To what? Not return the female to Earth? Don't be such a froden. Even if he wanted to, he couldn't. It would be a violation of the treaty.

I twitched when Quill thumped me on the back. "Galan, what troubles you?"

"Nothing, my king," I said.

I knew Quill didn't believe me. He was my oldest and best

friend and knew me better than anyone. It was difficult, if not impossible, to keep anything from him.

"Come, walk with me in the garden while my mate has her scan." Quill glanced at Sabrina. "Sadora, do you mind?"

"Not at all," she said.

"No," I said. "Stay with your mate. I am tired from the trip and will retire early."

I bowed to Sabrina and left the infirmary before Quill could argue.

CHAPTER 3

Ellis

I woke slowly, feeling better than I had in weeks. My head no longer throbbed and the weird heaviness in my lungs and the urge to cough had disappeared. Even the ache in my back was gone. I stared up at the ceiling, blinking until my vision cleared.

Was I still on the Draax ship? My stomach tightened. I had to be. Unless the Draax had turned around and returned me to Earth. That was a definite possibility, right? I couldn't remember much of what happened after sliding into that storage space to hide, but I had confusing images of a Draax with beautiful copper eyes and a mouth that did strange things to my insides.

And a sword, Ellis. Don't forget about the sword he had.

I scrunched up my face, trying to remember. After a couple of seconds, I cringed. Oh God, had I … had I thrown up on the copper-eyed Draax? If the sour taste in my mouth was any indication, I had definitely vomited on him.

Fuck.

I lifted a hand to my face, staring at the catheter embedded in the back of it. I followed the tube to the IV bag hung up on a metal pole next to the bed. The pink tinged liquid in the bag had to be gallberry serum.

Gallberry serum was like goddamn gold on the black market. And hanging just above me was my ticket to surviving my next encounter with Richie. If I brought him serum, he'd not only forgive me for giving the juice to Bailey, he'd probably get down on his knees and kiss my fucking feet.

You have bigger problems than Richie Bulchanini, you idiot.

I licked my dry lips. Damn straight, I did. I was still on the Draax ship. Hospitals on Earth didn't give the gallberry serum to lowers like me. The serum was reserved for the uppers – the rich and the famous. Which meant I was trapped on a Draax ship, and that was definitely a more pressing concern than Richie Bulchanini. I needed to figure out a way to sweet talk my way out of imprisonment or…

I slapped the hand not attached to the bag of liquid gold behind my ear. The bulge of the translator was gone, and I breathed a sigh of relief. The thing was killing me, I had no doubt of that, and apparently, the Draax had removed it. But why?

I touched my throat, manipulating the spot where the voice translator was. I couldn't feel it either, so I carefully sat up in bed and studied the room.

Well, shit. The room was too big for me to still be on the ship. I knew that right away. It housed numerous hospital beds and a few large pieces of machinery and… oh fuck me.

I studied the Draax standing at the counter with his back to me. He wore a white coat that reminded me of doctors' lab coats on Earth. A hologram screen was to his left, and he studied the screen occasionally before staring at the test tube in his left hand. His right hand tapped away at a tablet on the counter.

My heart pounding in my chest, I eased back the tape on my hand and, holding my breath, yanked the catheter from my hand. I ignored the blood oozing out of my hand and quietly slipped out from beneath the sheet.

I was still dressed in my clothes, but the bandage that bound my small tits had been removed. I stared longingly at the bag of gallberry serum, but what use was it to me? I couldn't exactly sell it on the black market if I was on the Draax planet, and I was confident that's where I was. I had no idea why they hadn't just tossed me out of the ship into the blackness of space, but I was a fool to stick around and wait for them to do whatever they had planned.

Did the Draax have prisons? Probably, and I had no wish to see the inside of one. I needed to get the fuck out of here and now.

My backpack was sitting on the floor next to the bed. I picked it up and slipped the straps over my arms, its familiar weight on my back comforting me a little.

Years of fighting for survival had made me a quiet little mouse. The Draax at the counter didn't hear a thing as I glided silently across the room to the door. My heart still hammering and blood dripping out of my hand, I eased open the door, keeping my gaze trained on the broad back of the Draax.

He didn't turn, and I glanced out into the hallway. It was a wide hallway but short, with blind corners at either end. It was currently empty. Hopefully my luck would hold out just a little longer.

I took one final look at the Draax before stepping out into the hallway. I shut the door slowly, wincing a little at the click as it closed. My hands were sweating, and I was feeling weak and a little faint. The urge to cough had returned, and I swallowed it down before turning left and jogging toward the corner.

I needed to find my way out of the building and find a place to hide. I knew it was summer on Draax, so at least I wouldn't freeze my ass off. Maybe I'd even find a –

I stared wide-eyed at the Draax who rounded the corner. He made a startled grunt and stopped, his gaze sweeping over my body. His dark hair was longer, and he had blue eyes. I made my own sound of surprise. I'd never seen a Draax with blue eyes before. Didn't even know that was possible.

Ellis, get the fuck out of here!

Right. Time to run.

The Draax stepped toward me, and I turned and raced down the hallway to the other end. Just as I made the corner, a second Draax appeared before me. I tried to stop, but my shoes skidded on the smooth stone floor. I crashed into the Draax with a loud grunt and fell backwards onto my ass. The impact jarred a cough from my throat. I tried to scramble away, but the Draax was quick. His big hands gripped my arms, and he lifted me to my feet. I stared into familiar copper coloured eyes.

Shit. *Double* shit.

Keep your cool, Ellis. You've talked your way out of worse jams than this, right?

Right.

"Um, hey," I said. "I'm Ellis. I met you on the ship, right?

Sorry about the whole vomiting thing. I wasn't feeling all that great."

The Draax cocked his head at me before saying something in his language.

Right. No more translators.

I coughed again. I was so fucked I could practically taste dick in the back of my throat.

The other Draax had joined us, and he said something to the copper eyed one. The Draax shook his head before staring at my hands. A frown marred his admittedly perfect looking face, and my breath caught in my throat. He was angry with me.

It'd be hard to talk them out of killing me or throwing me in prison without a translator. Shit, why had I never tried to learn any of the Draax language? I was gonna die because of laziness.

I realized the Draax was rubbing his thumb over my hand. I glanced down and immediately felt a little woozy at the blood that was smeared across my hand and still dripping out, which was weird because the sight of blood – even my own – had never bothered me before.

The ache in my back had returned, and it was difficult to breathe. I coughed hard, bending over with the force of it. Shit, on top of everything else, whatever nasty lung infection I was brewing was starting to hit me hard. Weird that the gallberry serum hadn't helped, but maybe I'd only been on it for a little bit. Truthfully, I had no idea how much time had passed.

My coughing fit finally eased, but I stayed bent over as I drew in a ragged breath, not particularly enjoying the whistling wheeze my lungs made. I glanced up at the two Draax. The blue eyed one was leaning against the wall. His look didn't scream I'm gonna chop you up into small bits with my shiny sword, but it wasn't a friendly look either.

I shifted my gaze to the other one. He had what almost looked like sympathy in his copper eyes and when I realized the heavy warmth circling my upper back was his hand, I quickly straightened and stepped away.

The blue eyed Draax's hand shot out and caught my arm. I froze like a scared mouse as he shook his head at me. I wasn't typically such a chicken, but I was tired, terrified, and definitely freezing despite my thick hoodie and sweat sliding down my back.

My legs were overcooked noodles, and I locked my knees to keep from collapsing to the floor again as the blue eyed Draax tugged me back down the hallway. I staggered forward a few steps, and my locked knees gave out. Before I could hit the floor, the copper eyed Draax caught me.

He cradled me in his arms, and I stared numbly at him as he carried me toward the room I'd escaped from. The door flew open, and lab coat Draax burst into the hallway, his eyes wide. He stared at the three of us, relief crossing his face before it turned to annoyance.

He said something and disappeared back into the room. We followed him in, and the copper eyed Draax set me back on the bed before pulling off my backpack and setting it on the floor. Lab coat Draax brought over two round green rings connected by a black chain. He opened one ring, and I didn't object when he slid it around my wrist and clicked it into place. The other ring was slid around the bed rail, and I blinked in surprise when both rings turned red the moment he clicked the second ring shut.

I studied the ring around my wrist before pulling experimentally. It immediately tightened, and I cringed, convinced that the red meant it would burn me, but the metal remained cool to the touch.

The lab coat Draax said something to me. He was clearly reprimanding me for pulling at the ring, but I ignored him. Both rings were completely smooth with no lock I could pick. There had to be some type of mechanism that opened it, but I couldn't see even a seam on either ring.

I pulled again, and the ring tightened further until it cut into my skin. Lab coat Draax huffed loudly and gave the other two Draax a *Can you believe this idiot* look before running his finger along the underside of the ring.

It loosened, and he very clearly admonished me in his language before turning away. The copper eyed Draax said something to him, and he turned back, staring at my hand before shrugging.

The copper eyed Draax pointed at the blood, and I could hear the irritation in his voice when he spoke. The other Draax walked across the room and returned with gauze and a bandage. He wiped away the blood and slapped the bandage over the hole before giving the copper eyed Draax an *Are you happy* look.

The Draax pointed to the bag of serum, and the one who'd bandaged my hand immediately shook his head. The copper eyed Draax spoke rapidly, his hands jabbing in the air as he pointed to me and the serum again. It was clear he wanted me hooked up to the IV again.

Lab coat Draax continued to shake his head, and the copper eyed Draax's voice rose in anger. A deeper scowl crossed the lab coat Draax's face, and he pointed at the door before making a shooing motion.

Copper eyed Draax brushed past him, and stalked to the far side of the room. He opened what looked like a fridge and returned with a bottle of pink liquid. Lab coat Draax said something, but he ignored him and opened the bottle before holding it out to me.

I took the bottle, sniffing at the opening, even though I knew what it was. What else could it be? Nothing on Earth was that glorious pink colour. The sweet smell of the gallberry juice filled my nostrils. It smelled a little like fresh, almost overripe strawberries.

The copper eyed Draax made a drinking motion. I stared at lab coat Draax, who rolled his eyes. I drank quickly, my eyes widening when the sweet liquid slid down my throat. I drank two big swallows before sucking in a breath and staring wide-eyed at the three Draax.

Oh my God, gallberry juice was fucking amazing.

I sucked back the rest of the bottle like I was dying of thirst, afraid that lab coat Draax might snatch it from me before I could finish it. I resisted my urge to lick the bottle's rim as the three Draax watched me. My face felt flushed, energy rushed through my body, and I was confident I could run a marathon if they asked me to.

I immediately wanted more, and I stared longingly at the fridge and then at the copper eyed Drax, but blue eyed Draax put his hand on his arm and said something before tugging him in the direction of the door. With a final look at me, the copper eyed Draax followed his friend out of the room.

Lab coat Draax returned to the counter and, ignoring me, studied the test tubes in front of him again. I stuck my finger in the narrow neck of the bottle and skimmed out some of the drops of juice that clung to it before sucking them off my finger. I set the bottle on the table next to the bed and coughed a few times, but he didn't turn around. I pulled up the sheet with my free hand, huddling under it as I studied the cuff around my wrist. I traced my finger around the smooth ring and pressed experimentally on the underside, but I couldn't feel a spot where the metal felt any different.

I searched for a hidden mechanism in my cuff for almost fifteen minutes. I jerked when the chime echoed through the room. I turned on my right side, cursing inwardly when I accidentally pulled on the cuff, and it tightened around my wrist, to study the Draax at the counter.

He hit a button on the tablet in front of him, and another hologram screen popped up. A dark-haired Draax spoke briefly to him, and lab coat Draax nodded a few times before, weirdly, bowing. The hologram screen disappeared, and the Draax rummaged through a drawer before standing beside my bed. He had a small black square box, more gauze, and a clear bottle of liquid in his hand.

I didn't object when he removed the bandage on my hand, cleaned away the dried blood with the liquid and the gauze and then placed the box slightly above the hole in my hand. There was a slight pinch, and I stared in amazement at the catheter sticking out of my hand. The Draax slid the thin needle out and dropped it into a container attached to the wall before reconnecting the tubing on the IV. He made a few adjustments and walked away.

He returned only a few minutes later, holding a small gun like object in his hand. Although it looked much newer and cleaner than the last one I saw, I knew exactly what it was, and, again, I didn't object when he pressed it behind my right ear and injected me. He pressed it in the hollow of my throat and injected it there as well. I winced at the sharp pain as he dabbed gauze at my throat and behind my ear.

At least he hadn't put the translator where the old one was. The area behind my left ear felt a little tender, not to mention weirdly wet and sticky, but when I reached up to touch it, the Draax grabbed my arm and pulled it away.

"Do not touch the area, human"

I would have fallen off the bed if I hadn't been cuffed to it. I hadn't expected to be able to understand him so quickly. When Emilio injected my first translators, it took almost four days for them to start working.

I reached to touch the area again, and the Draax scowled in annoyance. "Do not touch it, I said. For the love of Krono, are the translators not working?"

He tapped on the spot behind my ear and at my throat. I coughed before saying, "It works. I was just, um, surprised. The other translators took days to work."

"Yes, well, they were old models. The new ones the Vokine developed in the last six moons work instantaneously."

He frowned again. "This is a ridiculous waste of both serum and translators."

"Then why do it?" I said snottily.

Christ, it was like I wanted to be murdered by the Draax.

"Because my king told me to do so," he said.

Okay, not the answer I was expecting. "Uh, why did the king tell you to do it?"

"No doubt, Galan was in his ear the moment he left here."

"Is Galan the guy with the copper eyes?"

"Do you always ask so many questions, human?" Lab coat Draax said.

"What's wrong with asking questions?"

"What is your name?"

"Now look who's asking the questions," I said.

He huffed in annoyance. "Fine, do not tell me your name.

It matters not to me. You will be on your planet in a prison cell by this time tomorrow anyway."

I swallowed hard. "I haven't done anything wrong."

His annoyance turned to amusement. "Do you think we are stupid? We found the bottles of juice you stole from the shipping container in your backpack."

I didn't reply and he softened a bit. "Why were you stealing them? Are you what the humans call a lower?" He looked me over. "Your clothes are ragged and smelly, and it has been a while since you bathed. You must be a lower. Did you steal them for the black market?"

Like I was going to incriminate myself. I pressed my lips into a thin line and would have crossed my arms across my chest if the left one wasn't cuffed to the bed. "I'm innocent. I was set up."

He laughed. "You are funny, human. My name is Sigan. What is yours?"

"Ellis," I said. "Why is it so sticky behind my ear?"

"The old translator was leaking flux fluid into your brain. I opened the area, removed the faulty translator and flushed the wound with gallberry serum. It is still open to allow the last of the flux fluid to drain out. Although…"

He stepped closer, rummaging in the pocket of his lab coat and producing some more gauze. He tore open the packaging and wetted the gauze with the clear liquid before bending my ear forward. I winced when he cleaned the area, even though he was gentle.

"It should not be painful, human," he asked. "You just drank some juice, and the serum should also be helping."

"It's more that it's cold," I said.

He grunted in reply and finished wiping the area clean. I stared at the black and pink stained gauze in his hand as he stepped back. "It looks better. I believe the fluid has drained out completely, and the wound can be closed."

He left and returned with a silver pen-like object in his hand. "This will hurt a little."

I bit back my cry of pain when it felt like he was burning a line of fire into my skin. I squirmed, and his hand tightened on my shoulder before he patted it almost sympathetically. "Sorry, human. I thought the juice in your system would help. Here, I will bring you another."

He brought me a second bottle of juice, and I drank it as quickly as I had drained the first. He disposed of both bottles, and I took the opportunity to feel behind my ear when his back was turned. The skin still tingled, but I couldn't feel anything, not even a thin scar.

"Would you like to bathe now, human?" Sigan said.

"Yes," I said eagerly.

He unhooked my IV, and I watched carefully when he slid his finger under the cuff around my wrist. It turned green and opened with a small click, but I still couldn't figure out how the hell he'd opened it.

I slid out of the bed, and Sigan took my arm and led me toward a door on the far side of the room. "You may shower in there," he said. "Give me your clothes, and I will have them cleaned."

"Um, I'm not undressing in front of you," I said.

"I am not sexually attracted to you, human," Sigan said. "No Draax will be."

My face flushed bright red, and a memory I'd rather never remember threatened to surface.

Ukana. Ukana. Ukana.

The word echoed in my brain, making me feel both nauseated and ashamed.

"You do not have to be concerned about me asking you to mate just because I see you naked. Trust me. You are much too thin." Sigan was carrying on like he hadn't just sliced open my oldest and most painful wound.

I swallowed down the hurt and the shame, shoved it deep where it belonged and activated my sarcasm shield as I did so often. "As much as I enjoy your sweet talking, I'm still not taking off my clothes in front of you, Sigan."

"Sweet talking?" Sigan cocked one eyebrow as his tail waved in the air behind him. "What does that mean?"

Great. My sarcasm was lost on the Draax. "Look, I'll get undressed in the bathroom and toss my clothes out to you. All right?"

"That is acceptable," Sigan said.

He dropped my arm, and I stepped into the bathroom and shut the door behind me. I leaned against the door briefly before stripping off my clothes and wrapping one of the clean towels around me. I opened the door just enough to toss my clothes out and take the toothbrush and toothpaste Sigan handed me.

I turned the shower on and glanced at the door before quickly going through the cupboard under the sink.

"C'mon," I muttered. "This is like a hospital, right? There's gotta be a scalpel or something lying around that I can use to escape."

The idea of using a scalpel against Sigan's giant body was laughable, but it was my best plan. He wasn't wearing a sword around his waist like the other two Draax, so maybe he was more of a lover than a fighter. Besides, even a giant Draax like Sigan would have to submit to me if I was holding a damn scalpel to his throat.

Of course, that would only work if something other than

towels were in the cupboard. I sighed and stood up, staring at myself in the mirror over the sink.

"Ugh." My hair was dirty and stringy, and the whole right side was matted to my head with the sticky black flux fluid and gallberry serum. I lifted my arm and sniffed my armpit, wrinkling my nose at the smell. I smelled worse than a hydron pivoter in a havoc cruiser.

I brushed my teeth and then stepped into the shower, scrubbing my body and hair with the sweet smelling soap that dispensed out of a panel in the shower wall when I pressed the first of the two green buttons.

It felt fantastic to be clean, and I couldn't remember the last time I had a proper shower. Even though I was coughing again and my back was aching, I washed my hair and body again until my pale skin was pink from scrubbing.

I shut the water off and studied the panel on the wall before experimentally pressing the second green button. I shrieked and laughed when hot air blew from small holes in the shower's glass. It was like being inside a giant blow dryer, and I pressed the button twice before getting out of the shower and wrapping the towel around me.

I finger combed my hair as best I could, wincing at the tangles in my long locks. I coughed and tightened the towel around my body before opening the door to the bathroom.

"Hey, Sigan? Do you have a hospital gown or something I can wear until my clothes are…"

My voice died in my throat, and I stared at the copper eyed Draax standing before me.

CHAPTER 4

Galan

"Krey, where are you off to?" I left the garden and followed him down the hallway. Like Quill, Krey and I had known each other since we were children, and I didn't need to see the short, hard flicks of Krey's tail to know he was annoyed.

"I thought I was going to the dining hall to finally get some food in my belly, followed by my bed for a nap," Krey grumbled. He slowed down, allowing me to catch up to him. "What are you doing?"

"Walking in the garden," I said.

Krey scrubbed a hand through his hair, and I could see the weariness etched into his face. "Krono, are you not tired, Galan?"

I shrugged. I *was* tired, but while the gallberry juice I'd drank took away the space sickness, my stomach still felt as twisted up as the trunk of a darsinian tree. I couldn't have slept even if I'd tried.

After leaving the infirmary, I'd gone straight to Quill's private quarters. Angry with Sigan for allowing the little human to suffer, I could barely keep my voice measured when I asked Quill for permission to give the human more serum as well as translators.

He had agreed quickly enough, although I knew the agitation in my voice had left him curious. After he called Sigan, I made an excuse and left. He would ask me why I was so annoyed, and I didn't want to have to explain. Feeling so strongly for a human who I had just met and would probably break if I even tried to bed her left me perplexed.

Now you want to mate with her?

I flushed, my tail snapping back and forth behind me as I walked with Krey. No, I didn't. I just felt sorry for her. She would be returned to Earth within a day or two, where she would die a painful and miserable death while being locked away. No one deserved that fate, not even a thief. If I could make it a little easier for her while she was here, maybe even buy her some extra time with the healing juice of the gallberry plant, I would.

"Galan?"

I glanced at Krey. "Sorry, what?"

"I asked why you were walking in the garden and not relaxing like I want to be."

"Too wound up to sleep, I suppose," I said. "Where are you going?"

"Quill asked me to bring the thief to the council room. He and Teo wish to speak with her."

My steps slowed, and I hurried to catch up with Krey when he turned the corner. "You are taking her to meet them now?"

"Yes."

49

"She needs to rest."

Krey shrugged. "Our king demands it."

I clapped him on the back. "Go to the dining hall and eat, my friend. I will take the human to the council room."

Krey stopped and studied me for a moment. "That is kind of you, Galan."

I didn't reply and Krey squeezed my shoulder, the look on his face uncharacteristically solemn. "Your attraction to the human is not wise. Not only is she too small for you to bed, but she will be imprisoned for at least forty years. You know how the humans are about gallberry juice being stolen."

"Technically, she stole it from us, not from the humans," I said.

"So, what? You know as well as I do that the Planetary Treaty only allows humans to be punished for their crimes by Earth authorities. Even if that wasn't true, do you want her put in Iron Gate instead?" Krey said.

"No."

"I know you wish for a mate, old friend, but this tiny human is not the one," Krey said.

"I am aware. Besides, I am not attracted to her. I feel sorry for her. When Sigan scanned her, he found cancer in her spine and her lungs. She will not live long once she returns to Earth."

"That may be better for her," Krey said. "Earth prisons do not separate the males from the females. One as small as her could not possibly survive in a prison. Her early death will be a mercy for her. The male prisoners will most likely abuse her."

Krey's face had lightened to a pale green, a sure sign that he was upset. "The way human males so callously treat their females never fails to surprise me. Why do they not understand how precious a female is, Galan?"

"I do not know," I said.

His hands had clenched into tight fists, and his tail swiped through the air with hard strokes and jabs again. "Perhaps we should ask Quill to put her in our prison. Even the rakart who populate Iron Gate would never hurt her. They know the value of females."

"Go and eat, Krey. I will take the human to see our king," I said.

He nodded and we started down the hallway again, going our separate ways at the end of the hallway. A few minutes later, I opened the infirmary door, my eagerness to see the tiny human surprising me.

The human's bed was empty, and fresh anxiety poured through me. Had she tried to escape again? Sigan was sitting at his desk at the far end of the infirmary. He glanced up from his tablet when I said, "Sigan, where is the human?"

"Bathing." He pointed to the bathroom door. "I could no longer stand the smell of her."

I glanced at the bag of gallberry serum, and Sigan said, "Do not worry, Galan. I gave her the serum and implanted translators as the king requested."

I ignored the way he accented the word king and walked toward him. "Our king requests the human's presence in the council room. When she is finished bathing, I will -"

The bathroom door swung open just as I walked by it.

"Hey, Sigan? Do you have a hospital gown or something I can wear until my clothes are…"

The little female stopped speaking, staring wide-eyed at me as she clutched the towel around her body.

Krono, she was beautiful. Her eyes were a fascinating shade of blue that reminded me of the crashing waves of the Gardian Sea. Her pale skin, finally clean of the grime that covered it, was pink from the shower's heat, and her matted hair was now a shiny gold waterfall. I was suddenly itching to touch her hair to see if the locks were as soft as they looked.

The human squeaked nervously and backed away when I reached for her hair. My face burning, I took a step back as Sigan joined us.

"You look better, human." He sniffed at her. "You smell better, too."

"Uh, thanks. Do you have a gown or something I can wear?" She had her arms crossed over her tiny towel-covered breasts. I stared at her legs. They weren't perfectly smooth. I could see a few small scars on her right knee, and a long twisting scar ran down the front of her left shin. Still, I had a sudden image of those scarred legs wrapped around my waist, and my cock twitched against the confines of my briefs.

I cleared my throat as Sigan pulled a gown from a cupboard and handed it to her. "Here, human."

"Thank you." With one last look at me, she shut the bathroom door.

Sigan turned away, and I reached down and adjusted my dick. I was half-hard, and the image of the human and all of her pretty pale skin was etched into my brain.

Krono, I had to stop thinking about it before Sigan noticed my erection.

"Why are you here, Galan?" Sigan asked.

"Quill wishes to meet with the human."

I could hear the human coughing, and I frowned at Sigan. "Is she well enough?"

He nodded. "Yes. Although the cancer seems to be even more aggressive than I originally thought. I took a closer look at her scan while she bathed and discovered spots on her liver and her kidneys. My estimate of her life expectancy has dropped to a moon or less."

There was a soft gasp behind me, and I turned to see the human standing in the bathroom doorway again. Her gown was meant for a Draax male and hung on her like a sheet.

Her mouth trembling, she stared at Sigan. "Cancer? I have cancer?"

"Yes," Sigan said, although his tone was softer than it usually was. "I am sorry, human. You have a large tumour on your spine, and the cancer has spread to your lungs and other organs. It is why you cough."

"I... but I don't feel that bad," she said. "It's just a lung infection."

"It is not," Sigan said. "It is cancer, and you are going to die."

"Sigan!" I glared at him as the human slumped against the wall.

"Lying to her will not change the outcome," Sigan said.

"You could be... gentler about it," I said.

I liked our kadana, but he was not particularly compassionate for a healer.

"I am sorry, human," Sigan said. "I did not mean to upset you. But think of it this way: you will not have to live long in the Earth prison. That should cheer you, should it not?"

"For Krono's sake," I snapped as the human made a sound that was half laughter and half sob. "Sigan, be quiet."

I took a step toward the human. "Human, take a deep breath."

She stared up at me, her eyes as large and round as a diacus flower. Her pale skin was nearly translucent, and her lips had lost all their colour. I picked her up when she staggered and carried her back to her bed. I set her on the side of it with her legs dangling before pressing on the back of her neck. "Head between your knees, little human."

She bent forward obediently, but I kept one hand on her neck and rubbed her upper back with the other. "Take deep breaths."

She breathed deeply for a few minutes and when I was sure she wouldn't faint, I eased her upright. I studied her face. She wasn't quite as pale as before, and her lips were pink again.

"Sigan, bring me some juice," I said.

He brought it over, and I twisted off the cap and handed it to the human. "Drink this."

Her hands shaking, she drank the entire bottle of juice before wiping her mouth with the back of her hand. "Thanks."

"You are welcome, human," I said.

She made a face. "Ellis. My name is Ellis."

"I am Galan," I said.

"Nice to meet you," she said. "How many extra minutes do you think that bottle of juice gave me? Two? Three?"

"At least an hour," Sigan said.

"Sigan," I said as the female gaped at him.

Both Sigan and I jerked when the little female burst into loud laughter. We watched as she bent over, holding onto her stomach and laughing until tears slipped down her cheeks.

"This female is a strange one," Sigan said before walking away.

Ellis laughed harder until the laughter turned to coughing. She buried her mouth in the crook of her elbow, and I rubbed her back again until her coughing fit eased.

I was about to ask Sigan for another bottle of juice when he dropped one off on the bed beside her and returned to his desk. I opened the juice and handed it to her. "Drink."

She drank this one a little slower, swiping at her watery eyes. "Thanks. It's good."

I took the empty bottle from her as she rubbed her upper chest. "So, are you here to take me back to Earth now?"

"No," I said. "Our king has requested to see you."

"Right, there was a royal crest on the ship." She sighed and rubbed at her chest again. "I should never have snuck onto your damn ship."

I wanted to ask her why she was stealing the juice, but Quill was waiting for her, and he would grow impatient.

"Do you feel well enough to walk, human?"

"Yes." She slid off the bed, the hospital gown dragging on the ground behind her. She lifted it a little, and I stared at her bare feet.

"Sigan, where are the human's boots?"

"I threw them away with the rest of her clothing," Sigan said.

"Threw them away?" The little female stared indignantly at him. "What the hell? Those were my clothes, you dickhead. You said you were going to have them cleaned."

"The dirt was the only thing keeping them together," Sigan said.

She scowled at him and I hid my grin when she extended her middle finger to the kadana. I knew what that human gesture meant, and evidently, so did Sigan because he rolled his eyes and said, "Being rude will not get your clothes back, human."

"I will carry you," I said.

I reached for her, feeling a stupid sort of hurt when she pushed me away. "I can walk."

"Our floors are cold, and without your boots -"

"It's fine," she said. "I'm used to cold."

I hesitated before stepping back. "All right."

"Aren't you going to put those on me?" She pointed to the cuffs lying on the bed.

"Do I need to?" I said.

She shook her head. "No. I don't think I could outrun you even if my body weren't riddled with cancer."

Her face paled a little, and a trickle of admiration went down my back when she straightened her body and said, "C'mon, let's go see this king of yours."

Ellis

I WAS GOING TO DIE.

As I walked with Galan down the wide hallway, my brain kept shrinking away from the thought. I rubbed at my chest. Thanks to the two bottles of juice, my cough was gone again, and I didn't feel like I had cancer. I felt fantastic and healthy as a horse, as the old Earth saying went.

Yeah, well, you're not. You have cancer, and you're going to die. And fairly soon, if Sigan is to be believed.

I wanted to pretend that he was wrong, that his scanner had made a mistake, but it was a waste of energy. Not with the coughing the last few weeks and how, for the last year, the ache in my back had never really gone away. I'd chalked it up to sleeping on the streets, not a tumour. At twenty-three years old, who thought they would get cancer?

I took a quick peek at the green alien walking beside me. Lord, he was big. He could crush me like a bug if he wanted to. If we had sex, I'd have to ride him. It'd be the only way to...

What the fuck, Ellis?

Holy shit, where did that come from? Maybe I should ask Sigan to scan my brain again. It probably had cancer as well. It was the only logical explanation for why I suddenly imagined climbing the alien next to me like he was a big old tree.

It's called sexual attraction, not brain cancer, you idiot.

Yeah, well, it was pointless to be attracted to him, even if he did have a fantastic body and the sexiest voice I'd ever heard.

Don't forget about his eyes.

I looked up again, studying the way the light caught the copper in his eyes and made them appear to glow. I'd seen Draax with copper eyes before, but something about Galan's was...

His big hand grabbed my arm and pulled me to a stop. "Be careful, human."

I blushed furiously as we started walking again. Fuck me, I'd almost walked into a wall. What was wrong with me?

You have cancer, and you're going to die?

Yeah, yeah, I heard you the first time.

I tried to shove away the thoughts of my impending death. What good would it do? I was dead in a matter of months, and there was nothing I could do about it. Unless, maybe, I could gorge myself on gallberry juice before they shipped me back to Earth. How much juice did a person have to drink when cancer was in multiple organs and your spine?

Gallons, probably.

"What was that?" Galan glanced down at me, and I realized I had spoken out loud.

"Nothing," I said. "So, uh, is this place a castle?"

"Yes. You are in the home of King Quillan. He rules the western province."

"Do you live here?" I said.

"I do. I am the head of the King's Guard."

I glanced at the sword around his waist. "So, you protect the king?"

"And his queen and the princess," Galan said. "But that is only a small part of my job."

"Oh," I said. "Do you like being the head of the King's Guard?"

"Very much. What do you do for a job on Earth?"

For a moment, I was tempted to tell him the truth – that I sold juice on the black market. I was already going to prison for the next forty years, so what did it matter?

You'll be dead in three months.

"I, uh, repaired havoc cruisers and land vehicles," I said.

It wasn't a complete lie. I worked at a shop with Torra for a while and we *had* fixed cruisers and land vehicles. Sure, it was only for a few months so we could case the place, but it'd been my first and only real job. I'd been oddly proud of working there, and the owner, Horace, was kind to me.

Guilt wormed its way into my guts. I'd almost begged Torra to change her mind about robbing Horace. Hell, I *did* beg. It didn't work, and I was a fool to think it might. Torra did what she had to to survive, and, honestly, if it hadn't been for her, I would have been dead a long time ago. She was the toughest, smartest person I knew and taught me everything I needed to know about surviving on the streets.

Yeah, well, she lasted how long in prison before she died? Was it two months or three?

Fear was sending adrenaline shooting through my veins. If Torra, who I'd once seen take down three large men in less than two minutes without breaking a sweat, couldn't survive prison for more than a couple months, what chance did I have?

Forget cancer killing you. You'll be dead within a week.

I shuddered all over, and Galan stopped in the hallway. "Are you cold, human?"

"No." I *was* cold, and my feet had gone numb from the coolness of the stone floor, but if I told Galan that, he'd probably do something weird like carry me.

"Can I ask you a question?" I trudged along beside him when he started walking again.

"Yes."

"Where is everyone? I mean, for a castle, this place seems empty." We hadn't passed a single alien in the hallway, and we'd been walking for almost five minutes.

"It is the dinner hour," Galan said. "They are either in the dining hall or their living quarters."

"Oh," I said. "How many Draax live in the castle?"

"Many," he said. "Quill's home is large."

"What does… oh wow." I stopped in front of a set of open double doors. I stared at the lush garden in front of us. Warm light beamed down, and a light breeze carried the scent of flowers. I stepped inside, ignoring the stone pathway that wound through the garden in favour of the grass. It was soft and warm under my feet, and I stared upward at the large flock of birds sitting in a tree. They were about the size of a sparrow and bright orange with lime green beaks, and they were the source of the low beeps I could hear.

"What kind of birds are those?"

"Caterra," Galan said.

"Is that…" I squinted at the sky, shading my eyes against the bright light, "where's the ceiling?"

Galan chuckled, and it sent warmth down my spine. "In the warmer weather, the ceiling is retracted in the King's Garden to give the plants light and fresh air."

"Holy shit. He has a garden right in his house?" I said. "How big is it?"

"Large," he said. "Walking from one end of the garden to the other would take over an hour."

I blinked at him, trying to comprehend how big the castle must be. "How often do people get lost in this place?"

"In the cold season, the king opens the garden to the public so they may enjoy the warmth and the plant life. Occasionally, visitors will get lost and must be rescued. Come, little human, we must keep going."

I turned away reluctantly. I had never seen anything so beautiful and wished I could walk through the garden. Maybe if I asked nicely enough, they'd let me walk through it before I was sent back to Earth. It would be a good memory to have when I was being raped and murdered in prison.

Another full-body shudder, and Galan frowned at me. "Human, if you are cold, you must tell me."

"I'm fine," I said. "How much further?"

"We are here." Galan stopped in front of another set of closed double doors.

My stomach churned, and I hugged my torso. I was naked under the hospital gown Sigan had given me, and while I was thankful it was roughly the size of a sheet and billowed around my thin body, I still suddenly felt horribly exposed.

Shouldn't a person be wearing underwear when they meet a king?

"When you are introduced to the king, you must bow," Galan said.

"Sure, yeah, I can do that," I said.

Galan hesitated and then opened the left door, ushering me in ahead of him. The room we were in was on the smaller side. A window along the left wall filled the room with warm sunlight. A wooden credenza with a marble countertop ran along the right wall. A couple of jugs filled with pink liquid sat next to some empty glasses on the credenza, and my mouth watered. Gallberry juice. My sudden and intense craving for it was almost overwhelming.

I took a deep breath and forced my gaze away from the juice and to the middle of the room. A long table with four chairs on either side and a chair at the end took up most of the space. My heart thudded out an erratic rhythm as I stared at the two aliens sitting at the table.

They stood, and I stumbled forward when Galan pushed lightly on my back. We stopped in front of the larger Draax, who I knew instinctively was the king. I bit back a strangled laugh. Large was an understatement. Galan had to be at least 6'5", and the king still had a few inches on him. His body was as muscular as Galan's, and his dark hair was cut short. But where Galan's eyes were a warm copper and had kindness and compassion radiating from them, the king's eyes were an icy silver that didn't hold an ounce of compassion. I immediately looked down when his gaze landed on my face.

Fuck. I'd be lucky if the king didn't just kill me himself for stealing from him.

"Human, this is King Quillan of the Western Province. My king, this is the human Ellis."

I bowed, keeping my gaze on the floor even after I straightened.

"Hello, Ellis."

The voice was deep and, surprisingly, more kind than I imagined. I swallowed hard. "Hello, uh, your majesty."

"I asked Krey to bring the thief," the king said.

"You did," Galan said.

There was silence, and I diligently studied the cracks on the stone floor.

"This is Teo. He is advisor to the king," Galan finally said.

I nodded to the older Draax. His hair was more silver than dark, and his body was bent with age. He pointed to one of the chairs. "Sit down, human."

I sat, my knees unhinging at the last second so that I fell into the chair. Galan sat beside me as the king returned to the chair at the end of the table, and Teo sat in the chair to his right.

Teo had a tablet in his hand, and he scrolled through it. "You are being charged under your Earth's law for stealing gallberry juice. You will be -"

"It wasn't me," I said.

Teo looked up from his tablet. "What?"

"I didn't steal the juice," I said.

"You were found on a royal ship with juice from one of our shipping containers in your possession, human."

"Right," I said. "But I didn't put it in my backpack."

Teo studied me before turning to Galan. "Does she suffer from a head injury, Galan?"

"No," Galan said.

"Maybe brain cancer," I said.

62

Galan jerked beside me as Teo cocked his head at me. "As I was saying, you are being charged with -"

"But it wasn't me," I said. "I'm innocent."

"Who was it then?" Teo's voice held more than a hint of exasperation.

"Cheryl," I said.

"Who is this Cheryl?" Teo said.

"Well, I thought she was my friend, but then she convinced me to sneak onto a Draax ship and planted some stolen juice on me before running away and leaving me holding the juice. So, to speak," I said.

I was talking fast, my mind whirling as I spoke. There was no way in hell I was incriminating myself. I'd be given a lawyer when I returned to Earth, and even though the public defenders were notorious for not giving a shit about us lowers, there was still the chance I might get one with a shred of conscious who would try to keep me out of prison.

"Was there another human on the ship, Galan?" Teo said.

"No," Galan said. He was studying me with obvious confusion, but the king... was that amusement in his gaze? "There was only this human hiding in the storage space."

"I told you - Cheryl took off before you guys came on the ship. I'm surprised you didn't see her in the docking bay. Tall, blonde hair, real curvy?" I said.

Galan shook his head, and I shrugged. "She moves pretty fast when she wants to. Listen, I had no idea she planned to steal the juice. She told me she just wanted to see what the inside of a Draax royal ship looked like. I said sure, and the next thing I knew, she was shoving bottles of juice into my backpack. I told her no, I wasn't going to steal anything from you guys, but she had a gun and threatened me. But then she heard you guys coming on the ship and, like, took off."

"Out the same door that Galan and the others entered into?" The king raised one eyebrow at me.

"Uh, I'm not sure," I said. "I wasn't feeling very well. To tell you the truth, I was kind of dizzy and a little out of it. I'm chocked full of cancer."

"Yes, I heard," the king said. "Go on with your story, little human."

"I didn't have time to return the bottles to the shipping container, so I hid in the storage space. I planned to leave the bottles and get the hell off the ship, but I passed out, probably because of all the cancer. We were already in space when I woke up, and I was very sick. I vomited on Galan's shoes."

"Not mine," Galan said. "Krey's."

"Oh. Anyway, as you can see, there has been a huge misunderstanding. So, maybe," I smiled at Teo, "instead of turning me over to the cops, you could just drop me off somewhere on a beach? I'm not picky about which beach. I hear Mexico is lovely this time of year."

"You are lying to us, human," Teo said. "There is no Cheryl."

"You don't know that," I said. "There could totally be a Cheryl. In fact, there *is* a Cheryl, and she's the one to blame."

Teo hesitated before shaking his head. "It does not matter. It will be up to the authorities on Earth to sort the matter. You will be returned to Earth tomorrow morning. I have alerted the authorities in your city about your crime."

I swallowed again. The urge to cough had returned, and I tried to ignore it as Galan said, "Tomorrow morning?"

"Yes." Teo was looking over his tablet again. "Henden and Laos are making a trip to Vokine. They will take the human with them and return her to Earth before traveling to Vokine."

"It is out of the way," Galan said. "The jumpgate to the Milky Way is in the opposite direction. Krey and I could make another supply run to Earth in a few days and return her then."

Teo shook his head. "There is no need for another supply run so quickly, Galan. It is a waste of fuel to make an extra trip with another ship when Henden and Laos leave tomorrow."

"My king," Galan said, "if we give the human a few days, we can heal her of her cancer."

I stared in shock at Galan as Teo snorted. "It is an unnecessary waste of the gallberry plant. You know as well as I do that the human will not survive for more than a day or two in the Earth's prison. She is too small and weak."

"I'm stronger than I look," I said. "Plus, I'm innocent, remember? I probably won't even go to prison once I talk to my lawyer."

I liked that I sounded confident, even though I knew my chance of not being sent to prison was slim at best. Still, if the Draax could heal me before I left…

Maybe it's better if you die of the cancer, Ellis. The old Draax is right. You won't survive prison.

I ignored my inner voice. I might survive. I was small and quick, and I knew how to hide. And if that didn't work, I'd whore myself out to the toughest guy in my prison block in exchange for keeping me safe.

My stomach rolled at the thought, but I shoved any trepidations about my survival plans away ruthlessly. I didn't want to die, and I'd do whatever it took to survive.

"It won't hurt to heal her first," Galan said.

Teo sighed. "My king, it is a waste of resources. What will

your people say if they discover you wasted juice and ship fuel on a common thief?"

"Saving a life is not a waste," Galan said.

I appreciated his effort but could already tell the king wasn't going for it.

The king stared thoughtfully at me for a few minutes before shaking his head. "I am sorry, Galan, but Teo is right. It is a waste of resources."

"Quill," Galan said, "it is not -"

"Enough, Galan. I have made my decision. I am sorry, human, but you will be returned to your planet tomorrow morning," Quill said.

"Galan, take the human to the west wing of the castle. We will place her in one of the empty living quarters and post a guard outside the room for the evening," Teo said.

"No." Quill leaned forward. "Return her to the infirmary and have Sigan give her gallberry serum for the night. Tell him to give her as much juice as she can drink."

"Quill," Teo said, "it is a waste. I have read Sigan's report on the human. The cancer is throughout her body. A night of serum will not be enough to cure her."

"I am aware, Teo," Quill said. His gaze landed on me, and I saw a flicker of compassion in his eyes. "Galan, return her to the infirmary and have one of your men stand guard outside it."

"I will stand guard," Galan said.

"No," Quill replied. "You will return to your quarters and get some rest."

"Quill, I -"

"Enough, Galan," Quill said. "Return the human to the infirmary and then retire to your quarters."

"Yes, my king."

Galan grasped my arm, and he helped me to my feet. I bowed and said, "Thank you, uh, Your Highness."

"You are welcome, little human. I am sorry your fate is such a grim one."

I didn't know what to say to that, so I just nodded and followed Galan out of the room. His hand was still around my arm, and he was walking so quickly that I had to jog to keep up. His tail flicked back and forth in agitation, and his green skin had darkened considerably.

"Galan," I puffed, "can you slow down?"

He slowed, although his tail continued to cut through the air like a striking snake. "Sorry, human."

We walked silently for a minute or so before I said, "Thank you for your help."

He snorted angrily. "I was as useless as a botakin."

"What's a botakin?" I said.

"A small creature who lives in the forest and has no purpose other than as a meal for the groden," he said.

"What's a groden?"

"An animal similar to your grizzly bear," he said.

"Oh. You were helpful," I said.

Frustration coloured his words. "I was not, human."

"You were. I'm pretty sure the king is giving me gallberry serum tonight because of you."

"It will not be enough to cure you," he said.

"I know. But it'll probably give me a few more weeks, right?" I said. "That's better than nothing."

I meant what I was saying. Sure, it would have been fan-fucking-tastic to be completely cured of cancer, but when you were staring down the barrel of a three-month life expectancy, even a few extra weeks were a gift.

He stopped in the hallway and stared at me. I held out my hand. "Seriously, thank you."

He shook my hand, and the moment his rough, warm palm pressed against mine, my nipples went hard, and my brain went blank. I licked my lips, staring up at his mouth. God, he was so handsome. I'd seen plenty of Draax on Earth, but never one as good looking as Galan.

"Human?" Galan's hand squeezed mine, and dammit if my pussy didn't go damp. "Are you all right?"

"You're so pretty," I said.

He blinked, surprise registering in his beautiful copper eyes. My face went a bright red. Oh my God, I just told this giant warrior alien that he was pretty. What was wrong with me?

Ask him if he wants to have sex. You're going to die anyway, right? Why not bang a smoking hot Draax before you do?

My inner voice made an excellent point. Even if I somehow talked my way out of prison, I was dead in three months anyway. I should be living my life to the fullest, and at this exact moment, living my fullest life meant finding out just how big Galan's dick was.

"Human, are you all right?"

I took a deep breath. "I'm good. Galan, would you like to have…"

Ukana. Ukana. Ukana.

The words dried up in my throat and stuck like flypaper. What the fuck was I thinking? Galan would never sleep with me. No Draax would.

"Would I like to have what?" Galan said.

"Nothing. Never mind." I tried to drop his hand, my breath catching when Galan tugged me closer. The heat of his body was like a drug, and I could feel my body swaying toward his as he studied my face. Something flickered in his eyes, and the copper darkened to a beautiful burnt bronze. He inhaled deeply, his nostrils flaring as his gaze dropped to my mouth.

"That is a tiny human."

The voice behind us scared the bejeezus out of me. A hard pressure flicked around my waist and squeezed. I stared at Galan's tail wrapped around my waist before looking over my shoulder at the Draax standing in the hallway.

He studied Galan's tail before smiling at me. "Hello, tiny female. What is your name?"

"What do you want, Luka?" Galan said.

His voice sounded strange… strained and on edge.

The Draax blinked at him. "Nothing. I was headed toward the garden for my evening walk. I have never seen such a small female before. Is she new to the castle? Can she even clean or work in the garden? She looks so frail."

He held out his hand to me. "I am Luka."

I reached for his hand, wincing when Galan's tail tightened to the point of pain. "Ouch, Galan, stop that."

I tugged at his tail and, his face a dark green, Galan released me. I shook Luka's hand. "Hey, Luka. I'm Ellis."

"Ellis." Luka smiled at me. "That is a strange name."

"Uh, thanks, I think?"

"What part of the castle do you work in?"

Galan took my arm and pulled me past Luka. "We must be going. Goodnight, Luka."

"Goodnight," Luka said.

Still holding my arm, Galan practically marched me back to the infirmary.

"What's wrong?" I said.

"Nothing."

"You're pissed about something."

"I am not angry." He opened the infirmary door and pushed me into the room. "Sigan, the human will spend the night in the infirmary."

"I know." Sigan looked up from his desk. "Teo has already messaged me. Who will you assign to keep watch over her?"

"Adrix," Galan said. "I will speak to him now. Make sure you give her more serum and as much juice as she can drink."

"Yes, yes," Sigan said. He joined us at my bed, and once I climbed in, he attached the weird smooth cuff around my wrist again, tethering me to the bed.

"Is that necessary?" Galan said. "Adrix will stop her from leaving."

"I am not risking her touching my equipment," Sigan said.

"I won't. I promise," I said.

He snorted. "I do not believe you, human. You will remain cuffed to the bed."

"Shocker," I said.

My stomach growled, and Galan said, "Make sure she is also given food, Sigan."

My mouth watered, and my stomach growled again at the mention of food.

"When did you eat last, human?" Sigan said.

I thought back before shrugging. "A couple days ago... I think."

Galan muttered something I didn't catch before heading toward the door. "I will call the kitchen and have food brought to the infirmary."

"Galan, wait!" I glanced at Sigan, a little embarrassed at the eagerness in my voice. "Will I, um, see you again before I leave?"

Galan nodded. "I will stop by in the morning."

"Okay."

He left without saying goodbye. Sigan hooked me up to the IV and gave me a bottle of gallberry juice before returning to his desk. I drank the entire bottle and then flopped back in the bed to stare at the ceiling. All things considered, tonight would probably be the best night of my life. Sure, I was dying of cancer, and by this time tomorrow night, I'd be in a prison cell, but tonight I was warm, I had as much gallberry juice as I wanted to drink, and I'd have some food in my belly.

It was the best a liar and a thief could ask for.

CHAPTER 5

Galan

The castle was quiet this early in the morning. I stopped in front of Quill and Sabrina's private quarters and hesitated with my hand raised to knock. Our queen was not an early riser, and I risked waking her at this hour, but I had no choice. I'd seen Quill in the training room, clashing swords with Krey, and if I had any hope of speaking to Sabrina alone before the human was sent back to Earth, now was the time.

Ellis. Her name is Ellis.

I said her name out loud. I liked how it sounded on my tongue and repeated it before knocking on the door. To my surprise, it opened almost immediately.

"Galan, hi."

I bowed. "Good morning, my queen. I am sorry for waking you."

"I wasn't sleeping. Come on in."

I followed her into the room, smiling when Jovie slid off

the couch and skipped toward me. She held out her arms. "Up, Uda."

I picked her up and kissed her smooth cheek. "Hello, meena. Are you the reason your mama is awake so early?"

"She certainly is," Sabrina said. "She's lucky she's so damn cute."

Jovie rested her head on my shoulder, and I nestled her in the crook of my arm as Sabrina eased onto the couch. She rubbed her belly and smiled at me. "Quill isn't here. He went for an early morning sword fight with Krey."

"I know." I sat down on the couch beside her. "It is you I wish to speak with."

"Oh? About what?"

Quill would be angry with me when he found out what I was about to do, but I had to do it. I hadn't slept at all last night. My guilt and worry for Ellis kept me awake until keo rose in the sky and bathed my apartment in warm light.

"It is about the human in the infirmary," I said.

Jovie sat up and patted my face as Sabrina studied me for a moment. "What about her?"

I took a deep breath, praying to Krono that this would work.

———

Twenty minutes later, the door to Quill and Sabrina's living quarters opened, and Jovie squealed and bounced on my lap. She wiggled free of my grip and slid to the ground, running unsteadily toward Quill, who scooped her up and kissed her cheek.

"Good morning, little queen. Did you sleep well?"

Jovie hugged him, burying her face in his neck. He rubbed her back as he smiled at me. "Good morning, Galan."

"Hello, Quill."

He joined us in the living room, kissing Sabrina before sinking into the chair across from the couch. "I see our little queen did not let my sadora sleep in this morning."

"No, she did not," Sabrina said with a laugh. "She was awake about three minutes after you left."

"I told you last night to let your mama sleep this morning, did I not, Jovie?" Quill said to his daughter.

She giggled and relaxed against his chest, her tiny tail curling around his forearm as he turned to me. "You are here early, Galan."

I didn't reply, but Sabrina said, "He wanted to talk to me about something."

"I imagine he did," Quill said. "So, my queen, has he convinced you to convince me to keep the tiny human thief until she is healed?"

Sabrina glanced my way, and Quill grinned at me. "Do not look so shocked, Galan. I know you almost as well as you know yourself. Honestly, I am surprised you waited until this morning to speak to Sabrina."

"I agree with him," Sabrina said. "We should keep her until the gallberry juice heals her cancer."

"Of course you agree with him," Quill said. "Your compassion and generosity are no secret."

"Your queen's mercy is what makes her so loved by your people," I said.

"That is true," Quill said.

"We have more than enough of the gallberry plant to heal her," Sabrina said. "And I know for a fact that you just finished a trade deal with the Scuun that gave us, like, a mountain's worth of isotopes for the ships, so you can spare the fuel as well. Once she is healed, Galan and Krey will return her to Earth. It'll only be a few days, honey."

When Quill didn't reply, a familiar stubborn look crossed Sabrina's face. "This is important to me and to Galan, my king."

Quill smiled at her. "My queen, you know I cannot resist anything you ask of me. Galan also knows this, which is why he spoke with you when I was busy with Krey."

Sabrina's smug look made both Quill and me laugh.

"You're so getting lucky tonight," Sabrina said to Quill.

He laughed again. "I look forward to it, sweet sadora. But I will confess that Galan involving you was not necessary. I had already changed my mind about healing her. I planned to speak to Teo once we finished breakfast and let him know the human stays until she is fully healed."

I shouldn't have been surprised by Quill's confession. If my brain hadn't been so wrapped up in thoughts of Ellis, I may have even assumed he would change his mind. Despite Quill's outer appearance, he had a compassionate and kind nature.

Sabrina's smile widened as she stared at Quill. "God, I love you."

"I love you too, sadora. Galan, join us for breakfast." Quill said. "We will speak with Teo once we are done."

I wanted to return to Ellis, wake her, and tell her the good news, but I would not be rude to my best friend or his mate. "Thank you. I would like that."

There was a knock on the door, and Quill shouted, "Come in."

Teo stepped into the living quarters, bowing to Quill and then Sabrina.

"Good morning, Teo," Quill said. "You are just in time to join us for breakfast."

"Thank you, Quill," Teo said. "But I am afraid I did not stop by so early for food."

"What's going on?" Sabrina asked.

"The Emirans and Cillades are at war."

"Again?" Sabrina glanced at Quill. "Didn't the last war between them just end six months ago?"

Quill nodded. "What are they quarrelling about this time, Teo?"

"Who knows, my king." The disgust was evident on Teo's face. "It does not take much to set either race off, so it could be almost anything."

"Are the Emirans requesting our assistance?" Quill asked.

"No. Not yet. But both races have sent warships to each other's planet and are currently warring in space. Their battle is blocking the Tyranian jumpgate."

"For Krono's sake," Quill groaned.

Quill's annoyance was obvious, but I could hardly contain my grin. The Tyranian jumpgate was the jumpgate to Earth's galaxy. We were effectively grounded with the Emirians and the Cillades fighting around it. Quill would not risk sending a Draax ship to Earth, not when it could be caught in the crossfire of the Emira and Cillade war.

"Are there any of our Draax on Earth currently?" Quill said.

Teo scrolled through his tablet. "Neani and Venta are in the province," he paused and glanced at Sabrina, "I mean, the state of California. I have contacted them and informed them that they must arrange living quarters on Earth for now. I have sent messages to Earth's leaders, informing them we will not deliver gallberry juice for the foreseeable future. As well, I have contacted the Iowa authorities regarding the thief and told them we would be unable to deliver her before she died of the cancer sickness."

I stared at Teo in irritation. "Obviously, we will cure her cancer while she is here."

"Why would we?" Teo said. "She is a thief."

"She is a female," I said.

"A female who is too small to breed with," Teo said. "Even if she were not a thief, no Draax here would breed with her. Trying to carry a Draax child would kill her, even with a constant supply of gallberry juice."

I wanted to shake the old Draax, but he honestly meant no ill will toward the little human. He did not understand the value of human females beyond breeding capabilities.

"Not all Draax want children," Sabrina said with a glance at me. "Besides, with this new work program in place, human women have more value than being breeders, Teo."

Sabrina's cheeks were flushed, and I could hear a hint of annoyance in her voice. I couldn't blame her. She'd worked hard to convince Quill that hiring women to work on our planet, rather than just trading gallberry juice in exchange for them carrying our children, was a good idea. While Quill backed her on the new work program, it was still viewed by many Draax in the castle as a waste of human females.

"That is true, my queen," Teo allowed. "But even those working in the castle are healthy and large enough to carry a Draax baby."

Teo made a point. Every female who worked at the castle was on the bigger side with wide hips and the lush curvy body that we Draax found appealing. Quill had agreed to his queen's idea of a work program for the females, but only on the condition that the females who worked in the palace carried the gene necessary to breed with us. Although Quill often said he could not deny Sabrina anything she asked, he could not be persuaded to allow a female who was not breeding compatible to participate in the work program.

I supposed that wasn't entirely true. There was one in the program who was not breeding compatible. The woman named Candala was Evelyn's friend, and Sabrina had asked Quill to allow her to join the program as a favour to Evelyn.

"The human will be given serum and juice until she is healed," Quill said.

"As you wish," Teo said. "Once healed, I will send her to Iron Gate."

"What?" I jumped up from the couch, making Jovie cry out and cling to Quill in surprise. "You are not sending her there, Teo."

"She is a thief."

"I am aware," I snapped. "I swear to Krono, Teo, if you say 'she is a thief' one more time, I will -"

"Galan," Quill said. "Hold your tongue."

My nostrils flaring, I sank back onto the couch. Jovie's tail flicked out, and she brushed it along my forearm in a soothing manner. I made myself smile at her, and she tightened her tail around my arm before releasing it.

"What is Iron Gate?" Sabrina said.

"It is the prison just outside the city," Teo said.

"We can't send her to a Draax prison," Sabrina said.

"She will be fine, my queen. No Draax there will hurt her," Teo said.

"The prison is full of Draax rakart, and she is not going there," I said.

"What does rakart mean?" Sabrina said.

Quill thought for a moment. "An Earth word equivalent

would be scum. But even then, they would not hurt a female. No Draax would. Females are precious."

"She is not going to the prison," I said.

"She cannot stay here," Teo said. "You would risk the life of your king and queen?" He pointed to Jovie. "The princess? Be reasonable, Galan."

"She is small and weak," I said. "She is not capable of hurting them."

"You have no idea if that is true," Teo said. "The best place for her is Iron Gate. We will give her a separate cell from the other prisoners. Once the war between Emira and Cillade ends, we will return her to Earth for her imprisonment."

"No," I said.

Teo rolled his eyes. "What has gotten into you, Galan?"

When I didn't reply, he turned to Quill. "Do I have your permission to transport her to Iron Gate once she is healed?"

Quill glanced at me. "If she is kept here in the castle, she will need to be locked in her room, and one of your men must guard her whenever she is not in her room." His gaze turned to Sabrina and then Jovie. "If she hurts my mate or my child -"

"She will not," I said. "I will guard her myself, Quill. Your mate and child will not be in any danger."

"Are you sure this is what you want?" Quill said. "The war between Emira and Cillade could go for moons, as the previous one did. Do you want to commit to playing nanny to a thief for that long?"

"Yes," I said. "She is only one small female. How much trouble can she be?"

Ellis

"Is that really necessary?" I pulled the covers up and hid my hand under them when Sigan held out the cuff. "I almost wet the bed because I had to wait until this morning for you to uncuff me from the bed."

"You should not have tried to escape earlier," Sigan said.

"Oh, c'mon, you can't blame me for trying." I held out my hand, and Sigan slid the cuff around my wrist and closed it, tethering me to the bed again.

"I can blame you, and I do." He checked my IV and made a few adjustments while I hid my grin.

The way Sigan took everything I said so literally amused the hell out of me.

"Here, drink this." Sigan handed me a bottle of gallberry juice, and I drank it down, enjoying the warm flush of energy it brought.

"How are you feeling?" Sigan asked.

"Better. Be honest with me – how much extra time will this give me from the whole dying horribly of cancer thing?"

"It is impossible to predict an accurate length of time, but," Sigan looked me over, "probably a moon longer. Maybe a moon and a half. You are malnourished, though, and I assume food in prison will not be plentiful, so that will weaken you." He shook his head. "It will give you an extra moon. No more than that."

"Super," I said.

Depression was sinking into my bones, and I shook it off. An extra month was a gift.

Sigan patted my arm. "I am sorry it is such a poor diagnosis, human."

"Thanks," I said. "Honestly, I probably won't last a week before I'm murdered in prison anyway."

What almost looked like sympathy crossed Sigan's face. "Why did you steal the juice?"

"I didn't. It was Cheryl, remember? I was just in the wrong place at the wrong time."

He scowled before handing me another bottle of juice. "You are the most infuriating female I have ever met. I am glad not all females of your kind are like you, or I would never find a mate."

"So, you're single, huh?" I took a big swig of juice. "Haven't found a lady to be your breeding machine yet?"

His skin darkened. "I do not wish to find a breeding machine, as you so coarsely put it. I wish to find a mate. I respect human females, and if I am lucky enough to find one to mate with me, I will treat her well."

His tail thumped against the wall, and I felt bad for insulting him. "Sorry, Sigan. I didn't mean to insult you."

His tail thumped again. "We are not like your human males. We do not think females are below us, nor do we abuse them. Females are precious."

"Right, no, I get it," I said, even though I didn't. My track record with men wasn't exactly positive, and I couldn't wrap my head around the idea that a man – alien or human – believed a woman was precious. "So, um, why aren't you mated yet? You seem like a great guy."

His tail slumped to the ground. "I am in the database for the breeding program, but no female has chosen me yet."

Great, now he looked utterly dejected. First, I insult him, and then I depress him. "That's weird. You're handsome and smart, and you're like a Draax doctor, right?"

"Kadana," he said. "We are called kadanas."

"Why do you even need kadanas?" I said. "The gallberry plant heals you."

"It does. But as we age, it becomes less effective and eventually stops working. Plus, someone needs to help our females birth their young and guide our elderly to the other side. I also research human genetics, develop new and improved testing methods, and coordinate with humans on how to best administer the gallberry plant."

"So, you're a scientist, too," I said.

He just shrugged before giving me a funny little side glance. "You think I am handsome?"

"Um, yeah, sure," I said. Handsome probably wasn't the best word to use. Sigan didn't have the classic good looks of a movie star – if said movie star had green skin and a tail - but he did have very pretty silver eyes, and his body was as big and muscular as the rest of the Draax. "You have nice eyes."

Sigan folded his arms across his torso. "I am aware that I am not good looking. You do not have to lie."

Jesus, I was batting a thousand today.

"You're handsome," I said. "And I'm sure you'll be an excellent mate to a very lucky woman someday. There's probably so many Draax in the database that women haven't found you yet."

"Jarka says I am too blunt. He says I must soften my words and not speak the way I do if I wish to find a mate," Sigan said.

"Who's Jarka?"

"The palace chef and my best friend," Sigan said. "Perhaps he is right. Perhaps I do speak too bluntly. Do you think my words are too forward, human?"

"Well…" I hesitated, trying to think of a nice way to agree.

Sigan suddenly laughed. "Never mind, human. I have no

wish to mate with you, so your opinion holds no value to me."

I rolled my eyes. "That right there? That's what Jarka is talking about, Sigan."

Before he could reply, there was a knock on the door, and a woman walked in. She was carrying a tray in her hands, and the smell wafting from it made my stomach growl.

"Good morning, Sigan," the woman said.

"Hello, Inara." Sigan glanced at the device on his wrist. "You are here early this morning."

"Jarka knew I would be cleaning the infirmary today and asked me to bring breakfast for your… guest."

"Thank you. You can leave it on the table." He pointed to the table next to my hospital bed.

The woman, who was on the taller side with wide hips, dark red hair, and pretty green eyes, set the tray on the table. "Hello, I'm Inara."

"Ellis," I said.

She held out her hand, and I tried to shake it without thinking. My cuff locked up around my wrist, biting painfully into my skin. Inara stared at the cuff around my wrist, her eyes wide.

"Sigan, a little help here?" I rattled the cuff against the railing of the bed.

"Step back, Inara. This female is a prisoner and dangerous." He smoothed his finger along the underside of the cuff, and it loosened around my wrist, the bright red it had turned fading back to its usual dull shade.

A beeping sound emitted from the device around Sigan's wrist and he checked it before hurrying toward one of the inner doors in the infirmary. He opened it, and I caught a glimpse of some lab equipment as he stepped inside.

"Inara, I must check on a few of my tests. Do not go near the human while you clean," he said.

He shut the door, and Inara backed away, the smile on her face fading.

"I'm not dangerous," I said. "He was just joking."

"Sigan doesn't joke," she said.

"Jesus, you got that right," I said. "Look, I promise I'm not dangerous."

"Why do you have that cuff around your wrist then?"

"They think I'm a thief."

Her eyes widened. "Why would you steal from them? To be accepted into the program is a gift. Why would you jeopardize that?"

"I'm not a part of the breeding program. Besides, being in the breeding program is not a gift," I said.

Her forehead wrinkled in confusion. "I'm not a part of the breeding program."

"So, you're a nanny then?" I said. "I hate to tell you this, but looking after someone else's brats isn't a gift either."

"You're not here for the work program? There were rumours that they were bringing in more women, so I just assumed..." She looked me over. "I should have known. You don't have the body type."

"What are you talking about?" I said.

"I can't tell you," she said. "It's a trial thing, and not many people know. I assumed you were hired to work in the castle like the rest of us, or I wouldn't have said anything."

"C'mon, you gotta tell me now." I grinned at her. "Pretty please?"

"I can't," she said.

"I have a cancerous tumour on my spine, and it's spread to my lungs, liver, and kidneys," I said. "And because of the whole stealing accusation, they're sending me back to Earth today, where I'll be imprisoned. I'll be dead in like a week, so who will I tell?"

"Oh my God." A genuine look of sympathy crossed her face. "I'm really sorry to hear that, Ellis."

"Sorry enough to tell me about this work program thing?"

She smiled. "How can I say no after that? So, a few months ago, I found out I had brain cancer."

"Shitty," I said.

"Tell me about it." She shook her head. "But not surprising, right? Did you read the study that came out last year? They're predicting that more than sixty percent of us will get some form of cancer before we're sixty-five, and the numbers are only going to go up each year."

"Holy shit," I said.

"Right?" She glanced at the lab door before grabbing a chair and dragging it to the end of the bed. She sat down and slipped one shoe off before rubbing at her heel. "The government keeps saying it isn't the atmosphere that's causing all the cancer, but us lowers are the ones with the highest percentage of cancer, and we spend the most time outdoors or in crappy buildings, right? Most of us have shit jobs in buildings that don't have filtered air. The cancer diagnoses in middles and uppers are significantly lower. Like, forty-five percent lower."

I had no idea if what she was saying was true, but she was certainly passionate about the subject.

"So, you found out you had brain cancer…" I prompted.

"Yeah, so obviously, I applied for the breeding program right away and lucky me – I'm one of the seventy percent of women with the necessary gene to carry an alien baby."

"Lucky you," I said.

"You don't, huh?"

I shook my head. About four months ago, at a really low point, I'd gone in for the blood test to determine if I was breeding compatible. It had only taken seven years on the street for me to do it finally, and I wasn't sure if I was relieved or disappointed when I didn't come back as compatible.

Relieved. You know for a fact that even if you could carry their babies, no Draax would have asked you to breed a baby for them. It was a waste of time getting the test done.

Like always, shame and sorrow filled me up until I was almost drowning in it. Esther would still be alive if I had just tried a little harder, if I'd done a better job of seducing –

I shook myself out of my memories. What good did they do? Esther was dead, and that was it. Nothing I said or did now would change that. I'd fucked up, and maybe getting cancer was just karma's way of repaying me for killing my sister.

"Sorry," I said to Inara. "What were you saying?"

"I was asking when you were tested. If it was before three years ago, you might be breeding compatible. You might have the variant of the gene they discovered. I read that something like three to seven percent of women have it."

Man, this girl loved her numbers.

"I was tested this year," I said. "I didn't have the regular gene or the variant. Anyway, tell me about this work program thing."

"Right. So, I was breeding compatible, which was great. Only, when I went to the agency to look through the database of Draax males to choose one to breed with, I was introduced to Sabrina instead."

"Sabrina?"

"Our queen," she said. "She's amazing. She didn't say a word about being the queen of the Draax western province or anything, just said her name was Sabrina, and she was spearheading a new program and wanted to offer me the chance to participate."

She rubbed harder at the heel of her foot. "Basically, I'm a part of a trial work program. Rather than exchanging the juice for being a baby mama, Sabrina offered me the chance to work here in the castle. I'm just doing housekeeping, but I get free room and board, free food, and they pay me a weekly wage."

"But what about your brain cancer?" I said.

"Oh, they cured that right away with the gallberry juice," Inara said. "I can't participate in the program if I'm dying of a tumour, right?"

"Right," I said.

"Anyway, we had to sign a contract for a year, but at the end of the year, we're free to return to Earth with our earnings. Or, we could stay and keep working too, Sabrina says. As long as we follow the rules."

"What are the rules?" I said.

"Nothing too crazy. We aren't allowed to leave the castle without a Draax escort. We -"

"Why not?" I said. "Are they afraid you'll be hurt?"

"Oh God, no," Inara said with a smile. "Draax males are super sweet to females. I think they're more afraid that we'll meet a male outside of the castle and decide to quit our jobs to mate with them and have their babies."

"Mating is against the rules?"

"Well, not exactly. I mean, one of the rules is that we aren't allowed to," she made air quotes with her fingers, "socialize with the Draax males if you know what I mean, but that's only for the first three months. After that, we're allowed to date them if we want," Inara said. "But, honestly, the palace is huge, and so many Draax males work and live in the castle. If you're looking to get lucky, you won't need to look outside the castle, that's for sure."

"Date them," I repeated. "They don't want us for dating. They want us for breeding. I don't even understand why they're trying this work thing. What's the point? All they want from us is sex and babies."

She glanced at the door again before leaning forward and lowering her voice. "You make a valid point. Most Draax here just see us as potential mates, and I imagine once they're allowed to actively pursue us, some of the women in the work program will decide to quit and instead mate with them and have their babies."

"That's pretty damn sneaky," I said. "Luring women here with job offers when they just want them to be baby machines."

Inara frowned at me. "It isn't like that. The queen truly believes that if the Draax offer us an alternative to just popping out babies for them, it's better for them and us. One of the other women in the program, Candy, told me that she knew for a fact that Sabrina only approached lowers to be in the work program. She's trying to help us and improve our quality of life. As for the Draax, maybe they're only agreeing to this because their plan is to lure a woman away from the job and mate with them instead, but can you blame them? We're their only hope of not going extinct."

She sat back in her chair. "Look, don't get me wrong, the gallberry juice is amazing and without it, I'd be dead, but this opportunity is… well, it's the best thing that ever happened to me. I don't care if it turns out that it's only the queen who is determined to turn this into our new reality or if the Draax are just using this work program as a different way to get us on their planet as potential mates. What I care about is the money I'm making over the next year."

Excitement flooded her face. "With the money I make, I'll be able to get my own place on Earth and have a bit left over to start my degree through online schooling. With what I make here, as long as I find a part time job on Earth, I can keep going to school, and Wendy can live with me. Neither of us will have to worry about going hungry or being kicked out of some disgusting apartment in the middle of the night."

"Who's Wendy?" I said.

"My sister." Inara beamed with pride. "She's with my parents right now, but as soon as I get back home, she'll move in with me."

"So, I take it you're not planning on letting a Draax seduce you into staying permanently," I said.

"No, absolutely not. I hated leaving Wendy for even a year, and I'm definitely not leaving her permanently."

"Maybe she could get into the work program," I said. "If women start dropping out because the Draax convince them to be their mates, then they'll be looking for replacement workers, right?"

"Wendy is only twelve," Inara said. "She's too young for the work program. It isn't safe for her on Earth without me. Even after joining the breeding program, I planned to pop out a baby and return to Earth."

"Really?" I said.

"Yes. I know that makes me sound awful – what kind of mother would leave her child – but Wendy is like my child. I raised her, and at least I know my baby here would be well cared for by its father. Wendy only has me."

"I thought you said she was with your parents?" I said.

"She is, but," Inara's face pinched with worry, "they aren't great parents."

I was curious about what she meant, but it wasn't my business.

"Anyway," Inara stood, "I need to get back to work, and you need to eat before your food gets cold. I'm sorry about your cancer diagnosis, Ellis."

"Thanks," I said. I watched her walk to the broom closet before pulling my food tray closer.

I might have cancer and be dead in a month or two, but after nearly eight years of near-starvation, I wasn't letting impending death stop me from stuffing my face.

CHAPTER 6

Ellis

"Hey, Sigan?" I stepped out of the bathroom, my too-large gown billowing around my freshly washed body. "Is there a bathroom on the Draax ship returning me to Earth? Because I'm thinking I can probably drink at least another ten bottles of juice if there is. What do you think ten more bottles will give me? Another week, maybe?"

I rubbed the pot belly I had developed from breakfast and the four bottles of juice I drank. I already felt sloshy from the IV serum and all the juice, but I didn't care. I would gorge myself on juice if it gave me a few extra days.

Do you really want an extra few days in prison, Ellis?

"Sigan? Where'd you go?" I wandered toward the back of the infirmary.

"I asked him to give us a few minutes alone, little human."

I whirled around, my pulse kicking into high gear at the sound of Galan's voice. "Galan, um, hi."

I crossed my arms over my torso. When it was just Sigan

and me in the infirmary, I didn't think twice about the fact that I was naked under the thin hospital gown. But with Galan, it seemed to be the *only* thing I could think about.

"Hello, Ellis."

Goosebumps shivered to life on my skin. Holy crap, the way he said my name… why did it sound so friggin' sexy?

I squeezed my thighs together. I was not getting wet just from hearing Galan say my name. Nope, I absolutely wasn't because that was crazy, and I was probably just hopped up on the juice. That shit was a drug, and I was already hopelessly addicted to it. Christ, the withdrawal symptoms from the juice would probably kill me before my fellow prisoners did.

"You came to say goodbye," I said. Weird warmth infused my too-full belly.

Galan clasped his hands behind his back, and I stared at his flat abdomen. Wow, he liked to wear tight shirts, and I, for one, would not complain. Not when I could see the outline of his six pack. My gaze dropped to the front of his pants. It was a real shame he didn't wear pants as tight as his shirt.

Ellis, stop staring at his dick, you pervert!

I tore my gaze from his crotch, my cheeks burning with embarrassment. "Um, well, bye, Galan. It was nice knowing you. Thanks for convincing them to give me so much juice before I leave."

Oh my God, could I sound any dumber?

"Actually," Galan took a step closer, "you will stay with us until you are healed."

My mouth dropped open, and a loud buzzing filled my ears. I didn't hear what I just heard. I couldn't have.

"Wh-what did you say?" I whispered.

Galan grinned at me, and even in my shock, I couldn't

help but notice how straight and white his teeth were. "You will not leave this place until you are healed from cancer."

"Oh my God," I said. "Oh my fucking God. Are you serious?"

"Yes," he said.

I staggered over to a chair, sinking into it and staring wide-eyed at him. "How? Why? I mean…"

"Our king has agreed to allow you to stay until you're healed," Galan said.

"Why?" Suspicion overtook the shock. "What does he want from me?"

"What do you mean?" Galan said.

"He isn't doing this because he's a nice guy. He said it was a waste of resources, so why did he change his mind? He must want something from me. What is it?"

Galan frowned. "He does it because it is the right thing to do, not because -"

"I'm breeding incompatible," I blurted. "I can't carry a Draax baby."

That was a stupid thing to say. No Draax would mate with me anyway. Still, the smile on Galan's face stung like a bitch.

"That is good news," he said. "You are too -"

"Ugly, I know," I snapped.

The smile faded from his face. "No, you are too small to carry a Draax baby. Why would you -"

Sigan walked into the infirmary, holding his tablet in one hand. "Galan, are you finished talking to the human? Teo found me in the hall and explained the situation to me. I will remove the human's IV, and you can take her out of the infirmary."

"I thought I was being healed," I said.

"You are," Sigan said. "But since you will be here for who knows how long, thanks to the ridiculous war, there is no point in wasting the serum on you. The juice will heal you. It will just take longer."

"What war?" I said. My heart dropped into my stomach. "Did the Gokmards attack Earth again?"

The war between the Gokmards, a hulking and vicious bear-like alien race, and Earth had happened long before I was born, but I had seen holograms of the Gokmards. The thought of them attacking my home planet again made me sick to my stomach.

It would be foolish of them if they did. The Draax had saved us from them once before, and as part of the Planetary Treaty, they would assist us again if the Gokmards tried to take our planet a second time.

Of course, the breeding program between us and the Draax had developed precisely because the Gokmards were attacking our planet. The Draax had saved us from slavery and death, but they hadn't done it without expecting something in return. Their race was dying thanks to a lack of females. Saving Earth from a race of savage aliens was the perfect negotiating tool for breeding with our females.

"No," Sigan said. "Two of the planets in our solar system are at war again. For, no doubt, another ridiculous reason." He punched a few buttons on his tablet. "Their battleships are blocking the Tyranian jumpgate, and until they stop trying to kill each other, none of our ships can go to Earth."

"So, I'm being healed because you can't get me to Earth, not because your king is generous," I said to Galan.

"He had decided before we discovered the Emirans and Cillades were at war to heal you," Galan said with a frown.

"You owe our king your life, little human, and when you see him next, you will thank him for it."

Galan's voice was harsh, but I honestly couldn't blame him for it. I was acting like a total spoiled brat.

"I will," I said.

"Good. Sigan, remove her IV, please, so I can take her to her quarters."

"It is small and plain, and there is no window," Galan said, "but it has a comfortable bed, and the cold unit is stocked with gallberry juice and food."

He cleared his throat. "I asked Teo to give you living quarters with a separate sleeping area, but he said this would do. I am sorry, human."

"Are you kidding me?" I said. "This is amazing."

I wasn't blowing smoke up his butt, either. Where Galan saw a small plain room, I saw freaking paradise. The studio apartment had a tiny living area with a love seat and coffee table, a single sized bed and nightstand tucked along the far wall with a door on either side of the bed, and a kitchenette. There was even a small table with two chairs where I could eat my meals.

This tiny apartment was downright luxurious after years of living in literal cardboard boxes.

"That door leads to the bathroom," Galan pointed to the door to the right of the bed, "and that door is a closet. It has extra towels and space to put your clothing."

He glanced down at me. I was still wearing the hospital gown and tugged self-consciously at it. "Sigan burned my clothes, so..."

Galan was carrying my backpack, and he set it down on the floor. I did have a couple extra changes of clothes, but they were back on Earth. Wrapped in plastic and tucked into a cardboard box, and shoved behind a garbage dumpster in my favourite alley. Anything else that was important to me I carried in my backpack.

"Maybe I could borrow some clothes from some of the women who work here?" I said.

"You are much smaller than them," Galan said. "But I have left some shirts in the closet for you. They will sufficiently cover you."

"Thanks. That's thoughtful of you." I wandered over to the loveseat, running my hand along the smooth grey fabric. The apartment looked exactly like an apartment back home, and the furnishings were practically identical to Earth's. "Did you buy this stuff on Earth?"

"It makes our mates more comfortable if their new homes look like their homes on Earth," Galan said.

My stomach took the express elevator to my ankles. "Right. Um, what's your mate's name?"

I didn't actually want to know Galan's mate's name. She was probably some tall, gorgeous woman with nice big boobs, an ass that wasn't completely flat, and ribs that didn't protrude.

I rubbed at those protruding ribs as I waited for Galan's reply. It was stupid even to be attracted to him.

"I do not have a mate," Galan said.

My stomach returned to its rightful place as a weird sense of relief washed over me. "Oh. Okay. Why not?"

He just shrugged before opening the fridge and taking out a bottle of juice. "Drink this now."

I took the bottle from him, trying not to shiver when our

fingers brushed. Ooh boy. I had it bad for the big green alien. I was such an idiot.

Looking anywhere but at the way Galan's t-shirt stretched across his abdomen, I said, "So, can you tell me which way to the garden from here?"

"Drink, little human," Galan said.

I took a few swallows of juice, and he relaxed against the counter. "You need to drink lots of juice every day."

"That won't be a problem," I said. "I'm pretty sure I'm addicted to it already."

"Your body craves it because you are sick," Galan said. "Once you are healed, the cravings will diminish."

"Good to know," I said. "So, about the garden…"

He crossed his arms over his chest, and my mouth went dry when his biceps bulged against the sleeves and the fabric stretched even tighter across his broad chest. Good God, he was gonna bust right out of that shirt if he kept that up, and I, for one, was entirely on board with that.

"You are not allowed to leave your quarters without me or another Draax accompanying you," Galan said. "This is very important, human. The consequences will be dire if you are caught in the castle without an escort. Do you understand?"

"Yes," I said. "No roaming the castle on my own. Got it. I'll stay in my room."

He studied me with those gorgeous copper eyes until I made a show of drinking more juice. Jesus, it was like he could tell I was lying to him.

"Your meals will be brought to your living quarters, and I will take you for a walk through the castle in the morning and evening," Galan said.

"Sure, okay, sounds great. Thanks," I said.

What it sounded like was that I was Galan's new pet, but considering that the Draax were healing me and housing and feeding me after I'd stolen from them, I wasn't going to bring that up. But I also wasn't going to sit around like an obedient dog either.

I needed to check out the castle, find every exit, and plot my escape route for when the war ended. The Draax would have my skinny ass on the first ship to Earth, and that was the last thing I wanted. Not if I liked being alive, anyway.

As awful as this sounded, I hoped the war continued for a few months. I needed time to heal, scope out the castle, and steal enough supplies and food to help me survive on the Draax planet once I escaped. Eventually, I'd find my way back to Earth – I snuck on a Draax ship once before and could do it again – but the longer I stayed on Draax, the more likely Richie Bulchanini would think I was dead.

You're not going back to Iowa.

Well, I would try not to, but it's not like I could walk onto a Draax ship and ask them what part of Earth they were going to. I'd have to take my chances. If I were lucky, I'd end up somewhere warm like Hawaii. Of course, with my luck, I'd sneak onto a ship going to, I dunno, Canada or some other frozen wasteland.

I realized that Galan was staring silently at me, and I smiled at him. "This is fantastic. Thank you, Galan. I love my new place."

He glanced around the apartment, a frown marring his forehead. "It is small and plain," he repeated before walking to the door. "I must go. I have sword training with the recruits this morning."

My gaze dropped to the sword around his waist. "Right.

You guys are all slashy-slashy with the swords. Very…medieval."

His hand grazed the sword's handle, and I could see the confusion in his gaze. Apparently, deciding it wasn't worth his time to ask for clarification, he opened the door and stepped into the hallway. "Remember, Ellis, you are not to leave your room."

"I won't. I absolutely won't," I lied. "Have fun with your sword training."

Galan closed the door and I waited two minutes before walking over and trying the handle. It was locked – no surprise there – and I studied the lock for a few minutes before smiling. Jesus, getting out of this room would be like taking candy from a baby.

I reached for my backpack before pausing. It would be better to wait. To lull them into a false sense of security. Hell, they might even start leaving my door unlocked if they thought I was a good little pet and did what they said.

I finished the bottle of gallberry juice, set it on the small table, and then ran across the room and jumped on the bed. It was sinfully comfortable, and I stretched out on it and stared at the ceiling.

Despite being locked in my quarters, I was deliriously happy. I supposed this was how a death row prisoner felt when the governor called off the execution at the last minute. I rubbed my chest, my grin widening. I was warm, fed, and comfortable for the first time in seven years.

Don't get used to it.

I wouldn't. I might not be dying of cancer any longer, but I was still in a mess of trouble. But that didn't mean I wouldn't enjoy the soft bed and unlimited food while it lasted.

CHAPTER 7

Galan

I knocked on the door of the human's quarters before unlocking it and opening it. "Ellis? I have brought you some lunch. You must eat..."

The thought died in my head, and I stared wordlessly at the little human. She stood in the small kitchen, her tiny body bent as she stared into the fridge. She was wearing my shirt, and while it was just as baggy on her as the hospital gown, something inside of me strung tight at seeing her in my clothing. She was standing on one foot, the other rubbed up and down the back of one pale calf.

"Galan, what's this yellow stuff?"

I watched her foot slide higher up her leg and disappear beneath my shirt. My cock was starting to harden, and I wanted to join her. Wanted to kneel at her feet and slide my hands under her shirt. Wanted to feel the smoothness of her thighs before I pressed them open and buried my face into her bare pussy. She would taste sweet. Sweeter than warracot. Sweeter than gallberries.

"Galan?"

I tore my gaze away from her legs and walked briskly to the table. I set the tray down and sat with a thump in one of the two chairs. I had to sit. The hardness of my cock could not be concealed by my pants any longer.

"You okay?" Ellis was holding a container of warracot and staring at me.

"Yes. The food you hold is warracot. It is a fruit and tastes sweet."

"Okay." She set the container down before sitting in the other chair. My shirt was too large for me to see even the curve of her small breasts, but it didn't matter. I'd already seen them on the ship. Already knew how perfect they were.

My hands itched to cup them, and my cock was growing harder instead of softening. Krono, I needed to control my thoughts. The human would be returned to Earth as soon as the war ended. It was not wise to fuck her.

Why not? Ask her if she wants to fuck while she is here. There is no harm in asking.

There was plenty of harm. One, she was so small, I'd be lucky not to injure her during sex, and two, I wasn't looking for some casual fucking and hadn't been for some time. It was why I had left the Earth bar instead of finding a random female to bed when I was on Earth.

I wanted a mate, and the little thief sitting before me could never be my mate.

"Thank you for bringing me lunch." Ellis poked at the grundleswat. "Are you not eating?"

"I ate earlier. I am always hungry after a training session."

"Right. How did that go?" Ellis tried some grundleswat. "This is good. What is it?"

"Grundleswat. It's our main source of meat."

"Cool. I saw pictures of grundleswats in a Draax informational hologram at the library. They kind of remind me of deer."

I reached below the table and pulled the crotch of my pants away from my dick. "What did you do this morning?"

"Napped," she said with a grin. "Then I drank about four bottles of gallberry juice and had a bath."

Oh, Krono, I was not suddenly imagining her naked body in the bath.

She was already pushing her plate away, and I frowned at her. "You must eat more."

"I really can't," she said. "My belly is sloshing with all the juice I drank, plus I'm used to not eating much."

I studied the way the skin stretched tight over her cheekbones. "Are you a lower?"

"I am," she said. "How could you tell?"

"Your clothing was dirty, you smelled terrible, and you are too thin from not eating enough," I said.

Her mouth dropped open for a second before she laughed. Her laugh was low and throaty, making my tail wave excitedly.

She glanced at my tail before saying, "I'm not sure I would ever get used to how blunt and honest you guys are. Human men aren't like that."

"Where did you live?" I was immensely curious about the little human.

"Uh, actually, I was homeless," she said. "I lived on the streets."

"You are so small. How did you survive?" I said. "Krey

told me the area you live in falls below freezing in the cold months."

"I'm tougher than I look."

I couldn't see how someone so small could survive.

"How?" I persisted.

"Earth has homeless shelters, so I would try to stay in them as often as possible. If they were full, I slept in alleys under cardboard boxes. I had some warm blankets for a while that I sto – I mean, borrowed from the shelter, but some big dude with a hatchet and a terrible attitude took them from me."

She ate a piece of warracot, her face lighting up. "Ooh, this is so sweet. It tastes kind of like watermelon."

"You are lucky you did not freeze to death," I said.

"I did almost freeze to death once last winter. But I broke into a land vehicle, and it had a blanket in the back seat, so I just wrapped myself up like a burrito in the vehicle and hoped I didn't die."

She took another sip of juice. "Man, this stuff is so good. I can't stop drinking it."

"How did you get the scar on your leg?" I said.

She glanced at the scar running along the front of her shin before grinning. "That was a good one. So, for about two months, I hung around a real swanky uppers neighbourhood built near a small forest. There was an old treehouse in the forest – one of them must have built it for their kids and then forgot about it when their kids grew up. Anyway, it was perfect because I could shelter in the treehouse, there was a small stream in the woods that I could use for drinking water and bathing, and at night, I could sneak into the neighbourhood and go through their trash for food. Man, uppers waste a lot of food. I mean, a lot. I would find whole roasted chickens sometimes with, like, maybe a thigh missing, and that's it."

My stomach clenched, and my tail thumped against the floor. "You ate garbage?"

She shrugged, her face one of resignation rather than shame. "Yeah. You do what you have to to survive, right?"

When I didn't reply, she continued. "Anyway, one of the uppers caught on to what I was doing, he probably had security cameras or whatever, and one night, when I was going through his garbage, he came charging out of his house in his bathrobe with a gun in his hand and screaming he was gonna kill me."

She shook her head. "The crazy bastard started shooting at me, so I took off for the woods. There was a chain link fence with a gate separating the neighbourhood from the forest, but I wasn't anywhere near the gate, and the dude could move fast for an upper."

She laughed. "I wasn't exactly an expert at climbing fences or anything, but I scaled that sucker like a first-rate rock climber. But the barbed wire that ran along the top of it sliced open my shin as I was hauling my skinny ass over it."

She rubbed absentmindedly at the scar. "I made it back to the treehouse and tore up a blanket to wrap my leg and stop the bleeding, but I didn't have the money to go to the hospital. I holed up for a few days in the treehouse to let it heal, but I probably should have gotten stitches. I'm super lucky I didn't get an infection from it. But it took forever to stop bleeding so maybe that's why? Maybe it bled all the bad stuff out. I was really weak by the time it clotted, though. I could barely climb the rope ladder to get in and out of the treehouse."

I shook my head when she held out the container of

warracot toward me. After hearing her talk about almost being shot, of nearly bleeding to death, I wasn't sure I'd ever eat again. My stomach was in knots, and I couldn't understand how or why Ellis was being so casual about nearly dying.

What happened then?" I said.

"Well, the guy told the cops I was in the forest, and they showed up a few days later and sent the dogs in, so I had to leave. That was scarier than the guy with the gun because I couldn't run as fast with my injured leg, you know? I got lucky, though and got the hell out before the dogs got a good whiff of my scent."

She studied my face before saying, "You okay? You look kind of sick to your stomach."

"I still do not understand how you survived," I said.

"It wasn't all doom and gloom," she said. "For a while, I was friends with a group of people, and we all looked out for each other. Torra was the one who taught me how to boost... uh, how to repair ships and other machinery. She was good at stuff like that. Her dad was a mechanic and taught her a lot of mechanical stuff before he died. I worked at a repair shop for a guy named Horace. He was good to me and paid a decent wage. But that was only for a few months."

"What happened then?"

"Uh," she cleared her throat, "business got a little lean, and he couldn't afford to keep me employed."

"Why were you homeless in the first place? Where were your parents?" I said.

Her face closed off faster than a lokena could run. "We don't have a relationship. I left home when I was sixteen and haven't talked to them since."

"Why?"

She just shrugged. "What about you? Do you have family?"

"My father died when I was twelve. My mother is still alive and lives in the city. She remarried shortly after my father died."

"That sucks," Ellis said. "Why did your mother remarry so quickly?"

"She is human and either needed to remarry or return to Earth. She chose to stay here because she wanted me to grow up on my home planet."

"Holy shit." Ellis was staring at me like I'd grown a second tail. "You're half-human."

"I am," I said. "Most of the Draax around my age are half-human. Some are not. Quill's mother was a Draax, as was Krey's, but they were each one of the last of our females and on the older side. Quill's mother was a decade older than his father, and Krey's mother was two decades older than his father."

"Wow," she said. "You don't look half-human. Are any of you ever born, um, human coloured?"

"No," I said. "Our young ones are always green or purple. We carry the dominant genes."

"Oh, cool," Ellis said. "Do you like your stepdad?"

"No," I said. I didn't want to talk about my past or my family. It was too painful, and there was no point. My father had been a liar and a terrible mate to my mother, and he had cost us our home. Thinking about the loss of my childhood home made me feel sick.

"Are you okay?" Ellis said. "Seriously, I know it's hard to tell since you're already green around the old gills, but you really do look like you might throw up."

"I am fine," I said. "I no longer wish to speak of personal things."

"Sure, okay. I get it." She didn't seem upset with me, but I didn't know her well. She glanced at the door. "Hey, do you have time to show me the garden? I'd like to see it."

A big part of me wanted to say no. The garden would be full of other males, and the thought of them staring at her while all she wore was my shirt angered me. But I couldn't resist how the little female was staring so hopefully at me, so I shoved aside my misgivings and nodded.

"Yes, we can walk in the garden for a while."

Ellis

"Congratulations, human. You are cancer free."

I hopped off the hospital bed and joined Sigan at the scanner. I stared at the hologram screen in front of him. "Are you being serious right now?"

"Why would I joke about this?" Sigan pointed to the hologram screen. "Your lungs are clear, no spots remain on your internal organs, and the tumour is gone from your spine."

"Holy shit," I said.

"You healed much quicker than I anticipated," Sigan said. "Considering how malnourished you are and how big the tumour was, I am surprised it only took a week."

"It's gone," I said. "It's fucking gone!"

I shrieked with excitement and threw my arms around Sigan, hugging him hard. Sigan grunted in shock before patting my back awkwardly. I grinned up at him, my small body still pressed against his. "Thank you, Sigan. You have no idea what… ow!"

A long green tail wrapped around my waist was squeezing painfully. Before I could reach for it, the tail tightened, and I was yanked from Sigan's grip and up against the body of an equally tall, muscular Draax.

I stared up at the familiar face as his arm joined his tail around my waist. "Galan? What the hell?"

Galan had been standing at the door to the infirmary, looking at something on his tablet and holy shit, how fast and quiet was he to move across the entire infirmary like that without me hearing him?

"Do not touch the little female, Sigan. Ever," Galan said.

The easygoing nature I had grown to expect from Galan was gone. In its place was a hard and angry warrior. Anxiety laced with just the slightest hint of excitement filled my body. I tugged on his tail. "Hey, knock it off with the tail."

"Do you hear me, Sigan?" Galan said. "Do not touch her."

"I heard you, Galan," Sigan said. Despite Galan's anger, he didn't seem that concerned. "She was the one who hugged me. Besides, you know I have no sexual interest in the human. She weighs less than a maluken, for Krono's sake. Her fragile bones would crack under my weight."

"Enough with the fragile bones thing," I said. "I'm not fragile."

"I enjoy intense and vigorous fucking, and you are too skinny for that," Sigan said. "If we fucked, you would -"

"Speak about fucking her again, and I will cut out your tongue," Galan snarled.

A brief flicker of fear crossed Sigan's face before he scowled at Galan. "Control your temper, Galan. How you conduct yourself is unbecoming for the head of the king's guard. And release the female before you crack her ribs, and I have to give her more gallberry juice."

Galan's tail relaxed a fraction as Sigan turned and stalked to his lab at the back of the infirmary. He slammed the door shut behind him, and I glared at Galan. "You were super rude to Sigan."

"Come, little female," Galan said. His tail was still around my waist, and he walked toward the infirmary door. I had no choice but to follow or be dragged behind him like a disobedient child.

"Hey, I thought we were going for a walk in the garden," I said when he walked down the hallway toward my living quarters instead.

"Not now," Galan said.

"Why not?"

He didn't reply, and I stopped and tried to dig my heels in, snorting with frustration when my bare feet just slid along the stone floor. "You're being an asshole."

He completely ignored me, and after a few seconds, I started walking again, jogging to catch up with him. "At least tell me why we're suddenly not going to the garden."

"I am busy today," he said. "I do not have time to escort you for a walk."

"Okay, I get that, but can't we ask someone else to escort me? Adrix seemed nice when he brought me lunch the other day. Maybe we could ask him to -"

"You would prefer Adrix's company over mine?" Galan glanced back at me with hurt on his face.

"What? I didn't say that. I'm just saying that I know you're busy, so maybe someone else could walk with me in the garden."

He huffed out another angry snort before stopping in front of my door and yanking it open. "Inside, little female."

"Oh my God," I said when his tail practically tossed me into my apartment before releasing me. I turned to face him, my hands on my hips. "What is your damn problem, Galan?"

"I do not have a problem," he said.

"Then why can't I go for a walk in the garden? I'm cancer free, for God's sake, and I wouldn't mind celebrating. If Adrix is busy, let me ask Sigan. I know he takes a walk in the garden every day and -"

Galan stomped forward, and I backed up until my ass hit the wall, staring wide-eyed at him as he braced his hands on the wall on either side of my head and penned me in. "And you prefer Sigan's company to mine. Is that right, human?"

"What?"

"First, you hug him and then ask that he take you to the garden instead of me."

"You just said you don't have time to go to the garden with me. That's why I suggested Sigan," I said. "Why are you acting so crazy?"

"Why did you hug Sigan instead of me?" he said.

I stared at him with my mouth open. "I don't – I mean, he was right there, and I was excited, so I hugged him."

What almost looked like a pout crossed Galan's face. "Did you enjoy hugging him?"

"I didn't... not enjoy it?" I said.

Galan's face turned a dark green, and his tail lashed out against the wall with two harsh thuds. "You are not allowed to fuck Sigan."

"Holy shit," I said. "I hug him, and now you think I'm going to fuck him? What is up with you today? Did you get hit in the head during sword training this morning?"

"My head is fine," Galan snapped. "You are not to go around hugging other Draax males. It will give them the wrong impression, and they will pursue you for mating purposes."

"Okay, now I know you have a concussion or something. No Draax wants to mate with me," I said. "And I didn't hug you because any time I've gotten even remotely close to you this week, you flinch, get all stiff and weird, and act like you're gonna poke me with your sword."

His face went even darker, and I glanced first at his crotch and then at the actual sword hanging around his waist. "I mean poking me with your actual sword. Not your dick sword. I mean... I'm not asking you to poke me with your dick sword. Or your real sword."

Ellis. Please stop talking now.

I closed my mouth and folded my arms across my chest. Truth be told, this was the closest I'd been to Galan since he'd carried me around my first day here. The heat of his big body was making my insides get weirdly mushy. My nipples felt tight and swollen, and I had the strangest urge to step forward and rub my tits against him, just to see what effect it would have on him.

He'd run for the goddamn Draax hills, Ellis, and you know it. Galan is a nice guy, but he's not attracted to you. He always keeps two feet of space between you, and if you get any closer...

I sighed inwardly. If I got any closer, he did exactly what I accused him of doing. He got flinchy and weird, and an almost panicked look crossed his face. I was used to the Draax finding me ugly, but Galan's reaction seemed over the top.

"I do not get weird," Galan said.

"Uh, yeah, you do." I touched his chest, my palm resting against his heart.

He immediately stepped away, his tail lashing back and forth and the flush in his face deepening until the colour of his skin was a rich forest green.

I swallowed the ridiculous hurt that tightened my throat and said, "See?"

His nostrils flaring, Galan stalked out of my apartment. I hurried after him, stopping near the doorway. "Galan, will you ask Adrix to escort me to the garden?"

"No," he snapped before slamming the door and locking it.

"Jackass!" I stormed across my small apartment and hurled myself onto the bed. "What a jerk. It's the happiest day of my life, and he's ruining it."

I screamed into my pillow before flipping onto my back and staring at the ceiling. I had no idea what the hell Galan's problem was with me today, but I needed to forget about him and concentrate on my plan.

I'd been laying low for the last week, being a good little human and doing what I was told, but that was about to change. Now that the cancer was healed and I didn't have to worry about them withholding the gallberry juice as punishment, I was breaking out of my admittedly comfortable prison and exploring the castle. I had no idea when the war would end, but I needed to devise a strategy for escaping the castle the second it ended.

I slid off the bed and grabbed my backpack out of the closet, digging through it until my fingers touched the small leather case. I carried it over to the door and knelt before the lock. It was a simple pin and tumbler lock and I grinned to myself. Jesus, this was almost too easy.

I opened the leather case and took out my tension wrench and one of my hook picks. I slid the tension wrench into the lock and carefully used the hook pick to lift the pins one by one. The last pin lifted, and I used the wrench to turn the lock, my grin widening when it clicked open.

"I still got it," I said before opening the door and peeking into the hallway. It was empty, and I shut the door and studied the kitchenette before hurrying over and opening the cupboard under the sink. I grabbed the bottle of cleaner and a rag.

The odds of me not running into a Draax in the hallway were almost zero, but if they saw the cleaning supplies in my hands, they would probably think I was one of the women working in the castle.

Wearing nothing but Galan's shirt?

Shit. I'd forgotten about that. I set the cleaner and rag on the table and grabbed a large bath towel from the closet. Using a knife, I started a small rip in the towel and then yanked hard, tearing a strip of fabric from the towel.

I tied the strip around my waist and tugged on the shirt until the fabric overlapped the strip of towel tied around my waist. I checked in the mirror on the back of the bathroom door.

"Not bad, Ellis. Not bad," I said.

With the fabric overlapping the towel tie, it looked like I was wearing a shirt and skirt combo… if the shirt and skirt were the same colour.

I shrugged and grabbed my cleaning supplies. It would have to do. Besides, I doubted many of the Draax were fashionistas on human clothing. Not to mention that most of them wouldn't give my skinny ass a second look.

I took two deep breaths, opened the door, and stepped

into the hallway. It was still empty, and I closed my door, walked briskly down the corridor, and turned left. I headed toward the garden and the infirmary since it was the only route I knew.

Ahead of me at a t-juncture, I could hear voices and froze for only a moment before I straightened my back.

Act like you belong here, Ellis.

As two Draax turned the corner, I made a show of wiping at a spot on the wall with the rag. I smiled at them as they walked closer. They stared curiously at me, and I said, "Good afternoon, gentleman. Lovely day for cleaning, isn't it?"

"Hello, human," the one on the left said.

The one on the right studied my legs. Now that I'd made some adjustments to Galan's shirt, you could see my knees. The Draax stared at the scar on my leg until the one on the left elbowed him.

"Have a nice day," I said, walking down the hallway and around the corner. I released my breath in a pent-up rush. Ignoring my trembling knees, I hurried down the hallway to the next corner.

I passed by the infirmary and the garden without seeing another Draax. I was thankful for my luck, but at the same time – did this damn place not have any exits? How freaking big was this castle anyway?

Ten minutes and countless corridors later, I was hopelessly lost and no closer to finding an exit.

"Holy fuck," I muttered, "there's gotta be an exit somewhere or a front door for God's sake. They don't just parachute in through the open ceiling in the garden."

The problem, I decided, was that I was still in what appeared to be the living quarters section of the castle. Every door I'd tried in the random hallways was locked, and on occasion, I could hear voices behind doors as I walked past them. I needed to return to the garden and try a different corridor that didn't lead to living quarters.

"Now to find my way back to the goddamn garden," I said. I didn't have a terrible sense of direction, but the maze of corridors and hallways would have been too much for freaking Marco Polo.

"I should have left myself a damn trail of breadcrumbs." I peered up and down the hallway, trying to decide whether to go left or right at the t-intersection ahead.

"Left… I think. Yeah, no, it's left for sure," I said.

I froze when I heard voices coming from that t-intersection… one of them sounded familiar. I cocked my head, straining to hear… oh shit. I did recognize that voice. It was old blue eyes who had caught me during my first escape attempt.

Panic made my heart trip in my chest. I needed to hide and do it quickly. I backed up a few steps, glancing behind me as the voices drew closer. There was no way I'd make it to the end of the corridor before they saw me.

Think, Ellis! Think!

I grabbed the handle of the door closest to me. It was locked, and I backed away to the next one as the voices swelled in the hallway. Fuck, they would be turning the corner in seconds. The second door handle turned beneath my sweaty hand, and I opened the door and slipped inside just as the two Draax rounded the corner.

I closed the door with a quiet click and leaned against it with my eyes squeezed shut. My heart was racing, my breath was puffing in and out of my lungs, and my back was slick with sweat.

The low voices and heavy footsteps of the Draax grew

closer, and I held my breath as they walked past the door. Their voices and footsteps faded, and I slumped against the door.

"Fuck," I breathed. "That was close."

I opened my eyes and stared in mute surprise at the luxurious furnishings in the large living room to my left. The living room alone was bigger than my entire apartment and decorated in dark greys and rich burgundies.

"Holy shit," I said. "Look at this place."

I stepped forward and turned to the right to study the kitchen. "Shit!" I backed up, my ass hitting the door again, my heart roaring along like an airtrain, as I stared at the woman standing behind the marble topped island that separated the kitchen from the living area. She had long dark hair and blue eyes, and she held an identical bottle of cleaner in one hand and a rag in the other.

She had to be one of the women in the work program, a housekeeper like Inara. Although her lower half was hidden behind the island, I could tell she had the exact body the Draax liked. Tall and curvy in all the right spots. With tits like hers, she probably had to beat the Draax off her with a stick.

"Hello," she said.

"Uh, hey, how are you?" I said.

"Good." She sprayed the top of the island with the cleaner and wiped it with the rag before studying Galan's shirt. "That's an interesting look."

I laughed. "Yeah, thanks. I just felt like wearing something pretty today to clean. You know how it is."

Her laugh was genuine, and she cleaned another spot off the counter with the rag. "Are you lost?"

"Um, sort of. I mean, not lost, lost… I know I'm in the castle, but can't find my way to the front door. I don't suppose you could point me in the right -"

The knock on the door behind me made me drop my rag and slap my hand over my mouth. When Galan's deep voice said, "Sabrina? Are you busy? May I join you?" my heart almost joined the rag at my feet.

I bent and snatched it up before holding my finger to my lips. The woman stared at me in amusement as I crept toward the couch.

"Do me a solid, and don't tell the big guy I'm here, okay?" I whispered before dropping onto the floor in front of the couch.

I lay on my stomach, placing the bottle of cleaner and the rag on the floor beside me and staring under the couch as Galan knocked again. "Sabrina? May I come in?"

"Yes," Sabrina said.

Still staring under the couch, I held my breath as the door opened. The floor was spotless under the sofa. Damn… the woman could clean, I thought dimly as I tried to ignore the panic eating at my stomach lining.

"Hello, Sabrina. How are you?"

"I'm good, thanks, Galan. How are you? You look upset."

Sabrina… why was that name so familiar? I tried to think of where I'd heard it before as I watched Galan's feet walk over to the island.

"It has been a long day," Galan said.

"What happened?" Sabrina said.

Fuck, how did I know the name Sabrina?

I closed my eyes in thought and made a soft grunt of surprise when something hard and pointy poked me in the side of the head. I opened my eyes, staring at the tiny purple face looking down at me from the couch.

The little girl was maybe two years old, and her dark hair was scooped into two tiny pigtails. She blinked sleepily at me as her tail came down and poked me again in the side of the head.

I glared at her and pushed her tail away when she brushed it against my forehead. She sat on the couch, rubbing at the sleep creases on her admittedly adorable face. She used her tail to poke at my face again, and I batted it away, putting my finger on my lips when she opened her mouth.

"Shh," I said in a low voice.

Her tail brushed my hair before she whispered, "Hello, girl."

I waved at her, then held my finger to my lips again.

She mimicked me, holding one chubby finger against her mouth before smiling.

I glanced under the couch again, staring at Galan's feet. Shit, what did I do now? Also, who did this kid belong to, and why was –

I couldn't hold in my loud grunt when the toddler dropped onto my lower back. She was a chubby little thing, and it was like a bowling ball hitting me square in the spine. The toddler laughed, her tail tugging on my hair and her hands clapping.

"Surprise, girl! Mama, I surprise the girl!"

"Jovie, what…"

The toddler was lifted off of me, and I stared up at Galan, who held Jovie in his arms.

I waved at him. "Oh, hey, Galan."

"What in Krono…" Galan set Jovie down on the floor, and

she wandered away. I flinched when Galan reached for me, but he just grabbed my arms and hauled me to my feet.

"What are you doing in here, Ellis?"

"Um... I got lost?"

"How did you get out of your living quarters?"

Galan shook me lightly when I didn't answer. "Answer me, little female."

"Galan, it's fine."

We both looked at Sabrina. She was standing in front of the island and holding the little girl in her arms. My mouth dropped open at the sight of her belly. Holy shit. She was pregnant.

"My queen, I am sorry," Galan said. "I do not know how she got into your private quarters."

Motherfucking hell.

I stared wide-eyed at the queen, my sarcasm and usual smartass replies blanketed under the surety that I was about to have my head chopped off by Galan's shiny sword.

"What are you doing in the king and queen's private quarters, Ellis?" Galan's hands tightened around my arms. "You must answer me immediately before -"

The door swung open, and – oh, this just got fucking better and better – the king walked into the apartment. "Sadora, is Jovie awake from her nap? I will take her for a walk in the garden before... Galan?"

The king stared at me before turning his gaze to Galan. "Why did you bring the thief to my queen?"

There was a moment of silence. When Galan looked at me, I knew without a doubt that I had fucked him over big time. Regret and shame immediately coursed through me. I didn't intend to get Galan in trouble and didn't care if it cost me my head. I would make sure the king knew Galan had nothing to do with me being here.

"Answer me, Galan," the king said.

I craned my neck to stare around Galan's large body. "Your majesty, he didn't -"

"I asked him to bring her to me," Sabrina said. "I wanted to meet her."

The king frowned at her. "Sabrina, that little female is not to be trusted."

"I know, Quill," Sabrina said. "But I remember how bored I was when I first arrived and was locked in my room all day. I figured she'd like to meet some new people." She handed the toddler to him.

"Hi, Papa."

"Hello, Jovie." Quill kissed her cheek as he studied me and Galan. "Galan, if my sadora wishes to visit with the thief, I will allow it, but you must always remain with her. Is that clear?"

"Yes, Quill," Galan said.

"Good." Quill kissed the toddler's cheek again. "Meena, would you like to walk in the garden?"

She clapped her hands and screeched "garden" at the top of her lungs.

Sabrina laughed. "I think that's a yes. Let me change her first. Ellis, it was nice to meet you."

"Um, it was nice to meet you too, Your Highness." I made a clumsy curtsey and then bowed to the king as Galan's hand tightened on my arm.

Nodding to Quill, he marched me past the king and the princess and out the door. The minute the door closed behind us, I said, "Galan, I'm sorry. I didn't mean -"

"Hold your tongue, human."

There was no warmth in Galan's voice at all. Feeling sick, I followed meekly along as he led me through the maze of corridors until we were back at my room.

He pushed me inside, and I said, "I really am sorry. I didn't know who she was or -"

"How did you get out of your living quarters?" Galan's tail was flicking so quickly that it was a green blur.

"You left the door unlocked."

Lying came automatically to me. I'd spent the last seven years rarely able to trust anyone, and lying had kept me safe. I was extremely good at it, and my voice remained steady, and my gaze didn't shift from Galan's face.

So, why did I immediately feel so fucking shitty about lying to him?

"Krono!" Galan ran a hand through his dark hair. "This is my fault. If you had hurt the queen or the princess…"

"I wouldn't have hurt them," I said. "You know me better than that. I'm not, like, a monster, for God's sake. C'mon, Galan."

He stared at me, and the disappointment in his gaze was worse than the anger. "You should not have left your living quarters, Ellis. If the king knew what really happened, you would immediately be sent to Iron Gate. Is that what you want? To sit in a prison cell alone until the war ends and you are returned to your planet?"

"No," I said, "but it isn't fair that you keep me locked up in my room and refuse to take me for a fucking walk just because you're pissed that I hugged Sigan. I only get to leave this room twice a day, and you took that away from me because you were having a tantrum."

"I was not having a tantrum!" Galan shouted.

"Like hell you weren't!" I shouted back.

His tail banged against the wall before he stalked out of the room. He slammed the door shut and locked it, and his footsteps faded.

My hands shaking, guilt, anger, and regret all jockeying for a spot in my stomach, I ran to my bed and climbed in, pulling the quilt over my head and letting the hot tears fall.

CHAPTER 8

Ellis

The knock on my door made my pulse race, and shivers of anticipation run down my spine. I stood up from the loveseat, chewing on my bottom lip as the door unlocked. I don't know why I was so anxious. It wouldn't be Galan. It would be Adrix again bringing me lunch, just like it'd been for the last three days. I had a feeling I'd never see Galan again, not with how pissed he was at me.

The door opened, and just like I had expected, Adrix walked in carrying my lunch tray. What I didn't expect was the queen to walk in after him.

"Human, you will show respect to our queen and bow," Adrix said.

"Right." I bowed quickly. "Um, sorry, Your Highness."

"It's fine," she said as Adrix set my lunch tray on the table. She sat down on one of the chairs as Adrix stood behind her.

"Adrix, you don't need to hover," the queen said.

"My queen, your mate was very clear about what he

would do to me if any harm came to you while you visited with the prisoner," Adrix said.

"She's not going to hurt me," the queen said. "Are you, Ellis?"

"No, absolutely not," I said. "I promise."

"See? Why don't you wait for me outside in the hallway?"

Adrix's face turned pale green, and he shook his head. "My queen, I cannot do that."

"Not even if it's a direct order from me?" she said.

Indecision crossed Adrix's face before he said, "You know that my life is yours, my queen, but I cannot and will not disobey our king's orders."

"Yeah, okay. How about we compromise, and you relax on the couch or hang out by the door?"

Adrix glanced at me, and I held my hands up. "Adrix, I'm not going to hurt the queen. I know the king will lop off my head if I do, and I like the old brain bucket exactly where it is."

"He will kill you, human," Adrix said.

"Adrix!" the queen said.

"If you hurt his mate, he will kill you," Adrix said again. "He will show you no mercy or second chance. The last Draax who tried to harm her lost his life at the hand of the king. He will do the same to you. Do you understand?"

"Perfectly," I said.

I liked Adrix. He'd been kind to me the last few days and even sat and chatted with me once while I ate my meal, but I'd never seen this version of him before. A chill went down my back when he rested his hand on the handle of his sword and stared at me.

"Do not make me harm you, little human."

"Adrix, enough. She gets the point," the queen said.

Adrix walked over to the door and stood next to it. I stayed where I was, and the queen said, "Come and eat your lunch, Ellis."

I joined her, sinking into the chair across from her. I was hungry, but eating in front of the queen seemed... rude, somehow.

"You're not eating," the queen said after a few minutes.

"Um, I'm not that hungry, Your Highness."

My stomach growled with perfect timing, and the queen laughed. "One, you're obviously hungry and two, call me Sabrina."

I ate a few forkfuls of the blue rice-like grain called orechoke and some meat. "I'm sorry for walking in on you the other day, Your Majesty. If I had known it was your quarters, I would never have walked in like that."

"Call me Sabrina," she repeated. She rubbed at her belly. "Would you mind if I took some of your gallberry juice? Carrying this kid makes me crave it something fierce."

"Not at all." I stood, grabbed a bottle from the fridge, and handed it to her.

"Thanks." She took a long drink before shifting in her chair. "Look, before I met Quill and married him, I was a nobody, all right?"

"Were you a lower?" I asked.

"Just barely a middle," she said. "I worked as a nanny and lived with my sister. My sister had liver cancer, and I took the test to see if I was breeding compatible. I wasn't, so I joined the nanny program and was chosen by a farmer."

I blinked at her. "You're about as far away from a farm as you can get."

She laughed. "Yeah, I know. There was a mix-up, and I was sent here to Quill, and his actual intended mate, Evelyn, was sent to the farmer. It was in the cold months, and one of the infamous Draax storms had started, so we were isolated in the castle for a month."

"So, obviously, you're one of the women with the gene variant," I said.

"Yes." She drank some more juice before resting one hand on her belly. "I didn't like Quill at first. I thought he was arrogant and rude, but…"

A soft smile crossed her face, and I said, "But?"

"I realized I was wrong. Anyway, long story short, Quill and I fell in love, and we discovered the gene variant existed when I became pregnant with Jovie. We performed the mating ceremony shortly after that, and now this former nobody is the queen of the western province. Trust me, no one is more weirded out by the fact that I'm a queen than me."

"What happened to the other woman?"

Sabrina grinned at me. "Luckily, Evie fell in love with the farmer and his best friend. When the storm ended and Quill took me to the farm to tell the farmer I would not be his nanny, we discovered that Evelyn was perfectly happy to stay with her new loves. It's a friggin' miracle, really. What are the odds that one – they'd give us the wrong identification chips, and two – we'd both fall in love with the Draax we *weren't* supposed to be with?"

"So, Evelyn is in love with two Draax guys?" I said.

She nodded. "Yes. Bran and Court. Bran has a daughter named Bella, whose mother left her to return to Earth, but Bella thinks of Evie as her mother. And Evie and Court just had a baby boy."

"So, they're just one big happy family," I said. "I knew that

Draax liked to have threesomes with chicks, but I didn't realize it extended beyond the banging."

I winced at my coarseness. "Uh, I mean… sorry. That was a rude way to say it."

Sabrina laughed again. "Maybe, but accurate. It is unusual for two Draax to mate with one woman, but Bran and Court always knew they wanted to share a woman, and Evie is so happy with them."

I spilled some orechoke down the front of Galan's shirt and muttered a curse before giving Sabrina an apologetic look.

"As cute as you look in oversized Draax shirts, where are your clothes?" Sabrina asked.

"Sigan burned them while I was in the shower," I said. "And I didn't have any other ones in my backpack."

She laughed. "Sigan means well, but he has difficulty understanding females."

"Tell me about it," I said. "But to be fair, my clothes did smell pretty terrible."

"Yes, I saw you when you first arrived and were still unconscious. You're pretty lucky you stole juice from one of Quill's ships. Sigan said the faulty translator in your head probably would have killed you in another day or two."

"Oh, I didn't steal the juice," I said.

"Right. Cheryl stole it."

I jerked in surprise, and Sabrina grinned at me. "Your cleverness amused my husband."

She drank more juice, and I ate a piece of the citrus like fruit called jeanda. I glanced at Adrix and lowered my voice, "Thank you for what you did the other day. That was really nice of you."

"Truthfully, I did it for Galan," Sabrina said. "He's an amazing guy, and while he is my husband's best friend, if Quill had found out you escaped, it wouldn't have gone well for Galan."

"If you hadn't said anything, I would have told the king it was my fault, not Galan's. I wouldn't have let him get in trouble. I swear."

When she didn't reply, I said, "Is Galan okay? I haven't seen him for a few days and am worried about him."

Worried was an understatement. While I was reasonably sure he wasn't around because he was pissed at me, there'd been a large part of me that worried he'd gotten in trouble for what happened.

"He's fine," Sabrina said. "Busy."

"Is he?"

She paused. "No, at least no busier than usual. But he asked Adrix to keep an eye on you for now. He's upset with you but also with himself for being so careless in leaving your door unlocked. If you had escaped or hurt someone in the castle, Galan would never have forgiven himself."

Guilt streaked through me, and I stared at the table, worried that Sabrina would see it on my face. "I wouldn't have hurt anyone or tried to escape," I said in a small voice, entirely unlike my usual one. "I just wanted to do a bit of exploring."

"You asked me where the front door was," Sabrina said.

I kept quiet, and Sabrina said, "May I give you some advice, Ellis?"

"Yes."

"Try to see this apartment not as a prison but as a gift. I realize it isn't easy. I was in a somewhat similar situation to yours for the first few weeks I was here, but the alternative would be much worse. My husband is not always a patient

Draax, and if you keep trying to escape, he will have you sent to the Draax prison until we can return you to Earth."

I appreciated what she was saying, but she wasn't the one who would be imprisoned for the next forty years. As grateful as I was for the Draax king's kindness, I still needed to look out for myself. I'd learned the hard way that I couldn't count on anyone but me.

She was waiting for me to reply, so I painted on a sincere expression and said, "Of course. You're right. I'll follow the rules from now on."

Her look suggested that she didn't believe me, but she finished off her juice before heaving herself to her feet. "Ugh, my ankles are so swollen. I know many women love being pregnant, but I am not one of them."

"When are you due?" I asked as I stood.

"Another couple of weeks. It's nice to meet you formally, Ellis."

"It's nice to meet you as well, Your Highness."

She made a face and I smiled and said, "It's nice to meet you, Sabrina."

I followed her to the door, and Adrix opened it for her. "Come, my queen, I will escort you back to your quarters before I take the human for her walk in the garden."

"Thank you, Adrix." Sabrina paused in the hallway. "Remember what I said, Ellis. Okay?"

"I will. Thanks."

The door shut and locked, and I wandered back to the table. I sat down and pushed my fork around my half-eaten food. For the first time since I arrived, I'd lost my appetite. I hated that Galan was upset with me and even more that he was upset with himself.

Enough to tell him you lied?

My face went hot, and I pushed my food away before crossing the room to stretch out on the bed. Lying was what I did. Next to boosting ships and repairing mechanical shit, it was one of my best skills, and it had saved my ass more times than I could count. I'd never felt bad about lying to someone before, and these feelings of regret and remorse were foreign and unpleasant.

I didn't need to feel bad. Galan and I weren't even friends, for God's sake.

I SAT CROSS-LEGGED ON MY BED AND STARED ACROSS THE room at the lock on my door. My palms itched, and I traced the leather case on my lap. Picking the lock and leaving my apartment would be a colossal mistake. I knew that.

But it'd been two days since the queen's visit. Two days of nothing to do. Two days of eating meals, lying on the bed and staring at the ceiling, and twice daily walks with Adrix in the garden.

Two days of not seeing Galan.

There was a knock on my door, and I shoved the leather case under the sheet before standing. The door opened, and a woman with warm brown skin and pink hair stepped into my room and smiled uncertainly at me. "Hi there."

"Hello," I said.

A second woman walked in, and I said, "Inara, hi!"

"Hey, Ellis." Inara smiled at Adrix, who was standing behind them in the doorway. "Thank you, Adrix. We'll holler if we need you, okay?"

Adrix blushed, his gaze flickering to Inara's breasts for

the briefest of seconds. "You are welcome, Inara." He hesitated. "Your hair looks very pretty today."

"Thank you. I like your shirt," Inara said.

Adrix's skin turned an even darker green, and I could see his tail waving behind him like it was in a stage two hurricane. He glanced at me, the excited wave of his tail slowing. "Do not try to harm Inara and Candala, human."

"I won't," I said. "My murderous intentions are only at about a one today, and I need them to be at least a seven before I go all Lizzie Borden."

Adrix stared at me, and Inara laughed and said, "She's joking, Adrix. We'll be fine with her."

"I will wait in the hallway while you visit," he said.

He closed the door, and I walked over and stuck my hand out to the pink-haired girl. "Hi, Candala. I'm Ellis."

She shook my hand. "Hi there. You can call me Candy."

"So, are you guys here to clean or something?" I said.

"No," Inara wandered over to the loveseat and sat down. "Sabrina asked Candy to stop by and work her sewing magic for you, and I decided to join her just for a visit. I imagine you must be bored out of your mind."

"A little," I said. "What do you mean sewing magic?"

Candy laughed. "I'm a pretty good seamstress. None of the women who work here have clothes that will fit you, you're too small, but if you let me take your measurements, I'll make you some clothes."

"Seriously?" I said. "That would be amazing."

Candy had a small bag with her, and I watched as she brought out a tablet. "I won't be able to make a bra or underwear for you, but I can at least make you a few shirts and some pants, maybe even a couple pairs of shorts."

"Whatever you can do would be awesome," I said.

"Great, let's get you measured."

Fifteen minutes later, Candy had all of my measurements entered into her tablet, and the three of us were sitting in my small living room with bottles of gallberry juice. I'd dragged a kitchen chair over to sit in, and I shifted on the hard seat. "So, do you guys have the day off today?"

Inara nodded. "Yes, thank God. I had to clean the sparring room yesterday, and that's always a nightmare. I swear it took me three hours alone to scrub the blood off the floor."

"Blood?" I said.

"The Draax often spar with real swords, and sometimes they get cut so, you know… blood splatter," Inara said.

"Holy shit. That sounds like a good way to lose a limb," I said.

Candy laughed. "The Draax are pretty tough. And with this stuff," she pointed to the bottle of juice she held, "any damage they get from sparring is pretty much healed by the next day."

"Speaking of which," Inara said, "I heard they healed you from your cancer. That's pretty awesome."

"It is," I said.

"Adrix told me that you would be going to prison on Earth as soon as the war between the Emirans and the Cillades ended," Inara said. "I'm really sorry, Ellis."

"Well, I'm innocent," I said, "so I expect a lawyer will get any charges dropped once I tell him my side of the story."

"Right, it was a woman named Cheryl who made you steal the juice," Inara said.

"Boy, word gets around fast in the palace," I said.

"No," Candy said, "word gets around fast to Inara, especially when it's something that Adrix knows."

"He does seem to have a thing for you," I said to Inara.

She blushed prettily. "No more of a thing than he has for any other woman working in the palace. He's just a flirt."

"Bullshit," Candy said. "I guarantee the second the clock strikes midnight tomorrow night and this three month waiting period is over, he'll be knocking on your door and asking if you want to mate with him."

"And when I say no, he'll move on to the next woman and ask her," Inara said.

"Doubt it," Candy said.

"Are you saying no because of your sister?" I said.

"Yeah. I'm not staying here a minute longer past the year I agreed to," Inara said. "I can't. Wendy needs me."

"Doesn't mean you can't bang Adrix for fun," Candy said. "The Draax will be fine with that. Trust me."

"I wouldn't feel right about it, at least not with Adrix. Sigan told me Adrix is looking for a mate, not just sex. I don't want to lead him on."

"Technically, aren't they all looking for a mate?" I said.

"They are," Candy said. "But some of them are more eager to be mated than others. My experience has been that there are plenty of Draax just looking for sex and not a wife."

"How do you know that?" I said.

"I banged a lot of Draax back on Earth," Candy said.

Her matter-of-fact tone made me giggle. "Oh, well, um, good for you."

Candy grinned at me. "I didn't do it just because. My son, Roden, was sick, and I used to barter sex with the Draax for juice."

"Um, isn't that illegal?" Inara said.

"Oh yeah, but I was desperate," Candy said. "Roden was worth the risk of going to prison."

"Why didn't you just join the breeding program?" I said.

"I tried. I'm breeding incompatible," Candy said. "Anyway, a friend got enough juice to heal Roden, and that same friend helped me get the job here on Draax. Even if it is just house-cleaning, I love it. I was a lower back on Earth and barely scraping by. Here, I have a nice place to live, food for Roden, as much gallberry juice as we want to drink, and a weekly paycheque."

"They are pretty generous with the juice." I took another drink, relishing the sweet taste. My intense cravings for it had ended once my cancer was healed, but I still drank at least three bottles of the stuff a day. "So, are you planning to stay after your year of work is up, Candy?"

"Probably," she said. "I like it here, and so does Roden. Mind you, he hasn't been enrolled in an actual school yet."

"Why not?" I asked. "Is he too young?"

"No, but Sabrina thought it would be best to keep him and the other two kids separate for a while. This new work program is still in the testing stages, and very few Draax outside the castle know about it. Sabrina hired a teacher, Luka, to tutor them in the castle. Once the year contract is up and as long as the program works out, Sabrina said we can enroll the kids in regular school. Roden likes Luka, but he's a pretty social kid, and now that he can move and breathe without issues, he likes participating in sports. I'm just hoping that the Draax kids aren't mean to the human kids."

"They won't be," Inara said. "All of them are half-human themselves."

"I know, but they're also green or purple and have tails. Roden will stick out like a raisin in a chocolate chip cookie."

"Ooh, I should make cookies this weekend," Inara said.

Candy laughed, and I took another drink of juice. "So, are

you going to date a Draax now that you're allowed to socialize with them?"

Candy shook her head. "No. I'm over the just bang them and walk away thing. I did enough of that on Earth, and while there are plenty of Draax who are cool with just having sex, the ones who are looking for a relationship are looking for a breeding compatible mate. They want kids, you know?"

"There's some who don't," Inara said. "Laos told me that the head of the king's guard isn't looking for someone who can breed. Crap, what's his name…"

"Galan," I said through weirdly numb lips. "His name is Galan."

Inara snapped her fingers. "Right. I see him all the time in the sparring room. He's hot. You should go for him, Candy-girl."

"How does Laos know he doesn't want kids?" I said.

Inara shrugged. "I don't know, I didn't ask."

"So, he could want kids," I said. "Which means he wouldn't work for you, Candy."

Candy studied me, and I could feel my cheeks heating up. "I mean, if it isn't true he doesn't want kids. If it's true, then you could totally mate with him."

"His living quarters are right there," Inara pointed to the wall of the kitchenette, "why don't you pop by and say hello."

"Hmm, tempting… but no," Candy grinned.

"He isn't there anyway," Inara said. "He's always in the sparring room in the afternoon."

I stared at the wall like I'd never seen it before. Galan was right on the other side of it? Holy fucking shit.

"Are you serious? Galan lives right there?" I pointed to the wall.

Inara picked at a hangnail. "Yup. Not two weeks ago, I

was mopping the hallway floor, and he walked out. I remember because I'd left the bucket right in front of his door and he tripped over it. Water went all over his boots and pants. He had to go back into his apartment and change. I felt terrible, but he was super sweet about it. Said it was his fault."

She finished off her juice. "You know, the Draax have better technology than us. You'd think they have auto-brooms and auto-mops like we do on Earth. Not that I'm complaining. If they did, I wouldn't have a job, right?"

I didn't reply. I was still staring at the kitchen wall like it was the first goddamn wall I'd seen in my life. Galan had been right beside me this whole time. Eating, sleeping, show-ering, maybe doing... other things."

My pelvis clenched tight, and I immediately shoved that dangerous thought right out of my head.

"Ellis?"

"Yeah?" How thick were the walls anyway? Were they, *put a glass to the wall and still not hear anything* thick?

"Ellis? Helloooo, Ellis."

I made myself look away from the wall. "Sorry. What did you say?"

"I said maybe I could ask Sabrina if you could hang out in the common room with us sometime," Inara said.

"Common room?" I said.

"It's just a big room with couches and hologram screens and shit like that," Inara said. "A bunch of us ladies often hang out there in the evenings as a social thing. I'll ask Sabrina if you can join us. You must be so bored."

"I am," I said. "Thank you for the offer, but I'm pretty sure the queen won't let me go to the common room, even with a Draax guard."

"You never know," Inara said. "It won't hurt to ask. Anyway, I should go. I told Rachel I would meet her in the garden to do yoga. Candy, you want to join us, babe?"

"Not this time. I want to get started on some of Ellis's clothes before Roden finishes school for the day."

The two women stood, and I followed them as they headed toward the door. "Thank you, Candy. This is really nice of you, and I appreciate it."

"It's no problem," Candy said.

Inara opened the door and smiled at Adrix. "It was nice to see you again, Adrix."

"You as well, Inara. Are you headed back to your living quarters now?" Adrix said.

"Actually, the garden," Inara said.

"I will walk with you," Adrix said.

Candy glanced back at me and mouthed, "Told you he liked her."

Adrix shut and locked the door. I waited until their voices drifted down the hallway before I ran to the kitchenette, pressed one ear against the wall, and plugged the other with my finger. I couldn't hear anything and after a few seconds, I muttered a curse and straightened.

"What are you doing, idiot?" I paced back and forth. "One, these walls are made of goddamn stone, you're not going to hear anything, and two, he's not even in his apartment. He's at the sparring room and…"

I chewed at my bottom lip as I stared at my bed. My legs a little unsteady, I crossed over to the bed, opened the leather case, and grabbed my tension wrench and my hook pick.

"Seriously, what are you doing, Ellis?" I knelt in front of the door and inserted the tension wrench. "This is a terrible idea."

It was the worst fucking idea in the world.

CHAPTER 9

Ellis

I opened my door, looked both ways and stepped out into the empty hallway. I knelt in front of Galan's door and went to work on the lock. Nerves made sweat slide down my back, but my hands didn't shake. They never did.

Galan's lock was just as easy to pick as mine. I was inside his apartment in less than two minutes. I shut the door and leaned against it, holding my breath as I strained to hear any noise.

Galan's apartment was bigger than mine but not lavishly so. Nothing like the king's living quarters, anyway. Galan's decorating tastes were minimal, with a few pieces of art on the wall, some pictures, and other knick-knacks on a large bookshelf. The bookshelf was sandwiched between two doors on the far wall. One was shut, but the other was open, and I could see part of a dresser and the end of Galan's bed. I crept across the living room, running my hand along the back of the couch before opening the door on the left. It was a bathroom, and I studied the towel hanging on the rod and the razor and shaving cream on the bathroom vanity before closing the door.

There were framed photos on the second shelf of the bookshelf, and I picked up the closest one. It was a picture of Galan, the blue-eyed Draax, and the king as teenagers. They were standing in front of a vast violet coloured ocean, wearing swim trunks. Their hair was wet and slicked back, and their arms slung around each other's shoulders as they laughed into the camera.

I traced Galan's face before returning the picture and picking up the next one. Galan was a teen in this one, too, but his face was solemn and drawn. He stood next to a human woman. She was pretty with long dark hair. Unlike Galan, she was smiling into the camera, but there was a hint of sorrow in her dark eyes. A toddler of about four held onto her left leg tightly, his green skin glowing in the sunlight, and she cradled a dark-haired, green-skinned baby in her arms.

The man on the other side of her was tall and muscular like all the Draax, and a sword hung at his waist. He stared directly into the lens, his eyes the colour of flint. A shiver went down my spine. This had to be Galan's stepfather, but he didn't look like a nice guy.

I studied the picture for a few more minutes before examining the books on the shelf. They were all written in Draax, and I moved on to the next shelf. I picked up the small origami paper figures and smiled a little before placing them back in their exact spot.

Okay, Ellis, you've had a look at his place. Go back to your apartment now before we get caught. Please?

My inner voice was right. I really needed to get the fuck

out of here. But I hadn't quite looked at his entire place, had I?

I stepped inside his bedroom as my inner voice practically screamed in frustration.

Do you want to go to Draax prison? Is that it, Ellis?

"I just want to take a quick look around," I murmured. "No harm, no foul."

I stared at Galan's bed. He was pretty damn neat for a bachelor. There'd been no dishes in the sink, the space uncluttered, and the furniture dust free, but he hadn't made his bed, and there was a pile of clothes on the floor in the far corner.

My heart thudding in my chest, I walked over to the bed and sat down. I placed my wrench and pick on the night-stand table and ran my hands over the rumpled sheets before lying down and resting my head on his pillow. I turned my head and buried my face into his pillow, inhaling deeply. It smelled like Galan, and shamefully, my pussy dampened.

Jesus, was I that hard up for sex?

Ellis! Get out of his bed. If he comes home and finds you in his bed, he'll –

He wouldn't catch me. He was at sparring practice. I curled up on my side. His bed was queen-sized and comfortable as hell. I stared at the other side of the bed, wondering what Galan would do if he woke up one night and I was lying beside him.

Uh, gut you with his shiny sword? What the fuck is wrong with you?

Nothing was wrong with me. Other than being hot for a Draax who was pissed off at me and probably hated me.

My stomach clenched, and I rolled over and stared at the closet. The door was halfway open, and I could see Galan's shirts hanging neatly across the rod. Fuck, I'd messed up with him and while I knew that he wasn't attracted to me and never would be, the thought that he now hated me made me feel fucking awful. He was the closest thing to a friend I had here.

He's not your friend, Ellis. Stop thinking that way. No one here is your friend. If the jumpgate weren't blocked, you'd be sitting in a prison cell on Earth. Just because the Draax aren't tossing you in their jail doesn't mean they're your friends.

That was true. And honestly, if I didn't get my skinny ass out of Galan's apartment and back to my own, I really would be sitting in a Draax prison. It didn't matter how much –

The distinct sound of a door opening and closing made my stomach hurtle its way upward and battle my heart for a spot in my throat.

Fuck! Fuck! Fuck!

I slipped off the bed and darted for the closet, easing past the shirts and trying to hide in the shadows as I pressed my back against the wall. I held my breath, the sweat sliding down my back again and my heartbeat so loud I could barely hear anything beyond its frantic thud.

I peeked between two of his shirts and clapped my hand over my mouth when Galan walked into view. He looked hot and a little tired, and I could see the back of his shirt sticking to him with sweat. He stripped off his shirt and tossed it onto the pile of clothes on the floor.

Sweet baby Jesus. Despite my terror, I was mesmerized by the sight of Galan's naked chest. Did he… fuck, forget six pack, he had a goddamn eight pack. My heart cranked up another notch, but it had nothing to do with fear this time. I studied the broad expanse of his chest. It was hairless, and his nipples were a darker shade of green than his skin. A thin trail of dark hair started just below his navel and disappeared into the waistband of his pants.

He scratched at his flat stomach, and I watched in breathless fascination.

Please take off your pants. Pretty please?

My inner pleading went unheeded. Instead of losing his pants, Galan stretched out on the bed. He tucked one hand beneath his head, staring at the ceiling as his other hand rested on his abdomen. Long minutes passed, and my ability to stand perfectly still grew more difficult by the second. I had no choice, though. If Galan even looked in the direction of the closet, he would see me. Or rather, he'd see my legs. Hell, I was lucky he couldn't hear me panting after him like a… oh my sweet baby Jesus.

My breath caught in my throat, the small whimper that tried to escape muffled by my hand clamped over my mouth. Galan had unzipped his pants. He had unzipped his pants and…

Okay, so admittedly, I hadn't seen that many dicks, but I'd never seen a dick as big or thick or… yummy as Galan's. I watched with wide eyes as he lazily stroked his cock. It went from half-hard to fully erect in less than a minute, and I stared in mute wonder as he continued to rub in long strokes.

Ellis! Stop looking!

I should have. Peeping on Galan masturbating was totally wrong in so many ways, but I couldn't look away. I just couldn't. One did not simply stop looking at a beautiful work of art, or a finely chiseled sculpture, or the most beautiful cock they'd ever laid eyes on.

I clenched my thighs together. I was wet and hot, and I wanted nothing more than to charge out of the closet, hop onto Galan and ride that big, beautiful cock. Instead, I stayed quiet and still, watching as Galan's hand pulled and tugged. His thumb stroked around the ridge, his quiet moans and gasps setting me on fire with pure and perfect lust. When he stroked the head of his cock and pale green liquid spurted out of the slit, my mouth actually fucking watered.

I swallowed compulsively, my nipples hard pearls against Galan's shirt and my pussy aching and throbbing so much I wasn't sure how much longer I could stand it. Galan's hand moved harder and faster, the veins in his forearm popping out as he gripped his dick. His groans grew louder, his motions more frantic as his hips rose up and down.

I couldn't help it. I *had* to touch myself. I couldn't stand here and watch Galan find his pleasure without finding mine.

I eased my hand down toward my crotch, barely noticing the soft scrape of the hanger as my elbow nudged one of his shirts. But, apparently, Galan had the ears of a goddamn fox because he was up off the bed and stalking toward the closet immediately.

I made a loud eep of surprise when he reached into the closet, and his hard hand closed around my arm. He yanked me out of the closet. "Ellis? What are you doing in my closet?"

"I, um…"

I couldn't think of a single fucking lie. Not when Galan's cock was still rock hard, not when it was so close I could touch it, not when precum covered the head and practically begged for me to lick it off.

"Human!" He shook me, and I dragged my gaze away from his magnificent dick and back to his face. "How did you escape your room again? Did Adrix leave the door unlocked?"

"No," I said, "I picked the lock. Just like I picked it the first time I escaped, and just like I picked the lock to your apartment."

Huh, apparently, being in the presence of the most beautiful dick in the universe was some kind of goddamn truth serum.

"You lied to me," he said.

"I'm sorry." I licked my lips, my gaze drawn back to his dick. Fuck, he was still hard. Was he trying to kill me? "I shouldn't have lied, but I… it's what I do. I'm a liar."

I couldn't resist a moment longer. Hell, no woman could. My fingers trembling, I reached out and curled them around his thick shaft. His breath hissed out between his teeth, and his hips shot forward, nearly pinning me against the wall.

His big hand grabbed my wrist and pulled my hand away. I couldn't stop my soft cry of dismay, but he pinned both my hands above my head and stared down at me. "What are you doing, human?"

"I'm sorry," I said. I couldn't seem to say anything else. I was so fucking turned on that even though I knew I'd be going to a Draax prison, I didn't care. All I wanted was a taste of Galan's dick before they dumped me in a cell, and I would die a happy woman.

He leaned down, his warm breath washing over my face. I arched, trying to rub my tits against his chest, but he leaned back, keeping my arms pinned against the wall as he studied my mouth.

"You lied to me, broke out of your room twice, and now you have snuck into my quarters," he said.

I tore my gaze from his cock, staring up at his face. To my

surprise, there was no anger on his features, just… oh fuck me sideways… lust.

"Galan, please," I moaned and pulled at his grip.

His hands tightened around my wrists, his gaze dropping to my mouth. I licked my bottom lip, heat flaming in my belly when his copper eyes turned the colour of burnt bronze.

"Please kiss me," I whispered.

I didn't expect him to do what I asked, so I made a startled whimper when his mouth pressed against mine. He brushed his mouth over my lips, coaxing and teasing them open so he could sweep his tongue inside.

I moaned and licked at his tongue as he explored my inner mouth. One big hand cupped my tit, and I arched again, pushing more of my breast into his palm. He teased my aching nipple with the ball of his thumb as he swallowed my frantic cries and slicked his tongue across my bottom lip.

He pulled his mouth away, his breathing harsh and his nostrils flaring. "Tell me why you were hiding in my closet and spying on me, little human."

"I didn't mean to," I said. "I just didn't want to get in trouble, so I hid in your closet."

"Where you watched as I touched myself," Galan said.

"No! No, I… I closed my eyes. I didn't watch," I said.

A flicker of amusement crossed his face as his hand squeezed my breast. "Lying to me again, Ellis?"

"I wasn't watching," I whispered. "I'm not a pervert."

"No? So, you were not hiding in my closet, with your nipples hard," he gave my nipple a little pinch that made me gasp, "and your pussy wet, watching me fuck my cock with my hand while I imagined it was your tight pussy instead?"

I couldn't think of a single reply. Me, the queen of smartass retorts, who always had an excuse or a lie to get me out of a tight spot, was speechless. Galan wanted me?

Galan dipped his head and licked my neck, his tongue tasting and teasing and bringing a surge of wetness to my pussy. Fuck, I was gonna start dripping all over the shiny stone floor any minute now.

"You have stolen from my king, lied to me, left your room when you were told not to leave, and broken into my quarters." Galan's warm breath against my ear sent shivers down my spine. "You need to be punished, do you not?"

"Maybe you could let me off with a stern warning?" My voice was breathless and needy with anticipation.

"You and I both know a stern warning is not enough, sweet human." Galan sucked on my earlobe as his thumb rubbed circles around my aching nipple. "I will give you a choice. I can punish you, or I can take you to the king, and he will punish you. Make your choice."

"You," I said as a funny little cramp of pleasure hit my belly. I had no idea what Galan's punishment would be, but I sincerely hoped it involved me on my knees with his dick in my mouth.

"Wise decision. The king is not as patient nor good natured as I am." His hand still around my wrists, Galan tugged me toward the bed. I squeaked in surprise when he released me and quickly stripped his shirt off my body and tossed it on the floor.

Before I could even think to cover my nakedness, I was flat on my back on Galan's bed, and he was hovering over me, his large body between my thighs and his hands planted on either side of my head.

"Galan, what… oh my God!"

My hands threaded into his hair when his hot mouth

closed around my nipple. He flicked at it with his tongue and circled the tight bud before sucking hard. I arched into him, moaning and panting as he teased both my nipples. When they were dark pink and swollen and so sensitive that I couldn't stand it, he kissed his way down my flat stomach. He nuzzled my ribs and pressed a kiss above my belly button.

"Galan, I thought I was being... oh fuck!"

His warm mouth kissed the small patch of curls at the top of my pussy, and my mind went as blank as a broken PAR phone. I fisted the sheet in both hands, staring wide-eyed at Galan as he glanced up at me before easing his big body down the bed. His tail wrapped around my left thigh and tugged while his hand pushed against my right thigh.

"Spread your legs for me, Ellis."

I let my thighs drop open an obscene amount, any embarrassment I felt eclipsed by the waves of powerful lust rippling through my body. Galan studied my pussy before smiling up at me. "Such a pretty pussy. I bet it tastes sweet."

His tongue slicked across my wet pussy lips, and I slapped my hand over my mouth to muffle my shriek of pleasure.

He stared at me again, his grin almost predatory. "Deliciously sweet. I think pussy eating is the perfect punishment for you. Do you agree, little human?"

"Yes," I said. "Oh God, yes. Please, Galan."

He laughed and licked my pussy again. "Be a good girl for your punishment, Ellis."

"I will," I panted, my body straining against the grip of his tail and his hand. "Just, please, will you... oh God..."

His rough fingers parted the lips of my pussy, and his tongue slicked over my aching clit. I cried out, my hips arching up again as he flicked the tip of his tongue across my clit. When he sucked on it, I almost shot straight up off the bed. His tail tightened around my thigh, and he braced one forearm across my lower belly, pinning me to the bed.

He tasted my pussy again, his tongue, his beautiful, wet, freaking amazing tongue, licking and flicking and driving me higher and higher toward my orgasm. It'd been almost two years since I'd had sex and even longer since I'd had my pussy eaten.

And holy fuck, I'd never had my pussy eaten like this. Galan was a goddamn master at it, and I writhed and squirmed and pleaded, my hands tearing at the sheets as he kept up his relentless assault.

Shamefully, I couldn't hold back my release, not with the firm pressure of Galan's lips wrapped around my clit. I had the common sense to throw my arm across my mouth and dampen my scream as I came in a hard and roaring rush that sent flashes of light across my vision and made my entire body shake like I was being swept up in a tornado.

Galan cleaned the lips of my pussy with his tongue before easing to my side and stretching out on his back on the bed beside me. One hand rubbed my quivering thigh, the other rubbed his dick.

"Oh my God," I moaned. "Oh my God, that was… I don't even know what that was. It was so good."

"I am glad you are pleased, little human." I barely noticed when Galan shoved his pants and briefs down to his knees. His big hands cupped my hips, and he plucked me off the bed like I weighed less than a bug and settled me over his body.

Still weak from the best goddamn orgasm of my life, I sprawled across him with what I was sure was a stupid looking smile on my face as Galan smoothed his hand over my ass. "That was the best orgasm of my life. I've never come that hard before. I didn't even realize a girl *could* come that... oh!"

The head of Galan's cock pressed against my opening, and I immediately stiffened, my pussy clenching tight. I lifted my head, staring at Galan with wide eyes. It wasn't that I didn't want to fuck Galan, I did, but fantasizing about riding Galan's massive dick was utterly different from actually doing it. The dude's dick was the size of my damn forearm.

"Shh, Ellis," Galan said. "Relax."

He was gripping his dick in one hand, and I moaned when he rubbed the blunt head of it up and down my wet slit, bringing a zap of awareness to my sensitive clit.

His free hand squeezed my ass as he rubbed his dick back and forth over my pussy a few more times before pressing the head against my entrance again.

"Galan." I tried to squirm forward, and his tail wrapped around my waist, anchoring me in place as his big hands gripped my thighs and kept them spread wide around his body. "I think you might be too big."

"I will not hurt you, sweet human." His cock probed at my entrance, and I gasped when with a gentle thrust of his hips, he sunk the head of his dick into me.

"Oh!" I arched my back, my hands digging into his shoulders, as he kissed my upper chest and made another careful thrust. "Oh, fuck!"

He stroked my thighs. "Relax your pussy, Ellis."

"I'm trying," I said.

He kissed my chest again. 'You are not. Your little pussy is deliberately trying to keep my cock out."

"Probably because she doesn't want to be wrecked for life," I said.

His laughter made me and the bed shake. "Your pussy is very tight, but you can take my dick."

"We don't know that for sure," I said.

As we spoke, he was making small and measured pumps of his hips, and I could feel more of his cock sliding into me with every motion.

"There is only one way to find out," he said with a wicked grin and another pump of his hips.

"Easy for you to say, you're not the one who may never walk right again or… oh!"

I moaned, my fingers gripping Galan's shoulders until the tips went white. He had made one hard and final thrust, and I was stuffed to the fucking brim with cock. I took deep breaths, resting my forehead against Galan's chest as his big hands rubbed my back and his tail squeezed my waist.

"Such a good girl to take all of my cock, little human," he said.

"Thanks," I panted. "I've always been an overachiever."

He gripped my ass and kissed the top of my head. The humour had disappeared from his voice and now it was thick with need. "Your pussy is so tight, I must move. Are you ready for me?"

"I think so," I said. "But go slow, okay?"

"Yes. I will not hurt you, I prom -"

"For Krono's sake, Galan, where are you? You said you would be gone ten minutes, and it's been closer to …"

I shrieked in surprise when the blue-eyed Draax walked into the bedroom. I jerked wildly against Galan, wincing when there was a stab of pain in my pelvis. Galan groaned, his hands tightening painfully on my ass.

"Krey, leave us!" Galan snarled.

Krey tore his gaze from Galan's cock firmly embedded in

my pussy, and walked out of the room, shutting the bedroom door behind him.

"Fuck!" I said as Galan lifted me off of him. I scrambled off the bed, snatching up his shirt and dragging it over my head as Galan pulled up his briefs and pants and tucked his still hard cock out of sight. He grimaced and buttoned his pants before readjusting his dick.

"Galan, I -"

"Hush, little human." The warmth had seeped from his face, leaving – my stomach clenched – regret in its place.

He yanked his shirt on and took my arm just above the elbow, marching me out of the bedroom. Krey stood near the couch and my face flamed red when he stared at me.

Without speaking, Galan opened his door, led me out into the hallway, opened my door, and pushed me inside. "Stay here. Do you understand?"

"Yes," I said.

"Do not leave your quarters," Galan said. "You will be punished if you do."

His face turned a dark green, and his gaze flickered to my crotch for the briefest of seconds before he slammed the door in my face and locked it.

CHAPTER 10

Galan

"What are you doing?" Krey leaned against my couch, his arms folded across his chest and a look of disapproval on his features.

I ran my hand through my hair before grabbing a bottle of gallberry juice and chugging it down. My cock was still half-hard and throbbing and covered in Ellis's sweet cream. Krono! Her pussy was so tight and wet, and my balls ached with the need for release.

I stared at Krey, silently imagining how he would look with my fist in his face. I loved my best friend, but he had the worst fucking timing in the world.

"Stop looking at me like you want to punch me in the face and answer my question," Krey said. "Why did you take the thief from her room and fuck her?"

"I did not take her from her room. She broke into my room and was hiding in my closet."

"Krono," Krey said. "That little human is more trouble than she is worth. Why did you fuck her?"

"You know why," I said.

He studied me as I drank more gallberry juice. "I cannot understand your attraction to her, Galan. She is so small and thin. If I had not just seen it for myself, I would not believe she could even take your cock. Was her pussy tighter than other females?"

"Stop talking about her pussy," I said.

Krey glanced at my obvious erection before rolling his eyes. "She is a thief, and as soon as the war is over, she will be returned to Earth prison. It is a mistake to sleep with her."

"I know," I said. "I will not do it again."

"Will you not?" Krey said.

I hated how well Krey knew me. Keeping my tail steady, I said, "I will speak with the human and tell her it was a mistake that cannot happen again."

"I know you seek a mate," Krey said with sympathy, "but the small thief could never be your mate. Tomorrow, the waiting period ends for the females employed at the castle. There must be one who catches your eye."

"They are all breeding compatible," I said. "I will not take a breeding compatible female for my own when so many of our kind yearn for children."

"The one named Candala is not breeding compatible," Krey said. "She is very pretty and already has a child of her own. You should spend time with her."

"Perhaps." I drank more juice. Krey was right. The female was pretty, even with her odd pink hair, but I had no interest in her. I had no interest in any female who was not Ellis.

I stiffened, the bottle of juice halfway to my mouth. Krono, I was in real trouble if that was how I truly felt.

"Galan? What is it?"

"Nothing," I said. "I will speak with Ellis and tell her it was a mistake."

I stuck the bottle of juice back in the fridge. I didn't wish for Ellis to be my mate. I just wanted sex. I hadn't been with a female in moons, and the feelings Ellis drew from me were based on lust, not love. No sane Draax fell in love with a female he barely knew.

Ellis

IT WAS DINNER TIME BEFORE THERE WAS A KNOCK ON MY DOOR. It opened, and I jumped off my bed, smoothing Galan's shirt with quick, nervous jerks as Galan stepped into my apartment.

He held a tray of food in his hands and shut the door with his tail before carrying the tray to the table. I hurried over, my hope that maybe Galan didn't completely regret what happened dying when I saw the look on his face and the way he stepped back like he thought I might be infested with fleas.

I stood behind the chair with my heart thudding and shame billowing inside of me. "Hi, Galan."

"Hello, human."

"Um, how are you?"

"Fine. Sit and eat."

I sat down. "Will you join me?"

"I cannot. Human, what happened earlier was a," he paused and for a moment, that stupid bubble of hope grew in my chest again, "mistake. I should never have fucked you, and it will not happen again."

The hope bubble popped like it'd been poked with the point of a freshly sharpened pencil.

"Technically, we didn't really fuck," I said. "I mean, there was no actual fucking, just you making me orgasm until I saw God, and then, uh, penetration, right?"

His face darkened with embarrassment and holy shit, what was wrong with me? I seriously needed a goddamn off button.

"Anyway, you're right. It was a mistake, and it's my fault, and I apologize. I'd be really grateful if you didn't tell your king about me breaking out of my room. I won't do it again," I said.

I couldn't do it again. My damn tools were still in Galan's room.

"What happened between us is not your fault," he said. "It is mine. I will not speak of this to anyone, nor will Krey, but you must stay in your room. If you leave your room again without permission, Quill will have you sent to Iron Gate, and nothing I say will convince him otherwise."

"I won't leave again." I poked at the food on my plate. "How was your day?"

"Fine." He was already edging toward the door. "I am sorry, but I cannot stay and visit. I have prior commitments this evening."

"Oh, yeah, no, I get it. No problem." I stood and plastered a smile on my face. "Will I see you tomorrow?"

"Yes, most likely. Goodbye, Ellis." Galan left my apartment, locking the door behind him.

I stared at the food on my plate. My appetite had vanished for the first time since I woke up on the Draax planet. Unlike me, Galan was a terrible liar.

"HEY, HELLO!" I JUMPED UP FROM THE COUCH, SMILING excitedly at the pink-haired woman. "Candy, right? It's great to see you again."

"You too, Ellis." Candy's look was one part friendly, two parts *warning, Will Robinson, danger ahead*.

I immediately tried to rein in my enthusiasm. I was acting weird, but could you blame me? I hadn't spoken to anyone but Adrix for an entire week, and while I liked him well enough, it was quickly apparent that he wasn't that into me. Even on our twice daily walks through the garden, getting him to talk was like pulling teeth. Yesterday, in sheer desperation, I tried to speak to a random Draax we walked by in the garden, but Adrix had hurried me along and scolded me for talking to him.

"You must remember that you are not a guest in my king's home," he'd said with his tail lashing back and forth. "You are a prisoner, and it is only through the king's mercy that you are not at Iron Gate."

"This must be your son. Hi, I'm Ellis." I smiled at the dark-haired boy standing just behind Candy and carrying two sets of virtual reality goggles.

"Roden, say hello to Ellis, please."

"Hi, Ellis," Roden said cheerfully.

Adrix walked in behind them, setting a sewing machine on my small table. "Here you go, Candala."

"Thank you, Adrix."

He shut the door behind him as Candy set a bag on the couch. "I have your clothes ready."

"Thank you so much." I pulled out the four shirts, the

three pairs of pants and the pair of shorts. "These are amazing. Hey, shoes!"

Candy grinned at me as I held the shoes up to my feet. "One of the other ladies has pretty small feet. She had an extra pair of shoes she was willing to give up. Hopefully, they fit you."

I tried the shoes on. "Perfect, actually."

"Great," Candy said.

I pulled the pants on under Galan's shirt and buttoned them. "Thank you, Candy."

"They're a bit too long. I was afraid of that. Hop up on the chair, and I'll hem them for you," Candy said.

"Oh, it's fine. I can roll them," I said.

"It'll only take a few minutes. It's why I brought the machine with me. Roden, hang out on the couch for a while."

"Sure, Mama." Roden plopped down on the couch and stuck a pair of goggles on his face before hitting a button on the side. It glowed green and I watched with some amusement as Roden grabbed an invisible steering wheel and said, "Departure checklist complete. Ready for takeoff, air tower."

I hopped up on the chair, and Candy pinned the pants. "Okay, just give me a few minutes here."

"So, how are things?" I sat on the chair, watching Candy fiddle with the sewing machine.

"Good." Candy did something to the machine, placed my pants under a section of it, and hit a button.

I watched in fascination as the silver blur of the needle pierced through the fabric. Candy pressed another button, and a lever fed the pants through the machine.

"God, these new machines are crazy good," Candy said. "I had an old automatic sewing machine that belonged to my grandmother back on Earth, but when Sabrina found out I liked to sew, she had this new model brought to Draax. It's crazy fast, and I can just program it for simple jobs like this."

"That's cool," I said. "What else is new?"

"Well, the waiting period for us to socialize with the Draax is over."

"How is that going? Meet anyone interesting?" I was like a teenage girl desperate for drama. I usually couldn't give a shit about anyone's love life, but I'd never been so starved for human contact before.

"Oh God, no. I told you before that I'm not interested." Candy sat back in her chair. "To be honest, most of the women aren't. Everyone in the program is here to make money, and no one is willing to risk their job just for a bit of sex. Even if it'll be the best sex of their life."

"What happens if a woman did want to quit their job to marry a Draax? Is it even allowed?" I said. "Didn't you sign a year long contract?"

"There's a clause in the contract that states if you wish to marry a Draax and start popping out babies, it's an acceptable reason to end the contract."

"Of course there is," I said, rolling my eyeballs so hard they were in danger of falling right out of my skull. "This work program thing is bullshit. You know that, right? They only want women here for one thing."

Candy half-shrugged. "Maybe it is, and maybe it isn't. I know that Sabrina believes strongly in it, and even if it is just a," she hesitated, "way of luring women here in hopes they'll mate with a Draax, what of it? Everyone in the program was suffering back home either from malnutrition, abuse by people who were supposed to love them, or an incurable disease. Four of the women were on the verge of homelessness after losing their shitty jobs, and two were actually homeless. They joined the breeding program out of desperation, not because they wanted to give a Draax a baby. The work program allows them to do something more with their life, at least. It gives them a choice about whether they want to have a Draax baby."

She smoothed her shirt down before giving me a frank look. "Honestly, I'm not sure why you're so bitter about it. You were a lower, right? You know what it's like to struggle. Are the Draax perfect? No, but they're trying, at least. And they treat us way better than human males ever will."

I stared at the table, my cheeks hot and my shame at an all-time high. "I know. I'm being a bitch."

She sighed and leaned forward. "You're not being a bitch. You're used to not trusting anyone, and I get that. But I truly believe that Sabrina is doing a good thing for us. She's giving hope to women who didn't have much left to hope for. And you know what? The Draax may only be interested in one thing, but in the last week, when it became apparent that most of the women aren't interested in being," Candy made finger quotes, "courted, they backed off immediately. They respect us and our feelings, and that's a foreign concept for most of us."

Jesus, I was really feeling like a total dick now. I scuffed my foot along the stone floor. I wanted to tell Candy that I wasn't usually this awful, that deep down I was a nice person, but why would she believe me? Hell, I hardly believed it myself. I wanted to be a good person and see the best in others around me, but experience taught me that if people couldn't get what they wanted from you, you were disposable.

"I'm sorry," I said.

"You don't have to be sorry. I don't know your life story,

but I can guess there haven't been a lot of happy moments for you, and I understand that it colours your view. But don't judge the Draax for their way of life or what they do for the survival of their race. We owe them a lot as a race and, for some of us, as individuals. The Draax I slept with, the ones who were willing to break the law to barter sex for juice? They saved my kid's life. Were they getting something out of it? Sure. But how often do humans do something for nothing? Why should we expect that from the Draax?"

"You're right," I said. "I'm being judgemental as hell, and I suck."

Candy laughed. "Well, I'm so high up on my soapbox that the air's getting thin, so maybe we both suck a little today."

She muttered a curse when the sewing machine made a weird grinding noise and stopped. I watched as she pulled out threads, still muttering curses under her breath. When it became apparent that she needed all her concentration, I stood and wandered over to the couch, sitting beside Roden.

He took off the VR goggles. "Hey."

"Hey," I said. "What game are you playing?"

"It's not a game, it's a flight simulator," he said. "When I get bigger, I'm gonna be a fighter pilot for the Draax."

"Oh yeah? That's cool. I used to repair ships back on Earth. Flew them occasionally."

His eyes widened. "Seriously? You flew a Draax ship before?"

"Not a Draax one. But I've flown the havoc cruisers." I decided it was prudent not to mention that I'd stolen the ships.

"Luka says Draax battleships are different from human ships. He says they're better because they get technology from the Vokines. He says they're harder to fly than human ships, and I'll have to study and practice a lot."

"Ships are ships," I said. "How hard can it be?"

Roden handed me the extra pair of goggles. "C'mon, you can be my co-pilot."

"All right." I slipped the goggles on, swaying a little on the couch when the screen blipped, and the dashboard of a ship appeared in front of me. "This is cool."

"Super cool," Roden said. "Here, let me explain what you gotta do…"

"OH MY GOD," RODEN SAID. "YOU JUST FIRED THE GUNS INTO the back of the ship."

"Whoops," I said. "It's fine. Everything's fine."

"The engine's on fire. It's not fine," Roden said.

I was shocked when Candy's voice spoke directly behind us. "Okay, Roden, it's been an hour. We have to go."

"Mama, we're almost to the far end of the galaxy," Roden said.

"Sorry, big guy. We need to go. Shut it down."

He ended the program, and I slipped the goggles off my face and rubbed at the marks on my cheeks. "Sorry, Candy. I didn't realize so much time had passed."

"It's fine," she said. "I hemmed your other pants and it was nice for Roden to have company with his game."

"It's not a game, Mama." There was affectionate exasperation in Roden's voice. "It's a flight simulator."

"Right, of course," Candy said.

Roden cocked his head at me. "You learned the program pretty quick."

"Thanks," I said.

"You can keep my extra goggles and keep practicing. Maybe I'll come back in a couple of days, and we can fly again." Roden said.

"Sure," I said. "If it's okay with your mom."

"Fine by me," Candy said. "See you later, Ellis."

"Bye." I walked them to the door, smiling at Adrix when he stepped forward from his spot in the hallway. "I'm not trying to escape."

He grunted and then ruffled Roden's hair when the young boy stopped in front of him. "Hello, young human. How are you today?"

"Good. Can I hold your sword?"

"Roden," Candy said.

Adrix grinned at him. "You are too young to hold a sword this sharp and heavy. But have your mama bring you to the training room, and I will let you hold one of the wooden swords."

"Cool. Thanks." Roden held out his fist, and after a moment, Adrix shook it.

Roden laughed. "No, man, like this. Make a fist."

Adrix made a fist, and Roden bumped it. "You gotta pound it like this."

"Pound it," Adrix said before bumping his knuckles against Roden's again.

"Nice. It's an old Earth greeting," Roden said. "I'm bringing it back."

Candy laughed and put her arm around his narrow shoulders. "C'mon, kiddo, time for dinner."

They walked down the hallway, and Adrix motioned for me to step back. "I will bring you your dinner soon."

"Okay."

"You must eat more," he suddenly said. "Jakar is beginning to think you do not like his cooking."

I didn't reply. I hadn't had much appetite the last week, which was ridiculous because I could always eat, but now the food tasted like sawdust. Even the gallberry juice had lost some of its luster. It was hard to find joy in anything when all I could think about was a particular copper eyed Draax, who I'd never see again.

It was hard to admit, but missing Galan was a deep-seated ache that never really went away. Which was stupid because I'd hardly spent any time with him, right? A few hours together and one sexual encounter shouldn't have been enough to make me this lonely for him.

Only it did.

"Human, are you all right?" Adrix said. "You look ill. Are you drinking your gallberry juice?"

"I'm fine," I said.

"All right. I will return soon." He shut the door in my face, and I was alone again.

For a second, I thought about trying to jimmy open the door with the other picks in my kit before walking to my bed and curling up. Even if I could get it open, Adrix would be back in ten minutes with my dinner, so where exactly would I go without quickly being discovered and thrown into prison? This was a definite three strikes, and you're out scenario. There was a Draax posted outside my door almost constantly, and I had no one to blame except myself.

I'd ruined any chance of planning an escape because I'd gotten horny watching Galan touch himself. That was the truth – plain and simple. I was going to die in prison because I couldn't control my urge to masturbate while watching Galan masturbate.

Jesus, that has got to be the worst cause of death in the history of causes of death.

I rolled over and stared at the wall that separated my apartment from Galan's. He was so close. Hell, he could be in there right now, he could be thinking about me and touching himself, and I would never get the chance to see that beautiful giant dick again.

He's not thinking about you. He's over you, girl. Not even sure why he was into you in the first place, but I think the last seven days of zero contact proves he's come to his senses.

I closed my eyes. Yeah, Galan was over me, and that was to be expected. So, why did it feel so fucking shitty?

CHAPTER 11

Galan

"You want me to do what?" Melu scratched his head before wiping a rag at the ship's side.

"She worked on Earth repairing land vehicles and ships," I said.

"So? I do not need a human in my docking bay," Melu said. "I do not care if she can repair ships or not."

"You told Quill you were shorthanded," I said. "The human can help."

"We are making it work as is." Melu wiped at another spot on the ship. I'd known it would be a tough sell to convince Melu, the head of the docking bay, to allow Ellis to work in the bay, but I needed to try. The thought of her sitting alone in her quarters all day long was killing me.

Uzel, a younger Draax who wasn't more than nineteen and had only been working at the castle for a year, stopped next to us. "You were just saying this morning that if King

Quillan did not find another docking bay worker, you would quit in protest."

Melu scowled at him, but Uzel just grinned. "What? You said it. I do not see the harm in letting the female work at the bay. If she is good at repairing ships and land vehicles, she will be helpful to have around, will she not?"

"You only want a female to work here because you think it will give you a better chance at getting your dick sucked for the first time," Melu said.

I immediately turned on Uzel, scowling at him until he stepped back. "The female is not to be touched, Uzel."

He blinked at me. "I know, Galan. I have seen her walking in the garden with Adrix, and she is not attractive. Besides, she is a thief who will be returned to Earth after the war. A Draax would have to be a fool to try to mate with her when there is no chance of her staying."

"Go fix the vroha as I asked, and be quick about it," Melu said. His tone was gruff as usual, but it didn't seem to bother Uzel.

He walked away, and Melu folded his arms across his broad chest and leaned against the ship.

"Do you agree to have her here?" I said.

"She is a thief," Melu said. "And I heard she tried to escape and nearly killed a Draax in doing so."

"Oh, for Krono's sake," I said, "she did not try to kill a Draax."

Unless, I supposed, almost killing a Draax by having the tightest pussy in existence counted.

"But she is a thief," Melu said.

"Yes."

Melu glanced around the docking bay. "There are many things here she could steal or use as a weapon, Galan."

"She is not dangerous," I said. "She will be checked over every day before she leaves, and Draax will be around her while she works. Keep her busy enough with work, and she will have no time even to try to steal something."

"Melu, you grumpy old bastard, give the female a chance. At the very least, having a female in the bay will liven this place up a bit." Krey strolled up and grinned at Melu, his amusement over his use of the human's curse words as strong as ever.

"I should have known you would show up. Where Galan goes, you usually follow," Melu said, but the scowl on his face had disappeared, and his body had relaxed.

I could have hugged Krey in thanks. He'd saved Melu's life a few years ago, and Melu'd had a soft spot for him ever since.

"It is good to see you again, old friend." Krey hugged Melu. "Now, will you allow the female to work for you, or will I have to watch Galan keep asking until he wears you down?"

Melu snorted, glancing over at me before shaking his head. "Fine, we will try it. But if she steals from me or tries to escape in a ship, you will explain to King Quill what happened, Galan."

"She will not try to escape," I said, even though I had no faith that she wouldn't. "She will be chipped with a tracking device, and she knows how to repair ships, not fly them."

"She can start tomorrow," Melu said. "I will not treat her any differently than I treat the others. I do not care if she is a fragile human female."

"She is tougher than she looks," I said.

"We will see about that." Melu walked away, hollering at Uzel to join him at one of the dozen ships in the docking bay.

"Thank you, Krey," I said. "I know it is only because of you that Melu agreed to this."

"You are welcome," Krey said. "Are you sure this is a smart idea though? If she steals from Melu or tries to escape in a ship, Quill will put her in Iron Gate."

"You must make that clear to her," I said. "Make sure she understands clearly the consequences of breaking the rules."

"Me?" Krey said. "Why me?"

"It is best if I do not see the little female," I said.

Krey was staring at me with surprise in his gaze. "Why? Do you wish to be fucked so badly that you have such little self-control?"

I didn't reply, and Krey clapped me on the back. "Krono, Galan, you really should have found a female to fuck you when we were on Earth. With the war going on, unless one of the females in the work program agrees to fucking you, it will be a very long time before you feel the warmth of a pussy again."

I didn't bother telling Krey that it was only Ellis's pussy I wanted. What was the point? He would think I had gone mad, and, truthfully, he was probably right. I was feeling like I'd gone mad as of late. I had no appetite and could barely concentrate on training the latest recruits. The other day, distracted by thoughts of Ellis, a recruit's sword had slipped by my own and sliced my thigh open badly. I had bled more that day on the floor of the training room than I had in my last battle.

Every night I lay in my bed, staring at the wall that separated us and stopping myself from touching my cock. I don't know why I tortured myself that way. Not giving myself the release I so desperately craved was foolish, but what good was my hand once I'd been in Ellis's tight pussy?

"Galan?"

I shook off my thoughts of Ellis and changed the subject as Krey and I left the docking bay. "Have you convinced any of the women in the program to mate with you?"

"I have not tried," Krey said.

"Why not?"

He shrugged. "Many Draax are vying for their attention, and I do not believe a single female is interested."

"Truly?" I said.

"Yes." A smile crossed Krey's face. "Quill's idea to have all the females in the program be breeding compatible was a good one, but none of them being interested in us is a complication he did not anticipate."

"Sabrina chose females for the program who have lived difficult lives. For many, it is their first time having their own money and freedom. Is it any wonder they want to continue working?"

"No," Krey said, "but there have been many disappointed Draax in the castle lately."

"They will get over it. And perhaps the women will be more interested with time," I said. "Will you speak with Ellis for me, Krey? Will you be certain she understands the consequences of any attempt to escape from the docking bay?"

"Yes, I will speak to her." Krey clapped me on the back. "Come, it is close to dinner, and I am starving. Let us join the others in the dining hall."

Ellis

THE CLICK OF MY DOOR UNLOCKING HAD ME WHIPPING OFF THE
VR goggles and tucking them behind a couch pillow. I didn't
know if I would get in trouble for having them, but I wasn't
risking getting them taken away. They'd been my primary
source of entertainment for the last forty-eight hours, and I
didn't want to give them up. A girl could only surf the
Draax's version of the internet for so long. And considering
everything was written in Draax... well, it wasn't exactly
entertaining.

The door opened, and I grinned at the Draax, who walked
in. "Sigan!" I hurried over, ready to do something stupid like
hug him.

"Hello, human," Sigan said.

He almost looked happy to see me. Before I could hug
him, the second Draax walked in. I immediately backed
away, staring suspiciously at the blue-eyed alien, my eyes
dropping to the sword around his waist. I knew Krey was
Galan's best friend, but what if he'd said something to the
king about what he'd seen? What if the king was pissed and
had ordered my head to be chopped off for banging Galan?

*Did you bang him, though... I mean... you didn't even really get
to feel what it was like to –*

Shut up! Now is not the freaking time, brain!

I stared suspiciously at the device Sigan was holding in
his right hand. It was silver and cylindrical, and the end
narrowed into a ... shit... that was definitely a needle. Lethal
injection, maybe? I supposed that was better than getting my
head cut off.

"Hello, human," Krey said.

"Hey." I continued to back up until my ass bumped into a
kitchen chair.

"What is wrong?" Sigan said.

"Nothing. What, uh, what are you doing here, Sigan?"

He held up the needle. "To give you this."

"So, lethal injection," I said. "I can think of worse ways to die, I guess."

Sigan stared at me. "I have not missed your madness, human."

"Thanks, big guy." I stared at Krey. "You just couldn't resist telling the king what happened between Galan and me, huh?"

"What happened between the human and Galan?" Sigan turned to Krey.

"Nothing. The human's brain is probably rattled from spending so much time alone. You know how humans are, Sigan," Krey said. "They need to spend time with their own kind."

"Well, then, I guess this is a good idea." Sigan held up the needle.

"After all we've been through," I said. "Thanks a lot, Sigan. I thought you liked me."

"I do not dislike you, but I do not know you well enough to say I like you either," Sigan said. "Come here, human."

"I don't even get a last meal? One phone call to my family to say goodbye?"

"What is she babbling about?" Sigan said.

Krey shrugged. "I have no idea."

"Prisoners on death row get a last meal before they're killed," I said.

"Killed?" Krey said.

I pointed at the needle. "Lethal injection. Poison straight into the old veins."

Sigan rolled his eyes. "Oh, for Krono's sake. You are so

dramatic, human. You are not being killed. This is simply a tracking device that will go under your skin."

"So, you're not here to kill me with a poisonous injection?" I said.

"No. If I wanted to kill you, human, I would just break your neck. You are tiny and fragile," Sigan said.

"Sigan!" Krey elbowed him in the side, nearly making Sigan drop the needle.

"What?' Sigan glanced at Krey and then at me. "I was too blunt again, was I not, human?"

"You need to work on your inside voice," I said.

"I am sorry," Sigan said. "I would not kill you. I promise." He paused. "Unless my king demanded it."

"So close to acting like a normal human, Sigan," I said. "So close."

"I am not human," Sigan said.

"Yeah." I held out my arm when Sigan approached me.

"Normally, you would have been given a tracking and identification chip as soon as you set foot on our planet as per the treaty rules," Sigan said as he wiped antiseptic on my arm. "But because you are being sent back to Earth, we did not bother."

He slid the needle into my upper arm, and I winced. "Christ, how big is that tracking chip?"

"Smallish." Sigan wiped the spot of blood away. "You will not even know it's there."

I felt my arm where the needle had gone in. "I can feel it under my skin, Sigan."

He just shrugged. "Human skin is thinner than Draax skin, and you are still very skinny."

"Why exactly am I being tracked anyway?" I said. "You wanna see how often I go from the kitchen to the couch?"

Sigan glanced at Krey, who stepped forward with his hand on the handle of his sword. "You are being allowed out of your quarters, human."

"What? Seriously?"

"Yes. You will work at the docking bay daily, repairing our vehicles and ships. You cannot leave the docking bay without first asking Melu permission. Is that clear?"

"Yes." My voice was giddy. "This is awesome."

"Do you know how to fly ships?" Krey asked.

"Why?"

He stepped even closer, and I automatically moved closer to Sigan. Not that I thought he would protect me if push came to shove, but he didn't make me feel weak and afraid like Krey did.

"There is concern that you will try to steal a ship and escape," Krey said.

"I don't know how to fly a Draax ship." I wasn't technically lying. A game simulator was different from the real thing, right?

"Galan had to work hard to convince both the king and Melu to allow you this freedom," Krey said. "Trying to escape or perform poorly at your tasks will reflect badly on Galan. Do you understand?"

I nodded. "I do."

"Sigan, can you leave us, please?" Krey said.

"All right. Goodbye, human."

I swallowed hard. "Bye, Sigan."

When the door shut behind him, Krey marched forward. I backpedaled until my ass hit the far wall.

Krey loomed over me, his handsome face solemn. "If you hurt Galan, human, I will hurt you. Is that clear?"

"Yes," I said. "I won't hurt him."

"See that you do not," Krey said. "This is a gift from the king. You will be sent to Iron Gate if you try to escape from the docking bay. No second chances, no excuses. You will spend the rest of your time on our world locked away. Is that clear?"

"Perfectly."

He backed away, and I took a deep breath. "So, when does my new job start?"

"Tomorrow morning. Adrix will take you to the docking bay, and you will work until Melu says you are finished."

"All right. Who's Melu?"

"He runs the docking bay. He will not like you," Krey said. "He does this only as a favour to Galan. Keep your thoughts to yourself, and do not try Melu's patience. He is not as easy-going as I am."

"Right," I said. "Um, how is Galan doing?"

"He is fine," Krey said.

"Will you tell him I said hi?"

"No," Krey said. "It is best if the two of you do not have any contact. You are a thief and will be sent to prison as soon as the war is over. Spending time with Galan, hoping he will fall in love with you so that he will convince the king to forgive your crimes, is not wise, human. If you attempt to manipulate Galan in this manner, I will make certain you regret it."

"I'm not trying to do that," I said. Anger was taking over my fear. Who the hell did this Krey guy think he was? He didn't know anything about me and acted like I didn't care about Galan or that I didn't understand what he had done for me.

I stepped forward and glared up at him. "Do me a favour and quit judging me. You don't even fucking know me, you big green asshole. I'm not trying to manipulate Galan into anything. He's my friend, and I miss him, so I asked you to tell him I said hi. That's it. Stop thinking you know anything about me because you fucking don't."

The look of surprise on Krey's face faded and was replaced with... shit, was that admiration?

"You are feisty for a human," he said. "I still do not understand Galan's obsession with you, but I am beginning to think we could be friends."

"Doubtful," I said. "You're too much of an asshole."

He laughed before tapping me playfully on the forehead. "You are a cute little human."

"Make that condescending asshole," I said as he headed toward the door.

He laughed again and used his tail to open the door. "Goodbye, human."

"Bye, Krey."

CHAPTER 12

Ellis

"You are even smaller than I thought."

"Yeah, well, you're pretty short for a Draax," I said.

I suppose short was a relative word. The Draax was over six feet, but he looked short after being around Galan, Krey, and Adrix, who were all at least 6'5 or larger.

The short and grumpy Draax shot the young one a look when he snickered at my words. The young one turned a dark shade of green before clearing his throat. "Hello, human. My name is Uzel."

"Hi, Uzel, I'm Ellis."

"I am Melu," the grumpy one said. "You will do what I say when I say it, and if you give me any trouble, I will immediately inform the king of your disobedience. Is that clear?"

"You're a narc, I get it," I said.

Melu scowled at me. "What does narc mean?"

"It means you are a snitch," Uzel said. "You tell others in

positions of power about those engaging in illegal activity. Humans use it in a derogative manner."

"Uzel," I said, "don't be a tattletale."

"Tattletale?" Melu said.

"It means -"

"Krono, I do not care," Melu said with a roll of his eyes. "Will you obey my rules, human?"

"Yes," I said.

"Good. The bay floor needs cleaning. You will find what you need to clean it in the utility room. Uzel, show her the room."

"I'm supposed to be repairing the ships and land vehicles," I said.

"No, you are supposed to be working for me in the docking bay," Melu said. "The floor needs cleaning. If you do not wish to clean today, you can return to your quarters. It makes no difference to me."

"All right, all right, no need to be grumpy about it," I said. "I'll clean the floors."

I followed Uzel across the docking bay. Truthfully, I wasn't that upset about being relegated to janitorial duties. At least I was out of my room and doing something.

"Wow, this place is pretty big," I said.

Uzel nodded and stopped walking. "It is. This is the main section of the bay. The outside landing pad is there." He pointed to the far end of the bay, where a wide hangar door revealed an enormous circular stone area painted with bright red marks.

I studied the landing pad. The sun was shining, and I could smell fresh grass wafting in even over the smells of the docking bay. I wanted to run outside and roll around in the grass I could see around the edges of the landing pad. I couldn't remember the last time I'd spent so much time indoors, and while the garden was beautiful, I suddenly longed for bright sunshine and a warm breeze that wasn't ultimately surrounded by thick stone walls.

"It looks like a nice day," I said to Uzel. "Maybe you could show me the landing pad up close?"

"No," he said. "There is no need for you to leave the docking bay."

"I just wanted a bit of sun on my face," I said.

"It is not the sun here. It is keo," Uzel said.

"Sun, keo... tomato, tomahto," I said. "Wouldn't it be nice to get a bit of Vitamin D?"

"You are not allowed to leave the docking bay," he repeated. "If you try, Melu will return you to your quarters."

"Right," I said.

"We use this main area to repair the vroha ships," Uzel continued with his impromptu tour.

"Vroha are your battleships, right?" I already knew the answer. I'd been flying a simulated vroha ship for the last two days.

"Yes. The king's guard and the Draax military use the vroha ships."

"Why are they called vroha?"

"The ships are from an alien race called Vokine. They are named after the Vokine female who built the first one. We trade ships with the Vokine for gallberry plants."

"Plants, not juice? But I thought the plant could only grow on your planet," I said.

"Vokine is the rare exception. But even then, it only grows under certain conditions, and the healing potency of the plant is not as strong as that of those grown on our planet," Uzel said.

"The Vokines are one of your largest trading partners, right?"

"Yes. How much do you know of the Draax life, human?"

"It's Ellis, and I know some." I'd taken Draax studies in high school just like every other human, but considering I'd dropped out at sixteen and never graduated, I figured there was probably plenty I didn't know.

"The Vokine have provided us with much of our technology, including our battleships and the kyoden ships."

"What are kyoden ships?" I said.

Uzel pointed to a closed hangar door. "It is a larger luxury ship that Draax royalty and certain military ranks use. King Eastolf has three kyoden ships in the eastern province, but King Quillan does not see the necessity for more than one. He says it is a waste of space and fuel."

"You use isotopes for fuel, right?" I said.

"Yes. Through that hangar door," he pointed to a second one, "is where we repair our havoc cruisers."

"Right, you have Earth havoc cruisers," I said. "You trade us juice for them."

He nodded. "Yes. We used to use the malta ships from the Vokine, but we switched to havoc cruisers about a decade ago. Our planet has an abundance of the primitive fuel they run on, they are cheaper to repair, and they give human females a sense of home."

"Is that why you use our land vehicles as well?" I said.

"Yes. Our land travel technology was similar to yours, maybe even a little better, but these land vehicles are more familiar to females."

"You know we use air vehicles now, right?" I said. "Land vehicles are only used by the lowers who can't afford even a cheap air vehicle on Earth."

"We know," Uzel said. "We have begun to replace land vehicles with the air ones as well."

He started walking again, and I followed him. A vroha ship was in the bay with a large section of its outer shell stripped away. A few Draax were standing in front of the exposed machinery, and Uzel nodded to them as we passed by. They barely gave me a second look, and I wasn't the least bit surprised. None of them would be interested in seducing me in hopes that I'd quit my job and pop out little purple or green babies for them.

Galan doesn't want babies, remember? And he wants to have sex with you.

Eh, the jury was still out on that one. I'd chalk it up to a moment of madness on his part. He was horny, and I happened to be there and making it more than obvious I wanted to bang him. It wasn't surprising that he would look past my skinny, ugly body in the moment. But the ease with which he'd disappeared from my life made it even more suspect that he'd ever found me attractive.

"This is the utility room." Uzel opened a door near the third hangar. "Make certain you do a good job of cleaning. Melu will be displeased if you do not."

"Dude, I'm gonna clean this floor so hard," I said before holding out my fist.

Uzel stared at it. "What are you doing?"

"It's an old-school Earth thing," I said. "Roden and I are bringing it back. You bump my knuckles with yours."

Uzel bumped my knuckles before glancing at his hand. "I do not understand the point of bumping knuckles, but I will indulge you, human."

"It's Ellis, and thanks," I said. "Now, show me where you keep that mop."

Galan

I SAT DOWN NEXT TO MELU ON THE BENCH. HE GRUNTED OUT a greeting but kept his gaze on the waterfall before us. The evening was a warm one. The garden was teeming with Draax walking along the pathway in front of the waterfall, but they merely nodded in greeting and continued. Melu was not known for his good humour or his socializing skills.

"How is she doing, Melu?"

A look of begrudging respect crossed his face. "Better than I thought. She works hard and does not complain."

A caterra bird landed on a tree branch close to Melu's face. He studied its bright green feathers. "I did not allow her to do anything but clean the first few days. I figured she would whine about it, but she did not."

He reached a hand toward the bird, and it flitted off, diving and dipping through the air with an open beak to catch small bugs.

"Have you allowed her to repair ships yet?" I said.

"I gave her a havoc cruiser to work on a couple of days ago," he said. "She did well with it."

"Good."

Melu glanced at me. "I thought you would be at the docking bay every day to check up on her, considering it was your idea to have her work there."

I shrugged. "There is no need for me to check on her. You are more than capable of keeping track of your workers."

He snorted laughter. "I am. But if you think I do not see the look on your face when you ask about her, you are wrong, Galan. I may be old, but I have not forgotten what it was like to lust after a female."

"I do not lust after her," I lied. "And what is this talk of being old? You are not even forty yet."

He shrugged. "Too old for the human females to consider me a partner. At least not when they have Draax like you around."

"When was the last time you went to Earth?" I said.

"Moons ago," he said. "But I could not tempt any of the females into sleeping with me. They all wanted juice in trade."

I sighed. "Too many of our kind are willing to give them juice in exchange for sex. They do not care if it is against the law."

"It is the eastern Draax," Melu said. "Those rakart do not care about anything but themselves, and Eastolf encourages their behaviour. He does not care how his men lure the females to his province, only that they are there."

Melu wasn't wrong. The eastern Draax had always had a reputation of being hotheaded, and since King Cteri had died and his son, Eastolf began his rule, it had only gotten worse in the last decade or so.

"If Quillan is not careful, Eastolf will attempt to conquer our province. Just like his father did before him," Melu said.

"And just like Quill's father stopped Cteri, Quill will stop Eastolf. Eastolf desires power, but he would be a fool to think he can take Quill's," I said. "Our provincial military and King's Guard are the strongest in Odias."

"The north then," Melu said. "Eastolf will start a civil war with us or the north, mark my words."

The sound of soft and feminine laughter drifted over the rushing water. Both Melu and I stood when the three females rounded the corner. They walked down the path, and I smiled and nodded to them when they stopped in front of us.

"Good evening, little females."

"Hello. How are you, Galan?"

I smiled at the pink-haired woman. "I am well, Candala. How are you?"

"Good. Have you met Inara and Jane?"

"Not formally," I said. "It is nice to meet you."

"Nice to meet you. I'm Jane." The blonde woman with pretty blue eyes and generous hips shook my hand.

The redheaded woman smiled at me. "Sorry again about spilling the water on you."

"It was an accident, Inara," I said. "Do not worry about it."

I turned to Melu. "This is Melu. He is the head of our docking bay."

"Hello, Melu." Inara held out her hand, and I watched in puzzlement as Melu's face turned a dark shade of green, and his tail flicked out and whacked against the bench behind us.

"Melu," I prompted.

He gave Inara's hand a brief shake before staring at the waterfall.

Inara glanced at Jane and Candala, her cheeks pink and her face confused.

Candala made the barest of shrugs, and I cleared my throat. "Are you enjoying your walk in the garden?"

"We are," Candala said. "We just finished doing yoga." She held up a flat pink mat in her left hand. "Do you know what yoga is?"

"Of course," I said. "Many of the king's guard practice the art of yoga."

"Really?" Jane said. "That's weird. Although, I guess being flexible is a good thing in your line of work."

"Yes, I'm sure it's all about the flexibility and not another way the Draax tries to make us believe living on this planet is just like living back home," Inara said with a teasing grin.

I laughed. "Perhaps it is a little of both."

"We should get going. Nice to see you again, Galan," Candala said. "Melu, it was nice to meet you."

Melu grunted out an unintelligible reply. He was still studying the waterfall like he'd never seen it before, but when the females' backs were turned, his gaze swung to the one called Inara. He stared at her long red hair before studying her ass, his tail flicking rapidly and his meaty hands held in a tight fist behind his back.

I recognized the look on his face. It was the same one on mine whenever I thought of Ellis. A combination of lust and longing and frustration.

"Inara is a beautiful female," I said when they had disappeared down the path. "Her red hair is apparently a rarity on Earth."

Melu didn't reply, so I said, "You should ask her out. The waiting period is over."

He jerked all over before glaring at me. "Have you gone mad, Galan? She is too young for me."

"You are not an old man, Melu, no matter how hard you try to persuade me you are. Ask the female out. There is no harm in it. Unless you are afraid of a helpless little female?" I said teasingly.

If I were not the head of the king's guard, I was certain Melu would have punched me. As it was, he gave me a look that could melt steel and said, "Mind your tongue, Galan. I do not care if you are best friends with the king. It will not stop me from teaching you a lesson in manners."

I held my hands up. "I am only teasing, Melu. What has gotten into you this evening?"

"Nothing," he said. "Good night, Galan."

He walked away, and I sat on the bench again, staring blankly at the flowers surrounding the waterfall. It'd been almost two weeks since I'd seen Ellis and I had hoped my obsession with her would have ended. Instead, it was worse. I was barely sleeping or eating, and my need to see and touch her was a fire inside me that couldn't be doused.

I rubbed my hand through my hair. How many times had I almost gone to her in the night? Too many to count. Her apartment next to mine was an exercise in agony and self-control, but the idea of moving her to a different apartment further away made me unsettled and almost angry. I liked knowing she was right beside me and knowing I was close if she needed me. Even if I spent my nights staring at the wall separating us like a teenage Draax with his first crush. I'd even had a few fantasies where Ellis had broken into my apartment again and joined me in my bed.

She cannot. You have her tools, remember?

That was true. They were still sitting on my nightstand, and as the head of the king's guard, I was ashamed to admit that more than once, I'd been tempted to return them to her in hopes she would use them to enter my apartment again.

My job was to protect Quill, Sabrina, and Jovie and if anyone knew that I was considering giving Ellis back her tools of escape, they would think I'd gone mad.

You know she will not hurt anyone.

No, she wouldn't. It made me a real froden to believe that – I hardly knew her – but it did not quell my belief that she would never hurt anyone at the castle. She might be a thief, but that didn't make her dangerous to us.

I stood up and headed toward the entrance of the garden. I was glad that Ellis was doing well in the docking bay. Perhaps if she continued to prove herself useful, I could approach Melu about speaking on her behalf to Quill to allow her to join the work program permanently. The gallberry juice she had stolen was barely a drop in our supply. What would Earth care if they had one less human in their prisons?

Cheered by the possibility that Ellis might stay permanently at the castle, I felt the first rumbling of hunger in days. With a smile on my face, I headed back to my apartment.

Ellis

THE KNOCK ON MY DOOR HAD ME BOUNCING OFF THE COUCH with an excited grin. For the last two weeks, Inara or Candy stopped by my apartment every evening for a visit. I suspected that it would be Inara tonight, and my smile widened when the door opened, and Inara walked in.

I liked Candy a lot, and her son Roden was cute, polite, and fun to play with the flight simulator, but I felt a real connection to Inara. Maybe even a best friend connection.

What are you, twelve?

I flushed a little, but it didn't stop me from grinning like a fool at the redhead. "Hey!"

"Hi, Ellis." Inara dropped onto my couch as Adrix closed the door behind her.

I grabbed us both bottles of gallberry juice and joined her. The Draax had stopped posting a guy outside my door after they chipped me like a stray dog, which meant that Adrix had walked Inara to my room. I grinned at Inara. "Is Adrix still *accidentally* running into you in the hallways?"

She smiled a little. "Sometimes. Not as much as he was. Honestly, I'm impressed at how patient the Draax are. I don't think a single woman in the program is interested in dating them right now. We all just want to make money, you know?"

"That's what they get for hiring lowers to work," I said. "We're all desperate for money."

"True." She paused. "I met your boss in the garden earlier."

"Melu?" I said. "He was in the garden?"

"Yes. He was sitting with Galan."

I instantly forgot my surprise that cranky old Melu went to the garden. "How is he?"

"He seems as grumpy as you told me he is. He barely looked or talked to us."

"Not Melu," I said. "Galan."

"He looked the same as always, I think," Inara said. "I don't usually see him around the castle."

"Right," I said.

"Melu didn't look as old as you described him," Inara said. "He was kind of good looking, actually."

I made a face. "If you had to listen to him barking orders at you every day, you wouldn't find him good looking. Plus, he's old. Uzel told me Melu was almost forty."

She laughed. "That's not old."

"He could be our father," I said.

"No, he couldn't. Besides, I'm older than you."

"Only by two years. Do you seriously want to bang Melu?"

Inara shook her head. "No, I'm just saying he doesn't look the way I'd pictured in my head based on your description."

"What did you talk to Galan about?"

"Nothing, really," she said. "Yoga."

"Yoga," I repeated.

"Yeah. Apparently, the king's guard practices yoga."

I had an instant vision of Galan in the downward dog pose. Christ, was my mouth watering?

Inara poked me in the thigh. "You ever gonna admit your crush on Galan to me?"

I drank some juice and wiped my mouth with my hand. "Having a crush on Galan is pointless. As soon as the war between Emira and Cillade ends, I'll be living my best life in an Earth prison."

Inara scowled. "I hate it when you joke about that. It'll be so dangerous for you, Ellis."

"Yeah, I know. But if you can't joke about your impending death, what can you joke about?"

We lapsed into silence. Inara looked pale, and the freckles across the bridge of her nose were as visible as if I'd gone over them with a marker.

"It's fine," I said, even though it wasn't. "Maybe the war will go on for years. Candy said that Evelyn told her the last one was nine months."

"Maybe," Inara said.

I was being selfish. Inara only wanted to be here for a year, and if the war continued longer than that, she'd go crazy worrying about her sister.

"How was your day?" I said. "Did you talk to your sister?"

"Yeah," Inara said. "She had a good day. Mom was sober for once and took Wendy to a movie and out for dinner."

"What about your dad?"

Inara made a face. "He was out doing whatever drug dealers do."

She bit at a nail. Her nails were ragged and chewed, and

I'd learned quickly over the last week that bringing up her parents was a sure-fire way to have her nibbling on her nails.

"Sorry, Inara, I shouldn't have asked."

"It's fine," she said. "I just hate constantly worrying about Wendy. But I didn't have a choice about leaving. This is my best chance to give her a better life. Mom usually drinks away any money Dad gives her, and Dad doesn't give a shit about me or Wendy."

She chewed away at a second nail. "Wendy looks thinner to me. She says it's just the hologram, but I don't think she's getting enough food. Maybe I shouldn't have left. I could have found another job on Earth. It wouldn't have paid as well, but it would have been enough to keep Wendy fed."

"Are you forgetting that you had a brain tumour?" I said. "You had no choice, Inara."

She sighed, her hands dropping into her lap. "Yeah, I know."

"Your sister will be okay," I said.

"You don't know that!" Inara's usual sweetness had suddenly disappeared. "My parents are terrible, okay? And every day that I'm not with her, she's in danger. Every goddamn day, Ellis! You don't have a sister, so you have no idea what I'm going through or how -"

"I have a sister," I said.

Inara stared at me. "What? You've never mentioned her to me."

"Her name was Esther," I said.

I could see Inara's fingers tighten around her glass of juice. "Was?"

"She died when I was fifteen."

"I'm so sorry," Inara said. "I shouldn't have lost my temper or said -"

"You didn't know," I said. "It's fine, Inara."

I waited for her to ask me how Esther died. People always asked. They couldn't help themselves.

"What was she like?" Inara said.

"What?" I wasn't sure I'd heard her correctly.

"What was Esther like? Was she older than you or younger?"

I swallowed past the golf ball size lump in my throat. "She was younger. She was sweet… so goddamn sweet. Everyone loved her because she didn't have a mean bone in her body, you know? My parents they… they were disappointed in me a lot, but Esther… she was their perfect angel."

I swallowed again. "I wasn't jealous of her, if that's what you're thinking. Esther deserved to be my parents' favourite. I was – well, let's say I gave my parents a lot of grief from the time I was eight, and they were over it."

I laughed, but Inara didn't. She set her glass of juice down and took my hand. I studied her ragged nails, my throat burning and the back of my eyes stinging. "Esther never gave them any trouble. She was three years younger than me and she… she was so kind. To everyone. It didn't matter if you were a lower, middle, or whatever… Esther treated everyone the same. She was only twelve when she died, but she already knew that she wanted to go into social work and try and help the lower kids."

"She sounds lovely," Inara said.

"She was. She had bone cancer," I said.

"I'm so sorry."

"Me too. My parents didn't make much. We were," I laughed bitterly, "middles but just barely. Enough money to live in a small house in the suburbs but not enough money to buy the amount of gallberry juice Esther needed. By the time we found out she had cancer, it was all through her bones. They did chemo – my dad had health insurance through work – but everyone knew it wasn't going to cure her. They were doing it to buy Esther some time while my parents tried to figure out a way to buy enough gallberry juice on the black market. They figured out how to get the juice, but it fell through."

"I'm sorry it didn't work," Inara said.

"It was my fault." My voice was dull, like a chef's blade long since forgotten in the back of a drawer.

"What do you mean?" Inara said.

"It was my fault their plan didn't work. I messed it up, and Esther died because of me."

Inara squeezed my hand. "I'm sure that's not true. You were only fifteen. What could you have possibly done to mess it up?"

Ukana. Ukana. Ukana.

The words echoed in my head, and I winced. Every time I heard those words, I saw Esther's pale, thin face and her cancer ravaged body.

"I just did," I said. I couldn't tell Inara the reason why. It was too shameful. Besides, she wouldn't understand. To the Draax, Inara was beautiful. If it had been her standing in that room in her mother's best dress and heels that made her wobble, the Draax wouldn't have turned her away. They would have handed over the juice, and Esther would have lived.

"How?" Inara said.

I shook my head and swiped at the stupid tears running down my cheeks. "It doesn't matter. It was my fault, and Esther died, and my parents … they hated me after that. They tried to pretend they didn't blame me for her death, but they did. I could see it in how they looked at me... or rather, didn't look at me. One night, my mom, she... she had too much to drink, and she told me that she wished it'd been me who'd gotten cancer instead of Esther."

"Oh, Ellis," Inara said. A tear slipped down her cheek to darken the front of her shirt. "Honey, I'm so sorry. She should never have said that."

I shrugged. "She was right. It should have been me. Esther was good and pure and didn't deserve to die of cancer."

"You don't deserve it either," Inara said. "No one does."

We were still holding hands and I gave hers a brief squeeze before releasing it. "Anyway, I packed a bag and left home that night after my parents had gone to bed. I haven't seen them since."

"How old were you?"

"Sixteen," I said.

"They didn't try to find you?" Inara said.

"No. I was on my dad's PAR plan, and they never called or hologrammed me. At the end of the month, I lost access to the internet, and my phone was disconnected. My dad took me off the family plan." This time, my laugh wasn't even bitter. It was kind of funny when you thought about it.

"Unfuckingbelievable," Inara said. "What is wrong with them?"

"They were both in bad places," I said. "Esther was their world."

"You were their daughter, too," she said. "Where did you go after that?"

"I thought I could stay with a friend, but her mother kicked me out after a few days. I've been living on the street since then."

"Holy shit," Inara said. "I can't believe you survived for

seven years on the street. How did you make money to eat... where did you sleep?"

"I slept in homeless shelters if they weren't full and alleys if they were," I said. "It was only awful in the winter. I made some friends, and we all pooled what little money we had and lived in this one-bedroom apartment for a while. There were seven of us, and I slept on an air mattress in the living room with four other people, but it was better than the street."

"What happened to them?" Inara said.

"We were boosting ships, stripping them for parts, selling them, that sort of thing. They did a job and got caught. They went to prison."

"You weren't with them?" Inara said.

I shook my head. "I should have been. But I was sick that day. Had a stupid cold, and Torra told me to keep my sick ass in bed."

"Lucky," Inara said.

"I guess."

Maybe it was luck, but it made me feel like shit. I couldn't understand why someone like Torra, who, granted, maybe wasn't on the complete up and up, but who took a ton of us street kids under her wing, who taught us how to survive, how to stay safe, how to not starve, could go to prison and die there, and a fuck-up like me who killed her only sister got lucky.

Not that lucky. If it weren't for the Draax, you'd be as dead as Esther and Torra.

"Ellis? Why did you steal the juice from the Draax ship?" Inara said.

"I didn't. Cheryl did, remember?"

She laughed, and I grinned at her. "I was desperate. After

194

Torra and the others were imprisoned, I switched to the black market juice thing. You need a crew to boost and sell ship parts, and I would have starved before I found another one. It was going fine until I owed a guy a big shipment of juice that I used instead to save a friend from dying. The guy put a marker out on me, so I tried to steal the juice from the Draax ship to avoid being murdered by Richie for not bringing him the juice I owed him."

"Why didn't you just sleep with a Draax for it?" Inara said. "I haven't slept with a Draax before, but from everything I've read and seen, they're pretty good at sex."

"Seen?" I said teasingly. "Why, Inara, are you telling me that sweet little you watches Draax porn holograms?"

Her face flamed the colour of her hair, and she poked me in the arm. "Like you haven't watched it. Anyway, why didn't you trade sex?"

"Look at me," I said.

She looked me over. "What?"

"I'm ugly. The Draax won't sleep with me. Hell, half the time, they thought I was a boy... although, to be fair, I did dress like a guy."

"Well, you're a little smaller than they like, but you're not ugly," Inara said. "Don't say that again."

I just shrugged. "I knew they wouldn't sleep with me, so I didn't bother trying."

"How did you know? Had you tried before and -"

The knock on the door was a welcome relief. I wouldn't explain to Inara why I knew the Draax found me ugly. *Couldn't* explain it.

The door opened and Inara and I stood when Sabrina entered my apartment. We both curtsied, and I said, "Hello, Your Majesty."

Sabrina made a face and rubbed at her belly. "Hi, Ellis. Hi, Inara."

"How are you feeling, Sabrina?" Inara said.

"Like I'm gonna pop," Sabrina said with a laugh. She took Inara's hand and pressed it against her belly. "This kid has been doing summersaults for the last half hour."

Inara grinned at her. "Considering how close it is to your due date, you look amazing."

"You're sweet, but I know exactly what I look like and amazing ain't it," Sabrina said. "Ellis, how is it going in the docking bay?"

"Great," I said. "I love it."

"Melu isn't being too," Sabrina hesitated, "grumpy?"

"Nope," I said.

She studied me. "Is that the truth?"

"Well, he's cranky, but I can handle it," I said.

"Good. I have some news I think you'll like," Sabrina said. "I've spoken to Quill, and he has agreed to allow you to spend time with the other women in the common room and eat meals in the dining hall if you'd like."

"Holy shit!" I immediately covered my mouth. "Uh, I mean... sorry."

Sabrina laughed. "Trust me, it's fine. The other day, I had to explain to Quill why Jovie suddenly referred to my broken tablet as that rotten bastard. Anyway, you're now allowed to go to certain areas in the castle... the common room, the garden, the dining hall, the docking bay, and the pool. Bitta, our IT guy, for lack of a better word, has programmed your tracking chip to send an alert to Krey and Galan if you go outside the allowed areas. So, no wandering down unfamiliar corridors or looking for the... front door. Okay?"

"Yes," I said. "Thank you so much. I appreciate this."

"You're welcome," she said. "Stay where you're supposed to stay. If you break the rules, you'll lose these privileges immediately."

"I won't break them," I said.

"Good. Now," she sank on the couch with a low groan, "Jovie is with her dad, and I want to take advantage of this kid free time. Do you ladies mind if I join your visit?"

"Not at all," Inara said.

"The more the merrier," I said.

I grabbed one of the kitchen chairs and dragged it over to the couch. I could hardly contain my excitement. Finally, a small taste of freedom.

Don't fuck it up, Ellis.

I wouldn't. The last thing I wanted was to be stuck in my room again or, worse, sent to Iron Gate.

CHAPTER 13

Ellis

"Your yoga skills are not improving, human. This is a basic position."

"Sigan," I puffed as I strained to keep my balance in the chair position, "you don't have to put your mat next to mine at every yoga session. You know that, right?"

I fell onto my ass and begrudgingly took Sigan's hand when he held it out to me.

"If I did not, who would help you up each time you fall over?" Sigan said.

"Inara would."

"Don't drag me into this." Inara, her pale skin flushed and her legs quivering as she held the pose, carefully turned her head to look at me. "I'm only a step above you, and I've been doing this for years."

"It is true," Sigan said. "You are terrible at yoga as well, redheaded human."

Inara started to giggle, and when she lost her concentration, she gave up entirely and collapsed on her mat.

I sat cross-legged next to her, ignoring the look that Bitta – who was leading the yoga class – gave us. "Tell me something, Inara. Did you ever think you'd be on another planet, in a giant garden in the middle of a castle, doing yoga with a bunch of Draax warriors?"

"Nope," Inara wiped at some pollen on her yoga pants. "But I kind of love that the Draax are doing yoga with us. It's adorable, right?"

"Yes," I said.

"It is not adorable," Sigan said as he effortlessly moved into the next position. "It is an excellent way to maintain proper balance and flexibility. The king's guard take their duties seriously. Protecting our king requires them to be in excellent shape. Yoga is only one of the many ways they keep their bodies in perfect shape."

"Perfect is right," Jane muttered as she gave up and sat on her mat on the other side of Inara. "I swear, Krey has the best looking ass in the castle."

Krey was a few feet ahead of us, and Inara and I both studied his admittedly fine ass when he bent over into a pose.

"If anyone would make me forget that I'm here to work and not bone, it would be Krey," Jane said. "Those blue eyes of his and that body…"

She fanned herself before winking at us. "Anyone here get you thinking naughty thoughts, ladies?"

"No," I said.

"Not really," Inara replied.

"Uh-huh, sure." Jane's gaze had already returned to Krey's ass. "You keep telling yourselves that."

I didn't know about Inara, but it was true for me. As good looking and, okay, I could admit it, sweet the Draax males were, not one participating in the yoga class today did it for me.

I stretched out my legs and bent forward, easing the tense muscles in my back. While I'd enjoyed my week of new-found freedom, I still hadn't seen Galan once, and the ache I felt hadn't diminished. In fact, it had only grown. It wasn't just lust talking, either. I missed him. My urge to know everything about him was an unquenchable thirst.

I'd found myself lingering in the dining hall and the hallway outside our apartments, hoping I might run into him. I'd been tempted to knock on Galan's door more than once. But each time I worked up the courage, I'd lost it by the time I raised my hand to knock. He was ghosting me, making it more than evident that he wanted nothing to do with me, and how pathetic would I look if I just threw myself at him?

You could tell him you just wanted to be friends. Then, at least, you'd get to see him.

That was a good idea. Sure, I didn't *want* to be just friends, and not being allowed to kiss him or touch him or ride that deliciously thick dick again would be a massive bummer, but it was better than not seeing him at all. Besides, I'd told myself a thousand times that that day in Galan's apartment was nothing more than a moment of insanity on Galan's part, and I was frustrated that I couldn't convince myself it was true.

His ghosting me and his nearly supernatural ability to completely avoid me showed he regretted what had happened that day.

Girl, the look on his face ten minutes after it happened should be enough to convince you. Or when he outright told you it was a mistake. Write him a note and slip it under his door that says you know it was a mistake too and you're cool with being friends.

You're ruining his life, you know. If you weren't here, don't you think he'd be joining the garden yoga class, eating in the dining hall, trying to convince the other women to sleep with him?

I felt a wave of guilt that almost made me nauseous. I'd been so swept up in my own needs that I hadn't considered how this affected Galan. Of course he would miss his friends. Maybe, instead of telling him I was okay with being just friends, I should return to staying in my room so he didn't have to worry about running into me.

It's the right thing to do.

Yeah, it was. I was being a selfish cow and while I couldn't be blamed for trying to enjoy my freedom while I still had it, it didn't make my actions right. I would try the note thing about being friends, and if that didn't work, I'd stop hanging out with the others and stay in my room so that Galan wouldn't have to avoid his friends. Consider it practice for when I was living in a tiny cell and carving shives out of plastic spoons.

"Sigan!"

A Draax I'd never seen before came bursting around the garden pathway. He was sweaty and out of breath, and Sigan turned and raised his eyebrows at him. "What is it?"

"Come quickly. Our queen – she is in labour."

Sigan sprinted down the pathway, leaving his mat and water bottle behind.

"Holy crap," Inara said, "Sabrina's in labour."

The buzz of excitement from the Draax around us was kind of cute. Bitta clapped his hands at the front of the group. "She will not give birth in the next half hour. Let us finish our class."

He glanced over the others and pointed at us. "You three at the back. Stand up and finish the class, please."

I groaned but climbed to my feet before helping Inara to hers. "Oh God, if I make it through this class, it'll be a bloody miracle."

Inara laughed before giving me a playful slap to my butt. "You got this, girl. Let's show these Draax boys how it's done."

Galan

"I HAVE A SON, GALAN!" QUILL HUGGED ME HARD.

I returned his hug, the smile on my face so large my cheeks ached. "Congratulations, Quill."

"Thank you, old friend." He released me before hugging Krey.

Krey pounded him on the back and said, "I am happy for you, Quill."

Quill stepped back, his smile as bright as keo. "Thank you."

"How is Sabrina?" I said as Jovie slid off the couch.

"She is doing very well. He weighed almost ten pounds, and the delivery was hard on her, but Sigan gave her plenty of gallberry serum."

Jovie wandered over. She held a cup of gallberry juice and drank two big swallows before holding out her arms to Krey. "Up, Uda."

He picked her up, and she wrapped her tail around his arm before leaning contently against his chest. He kissed her cheek. "You have a baby brother, meena. Are you excited?"

She grinned at him. "Uda take Jovie swimming?"

Quill laughed. "She has met her baby brother but was uninterested in him."

"Is Sabrina still in the infirmary?" I said.

"No," Quill said. "She and Jota are in the bedroom. She did not want to stay overnight in the infirmary, and Sigan agreed she could leave. He is with them right now, but when he is finished, I will bring you my son so you can meet him."

"Your father would be pleased that you named your son after him," I said.

Quill nodded. "Yes, he would. I am thankful that my sadora agreed to it. It is a human custom to give them a second name. His second name is William, after Sabrina's father."

The door to the bedroom opened, and Sigan appeared. He carried Quill's son in his arms, and I smiled at the eagerness with which Quill took him. He pushed back the blanket, and I stared at the baby. He was the spitting image of Quill with plump cheeks and thick eyebrows, and thick dark hair.

"He is beautiful," I said.

Krey moved closer, and Jovie stroked her tail across her brother's cheek. "Baby."

"That is right, meena," Quill said, his voice thick with emotion. "This is your baby brother."

She stroked his cheek again before wrapping her tail around Krey's arm. "Uda, see baby?"

"I see him," Krey said. "You must be a very good big sister to him, Jovie." He kissed her cheek. "Look after him and protect him until he is bigger. All right?"

"Yes, Uda."

"My king," Sigan said. "Your queen asked me to remind you that her sister will be hologramming in a few minutes to see the baby."

"Right." Quill shifted the baby in his arms before smiling at us. "Do you mind if we cut this first introduction short?"

"Not at all." Krey set Jovie on the ground, and Quill took her hand. "Be with your family, my king. We will visit again in a day or two."

Quill gave us both a boyish grin before leading Jovie into the bedroom. Sigan had already left, and Krey clapped me on the back. "Come, old friend. The others are celebrating the birth of Quill's son in the garden. Let us join them."

With a grin, I followed Krey out of Quill's quarters and toward the garden.

Ellis

"They won't even let you have a sip of it?" I stared at Jane. "I get why they won't let me have any because, technically I'm their prisoner, but why can't you have some gall-berry wine?"

Jane settled herself on the bench next to me. "Because that stuff is super potent. Even a couple of sips would be enough to get us drunk."

"Seriously?" I studied the Draax, who were milling around the garden. Almost all of them had a wine glass filled with dark pink liquid.

"Yes." Candy sat down on my other side. "Evie told me she had half a glass once, and it knocked her off her ass. She passed out within twenty minutes."

"Well, now I really want to try it," I said.

Jane laughed. "You're so tiny that one sip would probably put you in a coma."

"If it's as delicious as it looks, I'm willing to take the risk," I said. "Although, again, I don't know why they're not letting the rest of you have some. I don't know about you guys, but drunk Ellis is horny Ellis."

"Girl, same," Jane said. "I swear, two tequila shots in, and I'm whipping off my shirt and dancing on the tables. Such a cliché but sadly… so true for me."

"Right? So, you'd think the Draax would want to take advantage of that," I said.

"It's why they're not letting us drink," Candy said. "They don't want us to do something we'll regret in the morning."

"So, they want to fuck you, but not enough to get you drunk and horny," I said.

"I keep telling you the Draax males are sweeter than human guys," Candy said. "Women are important to them."

"Honestly, I'm surprised they're even sending you back to Earth for your punishment," Jane said. "It was such a small amount of juice, and they're trying to convince as many women as possible to stay on their planet. It's weird that they aren't just forgetting you tried to steal the juice and offering you a year long work contract."

"They don't like how I look," I said, "and I'm breeding incompatible."

"What's wrong with the way you look?" Jane looked me over with a frown.

"These, for starters." I grabbed my small boobs and gave them a shake. "Draax guys do not believe in the old Earth saying, 'more than a handful is a waste.'"

Candy laughed. "They do love big tits."

"They like big everything," I said. "I'll never have the curves they like, at least not like you guys."

"Yeah, maybe you're a little thinner than they typically go

for, but I bet there's fifty Draax in the castle alone who are totally down with a slender girl," Jane said.

"It's not just the body. It's the face, too," I said.

Jane blinked at me. "What? You're super cute."

"Not to the Draax. They think I'm ugly."

"How do you know that?"

"They told me."

"No Draax would tell a woman that she's ugly," Candy said.

"Yeah, well, I guess I found the half dozen who would," I said. "Anyway, doesn't matter. I'm breeding incompatible."

"You know there are some who don't want babies." Inara showed up and squeezed onto the bench beside Candy. "I've already met four Draax in the castle who don't want kids, and that's not including Galan."

My chest tightened at just the mention of his name. We'd been in the garden celebrating the birth of the king and queen's son for over an hour, and I hadn't seen him once. Mind you, there were a ton of Draax in the garden, and I was pretty sure every Draax in the castle had shown up to celebrate. But still... it wouldn't be entirely unreasonable to run into him, right? I'd already seen Uzel, Melu, Sigan, and a bunch of the other Draax who worked in the docking bay. It stood to reason that I would see Galan eventually.

Unless he's deliberately avoiding you.

Yeah, there was that. Or even worse, he wasn't celebrating the birth of his best friend's kid because he didn't want to run into me in the garden.

My stomach clenched. That made me feel terrible. Galan deserved to celebrate with his friends. As nice as it was to be out of my room and around other people, I would leave. I could ask Sigan to message him and tell him I had returned to my room.

I stood up. "Have you guys seen Sigan? I need to talk to him."

"He was near the waterfall the last time I saw him," Inara said. "Want me to come with you?"

"No, that's all right." Inara would try to convince me to stay if she knew I was about to leave. "I'll talk to you later."

I walked away quickly before they could ask more questions. It took me only ten minutes to get to the waterfall, and although nearly a dozen Draax were gathered in the area, none of them were Sigan. I took the path that led further into the garden. The Draax were everywhere but most didn't even bother to look at me, let alone flirt with me.

I tried not to let it depress me. I didn't expect them to flirt with me, and besides, by now, all of them knew who I was and that I was a prisoner in the castle. Even if there was one who didn't find me ugly, most of them just saw me as a thief.

You are a thief.

My inner voice made a good point. Sure, I hadn't stolen anything while I'd been here at the castle, but this was the longest I'd gone without stealing since I'd ended up on the streets.

Maybe you're only a thief because you were forced to be one?

I contemplated that for a few seconds before shaking my head. Nah, that wasn't it. The only reason I wasn't stealing shit was because of this damn tracker in my arm. The places I was allowed to go to in the castle had nothing helpful to steal, which was a problem in my escape plan.

Escape plan? What escape plan? You haven't done a thing to even prepare for your escape. Too busy moping over the fact that Galan doesn't want anything to do with you anymore.

Ouch. That hit a little too close to the truth. I'd been so busy thinking about Galan that I hadn't even figured out how to gather the supplies I would need to live on the Draax planet after I escaped the castle. It's like I'd lost my damn mind and... oh, shit.

I turned a corner in the path and slowed to a stop, staring dumbly at Galan and Krey and the giggling human females with them.

I swallowed hard and stayed completely still. Maybe if I didn't move, they wouldn't see me. Their backs were turned to me, and the women were so busy flirting and touching the Draax that they wouldn't notice either.

As I watched, the woman closest to Galan rested her hand on his forearm. "Are you sure I can't have just a sip of that wine?"

Her voice was breathy and low, and while I'd seen her in the common room with the other women a couple of times, I'd never talked to her. She was beautiful with long dark hair and a plump, curvy body that I could only imagine made the Draax drool. Hell, I could practically see Krey drooling from here.

"It is too potent for you." Galan's low voice washed over me and after days of not hearing it, just the sound of his voice made goosebumps pop up on my skin. God, he was so fucking sexy.

"I have a pretty good tolerance," the woman said.

"We both do," the other woman added. She smiled at Krey. "I would love one little sip."

"Perhaps just one," Krey said.

Galan caught his wrist before he could hand his wine glass over. "Krey, do not."

"Sorry, little female," Krey said with a good-natured

smile. "The head of the King's Guard has forbidden it."

She pouted at him as the other female stepped closer to Galan. Jealousy and anger swirled in my belly, and I wanted to go over there and stomp her into the ground. Fuck, I was an idiot.

"Just one. Pretty please with honey on top?" she said.

"What is this honey?" Galan said. "Is that the liquid that your Earth sting beetles produce?"

The woman laughed. "Bees, they're called bees, and yes, that's honey."

"I've heard it is very sweet," Krey said.

"Almost as sweet as me," the woman flirting with Galan said. "Would you like to go for a walk, Galan?"

My hands clenched into fists. What happened to none of the women being interested in the Draax? Not that I could blame her, Galan was ridiculously hot, but the idea that she'd be hitting on my guy was infuriating.

Not your guy.

Okay, maybe not, but still... why should she get to ride his beautiful dick if I couldn't? That didn't seem fair or –

"Human, why are you standing in the middle of the path?"

I jumped about a foot when I heard Sigan's voice behind me. The kadana joined me, holding a wine glass in one hand.

"What are you doing?" he asked.

I made a shushing noise, but it was too late. The others had turned to face us. I studied Galan's face, smiling tentatively at him. He didn't look angry, but it wasn't a look of happiness on his face either. It was mostly just... bored.

For some reason, that was more upsetting than him being annoyed or angry.

"Hi there," the dark-haired woman said. "How are you?"

"Good," Sigan said. "What is your name?"

"I'm Lori, and this is Stephanie." Lori slipped her hand into the crook of Galan's elbow, and jealousy flared back to life in my belly.

"I am Sigan," Sigan said.

"And you're the thief." Lori smiled at me, and the look of contempt on her face made me bristle.

"I didn't steal anything," I said.

"That's not what I heard," Lori said. "I heard you stole a bunch of juice and then got so scared when you were caught that you vomited all over Krey's boots."

"She was sick, not scared," Galan said.

"A malfunctioning translator had made her ill and caused her to vomit," Sigan said. "I took it out."

"Oh." Lori looked me up and down. "You're so skinny. Do you have an eating disorder?"

My face flushed, but before I could reply, Sigan said, "Ellis is not nearly as thin as she was. She has gained significant weight now that she is fed daily meals. Her ass is much fuller than it was. Perhaps not as large as your ass, but it is no longer flat like it once was either."

I would have laughed if I hadn't been so pissed at the way Lori was still touching Galan.

"Right," Lori said. "Well, it's a good job you Draax like big asses, huh, Sidan?"

"His name is Sigan," I said.

"Sigan. Sorry." Lori smiled at Sigan, her gaze traveling over his face. "You're an interesting looking Draax, aren't you? I've never seen one with your... unique features before."

Sigan's face flushed a dark green, and he immediately turned around and walked away. I decided, between the way Lori was touching Galan and the way she spoke to Sigan, that it was a fine time for me to leave before I punched her right in her pretty face.

"You're a bitch," I said to her. "Talk to my friend again that way, and I'll kick your fucking ass."

"Nice language," Lori said. "Real lady-like." She smiled up at Galan, dismissing me completely. "Galan, are you ready for that walk now?"

I turned and stomped around the corner. "Sigan, where did you go?"

There was no sign of him, and I jogged down the path, taking random lefts and rights until I was deep in the garden with no sign of Sigan. I stopped and blew out my breath before lifting my hair off the back of my neck. It was after eight, but the sun – excuse me, *keo* – was still out, and the garden was warm and muggy. I slapped at a bug flying around my face before walking further down the path.

I was completely lost, but I didn't care that much. When I didn't show up at the docking bay tomorrow, it's not like the Draax couldn't track me down in the garden. I rubbed at the bump on my arm where the tracking chip was.

"Stupid Lori and her stupid pretty face," I muttered before pitching my voice higher. "It's a good job that the Draax like big asses, right? Don't you just love my big ass, Galan?"

I could hear voices behind me, one was definitely female, and I froze in spot for a second. Shit, it would be just my luck that stupid Lori and *I refuse to find him sexy anymore* Galan would walk the exact path I did.

I sprinted to the t-intersection, muttering another curse when both left and right were dead ends. Shit. The voices were growing closer. There was a thick grove of pale green bushes to my left, and I darted toward them, sliding past the soft green leaves and light blue flowers. There was a small natural clearing in the middle of the bushes, and I stopped in the middle before turning and peering through the leaves and branches at the path.

The voices grew louder, and I rolled my eyes when I realized it wasn't Galan and Lori. It was a pretty blonde woman and a Draax who I'd never seen before. I groaned under my breath when they both sat down on the bench. Oh great, it looked like they were settling in for a nice long chat, which was stupid because, frankly, this part of the garden was a bit boring and based on the way some of the bushes had overgrown the path, not many of the Draax even walked this way or...

I clapped my hand over my mouth, muffling my squeak of surprise when the woman and the Draax kissed. And not just a sweet little chaste kiss, either. They were already going at it, tongues flailing, lips devouring, hands... oh God, hands taking off clothes.

I took a step back, staring wide-eyed at the woman as the Draax stripped off her shirt before cupping her breast through her bra. She moaned and clutched at his broad back when he pulled the cup down and sucked on her nipple.

Holy shit.

The Draax unhooked her bra after a bit of fumbling, and the woman giggled at him. "You need more practice."

He grinned and cupped both of her breasts, rubbing his thumbs over the nipples until moans replaced her giggles. "Perhaps you will allow me to practice every day."

"Perhaps," she said as she arched her back.

I swallowed hard, more than a little turned on by the way the Draax was worshipping the woman's tits with his hands and mouth.

Great, now I was a pervert in the bushes, spying on people having sex. What was wrong with me?

I couldn't exactly waltz out of the bushes, so my choices were to close my eyes or try and slide out of the bushes on the other side and hope that there was a path.

The woman moaned so loudly that my gaze was drawn back to her. She was straddling the Draax's lap now. His shirt was gone, and she was dry humping the hell out of him as he cupped her ass and continued to suck on her nipples.

"Get it, girl," I said under my breath as her moans and cries grew louder.

Damn, I really did need to get laid if I was jealous over –

There was a low rustle in the bushes behind me, and a hand clamped across my mouth, muffling my shriek of surprise.

"Why are you hiding in the hydrana bush, little human?" His low voice whispered in my ear, and fuck if my nipples didn't immediately get hard.

"You scared the hell out of me, Galan," I whispered when he moved his hand. "Why are you spying on me? That's rude."

His low chuckle sent shivers down my spine. "I am rude? When you are the one watching Hingi and a female have sex?"

"They aren't having sex," I said. "They're only making out, and I didn't mean to spy on them. It just sort of happened. I'm not a pervert."

"First, you spy on me from my closet while I'm touching myself, and now you spy on Hingi while he's touching his female," Galan said.

"Well, when you put it that way, yeah, I kind of look like a pervert, but I'm not," I said.

The woman's moans were so loud now that I couldn't help but look. Shock ran through me.

"Holy shit."

While I was talking to Galan, they'd been joined by a third Draax and... holy double shit... the woman was completely naked and riding the first Draax's dick while she sucked enthusiastically on the second Draax's dick.

"She, uh," I swallowed hard, "looks like she's having fun."

"Indeed," Galan said.

His big hand cupped my breast, and I moaned when he toyed with my nipple through my shirt. "I have missed your sweet nipples, little human."

"They, uh, they missed you too," I said, groaning at how stupid I sounded.

His low chuckle made me arch into his hand. God, I was so wet. I was pretty sure I was about to have a damp spot on my pants. This no underwear thing was starting to be a real problem.

In front of us, the woman was still sucking hard on the Draax dick while the first one fucked her with rough strokes. Her moans of pleasure and delight were so loud I wouldn't have been surprised if the Draax at the far end of the garden could hear her.

My guilt growing at spying on her, I pushed away from Galan and shoved my way through the bushes. They were slightly bent and broken already, thanks to Galan, and it wasn't long before I was standing clear of them on the other side. A large tree was on the other side of the path, and I backed toward it as Galan emerged from the bushes.

He had a look of feral need on his face, and I licked my lips in nerves and anticipation when he backed me up until I felt the tree against my back.

He brushed one long finger over my nipples that were protruding against my shirt.

"Galan," I pushed his hand away, "we're right in the open. The path is right there."

"This is a quieter part of the garden," Galan said. "It does not have many visitors."

"Uh… there's three right on the other side of those bushes," I said.

"They seem to be busy," he said with a small grin as the woman's cries grew louder.

"How did you even find me?"

"Your tracking chip is linked to my vertex." He pulled a device from his pocket that looked remarkably similar to our PAR phones. "You see."

He pointed to the blinking red dot on the screen.

"Right," I said. I needed to remember that Galan had been ghosting me. Only, with him standing so close and touching me, it was kind of hard to remember that I was supposed to be pissed at him. "Well, if you'll excuse me…"

He didn't take the hint, leaning in instead and kissing my throat. "I have missed you, little human. I lay in bed every night and stare at the wall that separates us. I think about how tight your pussy is, how well you took my cock, how it sounded when you came on my face."

I moaned, my back arching when Galan slid his hand under my shirt and cupped my breast. "Do you lie awake at night and think about me, human?"

"Sometimes," I said.

"Only sometimes?" He arched a thick brow at me before slipping his hand into my pants. "Perhaps I should remind you of what you are missing?"

"Oh God, I… ohhh… oh, that's so good." My hand, which

was tugging on his forearm, clutched instead, and I rocked my pussy against his rough fingers.

He moved closer, bracing one arm on the tree above my head and kissing me with those slow and coaxing kisses that made me hot.

"I love how wet you are for me, Ellis." He kissed a path across my cheek to my ear and sucked on my lobe. "I want you to come for me."

"That's not a problem," I said.

He laughed and nipped at my earlobe before leaning back. He watched my face, his fingers rubbing small, firm circles over my clit as pleasure pooled in my lower belly. My legs trembling, my worry that we would be caught forgotten, I strained for my climax. I rose on my tiptoes when Galan slid two thick fingers into me and flicked at my clit with his thumb.

"Come for me, sweet Ellis," he whispered and then crushed his mouth down on mine, swallowing my cry of pleasure as I climaxed.

I shuddered wildly, clinging to Galan as I buried my face in his thick neck and tried to catch my breath. His tail was wrapped around my waist, helping to hold me up, and I could feel his hard cock against my hip.

He kissed my temple before easing his fingers out of my pussy and sliding them out of my pants. "You are beautiful when you come, Ellis."

"Thanks." My voice was muffled against his throat. "Your turn."

I reached for his crotch, leaning back and scowling at him when he caught my wrist. "What?"

"It is getting late," Galan said. "Come, little human, I will return you to your quarters."

"Are you fucking kidding me?" I said. "Galan, I don't want –"

Two Draax turned the corner and stopped, staring at both of us before their gazes dropped to Galan's tail, still wrapped around my waist.

His face a dark green, Galan let his tail drop before stepping back from the tree and onto the path. "Good evening."

"Good evening, Galan," the larger one said.

I joined them and smiled at the Draax. "Hey, I'm Ellis."

Galan made a weird growling noise, his tail whipping out to wrap around my hips again when the other Draax's gaze dropped to my tits. My nipples were hard against the thin fabric, and I resisted the urge to cross my arms over my tits.

Galan's tail tightened, making me wince, as he made another one of those weird growls. "Stop staring at her tits, Henden, before you feel my blade in your belly."

"Galan!" I elbowed him in the side. "Stop that."

"My apologies, Galan," Henden said. "But rest assured, I am in no way attracted to the small female."

Without another word, he and the second Draax continued down the path. I stared up at Galan. "What was that about?"

"He wants you for himself." Galan's voice was low and angry, and his skin had gone from its usual emerald green to forest green. "He cannot have you."

"He doesn't want me," I said. "Snap out of it, dude. You're the only Draax in the castle, hell, in the entire province, who wants me, so knock it off with the over-the-top jealousy. Also, your tail is squeezing me too tight."

He released his tail, letting it flick back and forth behind him. His copper eyes glowed in the golden light of the setting sun, and he took my arm almost roughly. "Come, human. It is time to return to your quarters."

CHAPTER 14

Ellis

"You know, you're being a real dickhead." I refused to step into my apartment when Galan opened the door. "You ghost me for two weeks, and then you corner me in the garden, make me come all over your fingers, and now you're gonna go right back to pretending like nothing happened."

"What do you mean by I ghost you?" Galan said.

"Ignored me, avoided me, pretended I didn't exist," I said. "You're running hot and cold, you know that, right? Why did you kiss me in the garden? Why did you make me come?"

"Because I have missed you," Galan said. "And when I saw you, I could not resist touching you again. It is why I have been," he paused, "ghosting you. I have no self-control when I am around you, little human."

Man, a Draax's honesty and bluntness were a refreshing change from Earth guys' mind games.

"I've missed you too," I said. "A lot. We were starting to be friends, right?"

"Yes," Galan said. "But I want to have sex with you as well, and there are many reasons why we cannot. It would be unkind of me to lead you into believing we could have a relationship when -"

"I'm not an idiot," I said. "I know we can't have a relationship. Even if you were willing to come to Earth to visit me in prison, I'm pretty sure I'd be dead before you could even request a conjugal visit."

His skin paled to light green, and his tail thumped against the wall. "Do not speak of your possible death so carelessly, little human."

I shrugged. "Hey, we all gotta go sometime, right? I made my choice, and now I have to live with the consequences."

"Ellis -"

I held up my hand. "I don't want to talk about what happens when I return to Earth, okay? I want to discuss you and me being friends with benefits while I'm here."

He didn't reply, and I said, "Friends with benefits is -"

"I know what it is," he said.

"Cool. So, what do you say? Are you in?"

It took me a few minutes to understand why he still hesitated. My stomach clenched, and hurt flooded through me, but I pushed it down ruthlessly. Of course, he wouldn't want the others to know he was banging me. One, I was a prisoner and a thief, and two, he might find me attractive, but none of the other Draax did. The Draax might be sweeter than human guys, but that didn't mean Galan wanted to be seen with the ugliest girl at the prom.

"I won't tell anyone," I said.

"It is not that I want to keep it a secret," he said, "but if the others found out, it would -"

"I know," I said. "I get it, and I'm perfectly fine with keeping it between you and me."

He stared at me, his copper eyes reflecting his internal war over whether he could trust me.

I stepped closer and rested my hand on his forearm. "Galan, I promise I won't say anything. I know I've lied in the past, but I'm not lying about this. I will keep it a secret. You can trust me."

"Are you certain you understand we cannot have a relationship?" Galan said. "That this can only be sex between us?"

"Yes," I said. "I promise I won't refer to you as my boyfriend or expect the girlfriend treatment. Just two people banging each other's brains out on a regular basis.

I grinned at him, but his face remained solemn.

I cleared my throat. "Or a semi-regular basis. Or, just for tonight if that's all you want."

Lord, could I sound any more pathetic? I wanted to walk back my words, maybe try to sound like I had a little pride, but I couldn't do it. The war would end, I'd go to prison, and then I'd die. This was my only and last chance to get laid, and that's why my desire to fuck Galan was so intense.

Is it?

I cleared my throat again. "I won't, uh, complain so much when we're having sex this time, I promise. I was just a bit nervous about your dick size the first time, but now that I know what I'm dealing with, I won't be such a whining chicken about it."

He frowned at me before closing my apartment door and taking my hand. We walked several steps to his apartment, and I followed him inside. He shut the door and wrapped his tail around my waist, pulling me close.

He touched my face before smoothing back my hair. "You did very well to take my cock, Ellis, especially for how little you are. Being apprehensive about it is nothing you need to apologize for."

I hooked my arms around his waist and smiled up at him. "Okay, cool. You ready to get naked?"

He laughed. "Yes, little human, I am ready to get naked."

I stood on my tiptoes, and he bent his head, pressing his lips against mine. The kiss started gentle and sweet but quickly turned heated. I sucked on his tongue when Galan slid it into my mouth and stuck my hands up the back of his shirt, running my fingertips over the large muscles in his back.

He tugged his shirt off, and I stepped back and stared greedily at his naked chest. "Your eight pack is very impressive."

I traced each slab of muscle, smiling when he moaned, and goosebumps appeared on his skin. The front of his pants was tented, and I cupped his cock, rubbing him through the fabric. His eyes went from copper to burnt bronze, and I arched my back when he cupped my breast. His thumb brushed against my nipple, and he bent his head and kissed me again. It was hot and feverish, and I fumbled at the button on his pants as he cupped the back of my skull and angled his mouth over mine.

He took the kiss deep, and I could feel the vibration of his groan when I finally succeeded in unbuttoning his pants and stuck my hand down the front of them. I wrapped my fingers around his thick cock and stroked him with slow, firm pulls.

His big hand cupped my ass and squeezed hard, his head

falling back when I kissed his chest. I sucked on his flat nipple, and his hips jerked against me, nearly knocking me over.

I giggled and kissed his chest again. "Let's take this to the couch, big guy."

He followed me without argument. I pushed on his chest until he sat but shook my head when he tried to tug me into his lap. "Nope, not yet. It's my turn to taste you."

He inhaled sharply, his gaze arrowing in on my mouth. "Take off your clothes first," he growled.

Lust burned in my belly, and I quickly stripped as Galan shoved his pants down his legs and off his feet. He sat on the couch, one big hand lazily stroking his cock as he stared at my naked body.

I told myself not to feel self-conscious about my small tits or my lack of hips. It was more than obvious Galan found me attractive. I didn't know why he did, but was now the time to wonder about it?

It definitely wasn't. Not when his big, beautiful cock was right there, the tip glistening with light green precum and practically begging me to lick it clean.

I dropped to my knees between his legs and smiled up at Galan when he immediately slid his fingers into my hair and cupped the back of my skull. His other hand gripped the base of his dick, and my smile widened when Galan pressed on my head.

"Impatient, are we?" I said.

"Little human, do what you said you would do," he said. "Suck my cock."

"So bossy," I said but leaned forward and licked the head of his dick. He groaned, and I stared up at him wide-eyed.

"What?" he said.

"Your cum tastes like gallberries," I said. "Do you guys do that on purpose so you get your dick sucked more often?"

He laughed so hard that the couch shook. "No, little human, it is a lucky coincidence."

"Sure, a coincidence," I said.

He kneaded the back of my neck before urging me forward. "Have another taste."

"Don't mind if I do," I said before sliding my mouth down over that gorgeous thick cock. I took him to the back of my throat and sucked hard. His loud moans and groans, the sweet taste of his cum, and the look of lust in those copper eyes made me even more eager to please him. I sucked and licked, varying the speed and pressure as I cupped his balls and gave them a gentle tug.

He cried out, his hips arching off the couch as I traced a path around the ridge with my tongue before licking away the fresh precum that coated the head.

"So good, sweet Ellis," he moaned, his hands tightening in my hair. He held my head steady and thrust into my mouth, slow, gentle thrusts that didn't make me gag or hurt my jaw. I loved how sweet he was and how careful and gentle he was, even though I could feel the power in his hands as he gripped my head.

I sucked hard, hollowing my cheeks, the taste of gallberries sweet on my tongue. He thrust back and forth a few more times. His cock was swelling in my mouth, and I made a frustrated groan when he pulled me off his cock with a loud pop.

"Galan, I want you to cum in my mouth," I said.

"I want to cum in your pussy." He hooked his hands under my arms and lifted me effortlessly into his lap. I straddled him and rubbed my pussy against his dick, cupping his head when he sucked on my nipples.

"Oh, oh, that feels so good," I said.

He gave my nipple a quick nip, and I squeaked and jerked on his lap. He grinned at me before cupping my ass and lifting me. "Put my cock in your pussy, little human."

I reached down and guided him in. I was soaking wet, but Galan took his time, lowering me slowly onto his cock until my pussy was stuffed full.

"Okay, sweet Ellis?" he said.

I took a deep breath and gripped his shoulders for balance. "Yeah, I think so. I need a minute or so."

He rubbed my lower back before sliding his tail around my waist. "Is it too much?"

I shook my head. "No, it's good."

I stared at the cords in his neck, at the sweat sliding down his temple, at the muscle ticking in his jaw. "Does it feel good for you, Galan?"

"Your little pussy is so tight," he said, his voice thick with desire. "It feels incredible around my cock."

Using his shoulders as leverage, I made a few cautious bounces, hesitating when Galan groaned, and his tail tightened around my waist. "Should I stop?"

"Krono, no," he groaned. "Move faster, sweet human."

I made a couple more experimental bounces at slow speed before quickening my pace. Galan's head was back, his eyes were closed, and sexy little moans escaped his mouth with every few thrusts he made.

My worry that it would hurt faded, and pleasure and need took its place. I clutched at Galan's shoulders, moving harder and faster, meeting each of his small upward thrusts. Fuck, his cock felt so good. When his big hand cupped my tit, I dug my nails into his skin and moaned, "Harder. Please, Galan."

He gripped my hips with his big hands and fucked me hard and rough. Pleasure shuddered its way through my body, and panting and moaning, I threw my head back and rode each one of his thrusts.

"I'm so close," I moaned. "Galan, I'm so close, I'm so…"

I trailed off, my breath catching in my throat and my body tensing as my orgasm rushed through me. I shook wildly, my fingers digging into Galan's skin, my soft cries drowned out by Galan's louder groans of pleasure. He made one final thrust, and hot warmth flooded my pussy as Galan shuddered below me.

I collapsed against him, the pleasure still coursing through my body. His heartbeat was strong and rapid beneath my ear, and I closed my eyes as the last of my orgasm fluttered through me. Galan's tail loosened around my waist, and I smiled when he rubbed my back with his big, warm hands.

After a few minutes, he said, "Are you all right, Ellis?"

"Yep," I said. "On a scale of one to ten, that sex was a hundred."

He laughed and kissed the top of my head. "I have never met a female who assigned numerical value to their sexual experiences before."

"Hmm." I yawned. It wasn't that late, but my orgasm had made me sleepy. I needed to get up and get dressed before I fell asleep in Galan's lap.

I clung to him when he stood up, wrapping my legs around his waist. His cock slipped out of me, and I patted him on the back, still keeping my eyes closed as he walked toward the door. "I need to put my clothes on first, big guy."

"You do not need clothes to sleep in my bed," Galan said.

I opened my eyes when he placed me on his bed. "I – you want me to stay the night?"

He slid into the bed beside me and paused, uncertainty crossing his face. "Do you prefer to go back to your bed?"

"No," I said quickly. "No, I'm good with spending the night."

"Good." He pulled the quilt up and spooned me, cupping my breast and kissing the back of my shoulder. "Good night, little human."

Galan

"You are in a good mood this morning." Krey sat down beside me on the bench in the sparring room.

I wiped the sweat from my face with the towel draped around my neck. "Am I?"

"Yes."

I shrugged. "Perhaps because I bested you in sparring again today."

Krey laughed. "You beat me at every spar session. It is why you are the head of the King's guard, my friend."

He wiped his bare chest with his towel. Other members of the guard were still sparring, and the clashing of their swords rang throughout the room. I watched a few of them, making mental notes of weaknesses to help them improve on.

"I know you fucked the little thief last night."

I jerked like I'd been zapped with a live wire and glanced at Krey. "And how would you know that?"

"Am I wrong?" he said.

"No," I admitted. "You are not wrong."

He sighed and leaned against the wall, setting the towel on his lap. "I knew I should not have let you go after her in the garden last night."

"Let me?"

"You know what I mean," he said. "That other female – the mean one – was interested in fucking you. She was angry when you left."

"Her name was Lori, and I am sure you were more than happy to fuck her," I said.

Krey shook his head. "No. Lori's comment to Sigan revealed her true nature. I had no desire to sleep with her."

"Nor did I."

"Because of your interest in the thief, not because of what Lori said to Sigan."

"It is only sex," I said. "We are friends with benefits – nothing more."

I kept my voice steady and made sure that my tail's movements were normal. Perhaps it would become the truth if I kept telling myself and others that Ellis meant nothing to me.

"Does the thief know that?" Krey said.

"Yes. She was the one who suggested it."

"If Quill or Teo find out you are fucking her -"

"No one will find out. Ellis knows she needs to be discreet," I said.

"Galan," Krey's hand landed heavily on my shoulder, "this is not a good idea."

I shrugged off his hand. "It is none of your business, Krey."

"You are my best friend, and if the others were to find out that the head of the King's Guard is sleeping with a thief -"

"Her name is Ellis," I snarled. My voice was loud enough that the Draax closest to us glanced over.

I schooled my features and lowered my voice. "I love you like a brother, Krey, and you are important to me, but continue to call her thief and disrespect her, and our friendship is over."

Krey stiffened next to me. "Krono, you are in love with her."

"I am not," I said. "But she is a good person who made a mistake and does not deserve your contempt."

"Galan," Krey leaned forward, "I like the thi- Ellis. I do. She is funny and smart, and Melu has even said good things about her. But it is madness to fall in love with her. She does not feel the same about you."

I didn't reply and Krey squeezed my shoulder. "Old friend, have you stopped to consider that she is using you to gain favour with Quill?"

I glared at him, and Krey said, "Hear me out, Galan."

"She would not do that," I said.

"You cannot possibly know that," he said. "You do not know her well enough. She will not survive even two days in the Earth prison. We all know that. Staying here is her best chance of survival. Your attraction to her is plain to see, and she may use that to her advantage. If you go to Quill on her behalf, his love for you means he could be persuaded to allow her to stay rather than be punished for her crime."

"Is that such a big deal? It was only a few bottles of juice. Does it seem right that she goes to prison over such a small amount?"

"No, it does not," Krey said. "But the Earth knows of her crime, and they expect her to be returned to them."

"It is our juice. We should be the ones to decide her fate," I said.

"You know it does not work that way. The treaty says that the humans will punish their kind for crimes committed, no matter who the crime is against. Quill's father's signature is on that treaty, and as the reigning king, Quill is obligated to obey it. He cannot break it no matter how much he wishes to do so."

I slumped against the wall. My ridiculous fantasy that perhaps Ellis's skill in the docking bay would convince Quill to keep her on our planet faded with Krey's words. Everything he said was true, and I was a froden for hoping Ellis would not be sent away.

"If she asks you to speak to Quill, you cannot," Krey said.

"She will not ask," I said.

He stared at me with disbelief, but I knew Ellis would never ask me to speak to Quill.

"She might," Krey said.

"You are wrong," I said. "Ellis is... she is not like the other human females. I know she is small and fragile looking, but I am beginning to think she is the toughest female I have ever met. She will not ask me for help in anything."

"I am worried for you," Krey sighed heavily.

"Do not be," I said. "I am not in love with her, and I am aware that she will return to Earth as soon as the war ends."

"Will you stop fucking her?"

I thought back to how Ellis looked this morning as she rode me. The light from the rising keo touched her blonde locks, making them look like spun gold as she leaned over me. Her soft cries of pleasure when I touched her clit, her intoxicating moans when I teased her nipples.

"Galan?" Krey prompted.

"No," I said. "I will not. We are both enjoying it, and there is no harm in continuing to fuck."

"There will be plenty of trouble if you are caught," Krey said.

"We will not be," I said.

"I hope you are right, brother."

Ellis

"C'MON, YOU STUPID PIECE OF CRAP!" I YANKED ON THE narrow tube, muttering a curse when it pulled free, and I almost fell on my ass.

I was standing under the silver belly of a havoc cruiser, the bottom hatch opened, and its insides exposed. I wiped the sweat from my forehead before studying the tube in my hand. A small hairline crack ran along one silver side, and I smiled triumphantly.

"I knew you were the problem," I said gleefully to the tube. "Wait until Melu sees this. He's going to be so pissed that I was right."

I walked out from under the havoc cruiser, rubbing absently at my thighs. They were sore, and my pussy was aching pleasantly from the sex with Galan early this morning. But it still wouldn't stop me from banging him again tonight.

If he wants to. He didn't mention anything about sex again with you, did he? Just said goodbye when you snuck out of his room this morning.

"Ellis?"

I glanced up, smiling happily when I saw Inara. "Hey, you. What are you doing here?"

"I came to see if you wanted to have lunch with me in the garden," Inara said. "Wait... do you even get a lunch break?"

Melu materialized behind Inara, his green skin weirdly dark and his big body tense. I grinned teasingly at him and raised my voice so he could hear it over the din of the docking bay. "Yeah, even as hardass and grumpy as Melu is, he lets us take a lunch break. Probably because he's so old, he needs a nap at lunch to keep up with the rest of us."

Inara rolled her eyes. "You and your old jokes. Seriously, Ellis, he isn't old, and he's good looking and in, like, amazing shape. I can only hope my future husband has a body like his when he's his age. I mean, have you taken a good look at Melu's ass? I bet you could bounce a quarter off that thing, and his chest is -"

"Inara," I said loudly, "please stop talking."

"What? Why?" She stared at me in confusion. "All I'm saying is that Melu's body is crazy hot and.... oh shit, he's standing right behind me, isn't he?"

"Yup."

Inara's face turned bright red, and she yanked on her hair as she slowly turned. Keeping her gaze on Melu's chest, she said, "Hello, Melu. It's, um, nice to see you again."

His tail lashing back and forth, Melu grunted out a hello before staring at me. "Do not be late returning from your lunch break, human."

He stalked away, his tail still whipping from side to side.

"Oh my God," Inara said. "I want to die of embarrassment."

"Don't worry about it," I said. "It probably gave him a

stiffy to hear that you think he's hot. If he can even still get it up at his age."

"You act like he's ancient. C'mon, let's get out of here. I only have an hour for lunch," Inara said.

After a quick stop at the kitchen to grab some food, we found a quiet spot in the garden to eat. I bit into my piece of poffin bread as Inara ate some warracot.

"How's your sister doing?" I said.

A pinched look covered Inara's pretty features. "My parents took her to see my uncle last night."

"Is that a bad thing?" I said.

"It's not great. He's involved in a lot of shady shit. Black market juice shady."

"Oh," I said.

Inara brushed some crumbs from her lap. "He made this joke once to my dad about how my sister and I would be worth a lot of juice on the black market."

"Holy shit," I said. "He actually said that?"

"Yeah."

"What did your father say?"

"He just laughed it off. Told me that his brother was always joking around and didn't mean it." Inara stared at the warracot on her fork. "Only, he didn't sound like he was joking. You know?"

"Yeah," I said. I knew guys like Inara's uncle. Men willing to do anything to get some of the gallberry juice. They could and would sell it at ridiculous amounts to desperate middles and uppers with sick family members and no breeding compatible females.

Or, in some cases, I couldn't stop the shudder going through my body, they would be willing to help middles trade other things for juice.

Ukana, ukana, ukana.

The disappointment on my parents' faces, the desperation that oozed from their bodies like a rotting stench that never went away, the paleness of Esther's sweet face... all of it flashed through my head.

My appetite vanished immediately, and I set the food aside. I could still see Esther's face, and I closed my eyes as nausea rocketed through my stomach.

"Ellis? Honey, are you okay?"

I took a deep breath and forced a smile in Inara's direction. "Yes, just fine."

"You look like you're going to barf."

"Nah, I'm good," I said. "So, any new gossip going on I should know about?"

Inara grinned. "You mean other than Rachel breaking down and banging two Draax last night at the celebration in the garden?"

I tried to look shocked. "Seriously?"

"Yup. She was in the common room this morning looking extremely pleased with herself," Inara said. "Apparently, she had a *very* good time."

"Good for her," I said with a laugh.

"Right?" Inara glanced around before lowering her voice. "Between you and me, I don't think Rachel was the only lady who had sex last night."

I studied her. "Did you have sex last night?"

"Of course not," she said. "I'm not getting involved with a Draax. I've never slept with one before, but apparently, they're amazing in bed, and I can't afford to be distracted by the best sex of my life. Wendy is my priority."

"Right," I said. "So, who else, uh, do you think had sex?"

As Inara named a surprisingly long list of suspects, I

nodded and smiled and hoped like hell that she didn't name me. Although, it would give me an excuse to tell her just how hot sex was with Galan. I was dying to tell someone – anyone – about my night with the sexy Draax. I'd never been one for kissing and telling, but apparently, amazing sex made me want to share all the details.

You can't tell her. I know you like Inara, but you don't know her that well, and you have no idea if she will keep your secret. If she doesn't and word gets to the king that Galan is having sex with you, Galan might get in trouble.

I sighed. There was no might about it. He *would* get in trouble. Maybe even lose his job in trouble, and I was not letting that happen. I couldn't live with myself if I destroyed Galan's life the way I seemed to destroy all of my loved ones' lives.

Loved one? Now you love him?

I pushed aside my inner voice. No, I didn't love him. That was ridiculous. Amazing sex wasn't enough to make you fall in love with someone.

Was it?

ELLIS

"I AM IMPRESSED BY YOU, SMALL HUMAN." UZEL DROPPED HIS arm around my shoulders before giving me a friendly poke in the ribs with his tail.

"Oh yeah? Why's that?" I liked the young Draax. From the start, he'd been friendly and pleasant to me and didn't ignore me like most of the other Draax in the docking bay.

"When you first started, I did not think you would be capable of repairing the vehicles and ships," Uzel said.

"Just because I'm a woman doesn't mean I can only clean and cook," I said. "Don't be sexist, Uzel."

"I know that. Before my mother married my father, she worked as an engineer on your planet," Uzel said. "I am aware that women can do more than domestic duties. I meant in reference to how small you are."

His tail poked my bicep. "You are stronger than you look."

"Hell, yes, I am." I flexed my arms until my biceps popped out. "Let me introduce you to Chaos," I kissed my left bicep, "and Fear." I kissed my right bicep. "These two ladies have helped me kick a lot of ass on the mean streets of Iowa."

"You have a very strange sense of humour," Uzel said.

"Thanks. I'm done for the day, are you?"

Uzel nodded. "Yes. Let us do the thing before we leave."

I laughed. A few days ago, I had taught Uzel a handshake involving fist bumping, hand slapping, hip shaking and, in his case, tail flicking. He'd been obsessed with it ever since.

I held up my fists, and Uzel eagerly bumped them with his own before we whipped through the rest of the handshake. He grinned, and his tail thumped happily on the floor when we finished.

"Thank you, small human," he said.

"Try to call me Ellis, would you, Uzel?" I said. "For goodness sake, you have a human mom. Didn't she teach you to call humans by their names or, I dunno, use contractions every once in a while?"

He shrugged. "She tried, but I take after my father, she says. All of my friends have human mothers, and none of us speak like humans do."

"Seriously?" I said.

As we left, he waved to a few other Draax still in the bay. "Yes. My mother says I did use contractions when she first taught me to speak, but I stopped using them by the time I started school. My friends were the same way."

"That's so weird," I said. "How does it sound in Draax when I use a contraction?"

"The Draax word is altered in only a small way, but it is noticeable. Males rarely use contractions, but females born to a human mother and a Draax father often speak in contractions and are more prone to acting like human females. But, since very few females are born, it does not seem to matter much."

"Wait, females aren't being born on Draax?" I said. "But the king and queen have a daughter."

"It was a huge celebration when she was born," Uzel said. "I was not yet working at the castle, but the celebrations within the city went on for days. In fact, our entire province celebrated her birth for nearly a week. Queen Sabrina received so many gifts from the commoners that they filled an entire room. It took her nearly six moons to open all of them."

"Wow," I said. "That seems excessive."

"Princess Jovie is the first female royalty born in nearly a century," Uzel said. "Our province will be the first province in Odias to have a ruling queen. We are lucky and blessed that Queen Sabrina grew a girl in her belly."

"How many babies are girls on average?" I said.

"I do not know. You should speak with Bitta. He is fascinated with this sort of stuff and follows many studies on it. He has a website predicting how many females may be born yearly. He is," he grinned at me, "what humans call a nerd."

I laughed. "I haven't heard the word nerd in forever. Do you think it's like one in five are females?"

Uzel shook his head. "No. If I had to hazard a guess, I would say more like one in a hundred babies born are female. I went to a large school in the city and did not have a single female classmate. Nor do my parents know any Draax who have female children. You humans have helped us escape extinction, but unless more females are born on a regular basis, we will need to rely on your breeding females for years to come."

We were almost to my apartment, and Uzel gave me another poke with his tail. "This is where we part. Goodbye, human. I will see you tomorrow."

"See you, Uzel." I walked the short distance to my apartment and let myself in, closing the door behind me. It was almost dinner time, and I wondered if I should join the other women and eat in the dining hall or wait around a few minutes and hope that Galan showed up and –

The knock on my door made me jump. I opened it, smiling at Galan when he stepped into my apartment and shut the door.

"Hey, how was your day?"

He didn't reply. He didn't look pissed off, but his tail was flicking back and forth in a decidedly agitated manner, and he walked toward me like a big cat stalking its prey. I backed up until I felt the wall against my spine as Galan penned me in with his hands on either side of my head.

I wasn't afraid. I was, weirdly, turned on, and all I could think about was how it had felt to ride Galan this morning. How thick and hard his cock was, the warmth of his mouth as he sucked on my nipples.

"What's going on?" I said.

"I saw you with Uzel in the docking bay," he said.

"Uh, yeah, I work with him."

He leaned down and kissed my throat, his breath hot against my skin. "He touched you."

"What?" I was finding it hard to concentrate, what with the way Galan was now cupping my tits.

"He touched you," Galan nipped my collarbone, "and you let him touch you."

"It was just a handshake," I said. "I've been teaching him a _"

"No. He put his arm around your shoulders." Galan pulled my shirt over my head, his copper eyes darkening when he saw my erect nipples. "Did you like it when he touched you?"

"Is this that jealousy thing again? Because I told you, you have nothing to be... oh fuck, oh, that feels..."

I arched into Galan's mouth, threading my fingers through his thick dark hair as he sucked hard on first my left nipple and then my right. His hand was unbuttoning my pants, and I didn't object when he yanked them down my legs. In fact, I might have kicked them off eagerly and reached for his pants.

Before I could undo them, he had dropped to his knees in front of me. He kissed the top of my pussy before slinging my right leg over one broad shoulder and cupping my ass.

"Galan, I..."

Rational thought faded when Galan licked my pussy. I leaned back against the wall, balancing on one leg, my other heel digging into Galan's back as he licked and sucked my throbbing clit.

"Oh God, that's so good," I moaned. I clung to his head, squeezing his skull as I ground my pussy against his mouth. He squeezed my ass hard as he teased my clit with the tip of his tongue. It didn't take long for me to climax, not with Galan's hot tongue working me over in that absolutely perfect way he had. I clapped my hand over my mouth, muffling my scream of delight as I came all over Galan's mouth.

He slid my leg off his shoulder and kept one hand on my hip as he stood. "Do not fall over, Ellis."

"Yeah, okay, I won't," I mumbled. I propped my body against the wall, my noodle legs quaking and the last of my orgasm still shuddering its way through my body.

Through half-closed eyes, I watched as Galan quickly stripped before picking me up. I expected him to carry me to the bed, and I gasped in surprise when he used his tail and left arm to lift me higher until my pussy pressed against his cock.

"Galan, what… ohhh. Oh fuck."

He slid his cock into my pussy with a slow, measured thrust. Stuffed full, I clung to his shoulders, my forehead pressed against his, our breath mingling. He pressed a kiss against my mouth. "I have missed your tight pussy, Ellis."

"You were just in her this morning," I said.

He laughed, and little tingles of pleasure flickered up my spine. "That is true, but it seems I cannot get enough of my little human's pussy."

"She can't get enough of you either," I moaned.

He pressed me up against the wall. "Put your legs around my waist."

I wrapped my legs around him, clinging to him as he pumped in and out of me. He cupped my face and kissed my mouth again. "Did you enjoy it when Uzel touched you?"

"What?" The pleasure was already beginning to grow in my belly again. I didn't know if it was the thickness of

Galan's cock or the way he fucked, but he was a magician at giving me an orgasm without even touching my clit, and I was here for it.

I squeezed around him, enjoying the sound of his harsh groan and the way it made him thrust hard into me. "Galan, stop talking and fuck me already."

He kissed me again, nipping hard at my bottom lip. "Did you like it? Do you wish to have Uzel join us in fucking?"

I stared at him in complete shock. His body went still, and he studied my face. "Do you, Ellis?"

"No," I said. "No, I don't want that."

"All right," he said.

There definitely needed to be follow-up questions, but apparently, up until this point, the fucking had only taken up a portion of Galan's concentration. Now, he was fully concentrating and, holy fuck, my desire to talk about whether Galan wanted a third to join us or not was lost in a haze of pleasure so amazing I wanted to live in it forever.

I closed my eyes and clung to Galan as he fucked me in a hard and steady rhythm. The pleasure grew, the sound of Galan's low groans turned louder, and when his thrusts became erratic and uneven, I squeezed my pussy around his cock as hard as I could and kissed my way up his throat to his ear.

"I missed your big cock," I whispered into his ear.

"Krono," he muttered. "Ellis, do not talk about such things, or I will not last much longer."

"I thought about it all day." I sucked on his earlobe, then kissed just behind his ear. "I love how thick you are, how good it feels when you're inside me and…. oh!"

He nearly flattened me against the wall with his thrusts, pounding into me until my climax washed over me in an unstoppable wave. My pussy squeezed him hard, and he moaned my name before driving deep and holding me still against the wall. The hot warmth of his come filled my pussy, and he made a few shuddering thrusts, muttering my name under his breath before burying his face in my neck.

I rubbed his back and squeezed his waist with my legs as he squeezed my thighs. He kissed my upper chest and eased out of me before lowering me to the ground. Before I could close my thighs, he reached between them and cupped my pussy.

I tried to pull his hand away, I was too sensitive for another orgasm, but he slid two fingers into my pussy. I watched in utter confusion when he pulled his fingers out and, without speaking, smeared his cum across my tits and upper chest.

"What are you doing?" I said.

His face darkened with embarrassment, but it didn't stop him from swiping his hand across my pussy again and wiping more of his cum across my tits.

"Dude, seriously," I said with a laugh. "Stop it. Now I'm definitely going to have to shower before I go to the dining hall, and I'm already starving."

He lifted me and carried me to my small bed, setting me down on it and crowding up behind me. He spooned me, cupping my now sticky breast and kissing the back of my shoulder. "I have food in my apartment. You can eat with me tonight."

"Sure," I said.

The bed was too small for the two of us, but I liked it. Cuddling with Galan was my favourite part of sex with him – after the mind-altering orgasms, of course.

He kissed the back of my shoulder again before resting his head on the pillow behind mine. "How was your day?"

"If you think we're just gonna talk about our day at work instead of the whole – hey, do you want a threesome with Uzel thing – you're dead wrong, mister," I said.

His low chuckle made me smile. "Most Draax enjoy threesomes."

"I know that," I said. "How, um, how many times have you participated in threesomes?"

"Many," he said. "But not for a long time."

"Who did you have threesomes with?"

"Usually with Quill before he mated, but also with Krey," Galan said.

"Oh, right, of course. That makes sense." I craned my head to stare at him. "Do you want to do a threesome with me?"

He studied my face. "Do you?"

"I asked you first," I said.

He squeezed my breast. "I want to please you. If being with me and another Draax pleases you, I will arrange for another to join us. Would you be open to it being Krey instead of Uzel? Uzel is young and most likely has never mated. It would not be wise to have him join us for his first time."

"I don't want a threesome at all." My voice was too loud, and I took a deep breath. "I'm, uh, I'm not trying to be difficult, but I'm not into the idea of having sex with two guys at the same time. I'm sorry."

"Do not be sorry," he said. "If that is not what you want, we will not do it."

"But if you want it, then -"

"I want to please you, remember?" he said. "I am happy with it only being us, little human."

"You sure?"

"Yes."

"Okay, good." I relaxed against him, stroking his arm with the tips of my fingers. "Honestly, even if I did want a three-some, you'd never convince Krey or any other Draax to sleep with me. They all think I'm ukana."

"Too young?" Galan said. "Why would they think you are too young? You are in your twenties."

"No, I said ukana," I replied. "It means ugly, not too young."

"It does not," Galan said. "Ukana means too young."

The blood roared in my ears, and I felt too hot and then too cold. Through numb lips, I said, "Are you sure?"

"Of course I am. It is my language, is it not?" Galan said. "Ukana means too young."

All that blood roaring in my ears was now draining away, and when I sat up and twisted my upper body to stare at Galan, I was immediately lightheaded.

"Too young," I whispered. "It means too young. Oh my God."

Alarm crossed Galan's face and he sat up, grabbing my upper arms when I swayed on the bed. "Ellis? What is wrong?"

CHAPTER 15

Galan

I stared worriedly at Ellis. I had never seen a human's face so completely drained of blood before. "Sadora, take a deep breath."

She didn't move, and I cupped her face. "Breathe, sadora."

She hitched in a breath and then another, her face still the colour of muldeva sand and her slender body quivering.

I propped her up against the wall and squeezed her hand. "Stay here."

I slid off the bed, grabbed a bottle of gallberry juice and returned to her. "Drink, sadora."

She drank a few swallows of juice, and I breathed a sigh of relief when some of her colour returned to her face. "Tell me what is wrong."

"Are you positive that ukana means too young?" she said in a timid voice that sounded nothing like her normal voice.

"Yes," I said.

Her bottom lip trembled, and her eyes were watering like she was about to cry. That sent what almost felt like panic rushing through me. I had never seen Ellis even close to crying, not even when she found out she had cancer. What in Krono's name was happening?

"Sadora, please," I said when she remained silent. "Tell me why you are upset."

She took another deep breath and drank more juice before pulling the quilt around her body. I sat beside her on the bed, leaning against the wall and resting my hand on her thigh. Not having to look directly at me seemed to help her hesitancy because she said, "I have – had – a sister. Her name was Esther, and she was a few years younger than me. She was sweet and lovely and... good. She wasn't like me, you know? Even as a kid, I was difficult and a pain in the ass, and I caused my parents a lot of grief. But Esther, she was special. Everyone loved her. She was so kind to everyone. It didn't matter what your social class was, Esther treated you the same."

I squeezed her thigh when she lapsed into silence. "What happened to her?"

"When she was twelve, she got bone cancer." She laughed bitterly. "We all seem to get cancer at some point, don't we?"

"Yes," I said.

"Inara says it's worse with the lowers. The doctors and the government keep saying the cancer isn't because of the atmosphere, but Inara says the numbers prove that it is. Anyway, my family were middle class but only a step above lower, you know?"

"Yes," I said.

"My mom had a hysterectomy after Esther was born, so

she couldn't even try the breeding program for the Draax to get some juice. But even if she hadn't had one, the Draax won't accept married women into the breeding program."

She glanced up at me as if waiting for my confirmation. I nodded. "That's right."

"Because you always hope to convince the woman to stay and be your mate and have more babies, right?"

"Yes."

She took another large swallow of juice. "Anyway, they sold a bunch of stuff to try and raise enough money to buy some juice on the black market."

She glanced at me again, but I kept my face neutral. The black market for juice was becoming a significant problem, but neither the Draax nor the humans had figured out a way to stop it from happening. But I couldn't blame Ellis's parents for trying whatever they could to save their child.

"They were not able to get enough?" I said.

"No. They even tried taking a second mortgage on the house, but the bank denied them. Esther was receiving chemo, but it was obvious that it wasn't working. The doctors told us she had maybe another month."

"I am sorry, sadora." I took her hand and squeezed it.

Her fingers were cold and clammy, and she clung to my hand in a tight grip. "One night, after Esther was in bed, my parents came to my room and told me they had found another way to get the juice. I was ecstatic."

She was near tears again, and the slight colour the juice had given her already leached away. "My dad had found a guy, I don't know how, and he never said, who was willing to help trade with the Draax for the juice we needed. He was like a broker. Do you know what that word means?"

"Yes," I said. "he receives money or juice in exchange for arranging the deal."

"Right," she said. "My mom said that I could save Esther. She said I would be working with the Draax for a couple of nights and needed to be brave and strong. I said I would do whatever they wanted me to do."

The laugh that spilled out of her throat was jagged and bitter. "I was so naïve. I had no idea what she meant by working, but I figured it out when my mom... when she..."

"When she what?" I was starting to feel sick, but what I was thinking could not be true. No parent would do that to their child.

"She dressed me in her prettiest dress and did my makeup and hair. Then she and my dad drove me to a hotel. The guy was waiting for us in the lobby, and he..."

She swallowed hard, and I could hear the click of her throat. "He looked me over and said that my mom had done a good job, that I looked real pretty and... older."

I reached out and pulled her into my lap, looping my arms and my tail around her waist and kissing her throat. "My sweet sadora, I am so sorry."

She stared across the room, her throat working and a tear sliding down her cheek. I wiped it away as she said, "We went up to the room, and I think I must have been in denial before this because I suddenly knew for certain what they wanted me to do as we stepped out of the elevator. I was so scared, Galan. I started to cry, and I..."

Shame practically radiated from her. "In the hallway outside the room, I lost my nerve and tried to run. But my dad caught me before I even made it to the elevator. I begged him not to make me do this, and he said... he said that if I didn't, Esther would die."

Rage made my tail squeeze around Ellis's waist, and I forced myself to relax. Being angry and wishing to gut Ellis's father with my sword would not help my sadora now.

"My mom told me that all I had to do was smile at the Draax and be friendly and just… just close my eyes and try to relax. She said it would hurt less if I didn't tense up."

I pulled her even closer, my chest aching as I imagined how afraid and alone my sadora must have felt.

She rested her head on my chest, and I stroked her soft hair. "I was scared, but I went into the room with my parents. There were two Draax in the room, and they were huge and scary looking. I was so afraid I thought I might wet my pants. But I didn't want my sister to die, so I tried to smile at them and tried to look pretty and happy. We couldn't understand the Draax, but the man had translators, so he spoke with them for us."

She paused and I kissed the top of her head and rubbed her back as my tail thumped against her hip. She took a deep breath. "The Draax looked at me and they – they got really angry. They started arguing with the man, I think, and he just kept saying that I was in perfect health and was willing to spend the night with them."

"Asshole," I said. I rarely used Earth's insults, but my anger couldn't be contained.

"The Draax kept saying one word over and over… ukana. They argued for only a few minutes, and then the Draax left the room. When my dad asked what happened, the guy said the Draax didn't want me. My mom asked what ukana meant, and the man said it meant ugly. The Draax thought I was too ugly to sleep with."

"It does not mean ugly," I said immediately.

249

"I felt so ashamed," Ellis said. "But the man said he would find different Draax."

"Krono, how many times did they try?"

"Three more times," Ellis said. "Each time there were two Draax and each time they got furious as soon as they saw me and started yelling ukana at the guy before they stormed out."

She took a deep and shuddering breath. "After the fourth set of Draax wouldn't trade juice for me, the guy got pissed and said it was pointless to keep trying. Said that all the Draax would find me too skinny and ugly. My parents begged him to keep looking for more, but he refused. He said it was a waste of his time."

Her small body curled into mine, and I held her tight, wishing I could take away the pain I could hear in her voice. "My parents were so upset with me. I said I was sorry and that I had tried, but they…"

"They what?" I said.

"They knew that Esther was going to die, and they were devastated. They couldn't even look at me. I'd failed them, and I'd failed my sister. She died two weeks later. She died because of me. Six months after she died, I ran away from home. My parents were barely talking to me. They were consumed by grief, and every time they looked at me, they didn't see their daughter anymore. They saw the person who had killed their child."

"Sadora, no." I cupped her face and made her look up at me. "You did not kill your sister. The Draax rejected you because you were too young. No Draax would ever sleep with a female so young. There was nothing you could do."

"I could have tried harder," she said. "I could have tried to look and act older. I could have tried not to be so afraid."

"No," I said. "Ellis, what happened is not your fault. Your parents should never have asked you to do this."

"Esther was dying. They were desperate, and I don't blame them for -"

"No," I repeated. "Do not make excuses for your parents, my sadora. What they did was despicable and wrong, and to use you in such a manner to save your sister is beyond comprehension. They should never have put this burden on you. Your mother could have easily bargained herself to the Draax but chose not to. She chose to send her child in her place."

She stared at me. The shock in her gaze made it evident she'd never thought of that. "I don't... why didn't she do that?"

"I do not know," I said.

"All this time," she whispered, "I believed it was my fault because I was ugly. I believed I killed Esther because I wasn't pretty enough or smart enough to trick the Draax into being attracted to me."

I kissed her cold lips and said, "You were only a child and too young for what they asked of you. Your parents were supposed to protect you, not trade your body and your innocence for a cure for your sister. Esther's death was not your fault, Ellis."

She stared blankly at me before bursting into loud sobs. Her thin body shook, and I cradled her to my chest, kissing the top of her head and murmuring soft words of comfort as she buried her face in my neck and cried.

I woke to the feel of Ellis's soft lips kissing a path across my chest. I reached down to smooth her hair back from her face. "Sadora, what are you doing?"

The pet name Draax gave their mates had just slipped out. I blamed it on only being half-awake.

"You were so sweet to me earlier," Ellis said. "I want to be sweet to you now."

She licked my flat nipple, and I groaned, my hand cupping the back of her head. "You do not have to do this. It is late, and I know your evening was difficult and -"

"Galan?" She kissed my sternum and moved lower down the bed. Her bed was too small for the two of us, and she was mostly lying on top of me, her perfect tits rubbing against my stomach, her thighs spread around one of mine.

"Yes, sadora?"

"Shut up and let me suck your dick."

I laughed, and she grinned up at me. Krono, she was so beautiful.

I arched when her stiff nipple brushed against the head of my cock. She wiggled down and kneeled between my open thighs, her soft hands stroking my inner thighs and her mouth hovering over my aching dick.

"Your cock is so beautiful." Her warm breath was both torture and pleasure on my cock.

"Ellis, please," I said. Begging wasn't something I normally did in bed, but the little female's mouth was so close to my cock, and I couldn't stop thinking about how good it felt the last time she'd sucked me.

"Do you want my mouth, Galan?"

"Yes, sadora," I said. "So much."

A smile crossed her face, and I cried out, my hands gripping the sheets in ecstasy when her wet mouth slid over my cock, and she sucked in a hard rhythm. Krono, she was so good at that.

I pulled her hair away from her face in a loose ponytail. Her hair was like silk against my palms, and I watched as she sucked at my cock. She cupped my balls and tugged gently, swallowing quickly when precum spurted from my dick in response.

"God, I love the taste of you," she said before licking up and down my shaft.

I gripped her skull and guided her mouth back over my dick, watching with feverish need as her lips slid down my shaft. She grabbed the base with one tiny hand, stroking firmly as she sucked. I thrust into her mouth, trying to stay gentle, trying not to overwhelm her, but the suction of her mouth and the low moans she made that vibrated around my cock were too much for me.

Holding her head tight, I fucked her mouth with hard long strokes. She stared up at me, her lovely blue eyes filled with trust, warmth, and another emotion that made my chest tight.

My sadora didn't love me, we barely knew each other, but it was easy to fool myself into thinking she did. Easy to pretend that she was my mate and we would spend every night together for the rest of our lives.

"Krono, little female," I moaned when she hollowed her cheeks and sucked hard, "you are so good at sucking my cock."

She pulled against my grip, and I released her immediately despite how close to coming I was. I groaned at the loss of her warm mouth as she smiled up at me. "I like sucking your cock, Galan. I like the way you look and the sounds you make when you're in my mouth."

"Then perhaps you should keep sucking." I sounded almost pathetically eager but wasn't even the least bit ashamed. No Draax would be able to resist the hot wetness of Ellis's mouth or the tightness of her pussy.

Just the thought of her being with another Draax instead of me filled me with jealousy. She squeaked in surprise when I gripped her arms and lifted her until she was straddling my hips.

"You are not to do this to another Draax," I told her. "It is only my cock you suck."

She blinked at me. "I don't want to do this to another Draax. Only you, Galan."

"Good." I cupped her tits, pulling lightly at her stiff nipples. "Fuck me, sadora."

She stared at me for a few seconds before reaching between us and gripping my cock. I groaned and moved my hands to her narrow hips, lifting her until she could press the head of my cock against her narrow opening.

Ignoring my urge just to slam my dick deep inside of her, I helped her ease slowly onto my dick, the tightness of her pussy making me grit my teeth. I'd never fucked a pussy as tight as Ellis's. Although I had downplayed her initial nervousness about fucking me, truthfully, every time we fucked, I was surprised all over again that she could take all of me.

She moaned quietly as she settled fully on my dick, her knees squeezing my hips and her hands resting on my chest as she leaned over me.

"So full," she breathed as I stroked her thighs.

I reached up and cupped the back of her neck, staring intently at her as she started to ride me. Already, I was close.

The combination of first her wet mouth and now her tight pussy, had me aching to come deep inside of her.

I moved my other hand to her pussy, stroking the soft curls before I rubbed at her swollen clit.

"Oh!" Her body shivered on mine, her pussy squeezing so tight I feared I would come right then and there.

I groaned and rubbed her clit harder. I needed her to come before I made a froden of myself and came before she did. "You feel so good, sweet Ellis."

"You too," she panted as she ground her pussy against my fingers and cock. "Really good. So… really good."

I squeezed the back of her neck until she looked at me. "You are not to fuck another Draax, sadora. Only me. Do you understand?"

My earlier assurances that I would do whatever pleased her, including finding another to join us in bed, had completely disappeared under a wave of intense jealousy.

"Yes," she said. "I won't. I don't want to. I only want you, Galan."

I pulled her against my chest, one hand rubbing her clit furiously as I fucked her with hard deep strokes. She cried out, her tiny body tensing as she came against my fingers, her pussy tightening with exquisite pleasure around my throbbing dick.

I shouted her name, my hips pumping hard as I came deep inside of her. She collapsed against my chest, and I stroked her smooth back as she pressed kisses against my skin.

Her voice muffled, her hand smoothing up and down my ribs, she said, "I don't want you fucking anyone else either."

I kissed the top of her head. "I will not, my sadora. You are the only one for me."

She kissed my chest, and I held her soft body even closer to mine. "Only you, sadora," I murmured into her hair. "Only you."

Ellis

"I SERIOUSLY CANNOT GET OVER HOW DIFFERENT YOU ARE now," Inara said. "Candy, she's different, right?"

"Yes." Candy sat on one of the couches in the common room the Draax had provided for the women working in the castle. "You're happy, Ellis." She paused. "Wait, that didn't come out right."

I laughed and lightly poked Roden, who was sitting on my lap. "Your mama looks cute with her foot in her mouth."

Roden looked up from the game he was playing on his vertex. "Mama has her foot in her mouth?"

He studied her before giving me a *you're a weirdo* look. "Hey, do you want to come to our apartment tonight and play with the flight simulator?"

"I can't, big guy. Not tonight."

He pouted at me. "You haven't come by once this week."

"I know. I'm sorry. I will definitely come by tomorrow night, okay?" I said.

"All right." We were sitting near the common room door and Roden jumped off my lap when he saw Luka walk by the open doorway. "Luka! Hey, Luka!"

Luka stuck his head into the room. "Hello, young human."

"Hey, what are you doing?"

"Going to the garden. Would you like to join me?"

"Yeah! Mama, can I?" Roden said.

Candy smiled. "It's may I, and yes, you may."

"Thanks!" He stuck the vertex in his pocket and bounced toward the door, taking Luka's hand when he offered it. We could hear him chattering to Luka as they walked down the hall and Inara smiled at Candy.

"Roden really likes Luka, huh?"

"He does."

"I bet he'd make a great step-dad."

Candy rolled her eyes. "I'm not interested in Luka. Besides, he wants children."

"Oh. Damn," Inara said.

"Stop trying to set me up with a Draax, butthead," Candy said. "I'm not trying to set you up with every Draax who looks twice at you."

"That's because you know I'm leaving as soon as my work term is done. Besides, I can't help it – I'm a romantic at heart," Inara said. "I want everyone to be in love and happy."

"Speaking of which…" Candy turned toward me, "Why have you been so extraordinarily happy lately?"

"I haven't been," I said. "I'm my normal grumpy self."

"Okay, I wouldn't call you grumpy," Inara said, "but you are kind of glowing and have been the last few days. If I didn't know better, I'd say you were in love."

I scoffed. "Who would I be in love with? None of the Draax look twice at me."

My voice stayed steady, and my gaze didn't waver from Inara. I had to admit that my history of being an excellent lying liar who lied came in handy from time to time. If they even suspected that I was so happy because I'd been banging Galan every night for the last week, it could lead to a major problem.

It's not just sex with Galan. You're also happy because you have a job, friends, and a place where you seem to fit in. And more importantly, you finally believe it's not your fault your sister died.

A little rush of giddiness went through me. While I still grieved for Esther and would always miss her, I had no idea the weight I carried over my guilt about her death until it was gone. That aching pit in my stomach, the sorrow and the regret that I couldn't do what my parents needed me to do was gone. I had tried my best to save Esther, but it wasn't my fault that I was too young.

After my initial confession about my sister, I hadn't wanted to talk about it again, but each night, after the lovemaking was over and I was warm and relaxed in Galan's arms, he brought it up. He assured me repeatedly that it wasn't my fault, that I was too young and that my parents had made a terrible decision.

At first, I hadn't seen the point of talking about it over and over, but now… I could admit that after each conversation, I felt a little better and believed a little more that it wasn't my fault. I started to think that maybe Galan had chosen the wrong occupation, and he'd make a killing as a therapist.

"I've seen a couple of Draax looking twice at you, Ellis," Candy said.

"Ooh, really? Who?" Inara said eagerly.

"One of the Draax who works in the kitchen – I don't know his name, but every time Ellis is in the dining hall, and he's serving at the buffet table, he gets a cute little smile on his face.

"Impossible," I said airily. "You're seeing things."

"Who else?" Inara said.

Candy's smile widened. "Galan."

I froze in place. Shit. Balls.

"That's awesome," Inara said. "He's super hot."

"He stares at her ass every time he's around her," Candy said. "And his tail does that flicky-flicky thing they do when a Draax is excited."

I arranged my face into a mask of boredom. "Oh please, you're seeing things, Candy-girl. Galan and I are friends, sure, but I am the exact opposite of what he's attracted to."

"How do you know that?" Inara said.

"He told me. We're friends. We talk. He's just like all the other Draax – he likes the curvy ladies."

"Oh." Inara slumped against the couch in disappointment. "That's too bad."

"Considering you're a thief headed for life imprisonment on Earth, Galan shouldn't even be friends with you."

The hair rose on the back of my neck. I knew that voice. I hated that voice. Irrational, maybe, but as Lori stepped into view, I couldn't even bring myself to fake smile at her.

"This is a private conversation," Inara said.

Inara's usual warm smile was gone, and I'd never heard her voice so cold. I could barely hide my surprise. Inara was friendly to everyone… usually.

"I'm just saying that Galan is the head of the king's guard. Should he really be best buds with you?" Lori said.

"We're not best buds," I said. "Mind your own business."

"Do you think you'll have a best friend in prison?" Lori said. "I heard that, on average, a woman lasts a week in prison if she doesn't find a guy to protect her in exchange for fucking him. Is that what you're going to do, Ellis? You going to whore yourself out to stay alive?"

Inara jumped up, her hands in tight fists and her face bright red. "Fuck off, Lori."

Lori gave her a brittle smile before studying me. "It's no

surprise you and Inara are friends. You're both rude and coarse and have filthy mouths."

"I'd rather have a filthy mouth than a stick up my ass," I said.

Lori just smiled and walked away. Inara collapsed on the couch, her face still red and looking like she would cry.

"Are you all right?" Candy said.

"I hate that chick," Inara said. "She's been a bitch since the day I met her at the Space Station. Always acting like she's better than us. She isn't. She's a lower just like the rest of us."

"Forget about her," I said. "She isn't worth being upset over."

"That's the truth," Candy said.

Before Inara could reply, two women walked by the couch and sat on the sofa beside ours. One of them was visibly upset, and she wiped at her face and blew her nose as the other woman rubbed her back.

"Poor Tasha," Inara said. "I feel so bad for her."

"What's wrong?" I said.

"Her grandmother was sick back on Earth. She went to Sabrina to see if she could go home to visit her, and Sabrina talked to the king, but he said no. With the war going on, he said it was too dangerous. She found out yesterday afternoon that her grandmother died."

"That's awful," I said.

"It is," Inara said. "Sabrina felt terrible, you could tell, but it's not the Draax's fault those other two worlds are at war, you know?"

We sat in silence for a few minutes before Inara glanced at Candy. "Have you seen the prince yet?"

Candy nodded. "I have. Evelyn visited a few days ago, and I saw him when we were together."

"Nice," Inara said. "Does he look like the king?"

"Spitting image of him. He's so chubby. He was over ten pounds when he was born, and he's gained a bunch more weight already. Sabrina said she can hardly keep up with feeding him."

A flicker of green caught my eye, and I glanced toward the doorway. Galan was standing in the hallway and staring at me. The way his copper eyes had already turned bronze made my pussy wet and my nipples hard. God, I was addicted to him.

He walked away, and I waited only a few minutes before standing. "I should go. It's getting late."

"It's not even seven," Inara said.

"Yeah," I made a show of yawning, "but Melu worked my ass off at the docking bay today, and I'm tired. I'm going to bed early. Night!"

I tried to walk normally across the common room and mostly succeeded. Hell, I even managed to walk at a regular pace through most of the castle. But by the time I reached our section, I was almost jogging, and my pelvis was throbbing, and I was shamefully turned on.

I stopped outside Galan's door and looked both ways before raising my hand to knock. The door opened before I could knock, and I grinned at Galan as I stepped into his apartment and shut the door behind me.

"Hi."

"Hello, little human. How was your day?"

"Fine," I said. "How was yours?"

"Good." He smiled at me, and I laughed before jumping at him.

He caught me, and I wrapped my legs around his waist as

he carried me toward his bedroom. I pressed a kiss against his mouth. "I missed you today."

"I missed you too," he said.

"Melu yelled at me twice because I was daydreaming about fucking you instead of fixing a land vehicle," I said.

He laughed. "I might have been thinking about fucking you as well. Only, instead of being yelled at, I was sliced with a recruit's sword nearly half a dozen times."

He set me down on the bed, and I immediately jumped to my feet, staring wide-eyed at him. "You got hurt? Let me see."

I lifted his shirt, but his torso looked normal. Before I could undo his pants and check his legs, he said, "They were shallow cuts, and the gallberry juice healed me in a short time. Do not worry, sadora."

I scowled at him. "I don't like that you're getting hurt because you're thinking about me. You need to friggin' concentrate when you're training."

"It is difficult when all I can think about is being in your tight pussy," he said with a flirty grin. "Perhaps if you weren't so tight or didn't take my cock so eagerly every time we fucked, it would be easier for me to forget about you during the day."

"Oh, so this is my fault," I said with a mock scowl.

"I think so," Galan said.

I reached around him and slapped him on the butt. "Keep talking that way, and I'll only fuck you once tonight instead of our usual twice."

He burst into laughter and picked me up again before laying me on the bed and kneeling between my thighs. He nuzzled my hard nipples through the fabric of my shirt, making me moan before grinning up at me.

"You cannot resist me, little sadora. Admit it."

"You're marginally appealing," I said.

He nipped at my collarbone as heat blossomed in my belly. "Only marginally? What do I need to do to change that?"

"Hmm," I tilted my head and pretended to think for a moment. "Probably pussy eating is your best chance."

"Is that right?" He sucked on my throat before nibbling along my jawline.

"Yes."

"Well then," he smiled at me before pressing a quick kiss against my lips. "Pussy eating it is then, little human."

CHAPTER 16

Ellis

"Galan, please," I moaned.

Galan lifted his head from between my thighs, his mouth soaking wet and a smug smile crossing his face. "Please, what, my sadora?"

"Please stop teasing. I need to come."

"I love the way you beg, sweet human."

I threaded my hands through his hair and pulled hard. If Galan wanted me to beg, I would beg. I needed relief from his teasing tongue, his firm lips, and his thick fingers. "Please, honey. Please make me come."

"Yes, sadora." His dark head bent between my thighs, and my hips arched up as he sucked on my clit. I came immediately, crying his name, my feet drumming on the bed, and my body shaking with pleasure.

He licked me clean before sitting up and wiping his face on the sheet. I waited for him to lift me on top of him. Our height difference made the missionary position virtually impossible, so most of the time, I rode him, or he took me from behind.

To my surprise, he lay beside me and tugged on my hip until I rolled to face him. He cupped my thigh and lifted my leg before sliding down a little and pressing his cock against my wet entrance.

I gripped his shoulder, moaning my pleasure when he slowly entered me. He took his time, stretching my narrow walls and filling me up bit by bit until he was fully sheathed.

I rested my hands against his chest as he smiled down at me. "Does this feel all right, my sadora?"

"Mmm," I said. "I like this position."

"Me as well."

I loved the intimacy of facing him this way, with every part of our bodies touching, his big hand cupping my thigh as he rocked his hips back and forth. I squeezed around his cock, and he moaned, his tail flicking over his hip to wrap around my waist. He held me tight against him, cupping my small tits and playing with my nipples as he fucked me with slow and gentle strokes.

I closed my eyes, and Galan said, "No, Ellis. Look at me."

My eyelids fluttered open, and I stared hazily at him as pleasure grew in my belly. "It feels so good, Galan."

"It does," he moaned. His hand cupped my face, and he ran his thumb along my mouth before smiling at me. "You are beautiful, Ellis."

"Thank you," I whispered.

"Do not look away," he said.

I stared up at him. The tenderness in his gaze made me catch my breath. He moved harder and faster, and I clutched at him as he gripped my ass and drove in deep.

"I cannot get enough of you, sweet sadora," he moaned. "You feel so good."

"I'm close," I panted. "Galan, I want to come."

"I want that too," he said. He reached between us and rubbed gently at my clit. "Come for me, my sweet sadora."

My hips bucked, and I cried out, staring at Galan as I came around his cock. My second orgasm was a little less intense but weirdly more satisfying. I kept my gaze on Galan as his breathing turned shallow, and the cords in his neck stood out.

He groaned, his back arching and his chest brushing against my nipples as, still holding my gaze, he came deep inside of me. His big body shook, his hand squeezed my ass hard, and the love and tenderness radiating from his beautiful copper eyes took my breath away.

I looked away, feeling close to tears as Galan held me tightly against him.

"Are you all right?" he said after a few moments.

"Yes," I said. "Are you?"

"More than all right," he said.

His cock was softening inside of me, and he pulled out. I didn't object when he reached down and took some of his seed to smear into my stomach and breasts with soft care. He did that every time we made love now, and I realized it was an almost necessary ritual for him. It made me sticky, but I liked it when he marked me that way.

I relaxed against his chest, closing my eyes and listening to his heartbeat slow into a normal rhythm. The tenderness and intimacy Galan had just shown left me ridiculously happy, but mixed in with that was alarm. We didn't have a future together and needed to remember that.

Galan

"Galan?" Ellis's soft voice, low and a little hoarse, nudged me awake.

"Hmm?" I said before spooning her closer. I loved having Ellis in my bed. Loved waking up to the warmth of her soft body.

"Your vertex is buzzing."

I released her reluctantly and turned on my back, grabbing the vertex from my bedside table. My mother was trying to hologram me, and I set the vertex down without answering it. I spooned Ellis again, kissing the back of her shoulder as she relaxed against me. It wasn't as late as I thought. I must have just fallen asleep.

"Are you not going to answer it?" she said.

"It is my mother. I will call her back later."

She sat up, clutching the sheet around her breasts. "I can leave so you can talk to her."

I tugged her back into my arms. "No, I want you to stay."

"Are you sure?"

I nodded, and she rested her head on my chest. I ran my fingers up and down the bumps of her spine, memorizing the feel of her soft skin. I'd been happier and more content the last week than in a very long time. Spending time with Ellis, touching and mating with her, soothed me in a way I'd never experienced before.

She is your mate.

I pushed that thought away immediately. Ellis couldn't be my mate. This had to be only sex between us. It was dangerous even to consider that it could be more.

Convincing Quill to allow the human to stay would break the treaty and cause issues with the humans. I couldn't ask him to do that to make me happy.

"Galan?"

"Yes?"

"Will you tell me about your family?"

I stroked her back again. "It is not a happy story, my sadora."

She glanced up at me before kissing my chest. "Mine wasn't exactly a happy tale either. I want to know. Please tell me."

I stared up at the ceiling, my fingers still trailing over Ellis's spine. "My father was a farmer. His gallberry crops were some of the best in the province. The king purchased crops from my father for use in the castle. It is how I met Quill when we were boys. My father would often deliver the crops himself to the castle, and the king would always request a meeting with him."

I watched the beams of light from the setting keo flicker across the ceiling. "Quill's father was a very... unique king. His father before him rarely met with the commoners or made public appearances, but King Jota did not shy away from his people. He would make many trips to the city just to talk to people, and he taught his sons to be the same way. Quill's father first started the tradition of allowing the Draax into the castle garden during the cold months so they could enjoy warmth and flowers, and both Quill's brother and Quill continued the tradition."

"The king has a brother?" Ellis said.

"He died a few years ago in a ship crash. Krey and I arrived first and discovered King Quodia's body. We had to tell Quill his brother had died," I said. My stomach tightened, and my eyes burned with unshed tears. Telling Quill his brother was dead had been the most difficult moment of my life, and even now, I could still feel the dread and the nausea at telling my best friend such horrible news.

As if sensing my discomfort, Ellis snuggled in closer. Her soft hand stroked my ribs, and she kissed my chest. "I'm sorry, honey. That must have been awful for all three of you."

"Yes." I took a deep breath. "As a child, my father would bring me with him when he went to the castle. When the king saw that I was the same age as Quill, he introduced us. We became friends quickly. My mother said we were two peas in a pod."

I smiled at Ellis. "Once she explained what the Earth saying meant, it described us accurately enough."

"How did you meet Krey?" she said. "You've been friends with him since you were a boy as well, right?"

"Yes. But that's a long story, and perhaps one best left for another time," I said.

"All right. Tell me more about your father."

I closed my eyes for a few seconds. My tail thumped against the bed, and Ellis kissed my chest again. "It's okay, honey."

"He had a gambling problem," I said.

"I didn't realize you had casinos here," Ellis said.

I knew what she meant by casinos. I had been to a few on Earth but hadn't enjoyed them, nor had Quill and Krey. We'd learned to limit our visits to bars and pubs. It was our best chance at meeting a female who would fuck us.

"We do not have casinos like on Earth," I said, "and while we have card games like Earth does, we rarely bet on them. Our gambling is in the form of races and sporting events."

"Ahh, like horse racing," she said.

"Sort of. Although we race an animal called a Cassowary. They are small and hairless mammals who tunnel through the dirt at great speed. Going to Cassowary races is the second most popular pastime on Draax."

"What's the first?"

"Reso. It is a game similar to your basketball," I said.

"So, your father gambled at the Cassowary races?" Ellis said.

"Yes. He used to go there every weekend, but as the addiction grew, so did his lies and the amount of money he spent. He started making larger bets and losing larger amounts of money. He hid what he was doing from my mother, and while she suspected that he was not entirely truthful, she had no idea how bad it had gotten."

"How bad was it?" Ellis said.

I swallowed hard. "He started selling gallberries to Draax, who would use them to bribe females on Earth to sleep with them."

"Shit," Ellis said. "He was a part of the black market?"

"Yes. He was caught after nearly a year. Earth military collaborates with Draax military to stop the selling and trading of juice outside of the agencies. My father was caught by our military and sent to Iron Gate. He died six moons later. Killed by another prisoner."

"Oh my God," Ellis said. "I'm so sorry."

"We were left penniless. We lost our home and the gallberry crops. My mother and I had nowhere to go."

"What happened?" Ellis said.

"Quill's father allowed my mother and I to stay in the castle until my mother found a new mate."

"Right, you said before that she remarried?"

"Yes. His name is Pakla. He is in the military. My mother

mated with him three moons after my father went to Iron Gate."

"Three moons," Ellis breathed. "Holy, you said she remarried quickly, but… wow."

"She had no choice. She was not allowed to work to support us and did not wish to rely on the king's charity for long."

"I'm still kind of surprised she didn't just pack you up and return to Earth," Ellis said.

"She did it for me." My throat was tight, and my voice was hoarse. "She knew living on Earth would be difficult for me and wanted me to be happy. I owe her a great deal for sacrificing her happiness for mine."

Ellis rubbed my chest. "Is she not happy with her new husband?"

"She is," I said. "She loves him, and he loves her. Very much."

"Is your relationship strained with her because of him?" Ellis said.

I didn't reply, and Ellis stared up at me. "You know that it's all right not to like the man your mom married, even if she married him to make your life easier, right?"

I swallowed hard. No one had ever said that out loud to me before, and it oddly eased the tightness in my chest a little. "He is not a bad man and an excellent mate to my mother and father to my half-brothers."

"But?" Ellis said.

"He did not care for me. I was a reminder that my mother had a mate before him. He was not cruel to me, but there was an obvious difference between how he treated me and how he treated his own two sons. Over time, my mother also transferred more of her affection to my brothers to keep the peace."

"Oh, honey." Ellis sat up and cupped my face. "I'm really sorry."

I shrugged. "I understood why she did it."

"Sure, but understanding and accepting it are two different things," Ellis said.

"I love my mother, Ellis. Very much."

"I know you do," Ellis said. "But it doesn't mean you have to pretend you're not angry or sad that she chose her new husband and kids over you. It's okay to feel angry or jealous."

"Were you jealous of your sister?" I said.

She hesitated. "Yes. I loved her but was jealous that my parents loved her more than me. Even if it was my fault."

"It was not your fault," I said.

"Just like it isn't your fault that your mother likes your brothers better," she said.

I paused before smiling at her. "You are my clever sadora, are you not?"

She shrugged. "Clever or maybe just an expert on ways that parents can fuck you up."

She laid back down with her head against my chest. "Do you think it's why you don't want kids, Galan? You're worried you'll mess them up like your parents messed you up?"

"A little," I said. "But I also enjoy my life the way it is. I have never felt the urge for children of my own."

"Me either," Ellis said.

"Not even with a human male?" I could hear the tightness in my voice. Even thinking of Ellis being with someone other than me was upsetting.

"No," she said. "Not that it matters now. Unless I can

convince the judge that I didn't steal the juice, I'll be in prison for the rest of my life. Not much chance of getting married or having babies in prison."

She smiled up at me, but I could hear the anxiety in her voice and see it on her face. My vertex was buzzing again, but I ignored it.

"Why did you steal the juice?" I said.

"I didn't. Cheryl, remember?"

I didn't reply, and her teasing smile faded. She traced a path down my chest with the tip of her finger. "I traded juice on the black market."

I suspected as much and hated that she'd been forced to break the law.

"Are you upset with me?" she said.

"No," I said.

She scanned my face. "I did it because I had no way else to survive. I wasn't like your dad. I didn't have a gambling problem or a drinking or drug problem. I was homeless and starving and -"

"Shh, my sadora, I know," I said. "I am not upset with you."

"Me and another girl, Bailey, worked together. She loved having sex with the Draax, so I had the translators implanted, and I would do the negotiating for the juice, and Bailey would sleep with them. We split the profits even. But Bailey did a job for another guy – a really bad guy – and when it went wrong, he blamed Bailey and beat the crap out of her. She was dying, so I used the juice I had promised to a guy named Richie Bulchanini to save Bailey's life."

"That was kind of you," I said.

"After Bailey healed, she split for her parents' place, but I couldn't return to mine, even though Richie had put a marker on us for the juice. I'd been gone seven years, and my parents had never once tried to find me. They were happy I left."

I rubbed her back as she stared up at the ceiling. "I needed a lot of juice, and I needed it fast, but with Bailey gone, I had nothing to trade for the juice. I knew I might get lucky and find a Draax ship delivering juice at the docking bay. Your ship was there. I tried to steal the juice... you know the rest."

I should have been admonishing her for breaking the law. Instead, I was thanking Krono she had. If she hadn't, I would never have met her, and she would have died. Panic shot through me at the thought of losing her, and my tail thumped hard against the bed.

"What's wrong?" she said.

"Nothing."

"Your tail says something is wrong."

I turned to my side to face her, pulling her in even closer and holding her tight. "Nothing is wrong, sweet sadora. I am only -"

The door to my apartment opened and slammed shut. "Galan, are you in here?"

Quill's voice filled the apartment, and Ellis stared wide-eyed at me. "Shit."

"Stay here," I said in a low voice as I climbed out of bed and quickly dressed.

"Galan? I hologrammed you, but you did not answer. Krey said you retired to your apartment after training. Are you here?"

"I am here." I left my bedroom, shutting the door behind me and smiling at Quill. "What is wrong?"

"Nothing." Quill sat down on the couch, and with a quick

look at the bedroom, I joined him. He studied me. "Were you sleeping?"

"A short nap," I said.

"That is odd. Krey said you were injured in training today. Do you need more juice?"

"No. Just tired. Not as young as I once was," I said.

Quill bellowed laughter before clapping me on the shoulder. "You and me both. Jota had both Sabrina and me awake for most of the night. He was a real groden last night. And Jovie was as wild as a lokena this morning."

"And yet I have never seen you happier. Being a father agrees with you."

"It does," Quill said. "How are you? We have not spoken much lately."

"You are busy with your family," I said.

Guilt crossed his face. "I am sorry, Galan. I am failing you and Krey."

"What?" I said. "You are not failing us. You are a king and have a mate, a newborn, and a toddler. We know your life has changed significantly in the last few years."

"But you and Krey remain single," Quill said. "I wish for you to have what I have, Galan, minus the children, of course."

I laughed. "The odds of me ever finding a mate are slim. You know that, Quill. Most females are not eager to leave their planet. And with the war going on and our ability to travel to Earth gone, my chances drop to zero."

"We received word an hour ago that Emira and Cillade have declared a temporary peace treaty."

"For how long?" I glanced at the bedroom again and willed my tail to stay completely still, but adrenaline had already started to pump through me.

"Only a day," Quill said. "It is the Emiran's Celebration of Athos, and the Cillades agreed to the temporary treaty so the Emirans could engage in their rituals. Teo suggested that Laos and Henden take the thief back to Earth while the peace treaty is on."

"No." This time, there was no stopping my tail from flicking and thumping. "It is too dangerous."

"They could return the thief to Earth and be back on Draax with a few hours to spare," Quill said.

"Unless something goes wrong. A ship malfunction or a delay in leaving the docking bay on Earth. At best, Henden and Laos would be trapped on Earth like Neani and Venta are. At worst, they would be caught in the Emira and Cillade war. Is that what you want, Quill? To put them in danger? Laos and Henden are two of my best men."

"I am aware of that." Quill's voice was calm. "But I wonder if your concern is for Henden and Laos or the little thief?"

I glanced at my bedroom again. "What is that supposed to mean?"

"I know you are friends with her," Quill said. "Even as distracted as I am, it has not escaped me that you sit with her in the dining hall and walk in the garden with her on several occasions."

"So what?" My voice was defensive. "It is not a crime to befriend the females, Quill."

"No, it is not," Quill said. "But this female is not like the others, no matter how much you might wish she was. She is a thief who must return to Earth and answer for her crime. It would not be wise to grow attached to her."

"Grow attached to her? This is sage advice coming from a Draax who fell in love with a woman who was not his mate,"

I said and immediately winced. "I am sorry, my king. Forgive me. What I said was beyond reproach, and I -"

Quill waved off my apology. "You know that I love you as a brother, Galan."

"I know. I feel the same," I said.

"Be careful with the little thief. She may seem kind and even seem to care about you, but remember that she is also desperate. She behaves now only because we have given her no choice. If she had the opportunity, she would leave this castle and you without a second thought."

"You do not know her the way I do, Quill."

"I suppose not." Quill squeezed my shoulder. "But trusting her is a mistake, Galan."

"Will you do what Teo asks and put Laos and Henden's lives in danger?" I said.

He shook his head. "I will not. I told Teo it was too risky. Neani and Venta will remain on Earth, and the little thief will remain here until the war ends."

After a moment, Quill stood. "Come, old friend. Join me for a walk in the garden."

I didn't want to. I wanted to return to Ellis and soothe and comfort her. She would have heard our conversation, and I needed to reassure her that I trusted her. But I could not refuse my king's request, so I nodded and stood. "I would like that, Quill."

CHAPTER 17

Ellis

"Ellis! Ellis, can you open the door?"

If I'd been asleep, I would never have heard the soft knocking or the low voice. But I wasn't asleep despite it being almost two in the morning. I couldn't sleep. Not after what I'd heard Galan and the king talking about.

I'd dressed and crept back to my room as soon as Galan left with the king. Part of me assumed Galan would join me when he was finished, but as the hours ticked by and he didn't show, I'd given up and gone to bed.

I couldn't sleep, though. Not after listening to Galan's conversation with the king. I'd dodged a huge bullet with this whole peace treaty thing, and it served to remind me that my time here was fleeting, and I needed to figure out how the fuck I was going to escape.

I suspected Galan hadn't joined me tonight because he believed I was angry and upset that he didn't trust me. But it wasn't that I thought Galan didn't trust me. I knew he did.

That was the problem. He shouldn't have trusted me. Not one bit. And it was killing me that he did.

Killing me that I was lying to the man I loved.

"Ellis? Are you awake? Please open the door."

I slid out of bed and padded across the apartment to open the door. Inara stepped inside, and I closed the door before turning on the kitchen light. "Inara, what's wrong?"

Her face was blotchy, her nose was swollen, and her fingers were ice cold when she grabbed my hands. "Ellis, something bad has happened."

"What?" I said. "Is it Candy or Roden or -"

"No," she said. "No, they're fine. It's my parents. They've been arrested for selling meth."

"Shit," I said. "When did you find out?"

"A few hours ago. Wendy messaged me. They raided our house, Ellis. Wendy was so scared. They put my parents in handcuffs and took them to prison and called social services for Wendy."

"Okay, it'll be all right," I said. "At least she's safe and -"

"No!" Inara clutched at me with her cold hands. "She isn't safe. Social services called my uncle. Because I'm here, he's the next of kin, so they called him, and he-he took her."

"Fuck," I said.

Inara started to cry again, and I led her to the table and made her sit down before grabbing some tissue. She blew her nose and wiped at her cheeks. "He has her at his place, and Wendy's so scared. He told her that she has to do what he says and that in a few days, she'll meet some very special friends of his and stay with them for a while."

"Oh, Jesus." My heart kicked up a notch, and the adrenaline surging through my veins made my head throb.

"He's going to sell her for juice," Inara said. "I know he is."

"Okay, it's all right," I said. "The Draax won't want her. She's too young and -"

"He's not selling her to the Draax," Inara said. "He's selling her to some human men who will give him juice for her."

"How do you know that?" I said.

"Wendy saw him hologramming with the men. She's freaking out. She hologrammed me, and she was crying and scared." Tears dripped down Inara's face. "I told her to call the police, but then my uncle – he showed up, and he grabbed her phone and told me to mind my own fucking business. I told him I was calling the cops, and he said to go ahead. That the police wouldn't bother even to show up. Then he ended the hologram, and I haven't been able to get a hold of her since. It just keeps ringing. He probably took her PAR phone."

"Did you contact the police?" I said.

"Yes," she said. "They took my information, and I gave them my uncle's address. They said they'd look into it, but the woman on the phone was barely interested and ..."

I sighed. "You're a lower, and they don't fucking care about us lowers."

"They don't," Inara whispered before bursting into fresh sobs. "I don't know what to do, Ellis."

"We can talk to Sabrina," I said. "Maybe she can talk to the king and -"

"And what?" Inara said. "They wouldn't let Tasha leave to see her dying grandmother, remember?"

"Yeah, but your sister is in danger. Plus, a temporary peace treaty is happening between Emira and Cillade right now, so there's a window to get to Earth. Maybe they'll let you go home."

Inara laughed bitterly. "They won't. The king won't risk his men to take me home."

"But if you tell them about your sister -"

"They won't care," Inara said. "Why would they? I'm just an employee."

I rubbed my forehead. I wanted to tell her she was wrong, but the truth was – I didn't believe that Quill would allow her to leave. Not if it put his men at risk.

"I don't know what to do," Inara whispered. "They're going to hurt her and…"

She swallowed convulsively, her face so pale that I thought she might pass out on me.

I stared at my arm before taking a deep breath. Fuck me.

"She's going to be okay," I said.

"She won't be," Inara said.

"She will. We're going to rescue her," I said.

Inara stared at me with her mouth open. "What? How?"

"I have access to the docking bay," I said. "We'll steal a ship at dawn and fly to Earth. Easy peasy."

"Have you lost your mind? We have tracking chips in our arms, and you can't fly a Draax ship."

"I've flown the vroha battleships before," I said.

"In a flight simulator with a ten-year-old," Inara said.

"So? It's basically the same thing," I said. "Look, these things practically fly themselves. All I have to do is fly it out of the Draax atmosphere. Once we're in space, I can program in the Earth's coordinates and let autopilot take over."

"What about the tracking chips?" Inara said.

I stood and opened a kitchen drawer, taking out a sharp knife. I pressed it against my skin and, ignoring Inara's horrified gasp, sliced the flesh open above the tracking chip. Grimacing, biting back my instinct to shout a string of curses at the sharp pain, I pulled the chip out and set it on the counter as Inara rushed over and clamped a dish towel around my bleeding arm.

"Jesus, Ellis, what the hell?"

"It's fine," I said. "I'll drink a few bottles of juice and be healed in no time. Do you remember where they injected you?"

She nodded, and in less than five minutes, her tracking chip was out, and she had a matching dish towel tied around her arm.

"This isn't going to work," Inara said. "There's no way we can steal a ship without them noticing."

"The first workers don't show up at the bay until seven," I said. "We leave at dawn, and we're gone two hours before they even know a ship is missing. The king won't send anyone after us because of the war."

"Ellis, we'll be in so much trouble," Inara said.

"Only if we get caught."

"I can't ask you to do this."

"You're not asking, I'm volunteering," I said. "I want to help save your sister, Inara. Let me."

For once, I wasn't lying. I couldn't save my sister, but I sure as hell could save Inara's.

"Ellis, are you sure?" Inara said.

"Yes," I said. "Meet me at the docking bay in a few hours, and we'll leave. But you know you'll have to go into hiding with Wendy, right? You'll be imprisoned for breaking your work contract with the Draax."

"I know," Inara said. "I don't care. Wendy is the only thing that matters."

"Then let's get the fuck off this planet and save her life."

Galan

"Galan?"

I lowered my sword and bowed to Laos before turning around. A Draax whose name I didn't know was standing in the doorway of the training room.

"What is it?" I sheathed my sword.

"Melu needs to speak with you immediately," the Draax said.

"Keep training," I said to the recruits, who had all stopped their swordplay to stare at the Draax. "I will return shortly."

I glanced at Krey, who sheathed his sword and followed me out of the training room. We made our way quickly to the docking bay without speaking. The bay was dead silent. The Draax who worked there had gathered in small groups and studied Melu without speaking. Melu was pacing back and forth near the landing pad, one hand clenched into a fist, the other holding a wrinkled piece of paper. We drew closer, and Krey dodged to the right when Melu's tail almost whipped him across the face.

"Melu, what is it?" I said.

He turned, the scowl on his face making his anger more than evident. "You said I could trust her, Galan. You swore she would behave."

My stomach clenched. "What did Ellis do?"

"What did she do?" Melu snarled at me. "Your little pet thief stole my fucking ship!"

I staggered back as Krey grunted in surprise beside me. I stared blankly at Melu as Krey said, "She could not have stolen a ship, Melu."

"She did!" he roared.

"She has a tracking chip in her," I said. "If she leaves the castle, my vertex -"

"This tracking chip?" Melu threw the chip at me. It bounced off my chest, and I caught it before it fell to the floor. I stared at the blood-stained chip, my guts churning as Melu waved a piece of paper at me. "She left you a note."

I took the paper from him, reading the three words with numb shock.

I'm sorry, Galan.

"Where did you find the tracking chip and the note?" Krey said.

"In the spot where my fucking ship should have been," Melu said.

"We don't know it was her," I said. "Someone could have taken the chip from her arm and -"

"Have you gone mad?" Melu said. "Or are you just so horny for the little thief that you have lost all of your common sense?"

Krey shoved Melu back. "Watch your tongue, Melu. Galan is the head of the king's guard, and you will show him the respect he deserves."

Melu glared at him, his chest heaving, and Krey stared coolly at him before placing one hand on the handle of his sword. "Do you wish to settle this with swords?"

"Krey, enough." I put my hand on his arm. "Do not -"

"Galan!"

Krono. I blew out my breath before turning. "What is it, Teo?"

"Quill wants to see you."

I glanced at Melu. "You told the king already?"

"Of course I told the king!" Melu snapped. "She stole a ship, Galan."

"Come, Galan," Teo said. "You as well, Melu."

The three of us followed Teo to the council room. Quill sat at the end of the table, and my stomach dropped when I didn't see Sabrina. My hope that our queen would convince our king to show mercy on Ellis died an immediate death.

"My king." Melu bowed, as did Krey and I.

Teo sat next to Quill, and Quill pointed to the other chairs. "Sit down, all of you."

There was a knock on the door, and Luka stuck his head into the room. "Teo? May I speak with you?"

"Later, Luka," Teo said.

"It is urgent," Luka said.

"Go, Teo," Quill said.

Teo heaved himself to his feet and left the room, closing the door behind him.

Quill studied me silently for a moment. "Has Melu told you what she did?"

"Yes," I said.

"I told you not to trust her," Quill said.

"She must have had a good reason," I said. "We must use the ship's tracking chip to go after her. She cannot fly a Draax ship, and the chances that she has crashed are high, my king. She could be injured or -"

"She removed the ship's tracking," Melu said. "And she can fly a vroha."

"How do you know that?" I said.

"Uzel told me she has been practicing with the flight simulator," Melu said. "She pretended to play with the pink haired human's child to gain access to the simulator."

I rubbed my forehead. "It is very different using a simulator and flying an actual ship."

"Not that different," Krey said.

I glanced at him, and he shrugged. "It is not. Sorry, Galan. She just needed to get it out of our atmosphere, and then she could have programmed the ship to fly to Earth."

"Krono," Melu said. "I knew we should not have trusted her. I knew the minute she had the chance, she would try to escape."

"She must have had a reason," I repeated.

"What I want to know," Krey said, "is how she knew there was a temporary peace treaty until this evening between Emira and Cillade. Very few Draax knew, and the humans certainly did not."

Melu glared at me. "Did you tell her, Galan?"

"No," I said.

I could almost feel my skin darkening. I hadn't told Ellis, but she had overheard my conversation with Quill last night. I knew she did. After our walk in the garden, Quill had invited me back to his quarters. I'd spent the evening with him, Sabrina, and their young ones. When I returned to my apartment, Ellis was gone. I'd wanted to go to her but decided to give her space. At the time, I believed she was questioning what Quill had said about me not trusting her, and I planned on reassuring her tonight that she had nothing to worry about.

"Then how in Krono's name did she find out," Melu said.

"I spoke with Galan about the peace treaty last night in his apartment," Quill said. "The thief was in his bedroom and, no doubt, heard us speak of it."

My tail thumped against the chair, and I looked away from Quill as Krey said, "My king, Galan would not sleep with the thief. He knows to do so would be foolish and unwise."

Quill sighed. "Neither you nor Galan has ever been able to lie for shit, Krey."

I winched. Quill rarely used Earth's curse words unless he was really angry.

"Galan is not -"

"Krey, stop," I said before gazing at Quill. "Yes, she was in my room, my king."

"Krono, have you gone mad?" Melu said. "What were you thinking, Galan? You should never have -"

Teo opened the door and stepped back into the room. "My king, we have another issue."

"What is it?"

"Another human is missing."

"For Krono's sake," Quill said. "Who?"

"Her name is Inara."

Melu's face went a pale green, and his entire body shuddered. "What did you say?"

"Inara is missing. We believe the thief took her."

"She kidnapped Inara?" Melu's throat worked as his face went from the pale green to the dark green of the beluca tree. He turned to me. "I will kill the little thief if she hurts Inara."

Krey rested his hand on Melu's arm. "Melu, calm down. Ellis may be a thief, but she would not hurt Inara. They are friends."

"I will kill her," Melu repeated, his gaze never leaving mine. "Do you hear me, Galan?"

"I hear you," I said. "But go anywhere near Ellis, and the last thing you see will be my sword as it cuts off your head."

Melu bared his teeth at me. "You think you can beat me,

you puny froden? I will slice off your limbs and bathe in your
_"

"Enough!" Quill said. "Melu, hold your tongue."

Melu shut his mouth with a snap, his body tense like
overstrung wire and his jaw twitching as he ground his teeth
together.

"Inara and Ellis are friends," I said. "If Inara is with her, it
is not because Ellis forced her to go. She would have gone of
her own free will. I am sure of it."

"Just like you were sure the thief would not steal my
ship?" Melu said.

"Melu," Quill said. "Enough. I know you are upset and
worried about your female, but now is not the time."

"Inara is not my female," Melu snarled.

Quill raised one eyebrow at him, and Melu bowed his
head. "Forgive my tone, my king."

"When did they leave?" Quill said.

"We are not certain. The ship was gone when the docking
bay opened at seven," Melu said.

"Did you return to the thief after you left my quarters last
night?" Quill asked me.

I shook my head no.

Quill glanced at his vertex. "It is just after seven. If we
assume they left when keo rose, they have been gone for only
a few hours. It will take them -"

He stopped when there was a knock on the door.
"Come in."

Bitta stepped into the room and bowed. "My king, forgive
the interruption."

"What is it, Bitta?" Quill said.

"The Emirans have contacted us. They have one of our
ships and, apparently, two of our humans."

CHAPTER 18

Ellis

"This is so bad, Ellis."

"It's fine." I popped up out of the ship's floor hatch. "Hand me that screwdriver."

Inara handed it to me before peering into the belly of the ship. "I thought this ship was repaired."

"I thought so, too." I unscrewed the access panel to the flux overflow. "I'm gonna kill Uzel the next time I see him."

Not that I would ever see him again. Either I'd get the ship fixed, and we'd haul ass to Earth, or we'd float around in space until the war started up again and we were blown to smithereens by the Emirans or the Cillades.

"Can you fix it?" Inara said.

"Yeah."

"Can you?"

"Maybe."

"Oh shit," Inara said.

"I can fix it, don't worry. I just need to -"

The ship jerked forward, and I went with it, slamming my head into an overhead pipe so hard that bright flashing stars immediately crossed my vision. A little lightheaded, I staggered up the short ladder and heaved myself onto the ship's floor.

Inara was sprawled out on the floor, and she sat up. "You're bleeding!"

I touched my scalp just above my right temple, wincing a little. My fingers came away bloody, and I closed the hatch before locking it. "It's okay."

"It's bleeding a lot." Inara opened up her small suitcase and grabbed a t-shirt before using it to stem blood flow. "You might have a concussion."

"It's a head injury. They bleed a lot," I said.

"We should have brought some juice with us," Inara said.

Yeah, we should have. I should have stolen a bunch of juice. Hell, just the amount of juice I had in my fridge in my apartment would have set me up for life on Earth. I could have lived on some beach and never had another care in the world.

So, why didn't you take the juice?

Because it was bad enough betraying and lying to Galan, I couldn't steal from him, too.

Yeah, well, your sudden case of conscience is going to make us starve.

Probably. But honestly, starving to death didn't seem that big of a deal. Not if it meant I wouldn't have to face a lifetime alone without Galan.

I swallowed down the bile that was rising in my throat. I had made my choice, and I needed to live with it. I was being all mushy and stupid for nothing anyway. The second the war ended, I would never see Galan again. Leaving with Inara meant that at least I wouldn't die in prison.

No, you'll die on the street.

The ship jerked again, sending both Inara and me flying forward. We staggered to our feet, and Inara followed me to the cockpit. She sank into the co-pilot seat with a soft gasp as she stared out the window. "What is that?"

"A ship," I said.

The ship in question was massive and fast approaching. Or rather, we were fast approaching it.

I swallowed hard as our ship was pulled forward with another teeth-rattling jolt.

"Why does the ship keep doing that?" Inara clung to the arms of her chair.

"I think that ship," I pointed to the enormous ship, "is using a tractor beam to pull us in."

"Do you think it's the Emirans or the Cillades?" Inara said.

"I have no idea."

"What do we do?" Inara said as the other ship grew closer. "Should we hide?"

"Our ship is so small that they'll find us in no time," I said. "How are you at hand-to-hand combat?"

"Not funny," Inara said as the alien ship's cargo hold opened, and we were pulled inside. The massive doors closed behind us with a skull-rattling thud. After a few minutes, a door large enough for a havoc cruiser to go through slid open in front of us, and a half dozen aliens stepped into the cargo hold.

"Emirans," Inara said.

"How do you know?" I studied the blood red aliens in front of us. They were over eight feet tall with reptile skin.

Their bald skulls gleamed in the light, and their yellow eyes had green pupils. Their limbs were long and skinny, and their drab brown robes hung on their skeletal frames.

They had three long digits on each hand topped with blunt yellow nails, and it was impossible to tell whether they were male or female.

"I took the alien species elective course in high school," Inara said. "I remembered the Emirans because they look so…"

"Weird?" I said.

"Yeah. Plus, they can spontaneously change their gender if needed."

"You're kidding me?"

"Nope."

"Do they have a good relationship with the Draax?" I asked.

"They do. I think."

"You think, or you know?" I said.

Inara gripped my hand as the aliens approached the ship. "Is the ship door locked?"

"We can't stay in here forever," I said. "If I don't open the cargo door, they'll force it open eventually."

I took a deep breath and pushed the button to open the cargo hold. "C'mon, let's go introduce ourselves."

Holding hands, Inara and I walked to the cargo hold. The door slid open, and we stepped into the hold. Inara gripped my hand so tightly I'd lost all feeling, but I didn't object as we stared silently at the aliens gathered in the hold.

"Hi," I said. "I'm Ellis, and this is Inara. Nice to meet you."

The aliens stared at each other before one stepped forward. It spoke, and Inara and I glanced at each other.

"You hear gibberish, yeah?" I said.

Inara nodded.

I stared at the alien and shook my head before shrugging. "We don't understand. Sorry."

"They won't understand you either," Inara said.

"Yeah, I know. But what else -"

"Where are your Draax mates, human females?" The alien was suddenly perfectly understandable.

"Hey! You speak English," I said to the alien. "Cool. I'm Ellis, and this is Inara. Um, what's your name?"

It would have raised eyebrows at me if it had any. Instead, in a *dear God, why is she such an idiot*, tone, it said, "I have switched to speaking Draax so that you may understand me. The human language is too primitive to bother learning."

"Right," I said. "So, uh, it's super nice to meet you." I took a deep breath and stepped forward, holding out my hand.

The alien skittered back from my hand, and the others made low gasps of disgust. One produced a glass bottle from its robe and sprayed the air with medicinal smelling liquid.

I stepped back toward Inara as the alien said. "Please do not touch us, humans. We have no idea where you have been. You are probably riddled with bugs."

"Okay," I said. "That seems like an overreaction, but we'll move past that. Our ship has broken down. I don't suppose you have any spare Draax ship parts lying around?"

"Where are your Draax mates?" The alien said.

"We don't have mates," Inara said.

"They are lying." A second alien stepped forward. "The Draax take the human females for mates and nothing more."

"Yeah, well, times change, buddy," I said.

"What do we do with them, Gwandole?" the second alien said.

Gwandole tapped his middle digit against his chest. "We will bring them onto our ship."

The gasps of horror from the others were almost comical.

"Gwandole, no!" The second Emiran said. "Who knows what infections and diseases they carry. Do you want the whole ship infected?"

"We're not infected with anything," I said. "Geez, relax, would you?"

Gwandole looked us over, his red, scaly skin wrinkling with disgust. "We will place them in a secure room while we wait for the Draax to arrive and thoroughly disinfect the area when they are gone."

"Oh, hey, no need to get the Draax involved," I said. "If you could just loan me some parts for our ship or maybe even have one of your guys drop us off on Earth, we'd appreciate it."

Gwandole stepped back. "Follow us, humans, and do not touch anything."

***

"Oh, c'mon," I said, "I'm not even touching that side of the glass."

I rolled my eyes as the Emira sprayed more yellow liquid on the glass that separated us and wiped it clean. He stared at me, and I smiled before deliberately licking a path along the glass.

He squealed in disgust and quickly sprayed the glass again as I rolled my eyes and walked away.

"Oh my God, they act like we're the grossest things they've ever seen," I said.

"Maybe we are," Inara said. She was sitting on the floor of

the empty room the Emira had herded us into, wiping down walls and surfaces as we passed with disinfectant spray like we were infected with the plague.

She wiped at the tears on her face, and I slid down the wall to sit on the floor next to her, slinging my arm around her shoulder. "It'll be okay, honey."

"It won't be," she whispered. "My uncle will sell my sister, and I won't be able to do anything to stop it because I'll be in prison for breaking my work contract with the Draax."

"You won't," I said. "When the Draax get here, I'll tell them I was trying to escape, and I convinced you to go with me rather than ask the Draax for help with your sister."

"I won't lie and get you in even more trouble," Inara said. "You wouldn't have tried to escape if it wasn't for me and Wendy."

"I would have," I said.

"Be honest with me," Inara said.

I opened my mouth to lie and instead said, "I planned to escape, but I kept putting it off."

"Why?" Inara said.

"Galan. I kind of, maybe, am in love with him."

Inara's mouth dropped open. "You're in love with Galan?"

"I think so. I've never been in love before, but I'm acting stupid about him. We've been sleeping together for a while now."

"Holy shit," Inara said. "Why didn't you tell me?"

"Because he could get in major trouble for sleeping with me," I said. "I'm a thief who's technically a prisoner of the king, and he's the head of the king's guard. He shouldn't have been sleeping with me, but we were attracted to each other and then…"

"Then?"

"Then I fell in love with him," I said. Tears were stinging the backs of my eyes, and my throat was burning. "Which is fucking stupid because he doesn't love me, and I'll be going to prison where I'll die, and he'll find another woman to spend the rest of his life with and never once think about me again. I had this plan to escape, you know? I was going to steal supplies, leave the castle, and hide on the Draax planet, but I... I kept not doing it. I told myself it was because the war was still going on and I had plenty of time to escape, but it was because I didn't want to leave Galan. I waited because the thought of never seeing Galan again killed me."

I glanced at her. "That's love, right? When the thought of not being with a person makes you wish you were dead instead?"

"I think so," Inara said. She touched my blood-soaked hair. "Why did you leave with me then?"

"Because you needed my help. Because I failed my sister, and I didn't want you to feel like you failed yours. Because I wanted to save Wendy."

Tears dripped down Inara's face. "Oh, honey. I'm so sorry."

"Don't be," I said. "I wanted to help you and Wendy, and I don't regret it. I do regret believing Uzel when he said the goddamn ship was repaired."

Inara hiccupped laughter before resting her forehead against mine. "I'm telling the Draax the truth, Ellis."

"No, you're not," I said. "You're going to tell them it was my idea."

"I won't do it," Inara said.

"Oh my God, it doesn't matter," I said. "I'm going to prison no matter what, remember? Think about your sister. If you play dumb and act like you really did think this was your best and only option, then the Draax will probably be cool with you tagging along with me. Plus, they might even be willing to figure out some way to help your sister."

"How?" Inara said.

"Maybe they'll talk to the cops on your behalf, get them to take your sister away from your uncle. The cops will be more inclined to help the Draax than they are us lowers."

"The Draax won't help me," Inara said.

"They might." I squeezed her hand. "Especially if you offer to bang one of them and pop out a baby."

Inara stared at me. "Shit."

"I know it's not ideal, but -"

"I don't care. If it's the only way to save Wendy, I'll do it."

"Okay." I squeezed her hand again. "So, we have a plan, right? I'll take the blame, and you play dumb. Once you're back on the Draax planet, you find the Draax you're most attracted to and offer to have his baby in exchange for helping your sister. Easy peasy."

"Easy peasy," Inara said. "Except for the part where you go to prison for life."

Her eyes watered, and I tried to smile at her. "Hey, it's all right. Maybe prison isn't as bad as everyone says it is."

Inara started to cry, and I wiped roughly at her cheeks. "Don't cry, honey."

"I'm so sorry, Ellis."

"It's not your fault. I'm the one who stole the juice. And the ship... remember that. This is all my fault, Inara. I was escaping and suggested you come with me to save your sister. You were upset and worried about Wendy and not thinking straight. Play that helpless girl card like your life depends on it, okay?"

"Yeah, okay," Inara whispered.

"You can't tell anyone about me and Galan. They'll send me to Draax prison until the war ends, so I won't be sleeping with him anymore, but you have to stay quiet about Galan. Promise me. If the king finds out he was sleeping with me..."

"I promise I won't say anything to anyone," Inara said.

We sat silently for a few minutes before Inara said, "What if the Draax tell the Emirans they don't want us back?"

"They won't. We're valuable to them, remember? Any moment now, probably Krey and Adrix will come walking through that door and -"

The door slid open, and Inara and I scrambled to our feet. We stared at the two Draax who walked into the room. Well, I was half-right about who they'd send.

The fear I'd been hiding from Inara about what could happen to us faded when I saw Galan. I wanted to rush to him, wanted to fling my arms around him and tell him I loved him and that I was sorry I ran, but I stayed where I was. The usual warmth on Galan's face when he looked at me was gone, replaced by the dark scowl of a stranger. There was a coldness in his copper eyes that I'd never seen before, and my hope that he might care for me, that I hadn't been just a female for him to fuck, disappeared.

Galan wasn't just pissed at me. He hated me.

CHAPTER 19

Galan

"Calm yourself, Galan," Krey murmured as we followed the Emirans down the corridor of their ship.

"I am perfectly calm," I said.

"Are you?"

"She lied to me. I trusted her, and she lied to me, betrayed me, and made me look like a froden," I said.

My body was vibrating with anger. I had automatically defended her to the others in the council room, but in the time it took to get to the Emiran's ship, my worry and belief that there had to be another reason she left had faded. Anger took its place. Ellis had lied to me, and as much as I wanted to, I couldn't think of a single reason why she had left other than to escape her fate.

Can you blame her? You know what will happen if she stays. If she is taken to Earth –

I shoved my inner voice out of my head. I did not want to

feel sympathy for her. I wanted her to have trusted me enough to ask for my help.

Krey sighed. "I wish she was the person you believed her to be, Galan."

"So do I," I said. "But she is not."

The Emirans stopped at a door, and Gwandole pushed a code into the panel next to the door. It slid open, and Krey and I stepped into the room. Despite my anger with her, relief swept through me when I saw Ellis standing next to Inara. Blood matted her blonde hair to her head, but she was alive.

I schooled my features and stared silently at her. My relief at her safety was disappearing, allowing the anger, betrayal, and confusion to return. My rapidly shifting emotions were playing more havoc with my stomach than space sickness did.

I loved the little human and hoped she felt something for me. To realize that she didn't tore at my insides.

I waited for her to say something sarcastic like she always did, but the silence dragged on. She dropped her gaze to her feet, and my stomach clenched. I could see a large wound just above her right temple, her scalp torn wide and blood still oozing from it.

"Did the Emirans do that?" Krey pointed to her head.

"No." She glanced at me. "I tripped and banged my head on the ship."

"Do not believe a word she says, Krey," I said. "Every word that comes from her mouth is a lie."

She winced, and the hurt that crossed her face immediately made me want to take back what I had said. Instead, I said, "What do you have to say for yourself, human?"

She pressed her lips together. "I told you I was a liar."

"You did. I suppose it is my fault for not believing you."

"No," she said. "Everything that's happened is my fault. I'm sorry, Galan. I didn't mean to hurt you."

"You did not," I said. "You mean nothing to me, human."

Her face went white, and regret poured through me. "Human, I -"

"Don't worry about it," she said dully. "I get it."

The other female, Inara, put her arm around Ellis's shoulders. "Ellis only did this to -"

"Be quiet, Inara," Ellis said.

"Ellis -"

"I said be quiet." A bit of colour had returned to Ellis's face, and she gave the other female a pointed look. "Don't say anything else."

"Neither of you say anything," Krey said. "Not until we are back on our ship. Move."

They followed Krey out of the room, Ellis refusing to look at me as she passed. The Emirans gave them a wide berth, and while I usually was amused by the Emiran's queasiness about humans, I found nothing funny in the situation this time.

We walked in silence to the docking bay of the Emiran's ship. Krey turned to Gwandole. "Thank you for rescuing our females. Once your war with the Cillades ends -"

Every Emiran in the room spat on the floor at the mere mention of the Cillades. I rolled my eyes, and Krey wiped some stray spittle from his pants before opening the cargo hold of our ship. "When the war ends, we will send men to repair our broken ship."

"Wait," Gwandole said when Krey tried to usher Ellis and

Inara onto our ship. "There is still the matter of our payment."

"Payment?" I raised my eyebrows at Gwandole. "For what?"

"For rescuing your females. For storing your broken ship," Gwandole said. "We should receive something in return, should we not?"

"You have received plenty from us," Krey said. "How often have we assisted you in your silly wars with the Cillades?"

The Emirans spat in disgust, and Krey gave Gwandole a tight grin. "No doubt, our assistance will be required again in this war."

Gwandole scowled, the middle digit on his right hand tapping away at his chest. "We will take one of the females as payment."

"Like Krono you will," I said, automatically stepping in front of Ellis.

"You have no use for them," Krey said.

"Not true," Gwandole said. "The human females sell for a hefty price in the Peleus system. Consider the price we will receive for her as payment for storing your ship."

He studied Inara and Ellis before pointing to Inara. "We will take the big one."

Four Emirans stepped toward her, and Krey's tail lashed out, wrapping around Inara's waist and tugging her back until she was pressed against him. His arm joined his tail around her waist in a possessive grip, and his other hand dropped to the handle of his sword.

"The female belongs to me. Touch her, and you'll regret it." His voice was soft, but I could already hear the bloodlust in it. The only thing Krey loved more than fighting was fucking.

Gwandole tapped at his chest again. "There are only two of you and," he glanced around the docking bay, "many of us. Surely one little female is not worth this quarrel."

"She belongs to me," Krey said, "and you cannot have her."

"You are outnumbered," Gwandole said.

I rested my hand on my sword. "There has been peace between us for many years. Will you destroy that over a woman and a broken ship?"

"Do you think you can defeat all of us?" Gwandole said.

"Yes." Krey's voice didn't waver. "Try to take my female, Gwandole, and your ears will ring with the screams of your dying brothers."

Fear flickered across Gwandole's face, and he waved the others back. "Fine. Take your females, but your king will hear of your insolence toward me."

Krey smiled tightly at him before turning and walking toward our ship. His tail was still around Inara's waist, and she had no choice but to go with him, taking his hand when he held it out to her.

"It was good to see you again, Gwandole," I said.

"Hmm," he said.

I made a short bow before turning toward Ellis. "Go, Ellis."

She walked quickly up the ramp, joining Krey and Inara in the cargo hold as I bowed again before walking up the ramp and closing the hold. The door closed with a heavy thunk, and Krey backed Inara against the ship's wall.

"Are you all right, human?" His tail squeezed around her waist, and he cupped her face, rubbing his thumb along her jawline as his gaze dipped to her breasts.

"I-I'm fine," Inara whispered. "Thank you for, um, not letting them take me."

Krey rubbed his thumb over her bottom lip, his nostrils flaring when her lips parted. "You are welcome, little female."

"Krey," I said. "We must leave."

He raked a hand through his dark hair before unwrapping his tail from Inara's waist and stepping back. His erection was evident against his pants, and he reached down and adjusted his crotch without shame. A smile crossed his face when Inara's face turned red, and she pulled nervously at her hair.

"I like your hair, little female," Krey said.

"Th-thank you," Inara said.

"Krey," I said.

"I know." He walked past us, and I made a come on motion to Ellis and Inara.

They followed us out of the cargo hold, and as Krey disappeared into the cockpit, I pointed to the chairs bolted to the floor of the ship's main cabin. "Sit down."

They sat beside each other, and Inara took Ellis's hand as I joined Krey in the cockpit. I eased into the co-pilot seat, ignoring the nausea in my stomach as Krey steered the ship out of the Emiran's cargo hold and blasted into space.

I let out my breath in a soft rush. "Krono, Krey, I thought you were going to murder all of the Emirans in the cargo hold."

He grinned at me, his hands gripping the controls loosely. "It would have been too easy."

"And stupid," I said.

"The Emirans offer us nothing, and I will gut every last one of them before I give them one of our females," Krey said. "I do not know why Quill even helps them with their ridiculous wars against the Cillades."

I shrugged. "Probably because his father did before him. Plus, the Cillades are dickheads."

Krey laughed. "Look at you, using the Earth's curse words."

I didn't reply, and Krey glanced over at me. "Go and speak with her, Galan."

"I have nothing to say to her."

"Bullshit," Krey said.

I scowled at him and stood. "She lied to me."

"She did," he said.

I rubbed my forehead, my tail banging against the seat before I turned and stepped out of the cockpit. Ellis and Inara were sitting where I'd left them. Ellis stared at the floor, but Inara stood up as I approached.

"Do you have any gallberry juice? Ellis's head is still bleeding, and I think she might have a concussion."

"Not on the ship," I said. "We will give her some when we are home."

"How did the Emirans know to contact you guys?" Inara said.

"They recognized the royal seal on the ship you stole as Quill's," I said. "Ellis, we need to talk."

"So talk," she said.

I glanced at Inara, who squeezed Ellis's hand. She glanced at the cockpit, her face flushing, before she said, "I'll, um, I'll go over here."

She walked away to the far end of the room, standing near the storage lockers and staring at the side of the ship.

"Why did you do it, Ellis?" I said.

"You know why," she said.

"Look at me."

She sighed and glanced up. Her eyes were bloodshot, her

face was pale, and blood still trickled out of her scalp. "I'm sorry I lied to you, Galan. But I had to leave, okay? I won't survive a week in Earth's prison. When I heard the king talk about the temporary peace treaty, I knew it was my only chance."

"Why did you bring Inara with you?"

"Her sister is in trouble on Earth. Her uncle has her, and he's a bad guy. He's going to sell her to some other nasty men in exchange for juice. Inara told me what was happening, and I convinced her to come with me to help her sister."

"You put her life in danger," I said. "If she had spoken to Sabrina, perhaps we could have…"

"Could have what? Helped her?" Ellis said. "Yeah, right. Like you helped Tasha when her grandmother was dying?"

"That is different. It was too dangerous with the war," I said. "We could not risk it. But with the peace treaty, perhaps Quill would have been convinced to allow Inara to go home."

"That's horseshit, and you know it. I heard you and the king talking, Galan. He wouldn't send any of his men to Earth, even with the peace treaty."

I gritted my teeth. She was right, but it was still incredibly dangerous for her to drag Inara into this mess, and I told her exactly that.

"It was dangerous of you to drag Inara into this mess. Flying a simulator is different from flying an actual ship. You could have crashed it, killing you both. The Emirans could have sold you to the highest bidder instead of contacting us. Do you know how much danger you put yourself and Inara in?"

"I do now," she said. "I'm sorry, but I had to try. I can't go to prison."

"You should have talked to me," I said. "You should have

asked me to help you to convince the king that you should stay and -"

"Now, who's talking crazy." She stood up, her tiny hands clenched into fists. "If the king even knew we were fucking, hell, if he even thought for a second that you wanted him to forget that I committed a crime, I'd be in your stupid Iron Gate before either of us could even blink, and you would lose your position as head of the king's guard. Is that what you want? Your whole life destroyed over a meaningless fling with a human?"

"Is that what this is? A meaningless fling?" I said. "I mean nothing to you."

"I didn't say that," she snapped. "But even if it was something more, we're both fucked in the head to think it could have worked. We can't work, Galan."

"You were not even willing to try," I said. I was talking foolishly, but knowing Ellis didn't care enough about me even to consider a different solution hurt me to the core. She'd abandoned me without a second thought, without even asking what it would do to me with her gone.

You know she had no choice. Quill will not break the treaty to save her, and she will die in prison. You know that.

I ignored my inner voice. I wanted to stay angry, wanted to punish her for leaving me, for frightening me and hurting me.

"You do not care about anyone but yourself," I said.

"That isn't true." I could almost see the hurt radiating from her.

"It is. All you thought about was escaping your fate, which you brought on yourself. You dragged Inara into this and did not even care that she might die. You thought only of yourself. You have no family or friends who love you because you are a selfish human who is incapable of loving anyone but yourself!"

I'd gone too far. I knew that immediately. I didn't need to see the agony on Ellis's face, hear the horrified gasp from Inara, or watch the blood drain from both their faces to know that.

Sick to my stomach, ashamed beyond belief for what I said, I reached for my sweet female. "Sadora, I should not have -"

The shrill whoop of the ship's warning beacon drowned out my apology.

"Hang on!" Krey shouted.

The ship veered sharply to the right, making my stomach roll and knocking me off my feet. My tail shot out and wrapped around Ellis's waist as she was flung sideways, catching her before she slammed into the ship's side.

"Inara!" Ellis shouted as I used my tail to pull her against my body. I climbed to my feet as the ship veered to the right again.

I picked up Ellis, and she pounded on my chest with her fists. "Inara! She's hurt!"

Moving quickly, I strapped Ellis into one of the chairs and gripped her chin. "Stay here. I will get Inara."

The ship was shaking and rattling, and I grabbed at the wall for support when Krey shouted another warning. This time, the ship veered to the left, and Ellis cried out when Inara's prone body rolled across the floor.

Holding onto the wall, I moved to the back of the room and crouched beside Inara. A large bruise had flowered across her temple, and when I peeled back her eyelid, I could see nothing but the white of her eye.

I rested my hand on her chest, relief flooding through me

when I felt the beat of her heart beneath my palm and the rising of her chest.

"Is she alive?" Ellis cried, clutching the bottom of her chair as she stared frantically at me.

"Yes." I picked her up and carried her to the chair next to Ellis, propping her in the seat and buckling her in. Her body sagged sideways toward Ellis, and Ellis put her arm around her, resting Inara's head on her shoulder.

"She hit her head against that." Ellis pointed to a large metal pipe that ran along the wall. "I saw it. She hit her head, and then she just fell -"

The ship made a stomach-turning dive, nearly flinging me into Ellis's lap. I grabbed the empty seat as Ellis stared at me with frightened eyes.

"Galan! Get up here!" Krey shouted.

"Stay here. It will be all right," I said.

I staggered toward the cockpit.

"Galan!"

I turned, staring at Ellis as she returned my stare with wide, frightened eyes. "Be careful."

I nodded and opened the cockpit door, dropping into the seat next to Krey's as the cockpit door slid shut. "What is happening?"

"The Cillades are attacking us," Krey said grimly. He pushed a button on the control panel, and a panel slid open in front of me. I stared at the weapon controls as Krey made another sharp right. "Do you even remember how to fire the ship's guns?"

"Yes," I said. "But it has been many years."

"You can steer the ship, or you can fire the weapons. Your choice."

"Fire the weapons," I said.

Krey's grin was fierce and way too cheerful, considering we were most likely about to die. "Wise move, brother. I love you, but you are a shit pilot."

I wrapped my hands around the controls and gave Krey my own not-quite-sane grin. "Are you ready, brother?"

Krey nodded. "To the end, Galan."

"To the end, Krey."

CHAPTER 20

Ellis

K rey had barely set the ship down on the landing pad outside the castle's docking bay before I heard the cargo hold opening. Feet pounded on the floor, and the door to the main cabin slid open. A wild looking Melu charged through, and I squeezed the unconscious Inara a little closer.

I had survived a space battle with the Cillades, only to be murdered by my boss. Super.

I tried not to cringe when Melu ran toward us.

"Melu, I'm sorry, I…"

I trailed off, watching silently as Melu dropped to his knees before Inara and cupped her face. "Inara? Inara, can you hear me?"

"She is unconscious," Krey said. He and Galan had joined us in the main cabin.

"She needs gallberry juice," Galan said. "I messaged Sigan before we arrived and asked -"

"I am here."

Sigan hurried into the room, followed by, I swallowed hard, the king and his advisor.

He knelt next to Melu and examined the bruise on Inara's temple. "I will take her and Ellis to the infirmary."

"No," Teo said. "The thief is to be taken to the west wing."

"She is bleeding, and it is a nasty wound on her head." Sigan glanced at me. "She could have a concussion or -"

"She will either live or she will not. Either way, she will not get another drop of gallberry juice from us. Adrix," Teo turned to Adrix, who had stepped into the room, "take her to an empty room and stand guard outside of it."

"Yes, Teo," Adrix said.

"My king," Sigan said, "she needs juice."

The king turned his silver gaze toward me. My throat went dry, and goosebumps popped out all over my skin at the look on his face. If Melu didn't kill me, the king would. I was sure of it.

"Adrix," the king said, "do as Teo commands."

"Yes, my king."

"Quill," Galan said. "I know you are angry, but Ellis's injury is severe and -"

"Enough, Galan," Quill said. "Do not ask me to show mercy on her after she nearly got you and Krey killed."

"Quill, she did not mean -"

"My head isn't that bad," I said quickly. "I don't need juice."

I was lying. My head was throbbing, and I felt sick to my stomach, and in the last twenty minutes or so, my vision had gone blurry. I wasn't even sure I could stand, let alone walk, but I didn't want Galan and Quill's friendship ruined because of me. Galan didn't love me, but he was a good person. The kind of person who didn't want to see anyone suffer, even someone he now hated.

"Melu, the female needs to go to the infirmary." Sigan tugged on his arm. "You must move so that I can help her."

I let go of Inara, and Melu unbuckled her before picking her up. He cradled her in his arms. "I will carry her to the infirmary."

He and Sigan left the ship, and I didn't object when Adrix unbuckled the strap across my lap. He stepped back, unsheathing his sword and holding it at his side. "Stand up, thief."

"Adrix," Galan said, "that is not necessary."

I heaved myself to my feet. The world tilted, and a wave of dizziness washed over me. I bent over, ignoring the steady patter of blood that dripped from my head onto the floor and took a few deep breaths.

"Ellis, do you feel faint?"

"Galan, step back." The king's deep voice was right over top of me. I flinched when his hand gripped my arm and pulled me upright.

Swaying, trying not to vomit, I squinted up at the king. "I'm sorry. I didn't mean for any of this to happen. I swear I didn't mean to put Galan and Krey in danger."

"But you did," he said. "As well as Inara."

He bent until his face was directly in front of mine. His silver eyes had gone a flint grey, and my knees trembled as he studied me. "You have used my generosity toward you as an opportunity to betray and lie and nearly kill both of my brothers. Tell me why I should not simply have your head removed from your body and be done with it, little thief."

"You should do it," I said. "I deserve it."

"Ellis, be quiet," Galan said sharply.

I could hear the alarm in his voice, but I felt only an odd sense of relief that I was about to die. Galan was lost to me forever. What was there left to live for?

What looked almost like a flicker of admiration crossed the king's face before he straightened.

"She does not know what she says, Quill," Galan said. "She has a head injury that needs treating. Let Sigan give her some juice."

"Take the thief, Adrix," Quill said.

Adrix took my arm, and I stumbled after him, trying to stay on my feet as another wave of dizziness overtook me.

"HEY, SIGAN. ARE YOU HERE TO KILL ME?"

The kadana rolled his eyes and hurried across the room. "I see the head injury has not cured you of your tendency to talk like a froden."

"What does froden mean anyway?" I said as Sigan crouched in front of me.

"Fool," he said.

"Well, if the shoe fits, right?" I said. "How is Inara?"

"She is still unconscious. She has swelling of her brain."

"Oh my God," I said.

Sigan opened the bag he carried and brought out a couple of bottles of gallberry juice, the silver pen thing he'd used on my skull when I'd first arrived, and a cloth and bottle of pink tinged liquid.

"She will be fine," he said. "She is receiving gallberry serum, which should relieve the swelling."

"Should?" I said.

"Will," he said. "She will wake in a day or two and be

314

completely healed." He wrinkled his nose. "It smells like vomit in here. Have you been throwing up?"

"Yeah," I said. "A few times."

He muttered something under his breath before standing and holding out his hand. "Stand up."

"Better not," I said. "That will definitely make me vomit."

He lifted me to my feet with another mutter and carried me into the small bathroom. His footsteps echoed in the empty apartment.

I still had double vision, and I squinted at the two Sigans as he sat me down on the side of the tub. I'd lost all sense of time after Adrix had brought me here and closed the door. The apartment was small like mine but empty of furniture. I'd sat on the floor, leaned against the wall, and waited to see if I would pass out, vomit, or die.

Vomiting repeatedly, with a few possible instances of blacking out, had won the war. I felt so fucking terrible that death would probably have been more kind.

Of course, the king could still take my head. Could and probably would.

"Yay for death by beheading," I croaked out and then laughed.

"You are not being beheaded," Sigan said.

"How long have I been in here?" I said.

"Only a few hours. I would have been here sooner, but Melu was in the infirmary and nearly lost his mind when I tried to leave. It took a long time for Krey to convince Melu that Inara would not die simply because I was not in the infirmary."

"He likes her," I said.

"Yes, I believe he does." Sigan left the bathroom and returned with his supplies. "Drink this."

My hand trembled too badly to hold the bottle of juice. Sigan held it to my mouth, and I gulped down the sweet juice, breathing a sigh of relief when it helped the nausea almost immediately.

"Better?" he said.

"Yeah. I don't think I'm going to vomit again."

"Good. Drink some more. Do you have blurred vision?"

"Yes."

He frowned. "I suspected you had a concussion. You should be receiving serum."

"Hey, I appreciate that the king is giving me juice," I said.

Sigan didn't reply, and a large stone wedged itself in the pit of my stomach. "Did the king give you permission to give me juice?"

"He did not *not* give me permission," Sigan said.

I immediately pushed the bottle of juice away. "What are you doing? You need to get out of here before Adrix tells the king that you're trying to fix me up."

"I told Adrix I was here to simply say goodbye before you go to Iron Gate, not to heal you," Sigan said.

"Oh God," I moaned. "Now you're lying for me? Sigan, you gotta go, buddy."

"I will not leave you here to suffer," Sigan said. "I am a kadana, and it is my job to help those who need healing."

"Not when the king might chop your head off for it," I said. "I'm fine, okay?"

"You are not fine," Sigan said. "You need juice for your concussion, and your wound needs to be cleaned and closed. Tilt your head back."

"No," I said. "No one else is getting in trouble because of me."

"You are tiny and weak," Sigan said. "I will easily over-power you if you do not do as I say."

"You're the worst, Sigan. You know that, right?"

"Yes," he said. "Tilt your head back."

I tilted my head back and tried not to wince when Sigan poured the pink liquid over the wound in my head. It burned, and Sigan squeezed my shoulder with sympathy. He used cloth and more liquid to clean the wound and picked up the silver pen.

"Shit, no," I said. "You're not using that thing on me again. It was like my skin was on fire the last time. I'd rather have an open wound."

"The wound needs to be closed, and the turing carver will close it quickly and efficiently," Sigan said.

"I'll just drink a lot of juice instead," I said.

"I could not smuggle enough in my bag to heal you of both your concussion and the wound."

"It can just heal naturally," I said.

"If it does not become infected, you will still have a terrible scar," Sigan said. "They will not give you juice in Iron Gate, human. You will be sent there in an hour or two, and it must be healed before then."

I blew out my breath and drank the rest of the juice in the bottle before gripping the side of the tub. "Yeah, okay. Do it."

He turned the carver on, and I squeezed his hand. "Hey, Sigan?"

"Yes?"

"Thank you."

"You are welcome, Ellis."

Galan

"WHY DO YOU STOP?" I SCOWLED AT KREY AND LOWERED MY sword.

"You are not paying close enough attention," Krey said. "I have no wish to gut you."

I bared my teeth at him. "The day you beat me in swords is the day I give up my position as head of the king's guard."

Krey wiped the sweat from his face. "I see your mood has not improved."

"My mood is fine. Let us fight." I raised my sword again, biting back my urge to smack Krey with the flat side of it when he shook his head and kept his sword lowered.

"I am fine," I insisted.

"You have not been fine since she was taken to Iron Gate two days ago," Krey said.

My hand tightened around the handle of my sword. "I do not wish to speak of her."

"I know you miss her."

"So what if I do?" I said. "She is gone, and I can do nothing about it. I cannot see her, I cannot talk to her, and I cannot touch her. I can do nothing but sit and worry that she is alone, that she is afraid, that she is dying from her head injury, and -"

"Sigan healed her head injury," Krey said.

I stared at Krey. "What?"

Krey grinned at me. "Sigan healed her before she was taken to Iron Gate."

"When? How?"

"He told Adrix he wanted to say goodbye to Ellis. When Teo arranged to take her to Iron Gate a few hours later, she was healed. Sigan is denying it, of course." Krey laughed. "Ellis told Teo she had always been a quick healer and then refused to say anything else."

Some of the worry in my chest eased. Of course, it was immediately filled with an ache for my sadora that nothing could or would ever ease.

"The Cillades contacted Quill. They said they attacked us because they believed we were going to attack them. They believed the Emirans had requested our assistance in the war again."

"Tell me Quill did not believe them."

"Of course not. But us being out there has not improved relations between us and the Cillades. The other three provinces have already messaged Quill about it. Eastolf, in particular, was livid and acted like Quill had started a war with the Cillades."

"Krono," I said. "What a mess."

"It is. The good news is – the Cillades and Emirans peace treaty is over, and they're back to war."

"How is that good news?" I said.

"For your female," Krey said. "Not that Iron Gate is great for her, but it is better than the Earth prison. The longer the war lasts, the longer she will live."

"Yes," I said. My face darkened, and I prayed to Krono that I could keep the guilt from showing on my face. Ellis dying was the least of my concerns. Because I had no intention of letting her be returned to Earth.

I turned away and took my time putting the sparring sword back with the other ones. I had reacted badly to Ellis trying to escape. It was because of fear for her safety, but it was no excuse for how I had spoken to her. Within hours of her being taken to Iron Gate, I realized that living without her was not an option.

I should never have been angry with her for trying to escape without talking to me. I'd never given her any indication that I loved her and had told her that this was nothing more than sex between us. Why would she have confided in me or asked me to help her? I'd been a damn froden, but Krono help me, I would make it up to her. I loved and needed her, and no one, not the humans, not even my king, would keep me from her.

I had already begun to make discreet inquiries about land for sale. Once I had something suitable for us, I would use my position as head of the king's guard to take Ellis from Iron Gate and escape with her. At Iron Gate, no one would question me about why I was taking Ellis, especially if I said our king demanded it.

Once Ellis was safe with me, we would disappear. Our province was large, and a small piece of farmland far away from the city would keep Ellis safe from discovery. I would never see Quill, Krey, or my mother again, but I would have my sadora with me, and that's what mattered. I was barely hanging on now with her being in Iron Gate, but at least I knew she was safe there. The thought of her suffering and dying in an Earth prison made me nearly mad with fear and anger.

I loved Ellis and would not allow her to be taken from me.

If she'll even have you. You hurt her. You said terrible things to her.

She would forgive me. She had to. I loved her and would spend the rest of my life trying to repair the damage I had done. I would show her that I loved her and explain to her that fear made me speak so cruelly to her.

"Galan?"

"Yes?" I refused to turn around.

"Look at me."

I glanced at Krey. "What is it?"

"What are you planning?"

"Nothing," I said as guilt made my tail thump on the floor. "What are you talking about, Krey?"

He studied me, his blue eyes burning into me. "Do you love her?"

"Yes." I wouldn't lie about that.

"She will die in the Earth prison."

"I know."

He scrubbed his hand through his dark hair. "Let me know when you plan the prison break, and I will help."

"Krey, I – I am planning no such thing."

He laughed and slung an arm around my shoulders before kissing the side of my head roughly. "Brother, when will you learn you can keep nothing from me? Your face betrays your emotions easily, and it has been so since we were children. For Krono's sake, try to avoid Quill as much as possible. He will see your plan as easily as I have."

"That will not be a problem. He is avoiding me."

"He will not admit it, but nearly losing both of us reminded him too much of the loss of his brother. He is struggling with processing what happened."

"He told you this?"

"Sabrina did," Krey said. "She is worried about you as well, you know. She said she asked you to come see her, and you have been making every excuse not to."

I sighed. "Our queen is very clever. I worry she will…"

"Figure out that you are going to break your little female out of prison and live in the wilds with her?"

Krono, Krey was good at reading me.

"I meant what I said, brother. When you need me, I will be there."

I shook my head. There was no way I was letting Krey be involved in any of my plans. When I quit my position as head of the king's guard, Krey would take my place, and he would do well. "I appreciate your support, but I am not planning on any prison break. You speak foolishly."

"I often do," Krey said. "Do you think the redheaded female would fuck me?"

I blinked at him. "What?"

"The redheaded female we rescued with your female. She is beautiful, and her breasts are incredible. Do you think she would be so grateful to me for rescuing her that she'd spread those smooth thighs of hers and allow me to pleasure her?"

"I do not know," I said. "She is still injured, is she not?"

"I ran into Sigan earlier this morning. She is starting to wake, he said. I would not be surprised if she is completely awake now."

I immediately pulled away from Krey and headed toward the training room door.

"Where are you going, Galan?"

"To shower and eat," I said. "I will see you later, brother."

Instead of returning to my quarters, I headed to the infirmary. It was lunch, and the castle corridors were mostly empty. It took me less than ten minutes to walk to the infirmary. I opened the door, stumbling to a stop.

Inara's bed was closest to the door, and I stared in surprise at Melu, who stood beside her bed. As I watched, he took a step back, the usual scowl on his face replaced by a look of utter shock.

"Please, will you consider it?" Inara was sitting up in the bed, her face flushed pink and her hands clasped between her breasts. "I promise I won't back out of our agreement. Once she's safe, I'll have sex -"

"What you ask is... I mean, it is not...I cannot..." Melu's face went dark green, and he took another step back before glancing at the door. Guilt crossed his face when he saw me, and without saying a word, he pushed past me and left the infirmary.

Inara started to cry, and I hurried over and sat on the side of her hospital bed. "Human, what is wrong?"

"Nothing," she said before scrubbing the tears from her face. "Um, hey, do you know where your friend Krey is? I need to speak to him."

"About what?" I said.

"None of your business." She swallowed hard. "I'm sorry. That was rude. Do you know where Sigan is?" She looked around the infirmary. "I need to leave."

"You are not well enough to leave yet, human. I told you that." Sigan had stuck his head out the door of his lab at the back of the infirmary.

"I feel fine. Please, I need to talk with Krey," Inara said. "Sigan said I've been unconscious for two days, and it's almost too late and..."

"Almost too late for what?" I said.

Inara pressed her lips together. "Is Ellis okay? Did they heal her head?"

"Yes," I said as Sigan disappeared into his lab again.

"Thank God. Can you, um, can you ask her to come see me?"

323

"She is at Iron Gate until the war ends, and then she will be returned to Earth," I said.

"What? She's in prison? Why aren't you just keeping her locked in her room here?"

"Because she stole a ship and convinced you to go with her. She endangered your life, and as a breeding compatible female, you are incredibly precious and -"

"Oh my God." Inara's face had lost all its colour. "It wasn't her idea, Galan. It was mine."

"What do you mean?" I said.

She grasped my hand, her fingers ice cold. 'You have to help her. She can't sit in a Draax prison when she was only trying to help me. It isn't right. If anyone should be in prison, it should be me. Please, find Krey for me. As soon as I talk to him and he agrees to help me, I will go to the king and tell him it was all me and ask him to bring Ellis back to the castle. Once I fulfill my agreement with Krey, I'll go to the Draax prison for life if that's what the king says, okay?"

"You want to go to Iron Gate?" What in Krono's name was the human talking about?

"All that matters is saving my sister and telling the truth about what happened with Ellis. Please, Galan, I have to find Krey."

She tried to rip out her IV, and I grabbed her hands, holding them tight. "Inara, tell me what is happening."

"I can't," she whispered. "You'll send me straight to Iron Gate, and I must speak to Krey first."

Her panic was so thick I could practically taste it in the air. I squeezed her hands and said the only thing I could think of to get her to trust me. "I love her, Inara. I love Ellis, and if you know anything that could help me convince the king to free her, you must tell me."

She stared at me, and I squeezed her hands again. "I love her. I swear to Krono I do."

She sucked in a massive breath of air and released it. "My parents were arrested, and my sister is in danger. A lot of danger."

CHAPTER 21

Galan

"Jesus, Quill, we need to help Inara's sister." Sabrina paced back and forth, rubbing Jota's back as he slept against her chest.

"I know, sadora," Quill said. "I will have Teo contact Earth's authorities immediately and ask them to remove her from this man's home."

Jovie climbed into my lap and patted my cheek. "Uda, sad?"

"No, meena," I said.

She frowned at me, looking so much like our queen that I couldn't help but smile. "Uda sad, Mama."

"I know, baby," Sabrina said. "But we're helping him not be sad. Can you call Teo right away, Quill? And what do we do if the cops refuse to help? They don't care about the lowers. I'm not sure your request will guarantee they'll help her."

"The uncle lives in the state of California," I said. "Neani and Venta are in California, and I thought perhaps…"

"Oh my God, Galan! That's brilliant!" Sabrina turned to Quill. "Message Neani and ask him to go to that godawful uncle's place and get Wendy. California's a large state, but they've got their ship, so it shouldn't take long to get to her. She can stay with them until the war ends, and they can bring her to Draax to be with Inara. We'll have them holo-gram Inara when they pick her up, so Wendy knows she can trust them."

A small smile crossed Quill's face, and Sabrina blushed. "If you agree, my king."

"It is a wise plan, my queen," Quill said.

"What if the uncle tries to stop them?" Sabrina said.

Quill shrugged carelessly. "He will not. You know the human males are nervous around us." He picked up his vertex to call Teo.

I pressed a kiss against Jovie's head, listening silently as Quill instructed Teo. When he was finished, he smiled at Sabrina. "Teo will let me know when they have the female's sister."

"Thank you, honey," Sabrina said.

I set Jovie on the couch and stood. "I will tell Inara."

"No, I will." Sabrina handed the baby to Quill. "You and Quill need to talk. Jovie, do you want to go for a walk with Mama?"

Jovie's tail flicked with excitement. She slid off the couch and skipped across the room to take Sabrina's hand. Sabrina kissed Quill on the mouth. "I love you, Quill."

"I love you, sadora."

Silence descended when Sabrina and Jovie left. After a

moment, I bowed and said, "Thank you, my king, for helping Inara."

Quill rolled his eyes before shifting the baby in his arms. "For Krono's sake, Galan, knock it off with this formal my king shit."

I couldn't stop my smile. "Sorry."

"You are my best friend and my brother. I hate that there is tension between us."

"There is no tension," I said.

Irritation flickered across Quill's face. "So, you have avoided me these past two days because?"

"You are avoiding me," I said.

Quill kissed the top of Jota's head. "Let us both agree we have been avoiding each other and move on."

"All right," I said. "With your permission, I will ask Teo to return Ellis to the castle until the war ends. She only tried to escape because she was trying to help Inara."

"She almost got you and Krey killed. You were lucky that Krey outmaneuvered their ship," Quill said.

"She did not know that would happen. None of us did. She should not be punished because the Cillades are dick-heads," I said.

Quill laughed, and Jota made a soft snort, his tiny tail flicking back and forth in his sleep before settling against Quill's chest again. "The Earth's curse words are always amusing, are they not, Galan?"

"Yes. Will you allow Ellis to return to the castle until the war ends?"

Quill studied me for a moment. "I suppose it would make it easier for you to escape into the wilds with her if she is at the castle rather than locked away in Iron Gate."

"For Krono's sake," I said, "can I keep nothing from you and Krey?"

"No," Quill said. "Hiding your emotions has never been easy for you, old friend. Although, I will admit that in this particular case, I simply asked myself what I would do if I were in your place, and your plan came easily enough to me."

"I have no plan. You are my king, and I have pledged my life to protecting you and your family," I said.

He laughed again. "Galan, you are one of the bravest and most loyal Draax I have ever known, but you cannot lie."

I rubbed at my forehead as my tail waved in the air. "I love her, Quill. I love her, and I cannot be without her. Being separated from her is driving me mad. She will not survive more than a few days in the Earth's prison. I will not give her up. Not even for you."

I hated that I was about to ruin my friendship with Quill, but I had no choice. I needed Ellis like I needed air to breathe.

Quill walked across the room and squeezed my shoulder. The look on his face was a mixture of humour and sympathy. "Old friend, do you forget that at one point, I was ready to give up my throne for the woman I loved? I would have done whatever was necessary to be with Sabrina. Believe me, I understand what you go through."

Tears pricked the back of my eyes, and my throat went tight. I did not deserve Quill's love or loyalty.

"Which is why I informed Earth's authorities this morning that we were forgiving Ellis of her crimes, and she would remain on Draax," Quill said.

My mouth dropped open, and my tail whipped back and forth. "I – what did you say?"

"The little female is yours if she will have you," Quill said. "You may bring her home from Iron Gate immediately."

"Quill," I was struggling to understand the enormity of what he'd done, "you have broken the treaty? Even before you knew that Ellis did this to help Inara?"

"I have," Quill said. "Old Teo nearly fell out of his chair when I told him."

"What did the humans say?"

"Do not worry about it," Quill said.

"Tell me, Quill."

"The authorities in Iowa are lodging a formal complaint with the Earth's United Nations, and I imagine I will be required to speak to them about why I have broken the treaty."

"You would risk our partnership with Earth for me?" I said. "Quill, I am not worth -"

Quill gripped the back of my neck, resting his forehead against mine. "You are my brother, Galan. I wish for your happiness as much as I wish for my own. You are worth it. Never believe differently."

My voice hoarse, I said, "I can never repay you, Quill."

"Of course you can," he said. "You can mate with your small, strange, sarcastic female and live a happy life."

"Thank you, brother," I said.

"You are welcome," Quill said. "Now, go retrieve your female from Iron Gate."

Ellis

ALL THINGS CONSIDERED, IRON GATE WASN'T THAT TERRIBLE. Sure, I was stuck in a small windowless room with nothing but a cot, toilet, and sink, but it was nice compared to some places I'd slept. It was clean and bug free, and that was probably more than I deserved.

Boredom was my biggest enemy. That and I tugged at the giant shirt I was wearing, ill-fitting prison clothes. The prison had given me their smallest size of prison uniform, but it was still miles too big. I wore the shirt like a dress and had given up entirely on the pants.

It wasn't like I needed to wear pants anyway. I saw no one but the guard who delivered my meals the last two days. I was given an hour to shower and exercise in the afternoon, but I saw no one else during my walk from my cell to the showers or in the exercise room.

If I didn't know better, I would think I was the only prisoner in the entire damn place.

I stood up from the bed and paced the tiny room. Fifteen steps from one wall to the other, touch the chipped stone just above the sink, turn, fifteen steps to the other wall. If the war continued for too much longer, I'd wear a path on the cell floor.

I supposed solitary confinement was better than death, but it gave me too much time to think about Galan. To remember the betrayal on his face and the anger in his voice. To relive the moment over and over when he said I was a selfish human incapable of loving anyone but myself.

He was wrong. So wrong. I loved him, and I would tell him so if I ever saw him again. I didn't care that he hated me now, didn't care that he thought I was a terrible person and probably regretted having anything to do with me. I needed him to know that I loved him. That I would love him until the day I died.

You'll never see him again, Ellis. You'll die without ever telling him how you feel. He'll never know. He'll find another human to fall in love with and never think of you again.

My chest ached fiercely. The agony of knowing that Galan hated me and would fall in love with another woman hurt worse than any physical pain. God, I had fucked up so badly. Maybe I could convince the guard to give me a pen and paper so I could write Galan a note.

And then what? You think they'll deliver your note to him?

I reached the wall and rested my forehead against the cool stone. No, probably not. But it was worth trying. Maybe I'd get lucky, and the guard would feel sorry for me.

The metal that covered the small window in the door slid open and the guard's face appeared. "Move to the wall, prisoner."

I moved to the wall farthest from the door, placing my hands in the spots marked and staring at the wall. It wasn't time for my shower or exercise, at least I didn't think it was – it was already hard to keep track of time – and my lunch had been delivered not long ago, so it wasn't dinner time.

The door opened, and I glanced over my shoulder, my jaw dropping when Galan entered my cell. My hands slipped from the wall, and the guard barked, "Hands on the wall, face forward, prisoner!"

I slapped them back into place and swiveled my head to face the wall.

"Leave us," Galan said.

I snuck a look over my shoulder. The guard looked like he might argue before thinking better of it and leaving. The door shut with a heavy clunk, and I turned to face the wall, my heart beating like a trapped bird against my sternum and adrenaline pumping through my veins.

"You can turn around, Ellis."

"Actually, the rules in the 'Welcome to Iron Gate' manual are clear. I have to stay like this whenever I have a visitor in my cell," I said. "Not that I've had many visitors, but I'm determined to win the 'most well-behaved prisoner in Iron Gate' trophy at the twenty-eighth annual 'Ironies' later this month. You get an extra toilet paper roll for winning, and I am down for that. They are weirdly stingy with the toilet paper in here."

"Ellis -"

"Is Inara okay?"

"Yes. She is awake and completely healed."

Some of the tension leaked out of my body.

"Please turn around, sadora."

I rested my forehead on the wall before turning around and staring at Galan. I soaked in the sight of him, resisting the urge to run straight to him and throw my arms around him. Fuck, I'd missed him. "I know what sadora means, you know. I asked Uzel, and he told me that Draax use it with their mates."

"Ellis, I am sorry for -"

"I love you," I blurted out.

Surprise crossed Galan's face. I took a deep breath. "You said I couldn't love anyone but myself, and I just wanted you to know you're wrong. I love you."

I chewed at my bottom lip. "I loved Esther too. I loved her so much and failed her, I know, but that doesn't mean I didn't love her."

"You did not fail her, sadora."

"I failed you, too," I said. "I should have talked to you and

333

told you that I loved you before I ran away, and I'm sorry that I didn't. But I won't apologize for not asking you to talk to Quill or not asking you to help me. I don't have a future and refuse to destroy yours."

"I love you too, sadora."

Tears pricked my eyes, and I stared at the narrow cot. "Well, aren't we just a couple of idiots."

"Inara told me the truth about why you stole the ship."

"I wanted to help her sister," I said. "And I failed to help her, too."

"You did not," he said.

I glanced at him, and he smiled. "Once Inara woke and found out you were in Iron Gate, she confessed immediately that you stole the ship to help her. I went to Quill and asked him to help Inara's sister. Quill sent Neani and Venta to help the young female."

"Seriously?" I said.

He nodded. "Yes. As I was traveling here, Quill messaged me. They have Inara's sister and she is safe. She will stay with them until the war ends, and they can bring her here to Inara."

I slumped against the wall. "That's amazing. Thank you for helping her."

"I am so sorry for what I said to you on the ship," Galan said. "It is not an excuse, but my fear for your safety made me say things I should not have. I do not believe you are selfish or incapable of love, I swear. You are the most giving human I have ever met, Ellis and I love you. I want you to be my mate."

Jesus, Galan was fucking killing me here. "I appreciate your apology. I forgive you for what you said, and I'm sorry for lying to you. Knowing that you love me makes me stupidly happy, but it doesn't change anything," I said. "As soon as the war ends, I'll be -"

"You will be with me, my mate," Galan said.

Shit, I liked hearing Galan call me his mate way too much. "That's a sweet thought, but -"

"Quill informed the humans this morning that we had absolved you of your crime and that you would be staying on Draax rather than returning to Earth for punishment."

My jaw dropped again, and I stared at Galan. I had to have misheard him. Solitary confinement insanity had already set in, right?

"What did you say?" I whispered.

"You are free, my sadora," Galan said. "Free to live your life on Draax. You are more than welcome to stay at the castle, and Melu has agreed to let you return to your job in the docking bay."

"Now I know you're talking bullshit," I said. "Melu hates me for almost killing Inara."

"He does not," Galan said. "No one hates you."

I stared wide eyed at him when he walked forward. His tail slipped around my waist and tugged gently. I walked toward him, stepping numbly into his arms as he bent his head and kissed my forehead. "I love you, sadora."

"I love you too," I said.

He kissed me hard on the mouth, and I threw my arms around his broad shoulders as our tongues touched and tasted. When he pulled away, we were both panting, and I could feel his erection against my abdomen.

"I have missed you, little human."

"I missed you too," I said. "How angry are the humans that Quill isn't sending me back to Earth?"

"They are unhappy, but Quill is not worried about it."

"Thank you for asking him to do this. I hope it doesn't change your friendship or -"

"I did not ask him to do it. He did it because he knows how much you mean to me," Galan said. "My plan involved stealing you from Iron Gate and leaving the city. I was going to find a small parcel of land to farm, one far away from this city where we could live our lives together without anyone knowing our past."

"What? Are you serious? You were going to stage a prison break and then become a damn farmer?"

He nodded, and I rested my forehead against his chest. "Oh my God, that's kind of romantic in a seriously fucked up way, but can I just say that I'm thrilled we didn't have to do that? I love that you were willing to give up your entire life for me, but I'm not sure I would have ever gotten over the guilt of forcing you to leave everyone you loved."

He tipped my face up, pressing a gentle kiss against my lips. "You would not have needed to feel guilty, my sadora. You are my life. I cannot live without you."

He wiped away the tear slipping down my cheek, and I smiled at him. "I love you, Galan."

"I love you too, my mate. Let us go home."

Keep reading for an excerpt from "Surrender," Book Four in the Draax Series.

SURRENDER EXCERPT

(DRAAX SERIES BOOK FOUR)

Melu

The door opened, and I froze on the couch, staring at Inara as she stepped inside my office and closed the door.

"Hello, Melu."

"Hello." My voice came out weird… strangled, and angrier than I intended.

I could see her throat working as she swallowed, could practically smell her anxiety, but she walked over and sat on the couch next to me. My tail thumped against the arm of the couch. She'd left plenty of space between us, but just being this close to her was torture.

"Why did you leave your party?" she said.

I shrugged, trying to breathe shallowly, trying not to think about the female next to me being naked, her mouth on my cock, her beautiful breasts filling my hands as she moaned around my cock.

Krono! My attempt at staving off an erection failed miserably. The bulge in my pants was extremely noticeable, and my skin darkened with embarrassment when the little female glanced at my crotch.

Instead of running away, she slid a little closer, and my breath caught in my throat when she rested her hand on my thigh.

"Inara," my voice was hoarse, "why are you here?"

"Do the Draax give birthday gifts, Melu?"

"Only to our young ones." I couldn't stop staring at her long fingers, couldn't stop wondering what it would look like to have them wrapped around my cock.

"Adults don't get gifts?" She shifted even closer until her thigh pressed against mine.

"Not usually." I couldn't breathe, couldn't concentrate. Why was she torturing me like this?

"I have a birthday gift for you. Can I give it to you?"

I stared at her perfect mouth and her flame-coloured hair before clearing my throat. "You did not need to buy me a gift."

She smiled, but I could see the nervousness in her face. "I didn't exactly buy it."

"What is your gift?" I said.

"I want to suck your cock."

My breath exploded from my lungs, and my cock stiffened into a hard spike. I'd heard her wrong. She hadn't said what she said.

"What?" I croaked, my hips arching when she rested her hand against my cock. "What did you say?"

She stared steadily at me even though her face was now the same colour as her hair. "I want to give you a blow job for your birthday. Will you let me?"

"Inara, I do not… that is… you are too young for me and _-"

"I'm not," she said. "Please, Melu. I want to do this very much."

"Why?" I said, trying to ignore the pressure of her palm against my aching dick. How long had it been since I'd felt a female's touch? Had a hand other than my own on my cock? Too long.

"Because I've never thanked you properly for saving my life in the garden and for your kindness to my sister." She reached for the buttons on my pants, popping them open one by one. "Because it's your birthday."

"Inara, we should not," I groaned as she opened my pants.

"We should," she whispered. Her hand traced the outline of my shaft through my briefs, and I was lost.

I reached down and freed my cock from the confines of my clothing, staring heatedly at Inara before reaching up and cupping the back of her neck. She smiled at me and leaned down. Her warm breath on the head of my cock was almost enough to make me lose control.

A groan escaped when she licked the head of my cock, cleaning it of the precum that already coated it. She glanced up at me. "The rumours are true. It does taste like gallberries."

"Please, sweet human," I groaned. "Your mouth. Suck me."

She slid her mouth over my dick, and I moaned loudly. Krono, my little female was so sweet. I swept her beautiful hair away from her face, holding it in a loose ponytail as I watched her suck my cock. She gripped the base of the shaft, rubbing lightly as she teased the head with her tongue. My hips rose and fell, and I cupped her breast through her dress and squeezed gently before rubbing her hip.

"Get on your knees on the couch," I said.

She glanced up at me, her mouth full of my cock, and I smoothed her hair back again. "Do it, sweet girl."

She got onto her knees on the couch, bracing one hand on my thigh and keeping the other wrapped around the base of my dick as she sucked. I immediately ran my hand over her upturned ass, squeezing and kneading the firm cheeks as she licked up and down my shaft.

I pulled her dress up around her waist, my lust intensifying when I saw the tiny pair of panties she wore. I rubbed her bare ass cheeks before tugging on the thin piece of material nestled between them.

She squeaked around my cock, and I rubbed her ass again. "Spread your legs, Inara."

She spread them eagerly, and I kept her hair wrapped around one hand so I could see her face when I slid my other hand between her legs and cupped her pussy.

Her panties were wet, and I growled my approval, then slipped my fingers under the material and stroked her pussy lips before rubbing her clit.

She pulled her mouth from my dick, crying out her pleasure as her hand squeezed my thigh. "Melu, please!"

"Keep sucking, sweet one," I said, using her hair to guide her mouth back to my dick.

She sucked eagerly, rubbing her wet pussy against my fingers. I smoothed her hair back from her face and rubbed her clit in light circles. "You look beautiful sucking my cock, little female."

The door to my office opened, and Krey strolled in. "Melu, you bastard, you cannot leave your own life celebration and expect…"

Inara tried to lift her head, her hand digging into my

thigh when I palmed the back of her skull and kept her mouth right where it was. "No, sweet one, keep sucking."

Krey shut the door and sat down on the couch behind Inara. He grinned at me. "I see you are enjoying your life celebration."

I stroked Inara's cheek with my thumb and smiled at her. "My little female is giving me the sweetest gift."

"Your little female's pussy is very wet," Krey said. "She has soaked through her panties."

Inara moaned around my cock when Krey stroked her ass. "It cannot be comfortable for her."

"No," I agreed. "Help her, Krey."

Krey leaned over and hooked his thumbs into the waistband of Inara's panties, tugging them off her ass and down her legs before dropping them on the floor.

"Krono, she has a very pretty pussy," Krey said.

I reached between her legs again, rubbing her swollen clit as I studied her face. I loosened my grip on her head, giving her the opportunity to lift her head and tell us to stop. She released my cock with a soft pop and turned her head to stare at Krey.

"Hello, pretty human," Krey said.

"Hi, Krey." Inara's voice was low and her lips were shiny with my precum. She licked her lips, and I stayed perfectly still. I may possibly have ruined the amazing gift Inara was giving me by not asking Krey to leave, but I had seen the way she looked at him. She wanted him as much as she wanted me, and I would allow her to have exactly what she wanted.

She smiled tentatively at me, and instead of telling both Krey and me to stop, she took a deep breath and sucked my cock with renewed vigor.

I groaned, twisting her hair in my hand and praising her softly as my hips rose. "Good girl, sweet one."

I glanced over at Krey. His pants were unbuttoned, and he had freed his cock. He stroked it slowly as he studied Inara's pussy. He drew in a shuddering breath before looking up at me. "Krono, I want to taste your female's pussy. May I?"

I stared down at Inara and watched the flare of fresh lust in her gaze as she looked up at me with her lips spread wide around my thick cock. I smiled at her and wiped away the saliva and precum from her chin.

"Yes," I said, "taste her, Krey."

ABOUT THE AUTHOR

Elizabeth Kelly was born and raised in Ontario, Canada. She moved west as a teenager and now lives in Alberta with her husband and a menagerie of pets. She firmly believes that a person can survive solely on sushi and coffee, and only her husband's mad cooking skills prevents her from proving that theory.

For more information about Elizabeth, check out her website at

www.elizabethkelly.ca

f facebook.com/EKellyBooks
📷 instagram.com/elizabethkelly_author
a amazon.com/Elizabeth-Kelly/e/B00EOHZ0MS
BB bookbub.com/authors/elizabeth-kelly

ALSO BY ELIZABETH KELLY

Tempted Series

Tempted

Twice Tempted

Forever Tempted

Breathless

Tempted Trilogy (Books 1-3)

Red Moon Series

Red Moon

Red Moon Rising

Dark Moon

Alpha Moon

Pale Moon

The Recruit Series

The Recruit (Book One)

The Recruit (Book Two)

The Recruit (Book Three)

The Recruit (Book Four)

The Recruit (Book Five)

The Recruit (Book Six)

The Shifters Series

Willow and the Wolf (Book One)

Ava and the Bear (Book Two)

Katarina and the Bird (Book Three)

Porter's Mate (Book Four)

Bria and the Tiger (Book Five)

Rosalie Undone (Book Six)

The Dragon's Mate (Book Seven)

Rise of the Jaguar (Book Eight)

The Assassin and the Bear (Book Nine)

Elora and the Crow (Book Ten)

The Draax Series

Reign (Book One)

Rule (Book Two)

Rebel (Book Three)

Surrender (Book Four)

Survive (Book Five)

Salvation (Book Six)

Harmony Falls Series

Sweet Harmony (Book One)

Perfect Harmony (Book Two)

Forbidden Harmony (Book Three)

Redeeming Harmony (Book Four)

Absolute Harmony (Novella)

Beautiful Harmony (Book Five)

Reckless Harmony (Book Six)

Seasoned Romance Series

Bet Your Heart on Me (Book One)

Take a Chance on Me (Book Two)

Place Your Trust in Me (Book Three)

Individual Books

The Necessary Engagement

Amelia's Touch

The Rancher's Daughter

Healing Gabriel

The Contract

A Home for Lily

Saving Charlotte

Shameless

The Fairy Tales Collection

Broken

An Unlikely Seduction

Holiday Romance

The Christmas Wife

The Christmas Rescue

The Christmas Nanny

The Christmas Boss

Sordid Games